The Immortal

THE IMMORTAL

Angela Hunt

WORD PUBLISHING
NASHVILLE
A Thomas Nelson Company

Published by Word Publishing, Nashville, Tennessee. All rights reserved. No portion of this book may be reproduced, stored in a retrieval system, or transmitted in any form or by any other means—electronic, mechanical, photocopy, recording, or any other—except for brief quotations in printed reviews, without the prior permission of the publisher.

Scripture quotations in this book are from the following sources:

The King James Version of the Bible.

Holy Bible, New Living Translation, copyright © 1996. Used by permission of Tyndale House Publishers, Inc., Wheaton, Illinois 60189. All rights reserved.

Holy Bible, New International Version. Copyright © 1973, 1978, 1984, International Bible Society. Used by permission of Zondervan Bible Publishers.

Library of Congress Cataloging-in-Publication Data

Hunt, Angela Elwell, 1957–
    The immortal / Angela Hunt.
      p. cm.
    ISBN 0-8499-1630-5 — ISBN 0-8499-4218-7 (tp)
    1. Immortalism—Fiction. I. Title.

PS3558.U46747 I53 2000
813'.54—dc21
                                                                                   00-036808
                                                                                   CIP

Printed in the United States of America
0 1 2 3 4 BVG 9 8 7 6 5 4 3 2 1

Author's Note

The apostle John wrote in his Gospel, "And I suppose that if all the other things Jesus did were written down, the whole world could not contain the books" (21:25). Did Jesus speak to a man while carrying his cross to Calvary? I don't know. Many legends suggest that he did.

This book is not inspired Scripture. Though it contains a great deal of truth, I'd like you to see it as a parable, a fictional tale with an outer layer of story and layers of deeper meaning underneath. All fiction rests upon an implicit conspiracy between writer and reader—the writer tells the story, and the reader, for a few hours at least, pretends *it really happened*.

I'm aware that asking you to believe in a two-thousand-year-old man is a little unusual, but thank you for allowing me the privilege. This fiction is based upon fact. As much as possible, when citing historical characters, events, structures, and information about the evolution of the legend of the Wandering Jew, I have taken pains not to contradict the historical record.

I'm not seriously suggesting that God might allow a man to live for two thousand years, but, like Vittorio Pace, I learned a long time ago that it's never wise to tell God what he can and can't do. So I am leaving the story in your hands in the hope that it will dwell in your heart for some time to come.

Thank you for journeying with me.

Angela Elwell Hunt
Angie@angelaelwellhunt.com

For them that think death's honesty
Won't fall upon them naturally
Life sometimes
Must get lonely.

—*Bob Dylan*

You search the Scriptures because you believe
    they give you eternal life.
But the Scriptures point to me!
Yet you refuse to come to me so that I can
    give you this eternal life.

—*Jesus, John 5:39–40*

ONE

L AST WEEK *PEOPLE* MAGAZINE CALLED ME "THE SEER."

I wasn't pleased.

They ran a nice article that made for great publicity, but the word *seer* conjures up images of crystal balls and hocus-pocus, and neither one has anything to do with my work. I rely on facts and evidence, not paranormal vibrations and intuition.

Once I dismissed a man based on something that felt strangely like a hunch, but in hindsight I found several revealing clues that must have tipped off my subconscious and tripped a mental alarm. Since then, I've learned to turn my eyes and ears into nets with which I catch the whispers, glances, sighs, and the barely noticeable gestures that are the real message carriers in this raucous world.

My business card says I'm a jury consultant and communications expert.

I like to think of myself as a people reader.

It was in my role as a jury consultant that I found myself perspiring in a New York courthouse on a cool morning in September.

"Men and women of the jury, my client's life lies in your hands."

Ross Colby, defense lawyer extraordinaire, paced before the jury box, his erect posture revealing his military background as clearly as his word choice. Most lawyers, including Howard Nardozzi, the prosecuting attorney for the state of New York, decorously addressed the "ladies and gentlemen of the jury," but I knew lawyers like Colby thought in terms of black or white, man or woman, guilty or innocent. And Colby desperately wanted these twelve men and women to believe that his client, U.S. Senator Chad Mitchell, was innocent of murder in the first degree.

From my seat in the first row of the spectators' gallery, I shifted slightly to study the twelve faces I had come to know nearly as well as my own. The law office of Wilt, Kremkau, Colby, and Stock had hired me in late February; it was now the seventh of September, and within a few hours we would all discover whether their decision had been wise. One of Colby's paralegals once let it slip that the senator had pressed Colby to hire Elaine Dawson, the jury consultant who rose to national prominence after the Marvin Maxwell trial, but apparently Elaine hadn't been available.

Her loss. My gain—perhaps. If the jury came back with a not guilty verdict, my star might rise as high as my former mentor's. But if the senator went to prison, I'd probably be pounding the pavement within a week.

I let my gaze rove over the assembled jury members while Colby continued his closing arguments. "Yes, Senator Mitchell did visit Stephanie Glazier on the afternoon of June 25, and yes, they did quarrel. He has freely admitted as much. Yes, they were involved in a romantic relationship. But that morning Senator Mitchell had confessed the affair to his wife, and he visited Stephanie Glazier's apartment for no reason other than to break off the liaison. When he left that apartment, Miss Glazier was alive and well."

A movement from the jury box caught my eye—Laurie Dorset, juror number ten, had shaken her head slightly. A headshake could mean many things—annoyance, boredom, even flirtation—but it was also a strong signal of disbelief. Would she create trouble during deliberations? I opened my case notebook and lightly drew a question mark next to her name.

As Colby continued his summation, I scanned the list of men and women who would decide the senator's fate. Juror number one, Alan Armstrong, was tailor-made for our purposes. A white middle-class sales executive from Manhattan, he despised the current conservative resident of the White House and practically worshiped the liberal senator.

Juror number two, a retired schoolteacher, had worn a stony expression throughout the pretrial proceedings, but once testimony was under way, her flinty glances melted into an almost maternal concern and affection. She smiled gently whenever the senator glanced in her direction and reserved her granite frowns for the prosecutor. Unlike the other jurors, who scarcely glanced up as they entered and exited the courtroom, Ms. Schoolteacher stared at the senator as she came in, literally inviting him to connect with her. The man could be as guilty as Cain—and most likely was—but she'd vote for an acquittal.

I put a check by numbers one and two. Juror number three was another certain vote for the defense. The sultry blonde, Veronica Wade, had been obviously salivating over the handsome defendant since day one of the trial. The prosecution had wanted to bump her from the jury pool but used up all their peremptory challenges before Wade could be excused.

Juror four worried me. A manager for the Hilton hotel chain, Elizabeth Mattingly seemed polite, respectful, and solicitous toward the judge and both lawyers. But I had noticed that she often pushed through the jury box as if the other jurors didn't exist, and more than once I saw her allow the courtroom door to close behind her even though a fellow juror followed at her heels. Polite to authority figures, rude to everyone else—how would her innate self-centeredness influence our case? After musing on the matter, I put a solid check next to her name. Anyone who routinely behaved so thoughtlessly would not be so attuned toward ideals of right and wrong that she would vote to condemn my client.

And the senator was an authority figure, so Ms. Mattingly would want to curry his favor.

I exhaled softly as I glanced over at Senator Chad Mitchell. If I were a wagering sort, I'd lay odds that Ms. Mattingly would be calling the senator after the trial, perhaps for drinks, perhaps for a job interview. She'd probably have to stand in line, of course, because I counted at least four female jurors who evidenced more than a professional interest in the defendant.

The defense had done a stellar job of painting the victim as a conniving tramp, and I couldn't help but notice that most of the male jurors had dipped their heads in agreement when Ross Colby began his defense by stating: "Stephanie Glazier's death was a tragedy—but so was her life. She collected men the way some little girls collect stuffed animals, but Stephanie Glazier was no innocent girl. She had to know that sooner or later one of her men would not appreciate being treated like a toy. One of those men lost patience with her immature games, but my client was not that man."

I looked over the rest of the list, checking off the remaining jurors, all men except for Laurie Dorset, the head shaker. Not much I could do about her now. My last-minute vote count was a futile exercise, at best— the most important part of my work had occurred during voir dire, when the jurors were questioned about any prejudices and/or opinions they might hold against the defendant.

Some people think voir dire is the art of picking the perfect jury, but it's really the skill of striking the worst jurors. We had successfully challenged and excused two clergymen, a woman whose teenage daughter had been murdered by an older man, a cop's wife, an abused wife, and a rabid proponent of the death penalty. Because the senator was a Democrat, we had also challenged five registered Republicans. They, in fact, were the first to be excused.

Closing my notebook, I returned my attention to Ross Colby. "I know you do not take this responsibility lightly," Ross was saying, his brilliant blue eyes sweeping over the rows of upturned faces. "And I know you will not disappoint. You are charged with upholding justice and deciding truth, and I know you have the intelligence to see the truth as these witnesses have presented it to you. Chad Mitchell was in his Manhattan office at the hour Ms. Glazier was murdered. Chad Mitchell had no motive for killing Ms. Glazier. Furthermore, Chad Mitchell had no *desire* to kill Ms. Glazier. Why would he want to bring the stain of shame upon his good name? He is a respected representative of the United States Senate and the proud father of four children. For what earthly reason would he risk his family and reputation by killing a woman like Stephanie Glazier?"

As Colby's rhetorical questions reverberated in the cavernous courtroom, I could almost see the progression of painted suggestions parading through the panelists' minds. They watched him with eyes wide and open; their heads followed Colby's pacing movements like entranced spectators at a slow-motion tennis match. They had forgotten that Mitchell had no evidence to support his alibi. They had either discounted or ignored the tearful testimony of Glazier's roommate. Stephanie Glazier had no other current male friends, the roommate testified, and no intention of breaking off her affair with the senator, for Stephanie had just discovered she was pregnant. Earlier in the week the roommate had heard Glazier call the senator and issue an ultimatum—marriage or exposure. That ultimatum had paid off in an unexpected currency.

Every instinct and skill I possessed assured me that Senator Chad Mitchell had murdered his mistress. Though outwardly he was the image of charm and respectability, several things about him didn't add up. First, the man had a tan—the backs of his hands were at least four shades darker than his palms, and that seemed odd for a man who supposedly spent ten hours a day laboring for the good people of New York State. His hands, furthermore, were soft and supple, with each finger tipped by a manicured nail. That told me the senator probably didn't acquire his tan outdoors visiting his constituents, but in a tanning salon. Our defendant was conscious of his public image, as were most senators, but Mitchell was also extremely vain.

The senator's clothing choices supported my initial observations. In court and in the law office, even after work hours, he wore ties color-coordinated to match the scarves in his coat pocket. His watch was a Rolex, his loafers Italian. Words flowed from his lips in the cultured accents of a man who'd been educated in Ivy League schools, and summers spent studying at Oxford had resulted in a British affectation of replacing "ay" sounds with "ah." The senator didn't ask women to dance—he AHsked them to dAHns. His carefully cultivated charm had not been lost on the female members of the jury, the press, or the public.

Every day for the last six months I had fought my way through the churning crowd outside the courtroom and taken my reserved seat in the visitors' gallery; every evening I caught a cab to the law offices of Wilt, Kremkau, Colby, and Stock, where the lawyers and I conferred about the day's events. While the associate lawyers second-guessed each other, Colby quizzed me about each of the jurors—what they'd been wearing, how their expressions had changed, and when their attention had begun to lag. I consulted my notes and responded, giving him a complete mental picture of each juror, then leaned back in my leather chair with a sigh of relief when he turned to crucify his associates for whatever lapses had occurred in the courtroom.

In all that time, Colby never asked me for my impressions about his client. If he had, I'd have said that Senator Chad Mitchell not only murdered Stephanie Glazier, but day by day he also was growing more confident in his ability to beat this charge. The first time I met the senator in Colby's office, I noted several indicators of nervousness—he flicked specks of invisible lint from his lapel, played with his pen, and even engaged in hand rubbing, that guilty gesture of appearing to wash the hands with invisible soap. Today, however, Mitchell sat erect in his chair, a smile upon his lips, his gaze forthright and direct, his hands calmly at rest, one at his belt, the other on the table. To display any more confidence, he'd have to prop his feet up on the desk and grin at the judge. The hand at the belt, furthermore, was an understated courtship signal, and the women in the jury box were picking it up like long-range satellite dishes.

It doesn't matter, I told myself, glancing down at the floor. Every American citizen was entitled to a full and capable defense.

Moving in for the *coup de grâce*, Colby walked to the jury box and braced his hands against the railing, leaning toward the panel members as if he would plead face to face with each of them if he could. "Let me remind you, my friends, that my client is cloaked with the presumption of innocence until proven guilty. The state must prove *beyond a reasonable doubt* that our outstanding senator murdered a helpless pregnant woman in cold blood." Colby paused and shivered, theatrically demonstrating that he found the idea incomprehensible. "The state has not convinced me. And I know the prosecutor has not convinced you."

The beeper at my belt vibrated softly, and I glanced down at the number on the screen. My office was calling, and I couldn't help hoping my secretary had good news. I'd had to clear our calendar for the Mitchell trial, and now that it was wrapping up, a huge stretch of white space dominated our calendar for weeks to come.

The prosecutor for the state of New York rose from his chair and faced the jury. In quick, no-nonsense words, he outlined his case: The senator's fingerprints were all over Ms. Glazier's apartment, and a neighbor had seen him enter the apartment at 9:00 P.M., well into the evening. Senator Mitchell claimed to be in his Manhattan office at that time, but not a single witness, human or mechanical, could affirm his assertion. The medical examiner had ruled that Stephanie Glazier died of strangulation at approximately 9:15 P.M., and security cameras in the apartment lobby had captured the blurry image of a man who looked remarkably like Senator Chad Mitchell at 9:20.

The prosecutor finished his remarks and took his seat. I edged toward the end of the wooden bench and leaned forward, studying the jurors' faces as the judge gave them his parting instructions. A quick appraisal of the twelve jurors and two alternates confirmed my earlier evaluation—it might take a few days for them to convince Laurie Dorset, but this panel would acquit Senator Mitchell.

I had staked my career on it.

As the jury stood and turned toward their exit, I rose from my seat and moved toward the double doors at the back of the courtroom, eager to get away before Colby caught me and demanded another dose of reassurance.

I slipped through the crowd of reporters outside the courtroom and wound through the marble hallways, finally ducking into a ladies' room. After a quick peek beneath each stall door to make certain I had the space to myself, I leaned against the wall in a corner, fished my cell phone from my purse, and punched in my office number.

Rory Metcalf, my secretary, answered on the first ring. "Fischer Consulting."

"Hi, it's me. You beeped?"

Rory knew better than to make idle conversation when I was

involved in a trial. I'd called him from rest rooms before, and though a ladies' lounge was often one of the quietest rooms in a public building, I never knew when one of the enemy camp might decide to pop in and eavesdrop.

"Nothing urgent, but I thought you'd appreciate your messages," Rory said, his voice clipped. "Floyd Wilkerson called this morning. He said it's urgent that he speak to you as soon as possible."

I groaned. Wilkerson was an officer at the bank where two years ago I'd taken out a short-term loan to establish my own litigation consulting office. The balloon payment on that loan was now six months past due.

Shoving the matter aside, I decided Wilkerson would have to wait. If this jury found Senator Mitchell guilty, I'd probably have to initiate bankruptcy proceedings.

"Hold Wilkerson. What's next?"

"Your sister called and wanted to know if you're still coming up this weekend."

"Call her back and tell her yes—unless we lose this case. If that happens, I'm locking myself in my apartment and sewing a sackcloth robe."

Rory ignored my melodramatic moment. "Karl called—are you two still on for dinner tonight?"

I held up my free hand and idly inspected the diamond in the center of my platinum engagement ring. "Sure. Call his office and leave word that I'll see him at the Rainbow Room at eight."

The plastic chatter of Rory's keyboard echoed over the phone line. "Got it. There's just one more thing." His voice took on a coolly disapproving tone. "Elaine Dawson called right before I paged you. She was watching the summation on TV and says you've got it all wrapped up."

A warm rush flowed through me, and for an instant I forgot that Elaine and I had gone from being best friends to archrivals in the last two years. Because she had been my mentor and employer, her opinion still mattered a great deal to me. It was nice of her to call . . . as long as her call wasn't designed to give me false confidence. If we lost this case, I knew she'd phone again and offer condolences, but she'd be secretly delighted that her position as America's foremost jury consultant was secure.

"Nice of her to notice us." I pulled myself off the wall, then turned and studied the empty stalls. "Anything else?"

"Nothing. I'll return these calls to Karl and your sister." He paused a moment, and I could almost see him smile. "I saw the summation too, and I've got to agree with Elaine. That jury was eating out of Colby's hand."

"Let's hope so." The door from the hallway opened, and a short woman with frowsy blonde hair entered and headed straight for the stall closest to me. I didn't recognize her, but one could never be too careful about security. "Gotta go. Speak to you soon."

I snapped the phone shut, dropped it into my purse, and moved to the sink. As I splashed water over my hands and checked my reflection in the mirror, I listened for sounds from the occupied stall. The district attorney had pulled some sneaky stunts in the past six months, and sending a secretary in to eavesdrop wouldn't be beyond the realm of possibility . . . even though there was probably no point in such shenanigans at this point. Senator Mitchell's fate now lay in the hands of twelve well-chosen jurors.

I dried my hands on a paper towel, tossed it into the waste can, and moved toward the door without seeing the frowsy woman again. The hallway outside appeared deserted, but as I moved down the marble-tiled corridor, I noticed that my footsteps seemed to have picked up an odd echo.

Disconcerted, I stepped to the wall, leaning against it as if I'd decided to wait for someone. A man stood about ten feet behind me, and his brows lifted as I turned. With one glance I registered his bald-ness, a certain thickness through his torso and shoulders, and his age—about fifty. An odd smile flicked across his face as my gaze crossed his, then he shrugged slightly and moved to the opposite wall, clasping his hands as if he, too, had decided to wait for the Mitchell jury in this deserted hallway.

I looked away as my survival instincts started clanging like a fire alarm. You can't live a week in Manhattan without becoming a little careful about strangers, and this fellow was obviously no New Yorker, any one of whom would have ignored my deliberate diversion and kept walking.

Without meeting his gaze again, I thrust my hands into my suit pockets and walked briskly back to the pack of paparazzi loitering out-side the courtroom. Safety lay in numbers.

Two hours later I was perched on a stool in Pravda, a Russian-themed lounge on Lafayette Street, the watering hole closest to the Manhattan courthouse. The place bustled with trench-coated reporters, and I enjoyed being among them. Years ago I discovered that media people were a secret weapon in the war against failure—like me, they made a living out of observing others, and their comments often confirmed or rattled my judgments about each day's proceedings. While any one of the press people could have identified me, few of them expected to find a member of Mitchell's defense team slumming with the press corps. So, perched near the end of the bar, I could sip my Diet Coke, quietly listen to passing comments, and measure my perceptions against prevailing conventional wisdom.

The couple seated to my right was proving particularly interest-ing. "The senator will be dining in his own apartment by the weekend," the man said, a swatch of wavy brown hair falling casually on his forehead. He wore a suit and tie—*television reporter*. Newspaper people didn't usually dress to impress, particularly if they were destined for a day of dodging traffic and scrambling for quotes amid the rabble.

The woman at his side, a blonde whose hair had gone coarse from too many chemical treatments, stirred her drink with her fingertip, then lazily brought her finger to her lips.

I rolled my eyes and looked away, embarrassed for the female species. Her blonde hair, tiny hair clips, and lace collar signaled femininity, but her gestures were about as demure as an oncoming train.

"I'm not so sure about the senator going free," she answered, her voice deep and husky. "Care to bet on it?"

I closed my eyes. Ten to one she was about to mention dinner someplace, and I'd bet my last cookie she wanted to lose that particular wager. She *liked* this guy, whoever he was, and her interest wasn't exactly focused on his intellectual qualities.

I could understand the interest. He was handsome and charmingly bewildered, and thick enough not to have picked up on her flagrant flirting. "You don't believe he'll get off?" The newsman turned the full wattage of his blinding smile upon the blonde. "Though the evidence clearly shows the senator is guilty, you can't forget who he is. He's a powerful man."

He had taken the bait; his smile said it all. Smiles come in three basic varieties—simple smiles, where the corners of the mouth lift without showing teeth; upper smiles, where just the top teeth are visible; and broad smiles, where you can practically count a person's molars. Of course, each smile comes in high and low intensities, and there are about as many variations as there are people, but you don't send a broad smile winging across the room unless you're expressing great pleasure and delight. No doubt about it, Mr. Newsman wanted the blonde, but he had no idea she wanted him almost as badly.

I shifted on my stool, suddenly bored with the tableau at my right hand. The man was an idiot, probably one of those cardboard suits who was paid to read the news and look good doing it. The blonde was welcome to him.

I picked up my glass and leaned one elbow on the bar, swiveling to look back at the crowd that had filled the room. A group of men at a table near the door erupted in laughter at a companion's punch line; a more discreet table of women buzzed in the corner, their eyes narrowed in concern and sympathy—for whom? The murdered woman or the scheming senator?

I took a sip from my glass and glanced toward the opposite corner, then felt an instinctive stab of fear as I recognized the bulky form propped against the wall. The bald man from the courthouse hallway stood there, his hands hidden in the pockets of his camel-colored overcoat, his gaze fastened to my face. As an icy finger touched the base of my spine, I broke the stare and glanced downward, then chastised myself for behaving so instinctively. When involved in a non-verbal power play, you should look up and away or to the side, but *never* down. Now he would know he had intimidated me.

I clenched my fist in annoyance at my own stupidity. Here I was, behaving like a submissive and helpless female, when the man probably had nothing to do with me. He could be anyone—a resident in my apartment building, a friend of Kurt's I'd met at a party, or someone who had read the *People* interview and thought I looked familiar. He hadn't looked away when I caught his eye in the courthouse, so for some reason he felt he knew me . . .

"Excuse me, Miss Fischer?"

I glanced up, surprised as much by the respectful tone as by the fact that someone had bothered to look at my face. The slim man standing beside me wore a white shirt, navy trousers, a tan trench coat, and a coffee-stained tie—the uniform of a newspaper reporter.

Grateful to be distracted from the man at the back of the room, I gave the reporter a tentative smile. "Do I know you?"

He pulled a business card from his pocket and expertly flicked it onto the polished bar. "Tom Brown of the *Times*."

I glanced at the card, then tilted my head and looked up. "What can I do for you, Mr. Brown?"

A steno pad and tape recorder magically appeared. "Would you care to predict the jury's verdict?"

"No comment."

The set of his chin suggested a stubborn streak. "Will you confirm that you are working for Ross Colby's law firm?"

"No comment."

"Come on, Claudia." He gave me a lopsided smile, no teeth showing. *Friendly, but unsure.* "We all know what you were doing in that courtroom every day. Just confirm it for me."

I parked my elbow on the bar and dropped my chin to my palm. "I never talk about my clients."

Brown shoved the steno pad and recorder back into his pocket, then gestured toward the bartender, his face screwing up in a conspiratorial grin. "Can I buy you a drink?"

I tapped a fingernail to the edge of my glass. "I have one, thanks."

"Can we talk off the record?"

"Not about my client."

"OK, then. I'd really like to talk about you and your work. I saw the *People* piece. Fascinating."

I sipped the watery liquid collecting among the ice cubes at the bottom of my glass as Brown placed his order. Just last week Rory and I had looked at our empty calendar and wondered if lawyers even read *People,* but here stood a reporter for the respected *New York Times.* An article might help, but timing mattered immensely. If Senator Mitchell was found guilty and a *Times* article came out immediately afterward, I'd become known as the jury consultant *least* likely to help a client win his case.

Still, it wouldn't hurt to hear what Mr. Brown had in mind.

"Why would you be interested in me?" I took pains to keep my voice light. "I'm just an ordinary person, trying hard to meet a need and make a living."

"I should hardly think life as a jury consultant is ordinary." Tom Brown accepted a scotch and soda from the bartender, then shifted to look at me. "I've spent every free moment of the last three weeks learning as much as I could about you, Claudia Fischer. And what I've learned is quite intriguing."

I forced a laugh. "Don't waste your breath, Brown. I don't flatter easily."

He took a quick gulp from his glass, then leaned against the bar and gave me a bright-eyed glance, full of shrewdness. "Flattery's not my style. I'm more of a researcher, and I always double-check my facts."

"Like what?"

He set his glass on the counter and pulled the steno pad from his pocket. He flipped a couple of pages, then lifted a brow. "You received your M.A. in communications with an emphasis in legal communication from San Diego State. You began your career six years ago working in Los Angeles with Elaine Dawson. You assisted her with several celebrity cases and left her firm just after the Hernandez brothers' trial resulted in two convictions for first-degree murder." He lifted his head and looked at me with a question in his eyes. "Her secretary intimated that your shoddy work lost that case."

I took a deep breath and flexed my fingers, waiting until the urge to strangle a certain secretary had passed. "I thought you double-checked your sources. If you had, you'd know that's not what happened."

I stood, ready to leave, but he caught my arm. "Then tell me your side of the story. I promise I'll get it right."

"I don't need this."

"Claudia"—his voice dropped to a deeper, more persuasive level— "in a matter of days, Senator Mitchell's trial will pass into history, and everyone on earth will want to know about the jury consultant who picked the panel. Do you want the world to know the full story? Or would you rather have them read your curriculum vitae as presented in a press release from Elaine Dawson's office?"

I gritted my teeth. Reporters could be as annoying as a whiny child, but Brown had a point. I had done very little work on the Hernandez brothers' case, but since I chose to leave soon afterward, I made a convenient scapegoat for the blot on Elaine's record.

Reluctantly, I lowered myself back to the stool. "Why did you call Elaine Dawson's office in the first place?"

Brown grinned as he pulled out the tape recorder. "Everyone knows she won the Marvin Maxwell case."

"I thought that was Tommy Coachman. I seem to remember hearing, 'If his prints don't show, you must let him go.'"

"Yeah, but it took a genius to pick twelve people who would buy into that poppycock." Brown flipped a switch on the tiny recorder. "So tell me what happened between you and Elaine Dawson."

I sighed heavily, then caught the bartender's eye and pointed toward my empty glass. He scooped it up. "You owe me a Diet Coke," I told Brown.

"The *Times* can afford it."

—

A fresh glass appeared before me. I took a sip, then turned to face the reporter. "I hate to disappoint you, but there was no big scandal. I wanted to start handling some of the actual casework. After six years, I knew I had learned enough to manage it. But Elaine is—well, she's one of those administrators who has to keep her finger in every pie. She always had to be—make that she always *liked* being—in the courtroom. She was happy to let her people do the background work, but she would never let any of us fly solo. So I finally resigned and told her I was moving east. Most of her clients are in California; I'm happy to work in New York."

"Are you still friendly?"

"Of course. Elaine phoned me just this morning, in fact."

Brown set the tape recorder on the bar and nonchalantly lifted his glass. "Did she call about the Mitchell trial?"

"No comment."

Brown smiled, acknowledging his sneak attack. "OK. So tell me— what's involved in the work of a jury consultant? You don't go to college and major in intuition."

"Intuition has nothing to do with it." I paused to frame my thoughts. Litigation consulting companies like mine assisted attorneys in witness preparation, credibility assessment, nonverbal communication analysis, venue analysis, and voir dire strategies. Boiled down to bare bones, the job largely depended upon demographic studies and body language. Most of my work relied upon a thousand little visual and audible clues I'd learned to recognize and interpret through experience. But I couldn't just rattle off a disconnected list of signals; they rarely made sense out of context.

"There's nothing magical about it," I finally said. "Anyone who likes to interpret statistics and watch people could probably be trained to do what I do. It's a matter of learning about individuals, of knowing

—

17

what makes them tick. It's just a matter of reading and understanding them."

"So how do you read people? Through body language?"

"That's only part of it." I took a deep breath. "First, through demographic studies we gather as much data as possible about the venue, so we'll know what sort of people we're likely to encounter in a jury pool. Then we gather information about each prospective juror—all from public records, of course; it's perfectly legal. While the lawyers for both sides conduct their questioning during voir dire, we take notes. We pay attention to what the jurors say as well as what they don't say. And we're not afraid to take chances—after all, many times our client's life depends upon our decisions. It's better to challenge a questionable juror than say nothing and have *that* juror convince the others your client is guilty."

A gleam of resentment entered the reporter's eyes. "Do you ever feel guilty about what you do? After all, Elaine Dawson's work resulted in Marvin Maxwell's freedom, and nine out of ten Americans today would tell you he murdered his wife and that other poor guy."

I frowned, resenting his question and his attitude. "American justice is not founded upon opinion polls, Mr. Brown. Every accused person is innocent until proven guilty beyond a reasonable doubt. Every defendant is entitled to the best defense possible."

"The best money can buy, you mean." Brown grinned at me, an odd mingling of cynicism and amusement in his eyes. "Tell me, Claudia—do you think you'll ever get tired of working for pond scum?" He lowered his voice and edged closer. "You and I both know the renowned senator killed that girl. I'm no expert at what you do, but I've been watching Mitchell long enough to figure that he sat down one afternoon with pen and paper and made two lists—one of reasons to keep her, the other of reasons to kill her. If he keeps her, he gets a few cheap thrills and he can swagger with the other guys who have trophy mistresses. But he also gets saddled with an illegitimate child, maybe even a nasty custody hearing and a public divorce. He gets smeared in a way not even the Teflon Senator can shake off. He gets hurt—badly."

The amused look suddenly left his eyes. "Did you know the bulk of the senator's fortune comes from his wife? If the current Mrs. Mitchell were to divorce her husband, the money for mistresses and campaigns and society gatherings would evaporate. Not all of it, but enough to cramp ol' Chad's style."

I crossed my arms and pointedly looked away. "It's a moot point; she'll divorce him anyway. You can't expect her to stay married after he confessed to the affair—"

"All I'm saying," Brown interrupted, picking up his glass again, "is that for the next few months I'm going to be checking up on Mrs. Mitchell's welfare. If the senator is cleared—and, due to your good work, I strongly suspect he will be—I'm sure Mrs. Mitchell will initiate divorce proceedings. If anything happens to her before the divorce is final—and, due to your good work, I strongly suspect something will—I'll be calling you again, Miss Fischer. I'll want to know how you can sleep nights."

It was a remark designed to sting, and it did. I stared in silence as Brown drained his drink, then picked up his recorder and snapped the power off. "Have a good night." The smile he shot me held a touch of malice. "I'll be in touch."

I gave him a black look. "Wait a minute, Brown—"

The oak doors of the pub burst open, and a red-faced cameraman leaned into the room. "They're back," he yelled, his eyes searching for his crew. "The Mitchell jury is coming back."

I glanced at my watch. They'd been out only three hours.

—

Waiting for a jury verdict—and I've waited for dozens of them over the course of my career—must be a bit like the experience of childbirth. Most of my friends are married and into the family scene now, and even though they were 90 percent sure of their babies' sex before the little darlings entered the world, an uncertainty still existed—what if the technician misread the sonogram?

What if I misread these jurors?

A high-speed verdict like this one almost certainly meant unanimous consent from the beginning of deliberations. The Marvin Maxwell jurors took four hours to declare the movie star innocent of a savage double murder, so I supposed this panel could find a senator innocent of one murder in only three . . .

Or they could look at the evidence and find undeniable guilt.

I flipped open my notebook again and studied the names printed there. Laurie Dorset might have wavered, but I didn't think she possessed the charisma or leadership skills to convince anyone else to change sides. Elizabeth Mattingly had leadership ability, but she had never demonstrated much interest in anything unrelated to herself. Alan Armstrong was a lifelong Democrat and appeared to approve of Mitchell, but he also had a wife and evidenced strong family values. In the jury room, could he have unveiled an aspect of his personality that I missed?

Exhaling slowly, I closed my notebook and loosely folded my arms across my chest. Too late now for second guesses and recriminations. The die was cast. The jurors had called the judge at four o'clock, and His Honor, eager to finish this extended case, had decided to reconvene at this late hour rather than prolong our misery another day.

Now the judge sat erect in his chair, his eyes on the empty jury box. At their respective tables, the attorneys for the prosecution and the defense waited silently. Senator Chad Mitchell sat in a wooden chair in front and to the right of me. Though he had crossed his arms and legs in a studied posture of nonchalance, I couldn't help but notice that a small drop of sweat gleamed on his upper lip. Not even the senator was totally confident.

Somewhere beyond the oak door in the front of the courtroom, the jurors were gathering their belongings, perhaps even exchanging addresses. They had been together for six months, more than enough time to form lasting friendships. Mindful of the waiting television cameras, the women would be smoothing their hair and applying lipstick, the men adjusting their neckties.

Finally the bailiff opened the door. Juror number twelve, Thomas Orr, entered first, his eyes downcast as he made his way to the first chair on the back row. The other jurors followed, several modeling Orr's hunched posture and lowered gaze.

My heart began to thump almost painfully in my chest. Chad Mitchell's wasn't the only life at stake here. If the senator went to prison, any lawyer acquainted or affiliated with the law firm of Wilt, Kremkau, Colby, and Stock would call on me about as quickly as they'd volunteer for an IRS audit. And if Tom Brown printed a story reporting that I'd been the jury consultant for the trial that sent Senator Mitchell to prison, I might as well leave New York State. Mitchell's supporters would hound me until my dying day.

I shivered, then rubbed my hands over my arms, trying to bring some warmth back into my body. Why was I expecting the worst? If the panel came back with a guilty verdict, the senator should bear the blame. One couldn't argue with facts, after all, regardless of what happened in other celebrity murder trials. I had done the best work I could do, and if the jury chose to vote according to their consciences instead of their politics, Colby should understand. After all, lawyers lost big cases every day.

The heavy door slammed with an emphatic sound, and the judge

—

21

rapped on his desk with the gavel. "Madame Chairman," he said, fixing Elizabeth Mattingly in a direct gaze. "Have you reached a verdict?"

"We have, Your Honor."

"The defendant will rise."

Senator Mitchell and Ross Colby stood behind the defendant's counsel table. The attractive Hilton Hotel executive handed a folded slip of paper to the bailiff, who handed it to the judge. I studied the judge as he opened the paper and skimmed it, but the man was skilled in the art of nondisclosure. "You may publish the verdict," he answered, and as he handed the paper back to the bailiff, I searched his face for some flicker of emotion, even a twitch of satisfaction or frustration . . . there was nothing.

As the bailiff opened the paper, Elizabeth Mattingly stood to her full height of five feet nine inches and faced the defendant. In that instant, I knew.

"In the case of the state of New York versus Mitchell," the bailiff read, "on the count of murder in the first degree, we find the defendant, Chad Myers Mitchell, not guilty."

Mattingly broke about a dozen rules of courthouse protocol as she flashed a heart-stopping broad smile at Mitchell. "Innocent of all charges, Senator!" she called.

The courtroom erupted. As Stephanie Glazier's weeping parents embraced each other, the senator hugged his lawyer, the jurors broke into applause, and the sea of reporters surged forward, recorders and pens at the ready.

The judge rapped for order, and the mayhem ceased almost as suddenly as it had begun.

I glanced at the prosecutor, who might well call for a polling of the jury to establish that the verdict had been unanimous, but Howard Nardozzi sat motionless, his gaze fixed to his legal pad.

—

After glancing at Nardozzi, the judge returned his attention to the panel. "Ladies and gentlemen of the jury, I'd like to thank you for the many months you invested in this case. You have done your duty as citizens, and we thank you. You are dismissed."

The courtroom waited in silence as the members of the panel stood and exited through their special doorway. I noticed that nearly all of them took a moment to send a congratulatory smile winging toward the counsel table for the defense—there were so many teeth showing, the courtroom could have been mistaken for a dentists' convention. Elizabeth Mattingly even grinned at me.

A whirlwind of giddy relief swirled in my head as the judge concluded the trial. At the moment of release, the press pack swept through the gate between the gallery and the courtroom, forming a solid phalanx around Colby and Senator Mitchell. I stood, hoping for a moment to congratulate my client, but soon realized that this was neither the time nor place for private congratulations.

"Senator Mitchell," one reporter called as I stooped to pick up my briefcase, "to what do you owe this overwhelming vindication?"

I expected Mitchell to say something about justice and his faith in the American legal system. I did *not* expect him to lean over the railing and lift me to my feet, his strong arm pulling me toward him in a ferocious bear hug. "I owe everything to my brilliant lawyer and this talented woman," he said, his bright smile dazzling against his tanned skin. "Ross Colby and Claudia Fischer believed in me. They believe in justice. They believe in the American legal system. And they, my friends, are why I am not only a free man tonight, but also an innocent one."

I tried to smile as the flashbulbs flickered, but I'm pretty sure I only flinched uncomfortably. I endured the weight of that iron arm around my shoulders for as long as I could, then ducked away and left the senator to face his public with his lawyer.

———

The pressing crowd let me pass without comment, but I caught Tom Brown's eye as I moved through the doorway. "Congratulations," he mouthed across the mob, but his somber eyes were as remote as the ocean depths.

I shrugged off the burden of guilt he thought I should be carrying and made my way into the crowded hallway. The excitement level there was as high as that of the courtroom, and a profound sense of weariness settled over me as I claimed my coat and fought my way into it. I glanced at my watch—6:30. With luck, I'd have just enough time to catch a cab, go home and change, and meet Karl for dinner.

The horde outside the courtroom showed no signs of dispersing, but I managed to thread my way through and reach the entrance lobby. I took a moment to smile at the guards who lingered at the security checkpoint.

"All finished?" Sam asked. He was an older man with an easy and congenial manner. We had often exchanged pleasantries when I passed through the checkpoint.

"All done," I answered. I paused beside the metal detector. "And I don't know when I'll see you again, Sam. My calendar's looking a little bare at the moment."

"Miss Fischer!"

As I glanced behind me I saw the strange bald man who'd been shadowing my movements. He was shouldering his way through the crowd, coming my way with his hand uplifted, his gait purposeful.

I turned to Sam. "I don't know who that man is, but I don't think I want to talk to him," I whispered, turning up the collar of my coat to shield my face. "Can you stall him for a moment? Give me long enough to catch a cab."

"I'll hold him for you." Sam spoke with quiet firmness. "You just go on, and I'll take care of this fellow."

Nodding my thanks, I hurried away.

—

Two

"To you, darling." Kurt lifted his goblet and lightly touched it to mine. "Congratulations on a job well done. Your trial was all over the news tonight. Even CNN did a piece on it, so that means you're getting international coverage."

I felt myself flushing under Kurt's compliment. "Well, it wasn't exactly *my* trial. And if the defendant had been anyone other than a United States senator, we probably wouldn't have gotten any coverage at all."

"But you did get it." There was something pleased, proud, and vaguely possessive in the way Kurt looked at me. "And tomorrow every lawyer on the eastern seaboard will know that Claudia Fischer is *the* jury consultant to hire for important cases."

I'll admit it—part of me reveled in his open admiration. But I resisted the unsophisticated temptation to crow right in the middle of the Rainbow Room and instead picked up my fork. "I certainly hope so. But there's no way of knowing what tomorrow will bring."

Kurt picked up his fork too, but then he leaned forward and lowered his voice. "Is the wolf still at the corporate door?"

"We'll be OK for another month." I stabbed at a piece of lettuce and tried to keep the worried note from my voice. "Colby promised me a bonus if we won. It will cover the balloon payment on the loan but little else because the trial took longer than I planned. We'll be in the black for about a month before expenses drive us into red ink again."

Kurt took a bite of his salad, his eyes gleaming blue and mischievous in the candlelight as he thoughtfully studied me. "You know I'd bail you out in a heartbeat," he finally said. "We can keep the deal on a professional level. My practice could loan you the money over a long term with a *very* attractive interest rate—"

"Thanks, Kurt, but no. I want to make it on my own."

"Don't be silly, Claudia." His lips thinned with irritation. "We're going to be married in less than a year, and then what's mine will be yours anyway."

"Not exactly—your practice and my firm will never be community property." I tried to glare at him, but I just can't be angry with Kurt when those summer sky blue eyes look up at me. I don't know how his parents ever disciplined him.

He shrugged off my objections and returned to his salad. "Then you'll just have to find another client—preferably one with deep pockets."

"I may have one." I paused until he looked up again. "I checked my messages just before coming here. According to Rory, I have an appointment tomorrow morning with a representative from the Global Union. The man's name is Darien Synn."

"Global Union?" His brows knit in puzzlement. "That name is familiar, but I've never heard of Darien Synn."

"Rory said the organization is based in Rome. I don't know much about it myself, but the appointment's not until eleven o'clock. I'll have time to scour the Internet and see what I can find."

Kurt's eyes were still abstracted, but they cleared as he shook his head. "It doesn't sound like a law firm."

"I don't know what it is." I stabbed at my salad again. "But as long as they want to talk business, I'll listen. Trials like Senator Mitchell's don't come along every year, so I can't afford to sit back and wait on the celebrity cases."

"Speaking of opportunities"—Kurt grinned at me, his eyes suddenly alight with mischief and inspiration—"I was thinking that maybe you and I should give a dinner party for the senator. You know, a celebration-type thing. Then you could introduce me to Mitchell, and I could—"

"Kurt Waldron Welton!" Aghast, I stared at him, knowing what suggestion lay on the tip of his tongue. "You aren't seriously thinking of trying to solicit the senator as a patient."

"Why not?" he countered, his golden brows rising nearly to his hairline. "Anyone would need counseling after a trial like that. After all, the man has been accused of murder, he is estranged from his wife, his children aren't speaking to him, and his career is uncertain. It's a wonder he hasn't sought out a psychologist before this."

"I am not going to let you accost my clients." I rolled my eyes, amazed that my fiancé could engage in what amounted to high-class ambulance chasing. "If Mitchell wants counseling, I'm sure he can afford to find his own shrink. Goodness, Colby employed two different psychiatrists during the trial. They both found Mitchell mentally competent and physically fit."

"Those were trial docs, Claudia; they say what they're paid to say."

"They were reputable psychologists, and they wouldn't lie . . . I don't think." I waved away the topic. "Enough, Kurt. I'm not throwing a party for Mitchell. I wouldn't care if I never saw the man again. If he wants to refer a client, I wouldn't refuse the work, but"—I couldn't stop a shudder—"something about him gives me the creeps."

"And that's ample evidence that he needs a psychologist." Kurt lifted his glass again and peered at me over the rim. "Think about it, Claude—you might be doing some other woman a great favor if you introduced me to the senator."

Feeling restless and irritable, I brought my hand to my forehead, shielding my eyes from Kurt's persistent gaze. Twice in the last few hours I'd been reminded that Chad Mitchell might be a walking time bomb, but what could I do about it?

Absolutely nothing.

Kurt turned his smile up a notch. "Come on, Claude, don't be mad."

"I'm not mad."

"Yes, you are. I don't have to be the Seer to read you like a book."

"That's not funny."

"Maybe not, but I know something that is. Today someone e-mailed me this list of messages for a shrink's answering machine. After the greeting, the voice says, 'If you are obsessive-compulsive, press one repeatedly. If you are codependent, please ask someone to press two for you. If you have multiple personalities, press three, four, and five. If you are paranoid, we know who and what you are. Stay on the line so we can trace your call.'"

I stared at him in amused wonder. "Kurt, I read those a week ago. They weren't funny then, either."

His eyes widened in pretend surprise. "You don't think so? I thought they were hilarious."

I looked up in relief as the waiter approached with our entrées. In less than sixty seconds Kurt would have his lobster, so he'd have to stop talking and eat.

Until then, he seemed determined to continue: "If you are delusional, press seven and your call will be transferred to the mother ship."

I closed my eyes and nodded, my attention drifting away on a tide of fatigue.

I thought I would pass out the moment my head hit the pillow, but not even the quiet sigh of passing traffic and the steady applause of fluttering oak leaves outside my window could lull me to sleep. An hour after going to bed I felt more wide-awake than I had been at dinner with Kurt, and I could find no explanation for my sudden second wind.

Muttering in frustration, I threw back the comforter, then realized I had covered Tux, the black-and-white stray who slept every night at the foot of my bed. Apologizing, I yanked the comforter off the cat. Tux opened one yellow eye and yawned, then curled tighter into a ball and went back to sleep. I scowled at him as I reached for my robe. Apparently my part-time cat didn't feel his responsibilities included keeping me company in the middle of the night.

Wrapped in the warmth of my heavy chenille robe, I padded to the computer on my kitchen table and punched the power on. As the machine beeped and flashed, I looked over the notes I had jotted down as I listened to Rory's message. Darien Synn—Rory had spelled the last name—represented the Global Union, was based in Rome, and was visiting New York for only a short time.

"I don't know what to make of this guy," Rory had said in conclusion. "He seemed polite enough on the telephone but didn't volunteer any information about the job. But I thought you'd want to see him."

Because you don't have any other work . . . Rory didn't need to add the obvious.

Once the computer finished its warmup routine, I clicked on the Internet icon. Almost instantly, the Excite search engine appeared on-screen, and I typed in my search criteria:

"Global Union" + "Darien Synn"

I tapped the enter key, then leaned forward as the ISDN connection whisked the search results to my screen. Global Union, or *Unione Globale,* as it was known in Rome, apparently had a Web page that featured Darien Synn's name.

I clicked on the link, and an instant later I found myself studying a lively Web page featuring a revolving globe, the blue flag of the European Union, and a color photograph of a strikingly handsome man with dark hair and even darker eyes. Was this Darien Synn? I leaned closer to read the caption: "Santos D. Justus, president and founder of Global Union, welcomes you to a new world through peace."

I lifted a brow. Well. If Darien Synn looked anything like his boss, tomorrow's meeting might be more pleasant than I had hoped.

The Web page offered little to explain why Global Union might be interested in a jury consultant, only a brief overview of the organization itself:

Global Union, headquartered in the heart of ancient Rome, is the culmination of a vision. Santos D. Justus, the Italian ambassador to the Western European Union, has long sought to find a common path for the people of the world to unite in peace.

The article ended with a quote from Justus:

The world's leaders have struggled to overcome national differences in the United Nations and other world organizations, but true change will only be implemented when it begins in the hearts of the common people. Those common people—rich and poor, young and old—share a dream of world peace and freedom. They are the foundation of Global Union.

The common people? I tapped my fingernails against the edge of the keyboard, turning the phrase over in my mind. How did Justus define "common people"? No matter what he meant, one fact was crystal clear—Justus was savvy enough to understand that the masses would never make a profound difference without leadership, and he had stepped forward to lead this particular herd. The name of Santos D. Justus, whoever he was, obviously carried some weight in Italy. And though he might be trying to organize a grass-roots political movement, from the look of his photograph, there wasn't a thing about Santos D. Justus I'd call *common*.

I skimmed the rest of the page and spied Darien Synn's name listed with the organization's board of directors. The remainder of the material consisted of politically correct drivel about peace being the only doorway through which an individual could find lasting happiness, and the Doorway of Peace lay beyond the Hall of Understanding . . .

Eager to leave the land of mystic lollipops and sentimental axioms, I clicked on the search icon, then typed: "Santos D. Justus"

The search brought up several links, most of which led to reports about the European Union and the Western European Union, or WEU. Unfamiliar with the latter organization, I jotted down the initials in my notebook.

Ten minutes later, after wading through several barely comprehensible bureaucratic reports, I had formed a clearer picture: inaugurated in 1955, the ten-nation WEU—composed of France, Germany, the United Kingdom, Italy, Spain, Belgium, the Netherlands, Luxembourg, Portugal, and Greece—was originally intended to provide for cooperation in economic, social, cultural, and defense matters. In recent years, however, the WEU had served mainly as a defense organization similar to NATO. As recently as the summer of 1999, certain voices within the European Union and the WEU had called for integration of the two groups, but not all nations in the two separate organizations were willing to unite.

I reached for my notebook and made a note of this particular conflict.

—

Could Synn or Justus be planning to take one of these organizations to court?

I bookmarked a couple of the more interesting pages, then yawned. A profound and peaceful weariness had settled over me like a blanket. I pressed the monitor's power button, making the room go dark. The heat came on as I wandered back to bed, and as the radiators clanged and hissed, I gathered my robe to my throat, my eyes burning from exhaustion.

It had been a long day, and a torturously long trial. I had earned a vacation, but until my firm had bankrolled a cushion of at least six months' operating expenses, I couldn't afford to take even a single day off . . . particularly if the coming day offered the chance to sign a new client.

I climbed under the comforter and felt Tux rearrange himself so his soft little body nestled against my leg.

We slept.

THREE

ALONE IN HIS APARTMENT, ASHER GENZANO SAT ON THE EDGE OF THE bed and leaned his elbows upon his knees. A small black-and-white television on the bureau cast a gray light over the spare furnishings, pushing back the gloom of early morning.

Outside his window, three ecological operators emptied a row of city-supplied Dumpsters into the churning jaws of a garbage truck. Through the quiet of dawn, Asher heard a baritone voice echoing over the nearly deserted piazza. "*I turisti sono difettosi quanto i residenti*," the man said, complaining that the tourists created as much trash as the residents.

The garbage truck whined and shifted its gears; the garbage collectors moved away. Asher leaned forward and focused on the television, tensing as the camera scanned a crowd of officials on a platform. After a panoramic shot of the European Union headquarters in Brussels, the cameraman centered on a dark-haired man who stepped forward and waved to the crowd.

"*Bonjour,* good morning," he called, lowering his hand to grip the lectern. His dark gaze scanned the crowd, then seemed to focus upon the television camera. "Ladies and gentlemen," he began, choosing to address the gathering in English, "it is with great humility that on behalf of my beloved Italy I accept the presidency of the Western European Union. Furthermore, it is with great pleasure that I announce the beginning of negotiations to unite the nations of the WEU and the

---

European Union. We will do *anything we must* to ensure peace for Europe and harmony for all the world's people."

A wave of applause rippled throughout the crowd, and an Italian interpreter spoke over the sound, interpreting the address for viewers in Rome.

The camera drew back, and the Brussels scene vanished, replaced by two newscasters from the local television station in Rome. The announcers smiled and briefly debated whether the new president, Santos D. Justus, might be able to accomplish what so many others deemed impossible, then the news broke for a commercial.

As a sensuous female voice extolled the elegance and comfort of Ferragamo shoes, Asher moved to the small desk in the front room, pulled his fountain pen from a chipped coffee mug, then drew a blue leather journal toward him. Carefully he opened to a blank page, smoothed the seam with his broad thumbnail, and began to write.

Is this the man? He speaks of unity and peace. He pleases the crowd and seems to possess an unusual charisma . . . like the others. Furthermore, he is Roman, of the people who destroyed the Temple, just as the prophet Daniel prophesied.

Asher paused, feeling suddenly limp with weariness. How could he know whether or not to proceed? He had walked into evil's lair before, betrayed nation and conscience and soul to be certain he had found *the one.*

His heart ached, torn by the familiar pain, the ageless remorse. Indecision was like a demon in his head, taunting him with what-ifs and supposing. What if this was not the man? What if this was not the place or the time? He could wait for more signs, he could fast and pray, but if he waited he might confront the man too late. And he could never be cer-

—

tain, not if he sat and worried forever, because the evil one always had others waiting for tomorrow and all the tomorrows beyond that . . .

Holy God, he wrote, the words coming faster now, *give me discernment.*

> *Show me what I must do, and guide my actions. I am ready to give all, Holy God, even if I must give my body to the destroyer again, I am ready. Show me the way to full forgiveness. Open the doors, and I will walk through them.*

The television commercials ended; the newscasters began to discuss a story about a tourist arrested for bathing in the Trevi Fountain.

Asher capped his pen, closed his journal, and carefully slid it into an empty space on the crowded shelf behind his desk. After slipping into a light jacket, he snapped off the television in his bedroom, then moved out of the apartment, carefully locking the door behind him.

FOUR

WHEN DARIEN SYNN ENTERED MY OFFICE PROMPTLY AT 11:00, MY first reaction was disappointment that Synn looked nothing like his employer. I had scarcely registered that fact when horror snaked down my backbone and coiled in my belly—the man before me was the bald stranger who'd been dogging my steps the day before.

"It is wonderful to finally meet you, Miss Fischer," Synn said, inclining his head in a deep nod as he stretched out his hand. "And I must apologize for what must seem like appalling rudeness. I fear I startled you yesterday when I saw you outside the courtroom. I would have spoken then but did not want to distract you at such a crucial hour. I tried to speak to you last night as you were leaving, but you must not have heard me call your name."

With difficulty, I set my panic aside and took his hand. The man's grip was firm and polite, and something in his down-to-earth manner made my previous anxiety seem foolish and paranoid. Smiling, I withdrew my hand and gestured to the guest chair in front of my desk. "Forgive me, Mr. Synn, if yesterday I seemed a bit unsettled. I'm always a bit on edge during a trial, and celebrity trials seem to attract . . . unusual people."

"I understand completely." Synn sank gracefully into the chair, a movement completely at odds with his square, stocky appearance. His blue eyes lit up with amusement as I took my seat and met his gaze. "I am sure you are wondering what matter would compel me to follow you during a trial."

"You are absolutely correct," I answered, tilting my head as I listened to his speech patterns. He spoke careful, educated English without a discernible accent, and that alone was enough to signal that he was Not From Around Here. Nearly everyone in New York had an accent of some kind.

"I must admit I am curious," I added, tenting my fingers. "What use would Global Union have for a jury consultant?" I tempered my smile. "Or perhaps you are here on behalf of someone else."

"You are correct on the first assumption; I am representing Global Union and my employer, Santos Justus." He nodded, his bald head gleaming in the fluorescent ceiling lights. "But we do not wish to hire you as a jury consultant. We wish to employ your skills for a different enterprise."

I lifted a brow. "Such as?"

Synn laughed softly. "I suppose we could use a woman with your unique abilities in many situations. But before I go further, I should ask what you know about our organization."

I smiled, glad I had done my homework. "I know Global Union is headquartered in Rome. I know you are a member of the board of directors, and Santos D. Justus is the founder and president. I believe you are committed to achieving world peace through a grass-roots movement, not solely through political means." I swiveled my chair slightly. "Did I get it right?"

Synn stroked his upper lip—a meditation gesture common throughout the world. He was thinking hard about whatever he would say next.

"You are absolutely correct, Miss Fischer. There are a few other things you might like to know about us. First of all, the organization's leadership now consists of the directors you mentioned—Justus, myself, and eleven other men and women, mostly Europeans. We came together two years ago, and Global Union has been little more than an idea since that time. Until a month ago, our headquarters was a post office box in Rome, our outreach only a Web page. That is all."

I smiled, though I couldn't understand where the conversation was leading. "And now?"

"Last month, one of our board members passed away, bequeathing a sizable fortune to our organization. Now that we are finally able to pursue our goals, we have purchased a building in Rome and are in the process of hiring a staff. We are putting feet to our dreams, Miss Fischer, and Justus wants to be certain we proceed properly. You are the key to our success."

I lowered my folded hands to the desktop, trying to be polite and pleasant even though I was beginning to wonder if he would speak in riddles the entire morning. "Perhaps you should spell out what you'd like me to do for you."

Synn leaned forward, propping one hand on his knee—the picture of eagerness. "We have hired a very skilled personnel director, Maura Casale, but the woman does not have your gift for seeing into the heart of an individual. We want you to come in for a short term—say, four to six months—and conduct separate interviews of prospective employees. Mrs. Casale will judge the qualifications of the applicants, but we want you to determine whether or not their personalities are suitable for service in our organization. We want to do good for the world, Miss Fischer, and we will require the most committed people we can employ."

I looked away and suppressed the urge to smile. I didn't know where his information had come from, but it sounded as if someone had painted me as a mind reader, which I certainly am not.

"Mr. Synn," I said, lowering my voice to a friendly tone, "I am honored by your trust in me, but I don't think I'll be able to help you. I cannot judge a person's personality or trustworthiness in a ten-minute interview. Sometimes it takes days before I am able to form a full picture of an individual. When I am working on a trial, for instance, we spend hours in voir dire, and I am able to observe the jurors as they respond to a number of questions about a wide range of topics—"

"You may take all the time you wish," Synn interrupted. "Each employee will be interviewed for at least a week, and those who are hired will work on a probationary basis for several months. We want you to quietly work among us. Interview our applicants and our present employees, get to know them, and alert us if you sense a problem personality."

"I don't *sense* things." I tried to mask my annoyance but probably failed. "I believe in the physical world, Mr. Synn, and I base my conclusions on hard evidence. But suppose you tell me what sort of things might indicate a problem personality?"

Synn looked at me, his bright, clear blue eyes direct. "Lying. Theft. Disloyalty. Pessimism. The same sort of things for which you might dismiss an employee, Miss Fischer."

Fire someone for being pessimistic? If that were the standard for Fischer Consulting, Inc., I'd have fired myself on several occasions.

I drew a deep breath. "I am honored by the offer, Mr. Synn, but I'm afraid I've never considered international work. I am working hard to establish a presence in the eastern United States."

"Which you have already done."

I narrowed my gaze at him, mentally conceding the point. "And I have to consider my firm. I can't just shut down my Manhattan office for six months."

"By all means, keep your office staff here. You will be busy in the months to come. The world is a small place today, and you can be certain Mr. Justus will refer other clients to you. He is respected in

Europe, and I know he will be lavish in his praise for your work."

The man really knew how to pile it on. Here I was, facing debt and disaster, and he was promising steady work for months to come. But I couldn't see myself as a glorified personnel director, and I didn't like the idea of working my way into the confidences of his employees in order to spy on them.

"I don't speak Italian, Mr. Synn. I can't read people if I can't understand what they're saying."

"Most of our people speak English as well as Italian; quite a few also speak French," Synn answered. "The European community is shrinking along with the rest of the world, and English and French seem to be the languages of choice. I promise you, language will not be a problem. Besides"—his smile deepened—"Italian is not a difficult language. I suspect you will have a gift for it."

Quelling a sudden urge to laugh, I rubbed a finger over my lips. He had baited me with friendliness and flattery while avoiding the promise of financial gain. I *was* flattered by the offer, a little intrigued by the idea of spending six months in Rome, but if this Justus fellow was operating on a shoestring budget, there was no way he'd be able to pay me enough to keep my firm afloat.

"The stipend," Synn said, impressing me with his own ability to read people, "would be most generous." He pulled a business card from his inner coat pocket, wrote a figure on the card, then leaned across my desk and handed it to me.

For a moment my brain went numb. "Nine *million?*"

Synn's mouth twitched with amusement. "Nine million *lire,* of course. At the present rate of exchange, that amounts to"—He pulled a calculator from his pocket and punched in a series of numbers— "$4,882.83."

"Per week?"

Synn nodded. "Plus living expenses." The corner of his mouth drooped in an apologetic expression. "The amount may be less than you are currently receiving, but we are a not-for-profit organization, after all."

Looking away, I did some quick calculations of my own. Nearly five thousand per week, for as long as twenty-six weeks—that figure alone would put my income at $130,000 for six months' work. Plus expenses, he'd said, so I'd be living free in Rome and could send most of the money straight back to Rory, who would pay the bills, interview clients, and line up the most promising cases for the remainder of the year. It would be inconvenient to be so far away from the important people in my life, but if an emergency arose, I could always fly home. And Kurt could afford the international calls . . .

Kurt! A grinning goblin of guilt reared his head, and I grappled with the little monster. I couldn't run out on Kurt, not with a wedding coming up, but he just might understand how this job could save my firm. Kurt might even like the idea of having an excuse to visit me in Rome.

I picked up the card and tapped it against the surface of my desk. "I'd like to think about it, Mr. Synn. When do you need an answer?"

Synn's bland expression shifted to a confident upper smile—reserved, yet friendly. "Monday would be good. I will be in town until late Monday afternoon, but then I must return to Rome."

"May I call you at your hotel with my decision?"

"By all means. I'm staying at the Ameritania, just off Broadway."

We stood, shook hands, and Synn left the room. I stood motionless for a long moment, his card flat against my palm and his offer uppermost in my mind.

I turned the card over. *Rev. Darien Synn,* it said, *Vice President, Unione Globale. 4 Via della Botteghe Oscure, Roma.*

The word *reverend* caught me by surprise. Synn hadn't mentioned any church affiliation, but perhaps, I supposed, it was only natural that a clergyman would be concerned about world peace and brotherly love.

I sank back into my chair and stared at the card. It might actually feel good to spend a few months working for peace. In Rome, at least, reporters like Tom Brown wouldn't be able to accuse me of aiding murderers for money.

I tried to call Kurt, but he was with a patient. I left my name with the office receptionist and hung up, still mulling over Synn's proposition.

Desperate to talk to someone, I stepped out into the reception area. Rory sat with the phone pressed to his ear, but he lifted a brow in acknowledgment when I sank into the chair by the side of his desk.

I shook my head, wordlessly telling him to take his time.

"I'd be happy to take your name and number, but Ms. Fischer doesn't usually take personal injury cases," he said, his voice as smooth as warm butter. "I'll pass the information along, but I suggest you find the best lawyer you can. Thank you for calling."

He hung up the phone, scribbled a note on a pink message pad, then tossed it into the desperation basket. Our office received about a dozen calls a week from ordinary citizens who thought a jury consultant would strike holy fear into insurance representatives, doctors' attorneys, you name it. I could have easily filled my calendar with those kinds of low-paying jobs, but I wanted to spend my time where it counted—with high-stakes trials in criminal or civil court. It may sound heartless, but when I established the firm I decided not to waste my time on run-of-the-mill cases. I firmly believe that our society has become too litigious, and I refuse to help people sue McDonald's for serving hot coffee.

—

"What did we charge Colby and company for our work on the Mitchell case?" I asked, sliding Synn's business card over Rory's desk.

"About eighty-five an hour, plus expenses, I think. I haven't finished the billing yet." He picked up the card and stared at the name on the front.

"He got the reduced rate, right?"

"The publicity was worth the trade-off." Rory turned the business card and gasped at the figure on the back. "Is this a joke?"

"What if I told you"—I couldn't stop a smile—"that Darien Synn promised me nearly $125 an hour for six months . . . while I work in glorious, sun-drenched Rome?"

Rory's narrow face twisted into a dry, one-sided grin. "Rome . . . Georgia?"

"No, you goof. Rome, Italy. *Roma.*"

Rory gently laid the card on the desk, then pressed his hands together in a prayerful pose. "Does Reverend Synn work for the Vatican?"

"He's a vice president of Global Union, and he works for Santos Justus. They want me to evaluate their staff for several months, that's all. It's a new organization, and apparently they want to make sure they've hired dependable people."

Rory let out a long, low whistle. "Seems an expensive way to go about it. You don't bring 'the Seer' in for routine observation unless there's a lot at stake."

I threw him a reproachful glance. "I'll have none of that talk in here."

"Sorry. So when do you leave for Rome?"

"I'm not sure I should take the job." I rested my elbow on the edge of his desk and propped my chin in my hand. "There are a lot of things to consider. First of all, there's Kurt. We're getting married in May, so this may not be the best time for me to leave the country."

—

Rory tipped his head back and grinned at me. "Haven't you ever heard of the Concorde? New York to London, then Rome's only a hop away. And Kurt could easily afford the airfare."

I ticked off the next item on my list. "What about my sister? Kirsten is due in four months, and I promised I'd help her when the baby comes. Travis is a handful, and she'll have to recuperate and take care of the newborn—"

"Your sister is married to a *pediatrician* who can certainly afford a *nanny,*" Rory argued, crossing his arms. "And so what if the little darling is two months old when you first see him? He won't remember that you weren't at the hospital to greet him."

I held up a warning finger. "I'm not thinking of the baby. Most women want their mothers around when babies come, and since our mother can't—well, I feel like I should be with Kirsten. She'd do the same for me."

"I still think she'd understand." Rory's tone softened. "You are not your mother, Claudia, and your sister must know that you need to lead your own life. Besides, you're going up there this weekend, aren't you? Ask her about it. I'd bet a week's pay that she'll tell you to go to Rome."

"I wouldn't gamble your paycheck; you don't know where the next one is coming from." I chewed on my lower lip and looked away. Rory and I had been together for two years and sometimes he seemed to know me better than Kurt. Maybe he was right about Kirsten. My sister and I were close and had grown closer since the crash, but it wasn't like I'd be deserting her forever. Sean would be there for the delivery, and maybe it was better for the two of them to share this special time alone . . .

"There's one other consideration—and it's important." A stack of folders lay on the desk by my elbow, so I pushed it out of the way

—

45

and leaned forward, as if being closer would help Rory understand. "This thing with Justus could be huge—it's *international politics,* for heaven's sake. I'll be working with some powerful European movers and shakers. If I do a good job, there's no telling what could open up next."

Rory cast me a wicked grin. "Elaine Dawson, eat your heart out."

"Wait." I pressed a fingertip to his forearm. "If I fail, though, I fail big. From what I gather, Justus stands on the verge of gaining a lot of international attention, and I'll be working in the spotlight. If this Justus fellow doesn't like my work, Fischer Consulting could be history. The same press people who are praising us today could eat us alive six months from now. It's a risk, Rory. I'm not sure I'm ready to gamble my career in an international arena."

"You took a greater risk when you broke off from Elaine." Rory's brown eyes were blazing with confidence. "You knew less then than you do now, and you established this office on nothing but chutzpa."

"Well"—I grinned—"I had a little more than that. I had the good sense to hire you."

The tip of Rory's nose went pink. "Yeah. Well, you've proved you can handle the personnel thing; you do more than that every time you evaluate a jury. I don't see why reading Italians should be any different than analyzing New Yorkers. I think you should go for it."

I leaned back and looked around the office. "You'd have to run things here. You'd have to take notes on interesting new clients, do some background work, check with attorneys and trial judges to work out the calendars if we get a big case. We wouldn't be free to work a trial again until next spring."

Rory swiveled his chair and crossed one leg over his knee. "I know the drill, Claudia, and I wouldn't worry. With all the publicity from the Mitchell trial, we'll have the calendar filled in no time."

—

"But what if I have to pass on a really interesting case because I'm in Italy?"

Rory threw me a frown. "It takes *months* to prepare the really interesting cases. You'll have plenty of time. By the time you get back, I'll have your calendar filled and the background reports done." His mouth curled in a one-sided smile. "The only thing you'll have to worry about is replacing me if I get a better offer."

"That reminds me"—I pushed myself out of the chair—"take your wife out to dinner on the company card, will you? Discuss business or something so it'll be deductible. But keep your wife happy—I don't want her to encourage you to look elsewhere."

"As if she would." Rory shot the words after me as I walked toward my office, then assumed his professional voice as the phone rang. "Fischer Consulting." I stopped and looked over my shoulder when I heard him say, "How nice to hear from *you*." He listened a moment, then cupped his hand over the mouthpiece and mouthed a name I understood immediately.

I hurried back to my desk, a little curious to discover why Elaine Dawson had decided to call twice in two days.

"Elaine?"

"Claudia, dearest, how are you? Congratulations, by the way, on the Mitchell trial. You're getting great press even out here—almost as much airtime as I got for that Ambrose Zoya case."

I swallowed my irritation. Ambrose Zoya, founder of a chain of discount clothing stores, had spent a considerable portion of his billion-dollar estate hiring a legal dream team to defend him against a series of sordid charges having to do with his ex-wife and stepdaughter. The media played up the coming legal battle and the tabloids followed

every gossipy rabbit trail, but at the time I was so involved with pre-
liminary work on the Mitchell case that I barely paid attention.
Ambrose Zoya's lawyer decided to settle before the plaintiff could call
the first witness, so with one stroke of the pen Elaine's work became
a moot point. My case, on the other hand, had gone to trial.

"I'm just pleased my client was vindicated," I answered, parroting
the party line.

"Really?" Elaine laughed softly, and at that moment I would have
given my last dollar for a good look at her face. If I could see her eyes,
I'd know whether she was merely being pleasant or if she'd picked up
the fact that I despised the client I had spent weeks protecting.

"Claudia, dear," she began, her voice taking on a businesslike tone,
"I called because I thought you might like a heads-up about a particular screwball approaching people in our business. He came by our office
last week, and I promptly sent him packing. After your victory, however, it occurred to me that he might appear on your doorstep."

"What sort of screwball?"

She laughed again, a delicate three-noted ha-ha-ha that set my
nerves on edge. "Oh, he's harmless, I daresay, but he wanted me to go
to Europe for six months. Can you imagine! He seemed to think I
would be honored to be the personnel director of some insignificant
political cult, World Peace Now or something like that. Anyway, I
turned him down and thought I'd let you know about him. He may
be calling you next."

All the doubts that had been lapping at my subconscious suddenly crested and crashed. What had I been thinking? Elaine was
probably right. Darien Synn was nobody, Global Union was little
more than a group of dreamers with a Web page, and I had nearly
convinced myself to leave my firm at one of the most crucial points
of its existence . . .

"Thanks for the information, Elaine." I smiled into the phone, knowing she would hear the smile in my voice. "I appreciate your thinking of me."

"You, ah . . ." She hesitated, and I knew the lack of visible contact frustrated her too. "You haven't seen him, have you? He's a stocky fellow, bald, about forty-five or fifty, with a rash of age freckles on his head—"

"Elaine." I forced a laugh. "I've seen about a dozen men who fit that description in the last twenty-four hours alone. This place was an absolute zoo last night, and the phone has been ringing off the hook with reporters. But if this man calls, I'll be sure to remember what you've told me."

"That's good." She paused again. "You're doing well? And your sister?"

"Kirsten is fine, thanks for asking. Another baby on the way, due in late December. She and Sean are thrilled, and Travis can't wait to have a baby brother or sister."

"Dear me, I have another call."

I smiled, knowing that Elaine would rather discuss bunions than babies. "I'll let you go, then. Thanks for the information."

I dropped the phone back into its cradle, then swiveled my chair toward the single window in my office. The view was typical for Manhattan—a wall of windows belonging to the gray office building across the alley. Though it was only three o'clock, the sky outside had already begun to darken. I knew the skies would grow dark earlier and earlier, now that autumn and winter were approaching . . .

I folded my hands and stared at a single window across the way. In the uncurtained rectangle I saw a woman sitting at a desk much like mine, but she was bent over her work, her hand driving furiously across a sheet of paper.

Who wrote in longhand anymore?

I tossed the question aside and pondered the real issue troubling me. Why would Elaine Dawson call me about Darien Synn? She had taken pains to keep the conversation light and casual, and she hadn't even mentioned the man's name. Was her call motivated by sincere helpfulness . . . or rivalry?

Though Elaine and I now pretended to be the friends we once were, I had not forgotten the hurtful things she said when I confronted her about my desire to take a more active role in the work. In a flash of defensive anger, she had called me egocentric, power-hungry, and a few names not fit for printing in a family newspaper. She must have known I'd quit—after all, predicting people's reactions was her area of expertise—but she hadn't counted on my willingness to move east and establish my own firm. I sincerely believe she thought I'd stay in L.A., where she could squash my fledgling efforts by the sheer force of her personality.

Was this call an attempt to prevent me from moving into the international arena ahead of her?

I swiveled my chair again, turning to face my desk. It did tweak my pride to know that Darien Synn hadn't called me first, but until last week I had been thoroughly tied up with the Chad Mitchell case. Furthermore, as far as I knew, Elaine Dawson *had* been available. Though she kept busy with work for various attorneys engaged in mock trials, Elaine hadn't handled a celebrity case since Mr. Zoya decided to come clean and pay his ex-wife for her mental distress and suffering.

Could she have called just to discourage me from taking the one client who could finally bring me out from her shadow? Or had she read something in Reverend Synn's personality or conversation that disturbed her?

I lowered my head to my hands, then peeped out through my fingers and stared at the phone. I would have loved to bounce some of these ideas off Kurt, but he would be tied up until late . . . and likely wouldn't understand, anyway. Though he made an admirable show of understanding all of my problems, this one felt just a little too catty and *female* to make much headway in his psyche.

I glanced again at my empty calendar, then tossed a new file labeled "Global Union" into my briefcase. "I'm heading out," I told Rory as I passed by his desk. "If anything comes up, I'll have my cell phone, and this weekend I'll be at my sister's house. I'll be back Monday morning."

Rory looked up, his eyes sparkling wickedly. "So—are you taking this show on the road?"

"The jury's still out on that one," I answered, tucking my briefcase under my arm. "But I'll have an answer for you Monday morning."

FIVE

I 'VE CAUGHT THE TRAIN TO THE HAMPTONS SO MANY TIMES I HAVE the schedule memorized—catch the 4:19 at Penn Station, change trains at the Jamaica station, arrive at East Hampton at 7:20 P.M. As the train whizzed past Westhampton, I pulled out my cell phone and told Kirsten I had managed to catch the early train after all. She said she'd meet me at the station.

Truth to tell, Kirsten's house was the closest thing I had to a real home, now that we'd sold my parents' house. I used my studio apartment in the Upper West Side just for sleeping, an occasional meal, and providing a warm nest for Tux from the hours of 10:00 P.M. to 7:00 A.M. In the last six months, I had barely spent eight hours a night in the place, dividing the rest of my weekday time between the office, the courtroom, and the law offices of Wilt, Kremkau, Colby, and Stock.

But the weekends belonged to my family, Kirsten and Sean and three-year-old Travis . . . and Kurt, of course, when he could get away. He managed to go to the Hamptons with me about twice a month, and Kirsten kept a spare room ready in case he decided to show up.

She was waiting for me, as usual, outside the station, propped up against her black 4Runner. I gave her a quick hug, patted her belly hello, then ducked to peek in the back window. Travis, who usually squealed out an affectionate greeting, was asleep, his tousled head propped against the stiff curve of his safety seat.

—

53

"Aw, look at him," I whispered, placing my hand on the glass. "A sleeping angel."

"A little devil is more like it." Kirsten blew a stray hank of hair out of her eyes, then opened the driver's door. "Come on, let's get home. I've got lasagna in the oven."

Sean's successful pediatric practice provided a lovely home for Kirsten and Travis, and as I studied my sister's reflection in the windshield on the drive home, I wondered if Sean made it home to her as often as I did. Despite Kirsten's happiness about the coming baby, I had noticed a strained tone in her voice of late, and her mouth took on a determined look whenever I mentioned Sean. She hadn't complained of anything, so she wasn't ready to discuss whatever was troubling her, but she couldn't hide anything from a sister . . . especially not me.

I turned in the seat to face her. "So, is Sean home or is he tied up in Manhattan?"

Kirsten turned to stare at something on the side of the road, literally blocking my question. "I heard about your trial," she said. "Congratulations. You must be glad it's over."

We chatted for a few minutes about how Colby had managed to snow the jury, and I told her how revolted I had been when the senator leaned over and practically grabbed me in a bear hug.

"The worst aspect of that trial is the possibility he'll kill someone else." I leaned my elbow on the car door and pushed my hair out of my eyes. Night had fallen outside, but the heated, cozy confines of the car felt safe—a feeling left over from childhood. "What if he does, Kirsten? Will some other woman's blood be on my hands?"

She glanced over at me, her eyes bright with speculation. "Does that worry you?"

"Why wouldn't it?"

"I don't know." She lifted her slender shoulders in a shrug. "I thought by now you would be like a lawyer, sort of hardened to it all. I mean, surely not all lawyers' clients are innocent. Which means that exceptionally good lawyers prevent exceptionally good criminals from ever having to account for their crimes."

She looked at me again, her lips twisted into a cynical smile. "I figured guilt was something you learned to live with. Everyone has to learn to live with things . . . that aren't so pleasant."

There. I heard a pleading note in her voice, a quiet signal that meant she was about to open up and share whatever had thrown that shadow onto her oval face, but then we passed the oak at the entrance to her driveway. The car slowed and turned, and something in the movement brought Travis awake.

"We home, Mama?"

"Almost, honey."

I turned in the seat, and saw Travis's wide blue eyes staring at me. He blinked slowly, then his perfect mouth widened in an O. "Auntie Claudie!"

"Hi, stinker." I reached out and tugged on the toe of his tennis shoe. "Are you ready for dinner? I'm starving for your mama's lasagna."

"Me too!"

The car coasted over the gravel driveway; the headlights lit up the front porch. The home was charming, warm, and welcoming . . . so why didn't Sean visit it more often?

I climbed out of the car, unbuckled Travis from his car seat, and settled him onto my hip, then followed my sister into the welcoming, empty house.

"OK," Kirsten said, lacing her fingertips over a half-finished plate of salad and lasagna, "here's reason thirty-nine why you shouldn't go to

Rome—you might meet a dark Italian who looks like Antonio Banderas. He'll sweep you off your feet and break your heart—"

"Kirsten!" I threw my napkin at her. "It's a good thing Kurt isn't here! I'm certainly not in the market for a man."

"She plays a good devil's advocate, doesn't she?" Sean said, grinning at me from across the table. Kirsten looked at him, her eyes wide and questioning, but his smile didn't change when her gaze crossed his. I watched them a moment, then sipped my iced tea, still unable to define or understand the undercurrents moving throughout the house.

Sean had come home just before eight, kissed Kirsten's cheek, rumpled Travis's hair, and retired to his office to return a couple of phone calls. Fortunately, we had just sat down at the dinner table, so he joined us a few moments later as if nothing whatsoever was out of the ordinary. He asked me about Kurt, congratulated me on the outcome of the Mitchell trial, and listened intently as I told them both about Darien Synn and the opportunity to work in Rome.

Kirsten had protested immediately, of course, wailing that I wouldn't be with her when the baby came, but after a few minutes her indignation cooled to a reluctant pout. I also told them about Elaine Dawson's odd call, and that's when Kirsten volunteered to play devil's advocate. "Let's just test your resolution," she said, straightening her shoulders, "and see if a trip to Rome is really in your best interests."

She plunged right in with questions about money, Kurt, risk and reward, and on those issues I managed to convince myself that going to Rome was a good idea. Now she snapped her fingers and leaned close so Travis wouldn't hear. "If you go to Rome," she whispered, "you'll have to fly over the Atlantic." She pulled away and lifted her brows as if daring me to counter *that* objection.

As casually as I could, I looked her straight in the eye. "So?"

"Come on, Claude." She flicked a basilisk glance at Travis, who simply went on eating his finger foods as if nothing in the world were out of the ordinary. "Can you honestly say you can fly over the ocean—over *that* spot—and not think about the crash?"

"What crash, Mommy?" Travis's treble voice cut through the silence.

"Nothing, honey. Eat your noodles."

I lowered my gaze and concentrated on prying a sticky slice of noodle from my plate. I knew very well what she meant, but the jet-liner crash that killed our parents had occurred in July 1996, years before Travis was born. I didn't think about it much anymore, but I hadn't flown over the ocean since it happened, either.

"You'll have to fly virtually the same route." An undercurrent of desolation filled Kirsten's voice. "Flight 800 was en route from New York to Paris, then it was going on to Rome."

With a sharp clatter, my fork fell to my plate. "Good grief, Kirsten." My voice went hoarse with frustration. "I thought you'd *want* me to take this job. You are actually beginning to sound as if you think I should stay here."

Her eyes welled with hurt. "I want what's best for you. And maybe it's best that you stay home. You'll be getting lots more attention now, and you may be walking away from all sorts of wonderful opportunities if you take off and go to Rome."

"On the other hand," Sean interrupted, a faint line between his brows as he felt his way into the conversation, "you might find it refreshing to work for the *good* guys for a change. You can't feel good about Mitchell walking away from that trial with blood on his hands."

The dining room went as silent as a church. Kirsten's blue eyes, as dark as gun barrels, grazed her husband's face, then trained in on me. "He didn't mean that, Claudia. You only do what you have to do; we understand that."

I forced a smile. "It's all right. It's a job, like anything else. I'm not supposed to care about whether or not the defendants are innocent—"

Sean ignored Kirsten's sharp glance and aimed his fork at me. "Still, Claudia, I doubt Sir William Blackstone ever dreamed people like you would exist when he wrote his *Commentaries on the Laws of England.* A trial by jury is supposed to be a trial by peers, not hand-selected people who are chosen on the basis of whether or not they're likely to favor a certain verdict. At the time our legal system was instituted, no one had ever conceived of jury consultants, mock trials, or computers that predict trial outcomes."

"What are you saying?" Kirsten said, each word a splinter of ice.

Sean shrugged and smiled at me. "I think Claudia might find it refreshing to work for people who are interested in helping others instead of empowering themselves. From what I've read about Santos D. Justus, he's honestly philanthropic."

"Mama!" Travis pounded the table. "I want bread!"

"Ask your father." Resentment edged her voice.

Ignoring Kirsten's growing irritation, I urged my brother-in-law to continue. "What have you read?"

"Not much." Sean broke off a piece of garlic bread and placed it in Travis's grasping hand. "But last week there was an article in *Newsweek* about his peace movement. International Unity . . . or something like that."

"Global Union?"

Sean snapped his fingers. "That's it. The article described Justus as a local fellow who hit the big time. Apparently he began his career serving a single term in Italy's Chamber of Deputies, which is like our House of Representatives, then decided he liked politics. He's now serving as the Italian ambassador to the WEU."

I swallowed another bite of lasagna and considered this latest bit

of information. Obviously, I'd have to do more homework before officially accepting a job with Global Union, but I couldn't deny that
Sean's comment had hit a sensitive spot. It *would* be nice to work for
honorable people for a change . . . if Darien Synn and Santos D. Justus
were as honorable as they seemed. Maybe doing good in Europe
would counteract the queasy feeling that rose in my stomach every
time I remembered Senator Mitchell's smug smile . . .

"Thanks for the info," I told Sean, lifting my head in time to catch
him sending Kirsten a really pointed look. I glanced away, not wanting to intrude on the unspoken war of sharp glances and prickly
tones. As an afterthought I added, "I'll keep it in mind."

After helping with kitchen cleanup, I went out to Kirsten's front porch
and sat in her rocker, my arms and shoulders covered with a soft chenille afghan I'd plucked from the back of her sofa. With its scents of
salt water and burning fires, the velvet dark seemed to enfold me like
a gloved hand. Out beyond the dunes, the incessant roar of the sea
provided steady background music, like the swishing sounds of an
exotic percussion instrument caressed by skillful fingers.

For the moment, it seemed, Sean and Kirsten had called a truce.
Sean disappeared into his study after dinner; after helping me in the
kitchen, Kirsten went upstairs to put Travis to bed. The ensuing quiet
gave me time to think, but after ten minutes of rocking in time with
the sea, I knew what my decision would be.

I wanted to go to Rome. The idea, inconceivable at first, now
beckoned like an exit sign in a dark and suffocating chamber. Sean
was right; I needed to work for something honorable. Rory was right
too; I needed to escape from Elaine Dawson's shadow. And despite my
affection for Kurt, some voice inside whispered that I needed to go to

Rome for the sake of my impending marriage. It wasn't a hunch, and I don't believe in presentiment. Perhaps it was my subconscious insisting that I needed one wildly independent adventure before marriage, I don't know. I just knew I wanted to go.

I also know that I'm different from most young women my age—I never wanted to be married. While my friends in high school were dreaming of husbands, I concentrated on college applications. And in college, while my friends fretted about their future matrimonial prospects, I dreamed of working in Elaine Dawson's firm. My college roommate got married the day after graduation; I served as her maid of honor, went back to the dorm, chucked the froufrou satin dress and shoes, then picked up my suitcase and took a cab to the airport. Two days later, I was answering telephones at Elaine Dawson's firm and studying books on body language.

Two years later, I was content to be Elaine's executive assistant . . . until an emergency television bulletin informed me that TWA Flight 800 had gone down over the Atlantic, killing all 212 passengers and 17 crew members aboard. My parents had been aboard that jetliner, bound for Rome to celebrate their thirtieth anniversary.

"I can't wait to see Rome," my mother had told me in our last phone call. "Palatine Hill, the Colosseum, the Pantheon. I've always dreamed of visiting the Eternal City."

The shrubs beyond the porch vibrated softly with an insect hum as I blinked the sounds of the past away. "Maybe that's why I hear Rome calling me," I whispered. "Maybe I'm supposed to take the trip my parents never finished."

Maybe I just wanted to see if Rome was worth the suffering I'd endured on her account.

As the screen door creaked on its hinges, the chirping of the night creatures ceased. I knew without looking that Kirsten had come out to join me. She stood in the sudden silence for a moment, then moved heavily over the wooden planks and lowered her increasing bulk into the swing at my side. She exhaled a long sigh. "Finally. That boy fights sleep."

We sat for a moment in a companionable silence broken only by the rhythmic groan of the rocker and the metallic creak of the porch swing.

"I know I'm being selfish," she finally said. "Wanting you here when the baby comes. If you want to go to Rome, don't let me stop you."

"I could come back." I turned my head to look at her. "Sean could call when the baby's born. I don't know how busy I'll be, but I'm sure I could take a few days and come help you."

A reluctant smile tugged at the corners of her mouth. "I'd love it if you could, but you really don't have to. Sean's mother has offered to come. I've never been able to stand the woman, but Travis adores her."

Beyond the porch, the wildlife had accepted Kirsten's arrival. The darkness came alive again with creatures that chirped and buzzed in the dark. I listened to the mingled sounds for a moment, then reached out and touched Kirsten's arm. "You know I'd come if you needed me."

"I know."

"For anything, Kirsten." I leaned forward until she looked into my eyes. "I don't know what's going on between you and Sean, but if there's anything I can do—"

"It's just the seven-year itch." Sighing, she shifted her weight and crossed one ankle over the other. "We just need to spend more time together, that's all. He works too much, and I'm too much into the preschool set. After the baby comes, we'll need to find some time to get away together, just the two of us."

I nodded, grateful she hadn't denied the stress that would have been obvious to anyone with eyes.

—

"You don't need to worry about me." Her hand covered mine. "I know this Rome thing is a great opportunity. Mom and Dad would want you to take it. Mom always did love that city—*Roman Holiday* was her favorite movie."

I squeezed her hand. "Thanks, K."

We separated, then she pulled something from the pocket in her heavy sweater. "I found something for you. Mom gave it to me a long time ago, but I never dress up anymore. You'll be able to put it to good use."

The light from the living room window reflected off a lovely piece of jewelry—a gold circle on a delicate chain. I had seen it before; it was a ladies' pocket watch designed to be worn as a necklace.

"I'd nearly forgotten about that." I took it from her and ran my thumbnail along the curved edge. When it sprang open, I saw the delicate watch face and the blur of words inscribed inside the cover. "What's this engraving?"

"It's a Benjamin Franklin quote: 'Do not squander time, for that's the stuff life is made of.' Dad gave it to Mom on their tenth anniversary." Kirsten looked at me with dewy moisture in her beautiful eyes. "Go to Rome, kiddo, and live it up. Then you can come home and tell me all about it."

"Thanks, Sis." I leaned forward to embrace her, then we parted and enjoyed the night sounds until the advancing chill sent us in to the warmth of the fire.

Six

Dawn came reluctantly to Rome, glowing sullenly through a cloud-dark sky. Asher stared at the gray morning through his window, then pulled on his navy trench coat in case of rain. After leaving his *appartamento,* he walked the few blocks northward to Montecitorio Palace, the seat of the Chamber of Deputies. The Eternal City had risen with him on this misty Monday morning, and as he stretched his legs the city likewise seemed to shake out its limbs and stretch to face a new day. Televisions blared through open doorways; merchants lifted their awnings and swept the sidewalk while automobile horns blared in the steadily thickening traffic.

At the street corner, under a group of scaly barked plane trees, a group of city sanitation workers blasted the sidewalk with a pressure cleaner, a stream of curses flowing as powerfully as the water. Asher suppressed a smile as he stepped into the street and strode past them. The object of their enthusiastic scorn was a carpet of bird droppings on the walkway, an inevitable sign of autumn in the city. For as long as Asher could remember, each fall swarms of starlings flew into the city from the north and roosted in the plane trees at dusk.

Though their presence mandated extra work for the sanitation workers and the necessity of umbrellas for pedestrians walking home at sunset, Asher had always liked the birds. He marveled as he watched them fly high above the ancient roofs and domes, turning simultaneously to veer in a new direction as if they were of one quick mind. How

—

did they learn to fly so effortlessly in unison? God, who had set the sun to measure man's day and the moon to measure his months, had set the seasons and the starlings to measure man's years. Asher had watched the starlings come and go more times than he wanted to remember. Still he liked the little birds.

On the *Via degli Uffici del Vicario* Asher passed Giolitti's, where a crowd had begun to fill the outdoor tables in the piazza. Many of the *onorevoli,* representing both the country's left- and right-wing parties, were present, all differences set aside as they shook out their copies of the daily *Corriere della Sera* and sipped espresso. Later in the assembly hall they would argue like in-laws, but the early hour and the socked-in sky seemed to have cast a drowsy spell over the politicians.

The main entrance to Montecitorio Palace lay just beyond Giolitti's. Asher slowed his steps as he approached it, then leaned against a street sign and slipped his hands into the trench coat's roomy pockets. Behind the dark lenses of his glasses, he surveyed the cars parked along the street. Only a few privileged citizens could obtain passes allowing them to drive in this part of the city, and fewer still were permitted to park. But surely the man he sought would be one of the fortunate few.

Even under a choked sun, this was a lovely part of town. The curving southern facade of the Palazzo di Montecitorio had stood for more than three hundred years, and the lovely cream-and-beige building had not lost an iota of its splendor.

Asher took a deep breath, then made a face and slowly exhaled the mingled scents of the city: the tang of the garbage bin hidden behind a hedge, the odor of dog excrement, the scent of baking bread. And always, the faintly metallic smell of diesel engine exhaust.

He had just begun to despair of fulfilling his quest when a blue Alfa Romeo, one of the *macchine blu* driven by people of power, insinuated itself through the traffic and nosed up to the curb. The driver, a dark-haired youth with a cheerfully insolent manner, stepped out and came around the front, nudging a pair of gawking boys out of the way as he bent to open the back door.

Asher stopped breathing as the man he sought stepped out of the car, glanced quickly right and left, then buttoned his coat and made his way through the crowd scattered about the portal of the palace. The driver waited a moment to be sure his employer was safely away, then locked the car and walked toward Giolitti's with a loose-boned, confident step.

Asher followed. He joined the queue before the counter, heard the young man order *caffè ristretto*, then placed his own order for an espresso. The young man picked up his drink, then took a seat. He lifted a brow in surprise when Asher joined him at the table a moment later.

"*Buon giorno.*" Asher lifted his mug in a mild salute, then took a taste and looked out across the piazza. The youth returned the greeting, then sipped from his cup again, apparently not caring that the crowd had forced him to share his table on this busy morning.

After observing the street scene for a moment, Asher turned toward his young companion. "Can you tell me," he asked, speaking Italian, "about your employer? Forgive me for being curious, but I saw him get out of your car this morning. His face is familiar, I think."

The young man's face broadened in a smile. "Signor Justus? The car is his; I am just his driver. But I can tell you he is a good man. A very respected man in Rome, in Italy, in the entire world."

"Ah, Signor Justus. I thought I would recognize the name." Asher took another sip from his steaming mug. "I have heard that he is a dedicated *romanista*. Is that true?"

The driver's dark eyes narrowed for a moment. "Are you *romanista* or *laziale*?"

Asher pulled a scarf from his coat pocket, then waved the yellow and purple insignia of the Roma soccer team before the young man's eyes. "I have been romanista for more years than you could imagine, friend."

The young man's reserved expression melted in an outpouring of excitement and relief. "I am Angelo Mazzone," he said, clasping Asher's hand in a warm grasp. "And I am pleased to meet another romanista!"

"Asher Genzano." Asher smiled, inwardly relieved that he had mentioned the correct soccer team. He had suspected that the athletic driver might be a *tifoso*, a fellow with soccer fever, that Santos D. Justus might be romanista, for the politician wore a yellow scarf around his throat at the championship match last year. A Lazio fan would have worn blue or white.

"Tell me, Angelo," Asher said as he folded his hands on the table, "if the rumors I hear are true."

"Rumors?" The word burst from the driver in a gasp. "If you have heard something evil, do not believe it. Santos Justus is the most fair man—"

"I have heard nothing bad about him," Asher interrupted, deepening his smile, "but I have heard he is hiring people to work for Unione Globale. Is this true? Might I find a job there?"

Surprise blossomed on the younger man's face. "You, my friend, do not look like you need a job."

Asher squinted with amusement. "All men need to work, Angelo. Of what use is life, unless it is directed toward a purpose?"

Angelo shrugged slightly. "Unione Globale is hiring, but not many common workers. There is a need for skilled people—"

"How skilled?"

The young man scratched at the slight growth of beard on his jaw. "Educated people. Last week *Il Presidente* hired two professors from the university."

Asher looked down, not wanting to reveal the small surge of excitement flowing through him. "A man so bright, hiring professors? What ever for?"

"Historians, Signor Justus called them. They are to keep records and such. I believe there is talk of opening a library."

Asher cleared his throat and struggled to be patient. "Has Signor Justus a need, perhaps, for interpreters? I have had some experience as a translator."

The chauffeur's smile broadened in approval. "*Si*, I think he would like a translator. I overheard him speaking to *Il Direttore* about an American who will be coming to work for Unione Globale. She speaks no Italian and hasn't time to learn."

Asher extended his hand, content with this small but satisfying victory. "Perhaps I will call upon Signor Justus—at his office, of course."

"Tell him Angelo recommended you." The youth enthusiastically shook his hand. "And it wouldn't hurt to mention that you are a romanista."

"*Si, grazie.* That is an excellent idea." Asher stood, then patted the youth on the shoulder. "If God wills, I will see you again, Signor Mazzone."

The driver grinned up at him. "*Arrivederci*, Asher Genzano."

SEVEN

I WOULDN'T HAVE MINDED IF KURT WANTED TO DROP ME OFF AT THE LaGuardia Delta terminal, but he insisted on parking and escorting me all the way to the gate. We sat for a few moments in the vinyl chairs, idly watching people and making dull conversation while the other passengers checked in.

It was there, sitting in the gate chairs, that I noticed something odd. Maybe it's because I was mentally detaching from Kurt already, or maybe my brain was just moving on a different track. In any case, as we sat there with our eyes fastened to the open area where people hurried back and forth, I realized that Kurt wasn't *just* sitting. Whenever he saw an attractive woman, he adjusted his position and sent out a courtship signal.

At first I told myself I was being paranoid. But then a Meg Ryan wannabe walked by, and Kurt moved his arm, physically grasping the back of the empty seat next to him. That, as any student of body language will tell you, is an obvious invitation to "sit here" and a subconscious attempt to demonstrate the dominance of space. If the blonde had met his eye, I wouldn't have been surprised to see him perform the gaze/smile/gaze/break gaze/return gaze/smile/approach ritual . . . well, maybe not the approach. I *was* still sitting right beside him.

"Kurt Welton," I drawled, distinct rebuke in my voice. "You are watching that blonde!"

He turned and abruptly gripped my hand. "Am not. Now—are you sure you have everything you need?"

I felt the corner of my mouth twist with exasperation, but what could I do? He was a man, after all, and I was on my way out of the country.

I tapped the leather attaché case by my side. "Passport, visa, notebooks, and tape recorder. Plus about a hundred articles on the Global Union. My refrigerator is empty, my neighbor is taking care of Tux, and Rory will handle everything at the office."

Kurt leaned closer and breathed a kiss into my hair. "I'll miss you."

"I'll miss you too," I answered, though I felt a long way from homesickness or honest regret. In the past week I'd been so busy arranging my trip that I hadn't had much time to think about Kurt at all.

Overcome with a sudden surge of guilt, I slipped my hand around his neck and gave him a quick kiss. "There's always the telephone, you know, and e-mail. Just remember that Rome is six hours ahead of New York. If you wait until evening to call me, you'll be dragging me out of bed in the wee hours of the morning."

"Maybe I'll call at midnight—so my voice will be the first thing you hear in the morning." He waggled his eyebrows Charlie Chaplin style, ruining an almost-romantic moment.

"I hear the pace of life is a little more relaxed in Rome," I said, pulling away. "So don't you dare call me before seven Roman time. I'm planning to sleep late, take siestas in the afternoon, and go to bed at sunset. I need to catch up on all the sleep I missed during the Mitchell trial."

One of the flight attendants announced that the flight was ready to begin boarding, so Kurt stood and helped me to my feet. Darien Synn had insisted upon furnishing me with a first-class ticket to Rome, so I'd be among the first to board.

Kurt pulled me into his arms for a farewell embrace. As I stood nestled against him, I closed my eyes and told myself I would miss him dreadfully. Even though I didn't feel any overwhelming sentiment at the moment, there were bound to be times when I'd long for the sight of a friendly and familiar smile . . .

"I'll miss you," he said again.

I pulled away and looked up, studying his face. I saw no sign of objection in his blue eyes, no passionate desire for me to stay. The only emotion I could read was a faint flicker of jealousy—probably springing from the fact that I'd be mingling with international personalities Kurt would give his last Valium to include on his star-studded patient list.

I reached up and patted his cheek. "Don't worry," I said, feeling a smile tug at my lips. "Perhaps I'll discover that Santos Justus has a hidden personality disorder. I promise to toss your name into the hat when they search for a psychologist to treat him."

His brittle laugh confirmed my suspicion, but he didn't comment, just pressed a kiss into my palm, then released my hand. "I'll call you," he promised as he backed away. "And I'll miss you every day."

I waved in reply, then picked up my briefcase and turned toward the gate. As I handed my boarding pass to the flight attendant, it suddenly occurred to me that several times Kurt had promised to miss me . . . but he hadn't said a single word about love.

Eight and a half hours later, I stepped off the plane and into Rome's Fiumicino Airport. I walked down the gangway on puffy ankles, a little amazed that I had done little on the flight except think about the task ahead. Kirsten's worries that I might brood over Mom and Dad were totally unfounded. My thoughts did veer toward them as the plane tilted away from LaGuardia and flew out over an expanse of ocean, but then I pulled out a folder of research materials and pushed the melancholy thoughts from my mind. I would always miss my parents, but scar tissue had successfully covered the gash in my wounded heart.

I saw no one at the gate to meet me, so I proceeded to baggage claim and stood in a long line for customs. After having my passport and visa checked, I stepped out into the open lobby and spied a sign with my name written in bold letters. A young man with dark, curly hair held it toward the arriving passengers.

I walked up to him and summoned the energy for a smile. "I'm Claudia Fischer."

His face split into a wide grin. "Signorina Fischer? No one told me to expect a *beautiful* lady!"

To my annoyance, I felt myself blushing. "Thanks. Are you from Global Union?"

"Si. I am Angelo, your driver. I am to take you to your *residenza*. You are to stay at the Vittoria, a very nice house." He reached down to take the handle of my suitcase. "Let me carry that for you."

I fell into step beside Angelo, only too happy to let him drag my suitcase through the airport lobby. "A house?"

"*Residenze* are apartments with all the comforts of a hotel. You will enjoy your stay."

"I'm sure I will."

At that moment I would have enjoyed any room with a mattress in it. The trip had left me feeling weary and strangely out of sorts—I had left New York at four in the afternoon and flown through a dark sky without sleeping more than a couple of hours, yet here another day was dawning. The airport bustled with activity, and the parking lot outside the building was filled with small cars seemingly intent upon edging one another out of any available parking space. Dutifully following

Angelo into the brightness of an almost blinding sun, I stepped over a curb, then shrieked when a whining motor scooter appeared from nowhere and blew past, missing me by inches.

Angelo looked back and grinned. "Did he startle you? You must not let the *vespistas* bother you. They are like flies, always buzzing around."

The word bewildered me until I saw another motor scooter, this one safely chained to a concrete post. The scooter had *Vespa* written on it, obviously a brand name, so the youths who rode the whining little scooters must be vespistas . . .

I stopped, unbelievably grateful when Angelo halted beside a blue sedan. He hit a button on his key ring, nodded in satisfaction when the vehicle chirped obediently, then moved to open the trunk.

"You speak very good English, Angelo," I called, determined to make a friendly impression before I passed out in exhaustion. "Where did you learn?"

He slammed the trunk shut, then came around to the passenger side and gallantly opened the back door for me. "Television, mostly. Everyone wants to learn English, but it is not taught in most schools. The teachers favor French, German, and Spanish."

I nodded numbly and slipped into the backseat, then settled my briefcase on my lap. Angelo sprinted around the car and slid into the driver's seat, then cranked the engine and roared away from the curb with a recklessness that left me feeling a little breathless.

I had imagined I'd be bright and energetic on my first morning in Rome, but my brain felt as though it were wrapped in a layer of cotton gauze. The dissonant sounds of car horns, the whine of the wind, and the blur of unfamiliar buildings and pedestrians came to me through a thick haze, then faded into blackness.

The next thing I knew, Angelo's hand was on my shoulder, his voice near my ear. "Signorina Fischer, we are here. Your bag is in your room, and the mistress understands that you would like to rest."

Embarrassed to have been caught napping, I lifted my head from the upholstered seat. "Thank you, Angelo." I stepped out and groggily followed the driver into a yellow building, then through a tiled foyer and down a hallway. A short, red-headed woman shook her head in quiet sympathy as she surveyed my appearance, then pointed through the open doorway at what looked to my dazzled senses like a one-bedroom apartment.

"I am Benedetta Donatelli," she said, placing one hand on my shoulder as she pressed a key into my open palm. "If you need anything, you call."

I thanked the man and the woman and tried to maintain a polite smile as they closed the door and left me alone. After locking the door, I tossed my attaché case onto a table, then kicked off my shoes. Beyond the small sitting room lay a bedroom, and the coverlet looked neat and clean. I sat on the edge of the bed, intending to lie down for just a minute, but then my cheek hit the pillow and my toes tingled with relief.

Overcome by exhaustion and jet lag, I slept.

The clock on the bedstand said two o'clock when I opened my eyes. Two o'clock? Day or night? Monday or Tuesday?

I lifted my head, overcome with a sense of confusion, and saw bright light pouring in from a window in the tiny bathroom. So—this had to be afternoon.

Overcome by a sudden and irrational conviction that I had missed my first day of work, I glanced at the pocket watch Kirsten had given me, still set for New York time. No—my watch said September 19, so I had only missed the morning of my first day in Rome. I didn't have to report to Global Union until tomorrow.

Groaning, I sat up and clutched at the edge of the bed. A window shade covered the window, but in the soft gray light I could see that the bedroom was pleasant and tidy, though decidedly simple. A double bed occupied most of the space, and a simple linen dresser scarf covered the small table at the bedside. A vase of fresh flowers stood upon a desk against the far wall, and a small television sat upon a stand near the door.

I shivered slightly as a cool breeze pushed at the shade covering the open window. I moved to raise the shade, then paused and peered out at a sloping street flanked by stone buildings in varying shades of gold and orange and red. A solid row of bumper-to-bumper automobiles lined each side of the narrow road, leaving barely enough room for another car to pass. An orange tabby cat stretched across the roof of one car and sunned itself, while a pair of motorcycles thundered by, shattering the quiet afternoon.

I leaned on the window sill and drank in the crisp, cool air. Though I had scarcely seen anything of the city, already Rome impressed me as being a bit of an oxymoron—the city had withstood the test of time, proving its strength and resilience, but the breeze and the little pink flowers in my window box seemed uncommonly delicate.

Leaving the window, I pulled my toiletry bag from my suitcase, brushed my teeth, and splashed water on my face. The touch of the cold water sharpened my senses and helped me to focus as I dried my skin with a thick cotton towel hanging in the bathroom.

Feeling better, I walked through the bedroom and entered the living room through which I'd staggered earlier this morning. Like the bedroom, this space was clean and pleasant and simply furnished. I had no way of knowing, but I suspected that Reverend Synn had done his best to make me feel comfortable and yet a part of Italy. He could have found a suite for me in any one of the luxurious hotels, but this pleasant place suited me very well.

A card on the desk caught my eye, so I picked it up. A stylish hand had carefully written:

Welcome to Rome, Miss Fischer. Please take the day to rest and make yourself at home. A driver will call for you tomorrow morning and take you to Unione Globale headquarters. Until then, if you need anything, please call my office.

A telephone number followed and a signature:

Santos D. Justus.

I whistled softly, impressed that the Big Man himself had taken the time to write a personal note. Apparently Synn hadn't been exaggerating when he said Justus was personally interested in having me work for his organization.

I propped the card next to the vase of flowers, gave them an appreciative sniff, then moved toward my suitcase. As I unpacked, I became aware of a strange sense of disconnection. I had nothing to do in the hours ahead—no appointments, no schedule, no responsibilities. No one waited to hear from me; no friends were planning on meeting me for dinner.

That thought had barely crossed my mind when another followed— I could drop dead in my tracks and hours would pass before anyone I cared about would know I was in trouble. The thought made me shiver.

I lowered my head and focused on my task, organizing my lingerie and jeans in the small dresser next to the wardrobe. This odd sense of disconnection was foolish, I told myself. It sprang from exhaustion and jet lag and insecurity. After all, I had just left Manhattan for the first time in over two years, so I was bound to have a few withdrawal symptoms.

Still, when I finished unpacking and stored my suitcase at the bottom of the wardrobe, sheer compulsion drove me to the telephone.

I pulled out my calling card, punched in the international access number, then mentally counted hours on my fingertips. Nearly three o'clock in Rome . . . equaled nearly nine in the morning in New York. Kurt would be on his way to the office, but Kirsten would be home.

I dialed her number, waited for what seemed an interminable length of time before the call went through, then heard the steady ringing of her telephone. When she picked up, I heard a note of exasperation in her hello.

"Kirsten? Are you OK?"

"Claudia! I'm fine, but Travis just spilled a bowl of cereal all over the floor." She giggled. "Are you homesick already?"

I laughed, relieved beyond words to hear a familiar voice. "I'm fine. I just wanted someone to know I made it. I got in this morning and slept a few hours, but I'm awake now. After a shower, I think I'll go out and explore the city."

"Your new client doesn't have you busy already?"

"I've got the day off. They must have known I'd be jet lagged."

"Well, if you go out alone, be careful. Watch for pickpockets and muggers. Keep your engagement ring turned around so the stone doesn't show—"

"I'm not a yokel, Kirsten. I'm used to big cities."

"Just be careful, will you? It's not like I can drop everything and run off to Rome if you get in trouble."

A surge of yearning rose in me, and suddenly I wanted to be in her kitchen wiping Cheerios off the floor. I struggled to speak over the

---

lump in my throat. "Well, I'd better get moving. My body gets confused if I sit too long—I'll be asleep if I don't keep moving."

"Take care of yourself, Claude. Love you."

"Love you, Sis. Take care of Sean and Travis."

"I will."

I placed the heavy phone back into its cradle and sat on the edge of the bed, fighting back tears. What was *wrong* with me? I came willingly on this journey, I looked forward to the challenges it presented, and I had decided working for Global Union would be great for the future of my firm. Santos D. Justus couldn't demand any more from me than Senator Mitchell had, and this was certain to be a far more pleasant experience than those stifling hours in that Manhattan courtroom . . .

But this was a different world, and I had no place in it.

A sludge of nausea oozed back and forth in my belly, whether from fear or jet lag, I couldn't tell. Then, in an impulse born from a childhood spent in Sunday school, I bowed my head and whispered a half-forgotten prayer: "God in heaven up above, look down upon your child in love. Guide my footsteps through this day, and keep me safe along the way. Amen."

I lifted my head and blinked away a veil of tears. Kurt would have laughed aloud if he had heard me recite those childish words, but something within me—he would call it my inner child—felt vastly comforted by the prayer.

I still didn't believe in God or miracles, but I recited the rhyme again as I went into the bathroom and ran the water for my shower.

EIGHT

THE NEXT MORNING, A BURST OF ENTHUSIASTIC RAPPING BROUGHT ME scurrying to answer the door. I opened it, expecting to see my driver, but there was no one in the hallway. A high-pitched squeal rang out from the end of the corridor, though, and an instant later I recognized the red-haired woman I had met the day before. My landlady came toward me, dragging a small, frowning boy with each arm.

"Signorina Fischer," she said, attempting a bow while the two boys struggled to escape her grip. "I am sorry for the disturbance. These are my sons, and they will not bother you again."

Looking down, I couldn't stop a smile. The children, who appeared to be five or six, were positively adorable. Dark, curly hair covered both their heads, and they looked up at me with dark eyes that sparked with mischief.

I squatted to look the twin imps in the eye. "What are your names?" I asked, speaking slowly in case they didn't understand English.

Their mother interpreted. *"Dirle i vostri nomi."*

The first little boy stuck his index finger in his mouth. "Mario," he said, shaping the word around his finger.

The second boy was braver. "Marco!" he announced, right before ducking to hide behind his mother's skirt.

Mama rolled her eyes at me. "I am sorry, signorina. They are such a handful. I will be back to clean your room as soon as I have delivered the mail."

I smiled and closed the door, a little curious about her last comment.

79

Her house was not large; in fact, I thought mine was the only apartment. How much mail could she have to deliver?

I didn't have time to debate the question, for a moment later someone knocked on my door again. This time the young man who had driven me yesterday stood outside, and he lifted a brow as I greeted him with a timid smile. "Signorina Fischer? Are you ready?"

"As ready as I'll ever be." I picked up my jacket, purse, and briefcase, and a moment later, Angelo seated me in the back of the luxurious blue sedan. As the car leaped from the curb and fought through the snarled traffic, I found myself studying the broad sidewalks and streets I had tentatively explored the afternoon before. I had been amazed at the variety of shops, restaurants, and monuments within walking distance of my residenza, and an unexpected thought popped into my brain: Why not buy an Italian designer wedding gown? I'd be putting my time in Rome to good use, and Kurt couldn't say I hadn't thought about him if I found and bought the perfect wedding dress . . .

"How do you like Roma?" Angelo called, catching my gaze in the rearview mirror. "Is it much like America?"

"In some ways, yes." I smoothed my skirt and pushed the hem toward my knees. For some reason I couldn't name, the bold, dark stares of Italian men made me want to run for cover. "But in other ways Rome is very different. I live in Manhattan, so I'm used to the crowds and the noise."

The driver braked abruptly to avoid a droning moped that veered into his path, then continued as if nothing had happened. "I want to go to America some day. I have family in New York."

I turned to watch two men on the street corner, both of whom were waving their hands to punctuate a vehement argument.

"If all American women are as beautiful as you"—Angelo's dark eyes held more than a hint of flirtation when I looked up—"I would like to leave tomorrow."

"Thank you," I said, turning to look out the side window again. "My fiancé would appreciate the compliment."

Angelo grinned and turned his attention back to the road, and a moment later we pulled up outside a stately building of brownish-red stone. I had not seen a single skyscraper in Rome, but this building was taller than average—I counted seven stories.

The driver opened my door, then grinned and announced, "The red palace. Home of Il Presidente's Unione Globale."

A sign on the outside of the building confirmed Angelo's announcement in English, Italian, and French. After thanking him with a smile, I went through the glass entrance doors, paused at the reception desk to give my name, and was immediately escorted into an office near the front of the building.

A dark-haired woman with snapping eyes rose from behind a desk, then took my outstretched hand between both of hers. "Signorina Fischer, how happy I am to meet you! I am Maura Casale, personnel director for Il Presidente."

The personnel director appeared to be forty-five, with jet-black hair that flowed from a center part and gathered at the nape of her neck in a soft ponytail. Her figure was curving and regal, her clothing understated and elegant. She moved with the graceful air of a woman who is at home in many worlds, and I could see in a glance why Santos Justus had hired her.

She gestured toward a chair, which I took, then Mrs. Casale picked up a phone, murmured something in Italian, then replaced it and smiled at me. "Il Direttore asked to be notified the moment you arrived," she explained. "He will be with us in a moment."

I was looking forward to finally meeting the charismatic Santos D.

Justus, but Reverend Synn appeared in the doorway a moment later. I had my second unofficial Italian lesson: Il Direttore and Il Presidente were not the same person.

"Signorina Fischer, a delight to see you again." Synn shook my hand almost as enthusiastically as the personnel director had. "We are so glad you have joined our team. We have much work for you to do."

"I'm happy to be here."

I stood, wondering what to do next, but Synn waved a hand in my direction and took a half step back. "I will leave you now with Signora Casale. She will explain our hiring procedures and make sure you are well acquainted with what we require in an employee. Thank you again, signorina, and if there is anything we can do to facilitate your stay in Rome, do not hesitate to let us know."

I turned my attention back to the older woman. Like most Italians I had seen on the streets, she wore a tailored blouse, a skirt of fine black wool, dark stockings, and low leather heels. I was wearing a suit too, but compared to the Italians' relaxed elegance, my cranberry-colored skirt and jacket felt a trifle gaudy.

"First, let me show you to your office," she said, leading the way. "You are fortunate, for you are on the fifth floor and in a private corner of the building. Il Direttore specified that you are to work without interruption if you so desire."

"Il Direttore is Reverend Synn, correct?"

"Yes." She flashed me a smile. "Reverend Synn is the director of our organization; Santos Justus is the president. You will find that people here usually address men of importance by their titles. It is a mark of honor and distinction."

I made a mental note to include this peculiarity among my list of things to remember about Rome and Romans. Already I had discerned that Italian traffic cops were more flexible than their Manhattan counterparts and that Italians' body language was much more expressive than Americans'. During my walk yesterday, I noticed that men routinely greeted each other with an embrace and a kiss, and it was not unusual to see women walking arm in arm along the street. The Italians were not afraid of human touch. Americans seemed positively stand-offish in comparison.

After a quick trip in the elevator, Signora Casale led me into a spacious office, far larger than the cramped space Rory and I rented in Manhattan. A pair of leather guest chairs sat before the mahogany desk; a leather sofa stretched out along one wall. Behind the desk stood a wonderful executive chair, with brown leather that looked as soft as butter.

"This is lovely." My eyes rose to the wide window, through which I could see the dome of St. Peter's Basilica in the distance. "Oh, what a gorgeous view!"

"Il Direttore thought you would like it." Signora Casale clasped her hands together. "When you are ready, you can call for me, and I will come up and explain our procedures."

"I am ready now, signora." I set my briefcase and purse on the desk, then gestured toward the couch. From her manner and words I could tell that this woman had been instructed to consider me her superior, but I wanted her as an ally, not an underling. I would need assistance in Rome, and Maura Casale seemed capable and willing to give it.

She moved to the sofa. Instead of sitting behind the desk, which would have reinforced my superior role, I sat next to her on the sofa, physically establishing my equality.

She smiled—a simple smile, no teeth showing—and waited for me to begin.

I turned the tables and invited her to initiate the discussion. "Why don't you tell me how I can help you and the people of Global Union?"

—

Her left eyebrow rose a fraction, then her smile relaxed slightly. "Unemployment figures in Italy are high," she said, resting her hands on her lap, "and we have had no shortage of applicants to fill our available positions. I don't know how much you know about Italy, but our people typically compete for jobs through a candidate evaluation process known as a *concorso.*"

She waited, brow uplifted, for permission to continue.

"I don't know anything about the concorso," I answered. "Please go on."

She nodded. "The concorso, which takes place over a three-day period, consists of a written exam and interview to test the candidate's skills. We also run extensive background checks, and no one who is not *raccomandati* for a job can proceed through the process."

"*Raccomandati?*" I tried the word out on my tongue. "Recommended?"

"Si." She smiled again, more naturally this time. "Ordinarily we would have no problem, for the Italian network is thorough and all applicants would be known to us, but Il Presidente wants Unione Globale to be an international organization. So we are hiring many foreigners and have no way to do a thorough check on their backgrounds. So Il Direttore suggested you might be able to assist us." She pursed her lips in a thoughtful expression. "I understand that you . . . read people's minds?"

"Not quite." I shook my head. "I read *people,* not their minds. People tell us many things through their body language, their expressions, even the clothing they choose to wear. I can tell a great deal about a person, but I can't read minds. No one can."

Her smile deepened into laughter. "Thank heaven."

"You've got that right."

We shared a laugh, then she took a deep breath and composed herself. "It is my understanding that you will interview the applicants after they leave my office. The applicants will not think this unusual, for they are accustomed to several days of interviews."

"That would work very well. I usually only need a few moments to get an overall picture of each personality, but occasionally I might need to call someone back." I pressed my hands together and tried to explain. "Some people are harder to read than others, and it will take me some time to adjust to the differences between Europeans and Americans."

"I understand."

She glanced toward the hallway, betraying her eagerness to get back to work, so I stood, signaling an end to the conversation. "Thank you, signora. You have been most helpful."

A relieved smile spread over her face. "Please call me if you need anything," she said, moving toward the door as she spoke. "I am at your disposal."

I smiled and watched her go, certain I had made at least one friend in Santos Justus's empire.

I had been at my desk only ten minutes—barely enough time to learn the whereabouts of paper, pen, and paper clips—when Il Direttore himself leaned through the open doorway. "May I have a private word?" he asked, regarding me with an intense but secret expression.

"Certainly." I stood as he entered and closed the door behind him, but he waved an excusing hand in my direction, then lowered himself into one of the two leather chairs facing my desk.

"You have met Signora Casale? She has explained our procedures?"

"Yes."

"Very good. Did she explain how we want you to conduct the interviews?"

85

"Not specifically." I picked up a pencil. "Why don't you tell me if you are looking for anything in particular?"

The line of Synn's mouth tightened a fraction. "Italy is not a stable country," he said, leaning closer. "There have been fifty-five Italian governments since the end of the Second World War, and with each election we face the possibility of another collapse. Global Union intends to remain above the fray of national politics, but we cannot deny that we must suffer along with our host country—and there are some in the Italian government who do not appreciate Justus's effort to focus upon world peace and cooperation."

He paused, apparently expecting me to respond. "So you are saying"—I sought the right words—"that we may encounter . . . *opposition* to our efforts?"

"Enemies, Signorina Fischer, from within and without." He sat back and crossed his thick arms across his chest. "Infiltrators. You must watch for signs of treachery. For liars. For cheats and thieves. We have hundreds of applicants and only a few available positions in Rome, so we want only the best and most loyal people. If anyone at all proves suspect in thought, word, or deed, do not hesitate to dismiss that person from the concorso."

In thought? Had they all read that blasted People *article?* I pressed my hands to the desk and leaned forward. "Reverend Synn, I can usually interpret a person's character, but I know no one who can read another person's thoughts."

Synn straightened, an expression of satisfaction showing in his eyes. "I believe you are up to the task we have hired you to perform. We have every confidence in you."

I offered him my thanks, but as he left the office I wondered if I had been transported to a place where people expected miracles I couldn't perform.

—

My first task was broad—before I could ascertain whether or not a particular person would be qualified to work for Global Union, I had to understand as much as possible about Santos D. Justus and the organization itself.

Rory had been kind enough to search out and print several articles about the man called Il Presidente, and I planned to glean as many additional facts as I could from the present employees of Global Union—assuming they'd be willing to talk to me over lunches and espresso breaks.

From the published news reports I learned that Santos D. Justus was born in 1949. Though several of the reports stated that he was born in Rome, not one mentioned his parents or any siblings. I thought that omission a bit odd. Either his background was completely unremarkable, or someone was trying to hide an unpleasant truth. An illegitimate birth, perhaps? Or was he trying to hide the real time and place of his birth? Thousands of people doctored their résumés every year, and politicians and entertainers were among the worst offenders.

I wrote *Background?* on my steno pad. In only two days I had learned that most Romans loved to talk, so I didn't think I would have much difficulty filling in the missing pieces. If Justus really was a native son, someone would be eager to brag about knowing him.

According to his official biography, Santos Justus hailed from the Lazio region of Italy, the west-central province that included Rome and Vatican City. Elected to the Chamber of Deputies at the tender age of thirty, his name shot from obscurity to prominence in a matter of months. No less than five of the articles in my folder made special mention of his charisma and gifted oratory. "In a city of rhetoric and bombast," wrote one reporter, "Santos Justus shines above his contemporaries. Though his speeches are often more philosophical than pragmatic, he has won the support of a fickle populace more thrilled by automobiles, soccer, and television than by politics."

An article in a 1985 edition of *Newsweek* featured a photograph of Justus with Pope John Paul II. I brought the photo closer and adjusted it to lose the glare from the overhead light. Though the black-and-white photo was small, I could tell that Justus was taller than the ailing pope and handsome in a polished JFK Jr. sort of way.

Reflexively, I glanced upward. Justus probably had offices on the top floor. If my spacious office was any kind of measuring stick, his must be absolutely palatial.

I kept reading. After serving five one-year terms in the Chamber of Deputies, Justus was elected to the Senate, where he served another five years. During this time, he apparently left his wife of six years, a Roman woman he married just before his election to the Chamber. No children resulted from their union, and the marriage was officially annulled.

I jotted the wife's name, Francesca Solano, on my steno pad. She was probably living a quiet and contented life as someone else's wife, but it wouldn't hurt to remember her name.

After serving his country for ten years, Justus apparently turned his attention toward international politics. In 1989 he became the Italian ambassador to the Western European Union. Now Italy served as president of that organization, so Santos Justus was not only Il Presidente to Global Union, but to the Western European Union as well.

I frowned at the page in my hand. Odd, that a man committed to peace would serve as president of a defense organization like the WEU. I would have expected him to aim for the ambassadorship to the European Union or even the United Nations—but, then again, Ronald Reagan and Margaret Thatcher had taught the world that the highway of military preparedness was often the most direct road to peace.

I glanced again at the photograph of Justus. As he extended his right hand to the pope, his posture was straight, his left hand calmly tucked in his pocket with the thumb exposed—the body language of confidence. The photographer might have intended to portray Justus as a religious man or a friend of the church, but the hand in the pocket told me he was not at all intimidated by his proximity to religious authority.

I considered this, then smiled in relief. If Global Union intended to change the world for the better, its leaders would do well to keep themselves distanced from established religions. Mankind had committed enough atrocities in the name of God.

After finishing the articles Rory pulled for me, I placed the copies into a folder, then stared at my nearly empty notepad. I had learned a lot about Justus's history and accomplishments, but very little about the man himself. When would I have the opportunity to meet him?

Five minutes later, the slim black telephone on my desk rang. Reverend Synn wasted no time with pleasantries before coming directly to the point—Il Presidente was presently giving a speech to the Chamber at Montecitorio Palace and hoped to be finished before noon. Would I like to join him and the director for lunch?

I answered yes, and Il Direttore said I should meet him and Signora Casale downstairs by the reception desk in half an hour.

I hung up the phone, feeling at once relieved and a little excited to meet the man who just might change the course of world history . . . and whom I had promised to help.

NINE

ASHER LEANED BACK AGAINST THE TRAVERTINE FACING OF THE STONE building and narrowed his eyes as the trio exited the red palace. He recognized Darien Synn from news reports, and he had seen the dark-haired woman on other occasions when he watched the building. But the second woman, a blonde with short, clipped hair, was unfamiliar to him. Asher pulled himself erect and followed, willing to wager his last lira that the blonde was the American Justus had just hired.

Synn walked at the newcomer's left side, shielding her from the commotion of the busy street, leaving the older woman to follow behind. The director of Unione Globale did most of the talking, occasionally pulling his hand from his pocket to gesture at a building. He was undoubtedly rattling off the typical information given to tourists while the blonde drank it all in, her head bobbing in silent agreement, her eyes wide with interest.

They walked at a brisk pace, dodging slower pedestrian traffic and hurrying through intersections, then stopped outside a crowded trattoria on the Via de Cestari. Synn spoke to the owner, and a moment later all three had been seated at a large circular table in the outdoor terrace.

From his vantage point on the sidewalk across the street, Asher stood and eyed the empty chair at the table. The seat was probably reserved for Justus, who had been scheduled to give a speech to the Chamber of Deputies at 10:00 A.M. The Chamber met less than two blocks away, so this would be an ideal meeting place.

—

Confirming Asher's hunch, a blue Alfa Romeo stopped next to the row of parked cars along the curb. As Asher leaned back against the wall, he saw the young man with whom he'd shared a cup of coffee step from the car. Angelo did not release his passenger, however, for before the chauffeur could move, Santos Justus alighted from the backseat, waved a cheery farewell to his driver, and left the young man to fight the traffic alone.

Asher grunted in satisfaction as the Alfa Romeo revved its engine and moved away, clearing his view of the diners on the terrace. Synn stood at once to introduce Justus, and the blonde woman stood as well, extending her hand to the politician. Both smiled and seemed genuinely pleased to meet.

Asher moved from the wall to a street post, still watching as Justus took the empty chair between Synn and the American, then said something to the dark-haired woman, who replied with a gracious smile.

Why bring in an American? Asher considered the question as he turned into the trattoria behind him. He placed an order for a light lunch, paid the cashier, and returned to the street with a drink and a sandwich, sipping his coffee as he thoughtfully considered the quartet across the street. They would not talk about business at lunch, he knew. Italians relaxed and enjoyed their meals, reserving work-related topics for the office and boardroom. But even though they would not talk business, the men and women across the road were certainly forming opinions of one another. Santos Justus would be interested in learning how the American woman could help his organization . . . just as Asher was.

Asher studied the diners a few minutes more, then turned and threaded his way through the lunchtime crowds. A pair of embracing teenagers with matching spiky, green hair shifted to let him pass; a Gypsy woman reached for his hand and offered to read his palm. Asher shook his head and left her alone to solicit another passerby. Her type had always been sprinkled throughout the crowds of Rome; even Hitler's occupying Nazis could not rid the streets of Gypsies. Mussolini enacted laws to drive the Gypsies out, and Nero had done the same thing, yet nothing could rid the city of their dark avarice . . .

Some things never changed. In the days of the emperors, Rome had been a bustling metropolis of thousands, not millions, but even then the city leaders had battled polluted waters, pickpockets, congestion in the city squares, and the ever-present beggars. In times of persecution, the beggars and Gypsies stayed out of sight, yet still they remained, sleeping in the fields, hiding in doorways, living in the ruins.

Asher had once heard someone say that life was one thing after another. He snorted in derision at the thought. Life wasn't one thing after another—it was one thing over and over. The evidences of evil waxed and waned with the seasons of mankind, but its source wielded as much power today as it had in the days of Hitler. The father of evil was patient.

Asher would wait with him.

TEN

SITTING IN THE GOLDEN GLOW OF A PERFECT SEVENTY-DEGREE DAY, I dipped another chunk of the delicious bread into a pool of spiced olive oil, then took a bite and returned my attention to my host. Santos Justus was everything I'd thought he'd be, but the articles and grainy photographs could not come close to depicting the man's vibrancy and charisma.

I doubted whether any camera could catch the depth of his allure. He was handsome, yes, with movie star appeal, which probably contributed to his success in a country where a television seemed to blare from every open window. He had a quick, bright smile, while his black satin eyes seemed to sparkle with a hidden secret. His dark, meticulously groomed hair surrounded a wide forehead. He wore an Armani suit that fit him perfectly, accenting his broad shoulders and narrow waist. His shoes had been shined and polished; his nails were neat and trimmed. Like Senator Mitchell, this man cared about his appearance, but though Justus was impeccable and impressive, he was also *likable*.

He was as easy on the nerves as on the eyes, and I felt instantly at ease in his presence. When we first met, his handshake had been warm and firm. He took time to greet Signora Casale, and by the answering blush upon her cheek's I surmised that she was not often invited to dine with Il Presidente. In fact, I noticed that she never looked at him directly, but cast him sideways glances, which spelled attraction in almost any language. Did Maura Casale nurse a secret infatuation for Il Presidente?

I mentally filed the question away and concentrated on my host. I had

---

expected that Justus would talk about my work for Global Union, but during lunch he adroitly steered the conversation toward his beloved Italy. With a graceful smile, he listed the sights I must see, the places I must go, and the foods I must taste before returning to America.

"You will find"—he paused as the waiter came forward to begin clearing the table—"that there is no place on earth like Rome and no people like the Italians. Our society is centered upon the family; our communities upon the town square, the *piazza*. Even Rome, as large as it is, has several distinct neighborhoods where everyone knows everyone else. I have a feeling you will enjoy your time in Roma."

"I've enjoyed it already," I answered, wiping my fingertips on my napkin. "And everyone in your organization has been most helpful. Signora Casale"—the woman blushed again—"has taken pains to make certain I understand the application process, and Reverend Synn has found me a charming place to live."

Nodding, Justus pulled a package of cigarettes from his suit pocket, silently offered it around the table, then shook one free. "We are glad you are pleased. Your *residenza* is in a singularly historic part of the city." He paused for a moment to light the cigarette, then shook the flame off the match. "Has anyone told you the history of our building?"

I shook my head, bracing myself to breathe cigarette smoke while I listened. People reveal a lot about themselves when they tell a story, particularly if it is a tale they enjoy telling.

He tasted his cigarette, but only a bare nip; he was eager to speak. "You will hear local residents refer to our headquarters as the red palace, but the designers of the building intended it to be a bank." Justus rested his elbows on the table and folded his hands together. "Instead of bankers, however, the Communist Party acquired the building shortly after the end of World War II. Some say the money to buy the building came from valuables that Communist partisans found on

Mussolini when they captured him on Lake Como while he was trying to flee with his mistress. Others say Moscow itself subsidized the investment. Whatever the source of funds, for years the Communists held court in our building, and guards rarely allowed citizens from the West even to enter the lobby. Their pet name for our headquarters was *il bottegone,* the big shop."

"What happened to the Communists?" I asked when Justus paused to draw on his cigarette again.

Smiling, he exhaled a stream of smoke. "The Cold War ended, and their funding dried up and blew away. They offered to sell the building for thirty-five million dollars American, but the real estate market in Rome had gone soft—so soft that Unione Globale was able to buy the building for a mere $20 million last year. Now we tread the same halls hardened Communists once trod . . . and we're quite grateful."

I repressed the expression of incredulity that threatened to creep across my face. Reverend Synn had mentioned a bequest that endowed the organization, but I never dreamed that bequest had consisted of millions. My mind's eye had conjured up a kindly gray-haired lady who dreamed of peace and donated a few hundred thousand dollars, but apparently Justus had financial connections far beyond the scope of my imagination.

"I am no expert on real estate," I offered, "but I think you got a real bargain."

"Sixty-five thousand square feet of office space in a prime international location," Synn said, lifting his wine glass. "The gods surely smiled upon us."

Something in me took note of his odd comment. What sort of minister referred to God in the plural? Trying not to reveal my bewilderment, I smiled at Synn as Maura Casale's hand fell upon my arm. "They say," she said, lowering her voice to a confidential tone, "that the rooms

—

on the upper floor once served as a love nest. Palmiro Togliatti, an international Communist leader, lived there with his mistress when his wife threw him out of the house." The corners of her eyes crinkled as she gave me a mischievous smile. "Apparently Signora Togliatti was much admired in the Chamber of Deputies, even for a Communist. And the unfaithful husband and his mistress, I've heard, spent more time quarreling than loving—"

"Signora Casale." Synn's voice held a note of reproach. "I am sure Il Presidente doesn't want to be reminded of these things. After all, you are speaking of his office."

The personnel director swallowed hard, her cheeks blazing brighter than the sunshine warranted. I felt embarrassed for her, but Justus reached out and affectionately patted the woman's arm. "Signora Casale meant no harm, Darien. And the story is fascinating. I can see why she wanted to share it with the signorina."

Our meal concluded, the waiter removed the last of our dishes, then presented the check to Justus, who promptly handed it to Reverend Synn.

"Well," Justus said, taking another drag from his cigarette. He put it in an ashtray to smolder, then turned his attention to me. "Now that our meal is done, perhaps you will allow me to speak of business."

"Please do."

He turned the full brilliance of his smile upon me. "We need your help with the concorso, of course, but another matter regarding our international work has arisen, and I think your unique skills may be of invaluable assistance. Would you be willing to attend a meeting or two in Brussels with me?"

Brussels? The capital of the European Union . . .

Suddenly my blood was swimming in adrenaline. Three weeks ago I would have been thrilled just to establish a reputation for quality work in the eastern United States, but from out of the blue I'd been invited to Rome. Now, as casually as if he were offering me another slice of bread, Santos Justus was inviting me to the European capital!

I lifted my gaze and tried on a casual, nonchalant smile. "I'd be happy to see if I can help."

Justus leaned back and picked up his cigarette again. "*Bene*. Wonderful. I will let you know more details as the time approaches."

Synn leaned toward his employer and gestured to his watch. "Were you supposed to meet someone after lunch?"

"Si, grazie." Il Presidente nipped at his cigarette one final time, then ground it out with a vicious twist of thumb and forefinger. As he stood, Justus turned his attention back to me. "Thank you for lunch. I am grateful for an opportunity to know you better."

He smiled at Signora Casale, held her hand for a moment in farewell, then slipped through the crowd milling outside the restaurant.

"Does he always travel alone like that?" I asked, craning my neck to follow his athletic form through the crowd. "Doesn't he have a body-guard?"

"I have tried to convince him it is foolish to walk about in the open," Synn answered, coming around to pull out my chair. "But he feels he is beloved in the Eternal City."

I stood, about to ask about the enemies Synn had told me to guard against, but Il Direttore was moving toward the cashier with a fistful of lire. I waited beside Signora Casale, silently wondering why Justus felt so safe in Rome. History had proved that public figures were not safe anywhere, especially at home. Hadn't Julius Caesar been stabbed to death on the steps of the Roman Senate? And Pope John Paul II had been shot in the courtyard of his own St. Peter's Basilica.

As Synn smiled and extended his hand toward the sidewalk, I joined him and Signora Casale, deciding to let Justus and his security people worry about his personal safety. After all, I had been instructed to watch for cheats and liars, not assassins.

I sincerely hoped the adversaries of Global Union preferred cutting words to automatic weapons.

Though I was more than a little intrigued by the idea of working with Santos Justus in the international arena, I resolved to focus first on the work he had hired me to do. To that end, I allotted several hours each morning for meeting and reviewing the present employees of Global Union. I promised Signora Casale that I'd spend my afternoons interviewing prospective employees from her list of recommended candidates.

On Thursday afternoon, my second day on the job, Maura Casale stopped by my office with several key staff members. Speaking Italian for their benefit, she referred to me in a string of syllables that seemed a haphazard mixture of "o's" and "ini's," then quietly bid me good afternoon and left me blinking in confusion. Though I think my technical title was "resource officer of the Global Union," I later learned that the employees of Global Union did not refer to me as *ufficiale delle risorse del Unione Globale*, but as *l'Americana*. Sometimes when I heard my title whispered in the cafeteria line, I doubted that the phrase was intended as a compliment. Who could blame them? I had been hired, in part, to watch them even in unguarded moments and search for signs of disloyalty. No wonder the senior staff members left my office so quickly.

Before concentrating on individuals, though, I had to learn about the Roman approach to business. I quickly discovered that no work ever transpired between the hours of noon and two o'clock (fourteen o'clock to the Romans). The average employee in our headquarters typically drank his or her breakfast (a cup of espresso) on the run, washed down a croissant (a *cornetto*) with another cup of espresso at eleven, then dawdled over a two-hour pasta lunch. They were earnest workers as long as they remained in their office environment, but apparently an invisible force field stood somewhere near the doorways of those offices and cubicles. When a Roman employee crossed through the force field, work ceased to exist or matter. Mealtimes were for relaxation and refreshment; walks in the park were inspiration for the soul. Business was *not* mixed with pleasure.

I learned this the hard way—on Thursday I joined a group of women employees in the cafeteria for lunch and casually brought up the long line of job applicants I'd seen in the lobby that morning. The women fell silent as a little flutter of indignation spread through the group. I had offended them, and later, when the conversation resumed its normal pace, I began to understand why.

The prohibition against business talk at mealtimes was actually a benefit in disguise. When people are relaxed, they reveal more of their authentic selves. So when I joined the employees of Global Union for the cornetto and espresso break at eleven, I found the cafeteria an ideal place to fulfill the first part of my responsibilities—reading the organization's present employees. Knowing that I was working while I sat and talked with the other employees helped ease the burden of guilt imposed by my American work ethic.

I learned more about Italians in my first few days on the job than I could ever have picked up from a book. I learned, for instance, that the American concept of personal space did not exist in Italy. Touches were freely given and feelings openly expressed. Complete strangers felt completely comfortable leaning close and touching my arm as we spoke; women thought it sweet, not strange, to stroke a friend's arm while they shared a confidence or talked about the weather. One afternoon while I sat alone at a table in the empty cafeteria, a man I had never met came in, served himself from the espresso machine, and sat in the empty chair *right next to me.* He didn't want to talk to me and he didn't know me; he just wanted to sit in that seat. Though his nearness made me uncomfortable, I soon realized that the Italians meant no offense by what most Americans would consider an invasion of personal territory.

On the first Monday of my second week, with Signora Casale's blessing I took a tour of the Global Union headquarters to get a feel for my surroundings. The security and employment offices filled the first floor; the cafeteria and employees' lounge took up most of the space on the third. I already knew that the Communists' former love nest on the seventh floor served as Santos Justus's personal offices.

On the second floor I found a mammoth library. The caretakers of this cluttered space, a man and a woman, looked up as I came out of the elevator. From their startled expressions I surmised that the library didn't receive many visitors.

Stepping forward, I met the Doctors Curvier—Millard and Patrice, husband and wife. Dr. Patrice greeted me with a distracted smile. She was a medium-sized woman with red hair too bright to have come from human DNA. Her green eyes flickered over my form from head to toe, then she gave me a flitting, close-lipped smile, said, "Bonjour, mademoiselle," and returned her attention to her work.

"Bonjour, Madame and Monsieur Doctor Curvier," I said, giving the historians the brightest smile I could manage in this dismal and dusty place. "Signora Casale said I should stop by and introduce myself. I am Claudia Fischer, the resource officer who will be working with Il Presidente for the next few months."

The woman pulled her glasses to the end of her nose and looked up from the document she had been reading. "A pleasure to meet you, my dear," she said, her voice heavy with a French accent. She reached out and tugged on her husband's sleeve, then proceeded to speak to him— about me, I think—in sign language.

—

Monsieur Doctor Curvier was obviously deaf, and though he answered his wife in fluent signs, I had no idea whether he signed in American Sign Language, European, or whatever. After watching the Doctors Curvier converse with one another, I began to suspect they had devised a language all their own.

"My husband and I are pleased to meet you," Madame Curvier said, turning to me after exchanging a series of flurried gestures with her husband. "What can we do to help you?"

I crossed my arms, mentally noting the gesture as a sign of my own defensiveness. "I just wanted to get a sense of all work Global Union employees are doing. I know you are sorting through stacks of old records—"

The lady made an abrupt *tsking* sound. "That is my husband's job. I don't bother with it. The dust makes me sneeze." She crinkled her nose, and I noted a gleam of amusement in her green eyes. "I am working on a different project for Il Presidente—a collection of biographies."

"Really?" I stepped forward and peered over her shoulder. "Who are you studying now?"

She waved her hand. "Many different people. Il Presidente wants to write a speech on the great peacemakers of the world, so I am pulling together facts about Edward VII of England, John of Gaunt, Jesus, Saint Casimir of Poland, Pope Clement VI . . ." Her voice drifted off as she idly touched her hair, then her gaze flew toward me. "Have you any suggestions? Can you think of any peace-loving Americans we should include?"

I bit my lip. "Um . . . Ronald Reagan? They say he brought about the end of the Cold War."

She tilted her head, considering my suggestion, then frowned. "Too controversial, too current. Il Presidente will be safer referring to men of ages past."

I smothered a smile, thanked her for her time, and walked back to

—

the elevator, only too happy to leave the stuffy room. The Curviers were unusual people, but I saw no signs of treachery or hostility in them. They were bookish introverts, very French, and very intelligent. I'd bet my wisdom teeth that they were also very boring at parties.

I skipped the third floor and the cafeteria, then stepped off at the fourth floor. This area, designed to house the Editorial and Publications Departments, was still largely unfurnished. A jumble of desks and office chairs filled the lobby, and painters and carpet layers occupied several offices. I quickly excused myself and took the elevator to the sixth floor, skipping the fifth. The only offices on the fifth floor thus far were mine and Rico Triccoli's, the man hired to oversee international chapters of Global Union. Rico traveled a great deal, and I had not had a chance to meet him.

The sixth floor revealed nothing unusual—only Reverend Synn's office, a data entry pool of nearly a dozen women, and the financial office, which stood behind locked double doors. I took the hint and moved on, smiling at the data entry operators as I walked past the half-wall that defined their space. As I rounded the corner, I heard whispers about l'Americana. Part of me wished there'd been time to take a basic course in Italian before leaving New York.

I stepped back into the elevator and pressed five, ready to return to my corner of the complex. And as the polished brass doors silently slid shut, I realized that Justus's personnel director had done a very good job of hiring faithful people thus far . . . without my help.

"So why were they so eager to hire me?"

The question hung in the air, shimmering like my reflection in the elevator's brass doors.

ELEVEN

ASHER TOSSED THE DAMP TOWEL OVER THE EDGE OF THE TUB, THEN checked his face in the mirror. Every hint of stubble had been whisked away, and the haircut looked good, not too severe. It wouldn't be wise to enter Unione Globale headquarters looking too eager.

He turned to the bed and picked up the shirt he had purchased with the designer suit in an exclusive men's store. The purchases would barely cause a ripple in his bank account, but the thought that he had spent the equivalent of an average Roman's two-month salary galled him. He hated spending money on clothes, but intuition told him the investment would reap rewards.

He shrugged his way into the shirt, fastened the buttons, slid a pair of gold cuff links into the holes at his sleeves. The suit fit him perfectly, as well it should, and the silky cotton shirt felt wonderful against his skin.

One corner of his mouth quirked downward when he caught his reflection in the mirror. Fabrics had vastly improved over the past generation, but what fabrics gained in texture, tailors lost in craftsmanship. With regular wear, this suit would last maybe five years, while others in his closet six times that age still looked as good as when he bought them. They were outdated, of course, but they just might last forever . . .

He slipped into his shoes, knotted a silk tie at his neck, and took a moment to rake his fingers through his close-clipped hair. He wore it shorter than he had a generation ago, and he preferred the shorter look.

Longer hair meant freedom from frequent barber visits, but he had never liked his hair bristling out over the tops of his ears. Perhaps his fondness for neatness stemmed from his youth—after all, the Romans of antiquity had clipped their heads, wisely recognizing that long hair could be dangerous in battle.

Asher straightened, flicked an imaginary speck of dust from his shoulders, then flashed a practice smile at the mirror. He had to appear earnest, intelligent, and quick. More than anything, he had to appear supportive.

Only one more ritual to observe. Girding himself with resolve, he moved to the desk in his sitting room, pulled the leather journal toward him, then lifted his fountain pen from its holder. After uncapping it, he hesitated for a moment, then began to write:

> *Today, Lord, I begin a new approach. I pray I will act while there is yet time to attain my goal. I have never felt as certain as I do today, I have never seen so many signs pointing to a single man, and yet I wonder if this is the path you would have me seek. If it is not, O God, show me another way. But if it is the path I am to tread, help me reach the soul of the wayward one before the enemy claims another victory.*
>
> *If Santos Justus is the man, lead me to him and open the door for a personal confrontation, Holy God. Clear my path. Give me strength and cunning and wisdom to defeat all those who would stand in my way—and I know there will be many. Give me the courage I will need to complete the task before me.*
>
> *I ask these things in the Name above all Names, in the Power That Fails Not. As you have cursed me, so send me forward to do your will. I am your penitent servant, Holy God, to use as you see fit.*

—

He paused for a moment to murmur his words aloud as a prayer, then put both pen and journal aside.

Squaring his shoulders like a Roman soldier under Tiberius Caesar's command, he stood and lifted his chin, then moved toward the door.

TWELVE

By Wednesday of my second week, Maura Casale and I had established a routine. I spent the mornings making notes on each of Global Union's present employees, visiting them if necessary. After lunch, the parade of job applicants began to move through my office at precisely half-past fourteen o'clock. Each hopeful applicant entered with his application and a colored badge in hand. The application was in Italian and virtually impossible for me to read, but the color-coded badges, Signora Casale had explained, were all I really needed to note. Blue badges indicated that the applicant was being considered for a minimum-security position. Orange badges represented jobs that would place employees in contact with classified materials, and red badges signified that the applicant was applying for a job that would place him or her in direct contact with Santos Justus. These applicants were to be carefully interviewed, for hours if necessary. We could not risk Santos Justus's life.

These interviews were more difficult than any I had endured thus far, for few of the new applicants spoke English as well as the other employees of Global Union. Furthermore, this wave of new applicants reflected Rome's international diversity.

The first applicant was a woman from Japan who carried a blue badge and spoke very little English *or* Italian. She was applying for a secretarial job in the financial office, not a high security risk, but certainly a position requiring discretion. We stumbled around a few comments and smiled a lot, but through all the confusion I picked up several positive impressions. Her clothing was conservative rather than flamboyant, which spoke of caution and tact, and her only jewelry was a wedding band and a simple gold watch, so she was practical rather than extravagant. She met my gaze without hesitation, which indicated a certain honesty and directness, and she evidenced the singular Asian custom of covering her mouth when she laughed—an indication of ingrained modesty. I signed her application and sent her out the door wearing a smile.

The second applicant carried a red badge, and my nerves tensed at the sight of it. The young man, an Italian who spoke tolerable English, told me he wanted to be a chauffeur and drive the *macchine blu*—the fast blue car favored by Italian politicians, including Justus. I asked him a few simple questions in English, noticing while he talked that he wore a wrinkled but clean shirt, cuffed trousers that had gone out of style three years ago, and well-worn leather loafers with a hole in the sole.

I asked for his file, signed it, and sent him out the door, then added his name to a separate list in a black-bordered file folder on my desk. Unfortunately, I could not recommend him for the job. His kind of dowdiness could mean many things, including a lower socioeconomic background (certainly not his fault), but it often signified preoccupation, sloppiness, and/or an "absent-minded professor" mind-set. *Any or all of the latter traits would disqualify the young man from a job as Justus's driver,* I wrote, *but he might be suited to working with the Doctors Curvier in the records room . . .*

The next applicant rapped on the door and entered before I acknowledged his knock. I looked up from my file to see a middle-aged man with thinning hair and a nervous manner lowering himself into the guest chair before my desk. He carried an orange badge and a manila file, which he slid across my desk without so much as a "good afternoon."

I opened the file and glanced at his application. This fellow, from Florence, was applying for a job as an editor in the Publications Department. Careful not to let my initial misgivings show in my expression, I asked him about his childhood. While he struggled to find the correct English words, I leaned back to watch and listen. He spoke in almost a monotone, unusual in any situation but certainly for an Italian, and frequently glanced down at the floor. He sat with his body turned partially away from me and kept his hands in his pockets as if hiding something.

When he had finished rambling, I launched into a silly story about my own childhood, noting that he kept his lips tightly closed, his eyes averted, and his hands in his pockets—classic signs of a secretive, guarded individual.

Sighing, I signed his file and dismissed him with a nod. I would add his name to the list of rejected applicants. If Global Union ever wanted to hire a spy, this man might be a suitable candidate, but I couldn't recommend him for Publications, where an open and friendly manner would prove invaluable.

Two other prospects followed in quick succession. The first was an Indian woman who wore a broad smile, upper and lower teeth showing, the entire time she sat in my office. A broad smile is nice, but it's not exactly appropriate in every situation. I added her name to the list of rejected applicants. The second was a young Englishman who chewed his fingernails during our entire interview. His obvious tenseness was bad enough, but when I saw that he was applying to work in the cafeteria, I sent him out the door with a cheery farewell, then rejected him as well. I didn't want those slimy fingers anywhere *near* my lunch tray.

The next applicant, another red badge carrier, looked like a typical Italian male, but his greeting caught me by surprise. "Miss Fischer?" he asked.

I gasped in disbelief at the sound of his perfect American accent.

"I am Asher Genzano," he said, thoughtfully ignoring my wide eyes and open mouth. "I understand you and I must have a little talk."

—

111

I stared in amazement while he placed his folder on my desk.

"May I sit down?"

I shook myself out of my stupefaction. "Please. Excuse me, I was just—" I couldn't stop a smile from spreading over my face. "You must have grown up in the States. Where—the Midwest?"

He looked down, his long lashes hiding his eyes, and smiled. "Sorry, but I am Roman to the bone. I have a particular gift for languages, that's all. And I like English. Despite its idiosyncrasies, I find it a very expressive language." He looked up and caught my eye. "I'm applying for the position of interpreter and translator."

I glanced at the file he handed across the desk, but Maura Casale's scrawled Italian notations meant nothing to me. I set the file aside. "Tell me about yourself, Signor Genzano."

"I was born in Rome," he began, his voice low and smooth, "and I have traveled for many years, to a great many countries in the Middle East, Asia, Africa, and America. I have spent a good deal of time in Europe, and as a result of my travels I have mastered several languages."

"How many?" I asked politely. I picked up my pencil to jot down a few notes, though I was actually more interested in how he spoke than what he said. He certainly dressed well; the suit he wore was beautifully cut and looked expensive. His leather shoes gleamed with polish, and he wore his hair in a neat style that would be equally suited for the boardroom or the soccer field.

Propping his elbow on the chair's armrest, he leaned toward me and rested his chin on his hand—a gesture of confidence—as a relaxed smile crossed his face. "How many languages do you need?"

I glanced down at the file as if I could find an answer there. "I know Il Presidente will require an interpreter who speaks French—"

"I do."

"—and German and Dutch and English, of course."

"I don't do everything well, but I do I speak those languages fluently."

I glanced up again, a little perplexed. The man sitting before me had all the charm and confidence of James Bond, yet I didn't see any of the typical markers of egotism in his manner. He did not preen, gesture flamboyantly, or attempt to center the conversation on himself. Instead, he seemed to be focusing on *me*—unusual for any nervous applicant— and he had exhibited self-deprecating humor, unusual in one so certain of his abilities.

"Forgive me for asking, but how old are you, Signor Genzano?" I flipped through his file, searching for a date. He appeared to be in his midthirties, but appearances could be deceiving. Common sense assured me, however, that it would take years of concentrated study to master the four languages he had mentioned.

"I'm not exactly certain of my age. There is no record of my birth date."

I glanced up, searching for any physical gesture that might indicate lying, but he sat as still as before. I thought I saw a faint flicker of unease in the depths of his dark eyes, but that could have been the light . . .

"No records? I find that hard to believe."

"I was born in a small and primitive village. My parents died when I was young, and I was not formally educated until much later in life."

I stared at him, baffled. "Surely you can obtain some sort of record. At a hospital, perhaps, or a church. Most churches keep records of infant baptisms, so if your parents were Catholic your name is surely recorded somewhere—"

"They weren't Catholic."

I lifted a brow. "Protestant?"

"Pagan."

He wasn't joking, for he sat perfectly still and his expression did not change. His gaze remained locked with mine; his body did absolutely nothing to betray him . . . if he was lying.

I propped my elbow on the desk and placed my chin against my palm, mirroring his posture while I puzzled through the mismatch of behavior and answers. Liars were always difficult to spot, but there were common telltale signs: restricted hand movements or hidden hands, touches to the face, or neck scratches. Collar pulls usually indicated an increased state of tension often due to lying. I once interviewed a potential witness who lied under oath and consistently revealed his deception by rubbing his nose; the more outrageous his lie, the harder he rubbed.

But Asher Genzano sat perfectly still with a relaxed, simple smile on his face. His chin was still cupped in his palm, so both hands remained plainly in view—there was no subconscious desire to hide them away.

Could he be telling the truth? I would be presumptuous to assume that Italy was so like America that every male over the age of two had a number registered with the Italian version of the IRS I knew primitive villages still existed in Italy, and perhaps it was possible that thirty years ago a young orphan boy could have grown up without an official record of his birth . . .

I made a mental note to ask Maura Casale how I should handle the situation, then pretended to study the file again. "Do you have family, signore?" I smiled politely. "A wife?"

"I am a widower." He spoke the words in a grave and solemn tone, yet I detected no crinkling of his eyes, no furrowing of his brow. The grief could not be recent, yet he was a relatively young man. So either he had married while practically still in adolescence, or he had felt nothing for the woman he wed.

I lowered my voice to a more sympathetic note. "I am sorry. Were you married long?"

He looked away and pursed his lips slightly; the gesture set alarm bells ringing in my brain. He knew the answer, he could count the years, but he did not want to tell me. Why not?

"A very long time," he said finally, meeting my gaze again. "Lifetimes ago."

Poetic hyperbole. I glanced at the file and resisted the urge to roll my eyes. The man was a romantic, but that didn't mean he wouldn't make a good interpreter. I scanned his application, looking for any word or phrase that might clarify his situation, but found nothing.

What could I do? The man was apparently gifted, and Global Union desperately needed a skilled interpreter. *I* needed an interpreter, and if this man was really good, I might beg to borrow him for these interviews.

But what could his reticence mean? The man was an enigma, and that did not bode well for his chances of earning a top security clearance.

After a moment of consideration, I closed his file and slid it across the desk. "The position of interpreter is an important one, and there are certainly security issues that must be addressed," I told him. "I cannot make a quick decision. I understand you have other tests involved in the concorso?"

My words displeased him; I saw clear evidence of that in his frown, but he nodded without any obvious signs of hostility.

"I would like to consider your application further, Signor Genzano. We must meet again before I can approve it."

He rubbed a hand across his face, then exhaled slowly and stood. I stood as well, extending my hand, which he took in a warm, solid grasp. "Grazie, I appreciate your time," he said simply, looking at me with some barely perceptible emotion stirring in his dark eyes. "I will look forward to our next visit. Until then, good-bye."

"*Ciao,*" I called as he turned to leave.

He stopped in midstride, then looked back over his shoulder and waggled a finger in my direction. "No, signorina," he said. "*Ciao* is how

—

you would bid farewell to good friends. In a business situation such as this, you must say *arrivederci.*"

My face grew hot with embarrassment, but I bowed my head in apology. "Thank you for the lesson. I will try to remember."

"You will learn a lot . . . in time." He gave me a gentle smile, and something in it reminded me of the way my grandfather had looked at me when he forgave me for playing with my grandmother's false teeth.

"*Arrivederci,*" he said, moving through the doorway.

I waited until he disappeared around the corner, then I sat down and circled his name on my appointment sheet. I would not have to test his language skills; Signora Casale would make certain he was qualified for the job he sought. My responsibility was to judge his character, and I was nearly certain Asher Genzano would prove to be an honest, humble, and honorable man.

So why couldn't I sign his application? His explanation for his lack of birth records was reasonable enough. His avoidance of my questions about his late wife might have indicated that he was uncomfortable discussing what could have been an arranged marriage that failed for some reason. And the fact that he spoke five languages fluently could mean only that he had studied hard and had an ear for intonation—he *had* said he had "a particular gift."

I opened my necklace pocket watch and sighed in relief when I noticed the time. Nearly four o'clock. I was tired, worn out from a hard day's work and the struggle to acclimate myself to a different time and culture.

Things would make more sense tomorrow.

—

Thirteen

Asher walked down the hall and found the elevator, then held the doors open when a breathless woman called out, *"Si fermi! Per favore!"*

A small woman with hair the color of a Santa suit hurried down the hall, then gave him a quick smile as she stepped into the elevator. *"Merci beaucoup,"* she answered, leaning against the back wall.

The abrupt switch from Italian to French startled him. A Frenchwoman? Asher crossed his arms and smiled as she pressed the button for the second floor. "You are from France?" he asked in French.

The woman looked at him with puzzlement in her eyes. *"Oui."*

"How long have you been in Rome?"

"Six weeks." Her hesitant smile deepened. "You are from France too, no? From Paris?"

"No, I am Roman." Asher glanced at the door as the elevator began its descent. "But I lived in France for many years."

"You speak like a native Parisian."

"Merci beaucoup, madame. I am applying for the job of interpreter here. I am not certain I will be approved."

The woman made a face. "And why not? It is a pleasure to hear someone speak my native tongue without butchering it. I shall speak to Il Presidente myself and make certain you are raccomandati . . . if you will give me your name."

Asher gave her a grateful smile. "Asher Genzano," he answered,

---

117

stepping back as the elevator doors slid open. "And thank you very much."

She stepped off the elevator, pausing in the hallway just long enough to give him a reassuring nod. Bowing his head in reply, he pressed the button for the first floor, then folded his arms and leaned against the wall as the elevator doors closed.

He had to get the interpreter's job. He was far more qualified for it than any man alive, and it was one of the few positions that would bring him into Santos Justus's inner circle. He knew he had impressed the personnel director, and a word of recommendation from the Frenchwoman would help, but the interview with the American had not gone well.

Who was she, and why did her opinion matter? He had tried to inquire about her role in the concorso when Signora Casale directed him to the American's office, but the Italian woman only murmured something about "resource officer" and "an important step in the process."

He chided himself as the elevator doors slid open. He should have prepared better before attempting this approach. He should have learned about the American and puzzled through the connections between her and Justus—then, perhaps, he would be able to understand why she had looked at him with reticence in her eyes.

He paused at the security desk to sign out, then caught the guard's eye. "I am to come back tomorrow," he said in Italian. "I am to see Signorina Fischer again."

"L'Americana?"

"Si." Asher slid the clipboard across the marble-topped desk at the security station, then adopted the most mournful expression he could muster. "Perhaps you can tell me a way to win her favor. I don't think she likes me."

—

118

The guard laughed as he picked up the clipboard. "At least you have been invited back. She has dismissed many people after just one meeting."

His words gave Asher a glimmer of hope. "She is a beautiful woman," he said, leaning one elbow on the desk. "Surely there is a way a man can work his way into her good graces."

"I wouldn't try it." The guard leaned forward confidentially. "She is an expert in what she does. If you bribe her with flowers, she will know you are not sincere."

"An expert? In questioning people?"

"In understanding people. This is not commonly known, but"—he gestured for Asher to come closer—"Il Direttore says she can tell almost anything about a person just by talking with him for five minutes. In America she works for criminals, helping them get away with murder in jury trials."

"*E terribile!*" Asher couldn't stop the expression from crossing his lips.

The guard shrugged and straightened himself. "What can I say? *E un americanata!* What else can you expect from the Americans?"

Asher murmured his thanks and left the building, his thoughts spinning.

FOURTEEN

As my last act of the workday, I picked up the computer list of applicants' names and noted with grim satisfaction that I had approved more applicants—for the lowest security level, at least—than I had rejected. For a while I had wondered if the change of culture had blurred my perceptions, causing me to see miscreants and goblins in the faces of ordinary working people. I ran my finger down the page, mentally summoning an image to match each entry, then paused as my fingertip touched Asher Genzano's name.

What should I do about him? Concerned about his uncertain past, I had called Signora Casale after the interview. She reported that Genzano hadn't been exaggerating when he said he spoke several tongues like a native; he spoke more languages than she could adequately test. She seemed surprised that I hadn't immediately approved him, so I quickly assured her I hadn't rejected him, either. I just needed more time. It was an important position, after all, because the interpreter would be traveling with Il Presidente and delivering his words to millions of people.

I hung up and fretted over his application. Signora Casale seemed to think I was some kind of mind reader who could see through people in an instant, but some individuals can't be read properly in a brief interview. Sometimes people who won't meet your eye in a conversation aren't deceitful or secretive—they're just terribly shy.

One juror in a California case refused to look Elaine Dawson in the

---

121

eye during three days of voir dire. The juror consistently sat with her body turned to the right and usually propped her head on her hand as though we were inconveniencing her by keeping her awake. Watching from the gallery, I had mentally categorized her as lazy, disinterested, and a lousy juror, but during a recess I met her in the ladies' room and noticed that a bright red birthmark marred her cheek, extending from just below the corner of her eye up into her hairline. She was none of the things I had supposed—just terribly self-conscious about a birthmark she couldn't conceal.

A woman I once pegged as a liar because she consistently rubbed her nose proved to have allergies . . . and a man who talked like Thurston Howell III on *Gilligan's Island* impressed me as a pretentious snob until I caught him studying a script during a coffee break. At that point I learned he was rehearsing for a play and had vowed to spend an entire week in character.

Though Asher Genzano had none of the particular markers that would ordinarily indicate a false, malicious, or perverse nature, something about his peculiar responses rang my alarm bells. I found myself wishing I had taped our conversation. My memory wasn't exactly clear, but I was certain I had asked a question that he answered with another question—a definite warning sign. Answering a question with a question didn't always signal evasiveness; the individual could be insecure, embarrassed, eager to please, or in need of clarification.

In a short burst of disconnected thoughts, I remembered that Kurt was prone to answer questions with another question. I supposed he often used that technique when dealing with his patients—after all, psychologists are notorious for never giving a straight answer. The question-and-question-again approach forces patients to think about things from another perspective. It sometimes annoyed me, though, when Kurt's psychological technique bled over into our daily lives.

—

"Where do you want to eat?" I'd ask, and he'd respond, "What do you feel like eating?" On and on we'd go, around and around, until I gave up and just pointed to the closest restaurant on the street.

Asher Genzano hadn't been quite as infuriating, but he had definitely evaded a couple of simple questions. That business about how many languages he spoke, for instance. Most polyglots would be proud to rattle off the name and number of tongues they had mastered. One of Kurt's friends spoke four languages, and we couldn't eat in any ethnic restaurant without his reminding us that we could travel to several different countries in his company without ever having to buy a phrase book. Yet Asher Genzano had never given me a number . . . why not? Did his silence indicate humility or false modesty?

I couldn't tell, and I knew I wouldn't find any answers in my office. I shook my head to clear it of frustrating thoughts, then swiveled my chair and scanned my computer mailbox for any late-arriving messages from New York. The huge computer seemed extravagant for a temporary employee; I used it only for word processing and e-mail. I could have managed with my laptop, but Reverend Synn insisted that I use a desktop linked into Global Union's intranet so I could access the organization's databases, Web pages, and interoffice e-mail.

Rory had shown me how to use the Internet to link my laptop with the Global Union computers as well as his desktop in New York. "Whatever you do, don't send personal information through the intranet," he warned. "Anyone with a master password to the server will be able to read your mail."

I had laughed. "Oh, yeah, like I care if Santos Justus hears about Kirsten's cravings for anchovies and peaches."

There were two messages in my mailbox now—a quick hello from Kirsten and a note from Rory. Kirsten's rambling letter could wait, but Rory reported that our office had received a call from the Boston mayor's office—Mr. Mayor was facing a possible indictment on rack-eteering charges. Would we be interested in his case?

I typed in a quick reply.

> Tell them we're not available until after March 1; see if you can stall.
> If not, let it go but send our regrets. Thanks, Rory.

I clicked the send button, then stood and slipped into my jacket. A glance out the window told me that the wind had picked up, so I hoped the brisk walk back to my apartment would clear my head. I gathered my purse and briefcase, then flipped the light switch and left my office in darkness.

Downstairs, I smiled farewell to the security guard, then zipped my official ID card through the electronic gizmo at the entrance gate. Only then did the deadbolt release and allow me to exit through the glass doors.

Outside, the sun balanced on the western horizon, gilding the high walls of the Vatican and the magnificent dome of St. Peter's. A light shower had fallen in the afternoon, and a cool wind blew remnants of rain from the plane trees lining the street. Eager to reach the warmth of home and family, my fellow pedestrians hunched beneath umbrellas and raincoats and scurried like rodents along the sidewalk. I had nei-ther family nor friends waiting at my residenza, but as I negotiated the wet stairs leading to the street I consoled myself with the thought of calling Kurt. If I reached my apartment by six-thirty, Kurt would be in the middle of lunch in New York. His secretary could forward my call to his cell phone.

I shivered, chilled and wet and suddenly overcome by the need to hear a familiar voice. I had spent all day talking to people, but none of them were friends. Even now, as I prepared to enter the stream of pedestrians on the sidewalk, no one would welcome me. But I would be OK if I could just get back to my room and hear Kurt's voice . . .

I lowered my head and set out in the direction of my residenza, lengthening my stride as the shadows stretched and the sun sank behind the Vatican. Though my apartment was located in a comparatively "safe" neighborhood, I didn't relish the thought of being accosted by a beggar or Gypsy. In New York, I met the hard luck stories with a quiet "sorry" and moved on, but here I felt as helpless as an infant left out in a cold and unfamiliar world. How could I gracefully escape from an Italian beggar when I couldn't speak the language? I made a mental note to ask Maura Casale how to say "sorry" in Italian.

"Excuse me, Miss Fischer?"

I glanced up, startled to be called by name. Asher Genzano stood beside me, darker and fuller in the lengthening shadows than he had been in my office. I stared at him, my gaze moving up and down his frame, as the muscles of my throat moved in a convulsive swallow.

What was he doing here? I suppressed a groan as my thoughts leaped from one assumption to another. He knew the interview hadn't gone well, and he had waited here to confront me, perhaps even to threaten me into giving him a position. Maura Casale told me unemployment was high in Italy, and Asher Genzano might be a desperate man . . .

I injected a note of iron into my voice. "What are you doing here, Signor Genzano?"

I stepped back as he lifted his hand, then I saw that his hand was empty—no gun, no tire iron, no knife. "Please," he said, his voice choked with sincerity. "Don't be afraid."

The gesture of openness eased my anxiety somewhat. I took a deep breath to quell the leaping pulse beneath my ribs, then met his gaze. "How can I help you, signore?"

A smile found its way through the mask of uncertainty on his face.

—

125

"Excuse my forwardness, but I thought I might offer to walk you home. The streets in this part of town can be . . . intimidating after dark. As you see, the sun sets quickly here."

I glanced behind him and saw that he was right. The sun had already dropped behind the dome of St. Peter's, bathing the Vatican walls in a rosy glow. Soon there would be no light but that from the occasional street lamp.

But did I want this man to know where I lived? I did not understand him at all, and this encounter had done nothing but increase my concerns about his character. Professional liars are difficult to detect, and psychopaths blend effortlessly into society . . . until they decide to act upon their buried hatreds. Ted Bundy charmed people in Colorado, Washington, and Utah before he was ever identified as a cold-blooded serial killer.

"Thank you, signor, but I prefer to walk alone." I forced my lips to part in a curved, still smile. "I appreciate your thoughtfulness, but it would not be appropriate for me to see you outside the offices of Global Union. It would not be fair to the other applicants."

"And you wouldn't feel safe."

The words alone would have sent a chill up my spine, but when I searched his face I saw nothing but sympathy in his eyes. He gestured toward an espresso shop across the street. "I understand, of course, but the night is cold and damp. Perhaps you would like a cup of coffee before you return to your *pensione?*"

I wasn't exactly sure what a pensione was, but the coffee shop did look inviting. At least a dozen people lounged at the tables both inside and outside the well-lit shop, and a tantalizing aroma wafted out from the place. I suddenly realized I could use a jolt of caffeine. The day had been a long one, and, aside from calling Kurt, I had no plans for the long, empty evening. Besides, I did need another interview with Asher Genzano. So why not have a cup of espresso with him?

—

126

"Now, *that's* a good idea." I had just stepped off the curb and taken a step toward the espresso shop when Genzano's arm abruptly blocked my path. I opened my mouth, about to protest, as a whining motor scooter sans headlights buzzed up out of the thickening gloom and passed us in a blur.

"One must be careful in the streets of Rome," Genzano said, lowering his arm. "The mopeds and scooters and motorcycles are not fond of obeying the traffic laws. The vespistas do not regard pedestrians. They have even been known to come up behind people on the sidewalks."

Grateful for the warning, I nodded, but as we crossed the street I wondered if I'd made a wise decision. In New York I would have considered having coffee with a potential juror as a conflict of interest, but since the Italians did not mix business and pleasure, Asher Genzano would almost certainly refrain from discussing his pending position at Global Union. I, meanwhile, could use the time to study him. And perhaps in this relaxed environment he would share things I could not pick up in the more strained atmosphere of the office.

He pulled out a chair for me at an empty table in the courtyard outside the shop, then stepped away to the counter. The marble tabletop bore the circular stains from at least a dozen previous espresso drinkers, and I used a rumpled napkin from the dispenser to try to rub away the marks. The Romans seemed more relaxed about cleanliness than Americans, and while I didn't expect the place to be as spotless as Disney World, I had hoped to find conditions a little cleaner.

Asher returned a moment later with two steaming cups of the rich, potent coffee Italians loved. I dropped two sugar cubes in mine, then poured in a stream of milk. When the smooth liquid lightened to the color of my favorite tan handbag, I felt it was safe to drink.

"Is the coffee to your liking?" Asher asked, his eyes coming up to study my face.

"Yes." I gave him a brief glance, then looked away. The piazza where we sat teemed with life. Next to us, an African woman struggled to hold a rambunctious little boy on her lap. The child kept trying to wriggle out of her arms, but I knew she would not want to release him in the crowd.

"Signor Genzano," I began turning my attention back to my host, "where do you live?"

He pointed vaguely down the street. "In a very old hotel." He paused to sip from his coffee cup. "I have lived there many years."

I nodded, thinking of the seedy Manhattan hotels that often rent rooms by the week or month. Asher Genzano didn't look like the typical transient; on the other hand, he *was* looking for work. The expensive suit could be the only decent outfit he had. "And what work did you do before?"

He lifted a brow. "Before?"

I knew I was teetering on the wall separating business and pleasure, but I couldn't help myself. "Before applying at Global Union."

"Ah." He pulled his coffee cup to him and wrapped both hands around it. "I have done many things in the past. I once worked in government. It was not an exalted position, but I served a Roman official, so I enjoyed a few advantages. Since that time I have held many jobs, but mostly I have worked as an interpreter. It seemed a natural choice, given my many travels."

"Did you travel much in your government job?"

A secretive smile softened his mouth. "We were assigned to Jerusalem for ten years."

I searched my memory for some recollection of news about Italian diplomats in Israel but found nothing. Then again, until now my work had never involved international politics.

At the table next to us, the wriggly little boy had managed to slip from his mother's arms. He obediently stood by her table just long enough for her to relax and pick up a magazine, then he began trotting through the crowd on chubby legs. The panicked mother dropped her magazine and rose to follow him, but Asher was quicker. He stood and caught up with the boy in three long strides, then scooped the toddler up just as the little imp was about to step into the streaming traffic. Genzano settled the protesting child on his hip, then waved at the mother and made his way back to us.

As she accepted her child, the grateful mother babbled her thanks in a language I had never heard. I stared, dumbfounded, when Genzano answered in the same tongue. The woman's eyes filled with wetness as he soothed her, then she took the toddler by the hand and moved away into the night.

Like Clark Kent back at the *Daily Planet,* Asher Genzano settled back in his chair and took another sip of his coffee. Superman's work was done.

"That woman"—I pointed toward the retreating figure—"what language did she speak?"

"Somali." His tone was utterly matter-of-fact.

"You've traveled in Somalia too?"

"I doubt you could name a country I've not visited."

As I wondered whether this remark sprang from conceit or confidence, an Asian woman called out Asher's name. She came to our table, warmly greeted him in another language I had never heard, then nodded and left us alone.

"A friend?" I asked.

"A housekeeper at the hotel," Asher explained. "Many Filipinos work as domestics in Rome. They are well educated but can't find jobs in the Philippines for which they are qualified. They are well paid here, however, and are able to send money to the families they have left behind."

I struggled to remember the language of the Philippines but couldn't recall it. "And she speaks—"

"A little Italian, but mostly Tagalog. Rome is a city of many nationalities." He coughed out a short laugh. "I suppose I could have learned to speak many languages without ever leaving home."

"I see." I drank the last of my coffee, then sat quietly, clutching my empty cup. I had not learned much about Asher Genzano on a subliminal level, but I had observed many obvious things—he was gentle with children, attentive to women, and possessed a truly extraordinary command of language. Perhaps he did have a gift. Then again, perhaps he had staged this entire evening for my benefit. He could have had both women appear here, just to demonstrate his linguistic skill . . . if that's really what it was. They could have been speaking pig Latin for all I knew.

My smile stiffened at the thought. "Thank you for the espresso," I said.

"You really should learn to speak a bit of Italian, Miss Fischer." His smile was easy, but his eyes were serious. "You will enjoy your stay in Rome much more if you do. You will find that people will be more eager to help if they feel you are making an effort to understand them."

I shrugged, realizing this bit of pop psychology was probably right on target. Not being able to communicate was inconvenient at best and terrifying at worst.

"I'll pick up an Italian phrase book tomorrow," I promised. "And in the meantime, good night."

"Buona notte," he answered.

I turned to leave, then, on impulse, I looked back to him. "Buona notte," I said, mimicking his accent as best I could. "And grazie . . . for the espresso."

He did not rise to walk me out, and I'm certain he sensed my reluctance to have him follow me. But I felt the warmth of his answering smile for a long time after I left the crowded piazza.

—

Fifteen

Asher finished his espresso, then turned to survey the sidewalk. When he was certain the American woman had vanished into the crowd, he stood, tossed both empty cups into a corner trash bin, then thrust his hands into his pockets and walked home.

Night had fallen, thick and dark, yet the street lamps pushed at the gloom and the laughter of pedestrians warmed the chilly air. Asher quickened his steps across the Piazza della Rotonda, passing the tall obelisk in the courtyard and feeling the hulking presence of the ancient Roman temple behind his back. Marcus Agrippa had named the building Pantheon, or "temple of all the gods," but authorities in the Middle ages claimed the architectural marvel for a church. Today it functioned as a tourist magnet.

The Sole al Pantheon sat across the street from the famous landmark from which it had taken its name. Built in 1467, the building now served as a four-star hotel for the tourists that descended upon Rome during all seasons of the year. All thirty rooms were presently occupied, as they would be for months to come. The flood of tourists slowed only in the miserable month of August, when the temperature often soared to over 104 degrees and native Romans fled the city for cooler climes by the sea.

Asher entered the foyer, nodded at the desk clerk on duty, and moved toward the hallway that led to his private apartment at the side of the building. Before he could reach the hallway, however, Signor Portoghesi, the manager, came running from a far corner of the lobby.

"Signor Genzano." The red-faced man inclined his head in a deep bow. "Excuse the interruption, signore, but there is a matter I must discuss with you."

Asher bit his lip, in no mood for trifling issues. "Can it wait until morning?"

"Of course, signore, but it is only a small matter. It seems that one of our American guests has caught her hair in the drain of the Jacuzzi."

Asher's annoyance turned quickly to alarm. "Was she injured?"

"Thank God, no. Her husband drained the water and cut her free. But she is in a temper and is threatening to take the matter before the civil courts if we do not—"

Asher silenced the man with a scowl. How like Americans to make a mountain out of a mistake resulting from their own foolishness. Who would try to swim in a Jacuzzi? He ought to let the woman take the matter before the civil court; after a day or two of filling out paperwork that accomplished nothing, she would rethink her litigious attitude.

"Tell me, Portoghesi," Asher said, scratching his chin, "have they been at the hotel long?"

"A full week, signore."

"Ah." A full week in one of the more luxurious rooms would result in a sizable balance due. Over the years, Asher had seen hundreds of people try to escape their debts—by slipping on the tiled lobby floor, claiming that valuables had been stolen in the dead of night, or feigning some other injury. One man even proclaimed that the aged painted and paneled ceilings had brought on a severe asthma attack, resulting in a huge physician's bill.

"Tell me, friend—did you see this suffering American woman?"

"Yes, Signor Asher. She was wet and breathless—"

"And her hair—had it been shorn off?"

"Only this much." The manager lifted his hand, indicating a space of two inches between his thumb and index finger. "It was not noticeable, but the wife was weeping about her beautiful hair . . ."

Rejecting the Americans' absurd complaint, Asher smiled at his manager. "Allow them to eat tonight in one of the best restaurants, Portoghesi—allow them to choose their favorite. Tell them the meal is our attempt to atone for their difficulty."

"And if a meal is not enough?"

Asher paused. He could dismiss their debt. He did not need their money. In truth, he did not want it. But he could not allow such people to continue a life of fraud and deceit.

"If it is not enough, let them go to the courts. Wish them Godspeed and send them to another hotel."

"Si, signore." Portoghesi smiled his approval. "I shall do as you wish."

The manager left, and Asher continued down the narrow hallway that led to his own rooms. He pulled the ancient key from its niche in the plastered wall, then opened the door and slipped into the dark foyer. Without pausing, he strode through the front room and entered his bedchamber, which stood exactly as he had left it except for a pair of fresh towels on the rod by the bathroom door.

The computer, his personal concession to the twenty-first century, sat upon a desk in the corner, the keyboard still protected by the rigid plastic cover that came with the equipment. If not for the maid who tidied up every morning, it would have been covered with the fine, sandy dust that blew into Rome during the autumnal sirocco winds.

He stared at the dead, unblinking eye of the monitor as he unknotted his tie and removed his coat. He was usually content to rely upon his memory, the community grapevine, and the university library for information, but now he found himself in need of knowledge that could not be obtained from any of his usual sources. He needed to know about Claudia Fischer, for she alone stood between him and the goal he had spent his life pursuing.

He took a moment to hang the suit coat on a wooden hanger, then replaced it in the wardrobe and moved to the computer. Sighing in resignation, he bent to press the on switch on the power strip, then stood and crossed his arms as the monitor crackled and something in the steel box whirred and came to life.

As the machine went through its electronic paces, he considered his last meeting with the American woman. She had been frightened when he approached her on the street, but the offer of coffee in a public place obviously appealed to her practical nature. As they talked, Asher felt the sharp prick of her questions and the speculation in her gaze. She was still evaluating him, but that was what he wanted. Let her test and question and study. He would give her the entire truth . . . if she really wanted it.

The computer had finished its warm up, so Asher sat down and logged on to the Internet. In a few keystrokes he had accessed a search engine; in another moment he had typed in the name *Claudia Fischer*. He slapped at the enter key, then waited while a series of links appeared on the screen.

After an hour of Web surfing, Asher had learned that Claudia Fischer was president and owner of Fischer Consulting, Inc., operating out of an office in New York, New York. According to her firm's Web page, Ms. Fischer's experience as a jury consultant encompassed several areas of litigation, including general business, wrongful termination, professional malpractice, and criminal defense.

The page offered little personal information—only a brief mention that Ms. Fischer had received an M.A. from San Diego State University in California. Nothing about a husband, children, or personal goals.

Nothing to indicate why she would be working with Santos Justus.

—

Sighing, Asher turned off the computer, then moved to his writing desk in the sitting room. After picking up a pen, he pulled his journal toward him.

I was nearly approved to work at Unione Globale when I encountered an unexpected obstacle—an American woman, Claudia Fischer. For some reason Santos Justus has placed her in a position of authority, and I sense that she does not trust me.

But why should she? If she knew the motivation of my heart, she would shun me like the devil himself. And yet . . . I wonder about her. Logic tells me she must be ungodly—indeed, there is nothing in her appearance, manner, or speech that leads me to consider her a believer. I have heard she works for American criminals, which would seem to indicate that her heart is dark and ruthless, yet I cannot believe she has sold herself to evil, for there is goodness in her too. She smiled tonight when I returned a child to his mother, and when I met her on the street I saw a flicker of loneliness in her eyes . . .

Holy God, prove yourself faithful. Grant me courage and perseverance, but above all, give me wisdom to overcome the evil that must arise in these last days.

I pray these are the last days. Please, Holy God, may they be.

Sixteen

True to my promise, the next morning I picked up an Italian phrase book at a newsstand. For the next two days at Global Union headquarters, I made an honest attempt to conquer the first chapter, "Useful Everyday Phrases." And while I struggled to inject *Piacere di conoscerla?* (How do you do?) and *Sono davvero spiacente* (I'm really sorry) into my conversations, I discovered Asher Genzano was right —people really did warm up to me when they realized I was trying to fit into their world.

By the end of the week, I had also approved Asher Genzano's application. I didn't want to. I fretted over my uneasiness for hours, then went down to Signora Casale's office, hoping to use her as a sounding board.

"Something about him is not right," I said, sliding my legs into the narrow space between her guest chair and her desk. "His residence, for instance. Don't you find it odd that he lives in a hotel?"

Maura Casale arched her fine brows into triangles. "Why shouldn't a man live in the building he owns?"

He *owned* the hotel? I sat back, stunned by the realization that the man who had appeared desperate for a job was apparently as rich as Midas. Roman real estate, I knew, was not inexpensive.

"So why does he want this job?" I whispered the question more to myself than to the personnel director, but Signora Casale took it upon herself to answer.

137

"Why shouldn't he want to serve the cause of world peace? He is an honorable man; I myself have interviewed him on three different occasions during the concorso. He is well qualified, he respects Il Presidente, and he yearns to do something good for the world. Are those not good reasons for wanting to work for Unione Globale?"

I could feel my cheeks flushing hotly. "If Il Presidente wants to hire Signor Genzano as a figurehead, why doesn't he just do it? There is no need to make him go through the concorso. There was no reason for him to sit through that interview with me—"

I stopped as my embarrassment turned to raw fury. Had Asher Genzano been toying with me in that first interview? Perhaps he knew his position in Global Union was secure; most wealthy men got whatever they wanted, particularly when they signed up with charitable organizations. *Want to be a vice president? Sure, just sign over a check. Want a building named in your honor? Our pleasure. Just write a check, and we'll do whatever you want . . .*

"Signor Genzano," Maura Casale was flushing now, scarlet stains appearing on her cheeks as she stared at me with glittering eyes, "has never even *met* Il Presidente. He has asked for nothing and received no special treatment. From what I can tell, he wants only to work with Unione Globale as a humble interpreter, as any man committed to the cause of peace."

My mouth dropped open, surprised again at this unexpected turn of events. A wealthy man who wanted to be treated like everyone else? Asher Genzano was more extraordinary than I had imagined.

Helpless to halt my embarrassment, I pressed my hands to my burning cheeks. "I'm sorry," I whispered, feeling like a complete and total failure. I had misread every clue. His elusive answers to my questions were not an effort to hide some unsavory aspect of his past; he must have meant only to disguise his wealth and position. He needn't have worried. I knew less than nothing about wealthy Roman families.

He wanted to work for peace, Signora Casale said. I should have accepted the man's desire at face value, but we Americans are cynical by nature. Ninety-eight percent of the people I knew in Manhattan were quick to sign on for do-gooder causes and just as quick to bail if no photographers or celebrities clambered around to add sparkle to an event. No one did anything without regard for personal gain . . . but for the life of me, I couldn't see what Asher Genzano would gain from following Santos Justus around the world like an obedient puppy. Some people, I supposed, did enjoy being part of a powerful person's entourage, but Asher Genzano had not impressed me as a hanger-on.

Signora Casale must have taken my silence for hesitation, for she slid reports from the office of the local *carabinieri* across her desk. "You'll see that Signor Genzano has no arrest record and no complaints lodged against him," she said. In a final effort to convince me, she followed the police reports with a yellow sheet of paper.

I picked it up. "What is this?"

"Intelligence test results." Her expression was locked in neutral, though I suspected she found my continued reticence rather annoying. "Signor Genzano scored a 148."

I made a face at the test results. So, the Wealthy Man I Would Not Hire tested well into the genius category. Add to that his savant's gift for language, and the sum equaled one convincing truth: Maura Casale thought I was a fool.

Knowing when I was beaten, I had dropped the report onto her desk and reached for his file. "I'll approve him. But I'll keep an eye on him too."

And as I signed my name to his employment record, I told myself

---

no harm would come from it. Something about Asher Genzano rang false in my ears, but I could see nothing in his character or manner to suggest he would be anything but a faithful and extraordinarily competent employee for Global Union.

Global Union, I discovered in the following weeks, could boast of a plethora of competent and faithful employees. Due to the rigors of the concorso, the organization hired only the crème de la crème, and peace-seeking idealists had flocked to Rome from several European nations. Each day I saw new faces in the cafeteria and met new applicants in my office. *Il Peacemaker*, the organization's official newsletter, reported that chapters of Global Union had been established in each of the fifteen European Union countries, and additional national chapters would be established within six months. By the end of the year, the editor enthusiastically prophesied, every nation on earth would have at least one chapter of Global Union operating within its borders.

One morning in the cafeteria, Reverend Synn sat at my table and sipped a cappuccino, pointing out new employees as we talked. "They are the lifeblood of the world's future," he said, nodding to a pretty young English girl who had been hired as a receptionist earlier in the week. "They will straighten the paths our forefathers have made crooked."

Accustomed by this time to his political grandiloquence, I smiled and let him talk. Like all vast organizations, I had discovered that in some ways Global Union was a world unto itself. The organization even had a few laws—albeit *unwritten* laws. First among them was a commandment never to speak ill of Santos Justus or Darien Synn. Anyone who dared question an order from the seventh floor or a suggestion from the sixth earned an icy stare, if not an outright rebuke, from the nearest bright-eyed idealist.

Nor, I noticed, did anyone speak of nations after Justus gave a speech about how the world was one unity and nations only artificial boundaries designed to keep people apart. After that, I heard no more whispers referring to me as l'Americana. My landlady and her neighbors seemed fascinated with the United States and things American, but everyone within the walls of Global Union apparently wanted to be one big, chummy family.

Justus wanted to bring people together not only on an international scale, but also within his own organization. Every Wednesday morning, at 10:00 sharp, every office emptied for the weekly convocation. From the lowest receptionist to Justus himself, the employees of Global Union gathered in the third-floor cafeteria. While employees filed in to sit around the luncheon tables or stand along the walls, Signora Casale took the microphone and led the gathering in an energetic Italian chorus. Her chesty alto echoed along the walls, and only after I had become partially conversant in Italian did I realize we were singing, "Peace, Peace, follow me to peace! We'll win the world; we'll save the children; we'll do all things through peace!"

An energetic pep talk, usually given by Il Direttore, followed the singing, then Rico Triccoli, the director of Global Union's international chapters, stood and announced how many new chapters had been chartered in the past week. Fervent applause followed his report, and then, if we were lucky enough to catch Il Presidente in town, Santos Justus himself would stand and speak for five or ten minutes.

I used to think of myself as somewhat jaded—when you live in Manhattan you tend to see and hear the best and worst of everything, including orators. I've had the privilege of hearing speeches by everyone from Reagan, the Great Communicator, to Clinton, the weepy "I feel your pain" president, so I really didn't expect Justus to move me in any particular way. But I must admit, the man had a gift. Like Reagan, he could stir hearts with star-spangled fervency; like Clinton, he could tell a story about a child in war-torn Somalia and leave his audience in tears. He spoke of hope, of peace, and of mutual respect and love. He spoke of the power of dreams and of the destructiveness of despair. But he never, I noticed, spoke of God. Was he trying to avoid a divisive topic? I couldn't tell.

In a city famous for being the home of the Holy See, I thought it odd that no one at Global Union ever referred to the Vatican. The pope and his vast legion of employees and guards affected the city in myriad ways—tourists flocked to St. Peter's, religious pilgrims knelt before statues and prayed in the ancient churches, and nearly every night a television newscaster reported the Holy Father's whereabouts and remarked upon his health. I myself had seen the great white helicopter that routinely transported the pope from his heliport in the Vatican Gardens to his vacation home at Castel Gandolfo in the Italian hillside. Despite the average Roman's indifference to papal trappings, the sight of that white helicopter was enough to stop pedestrians on the street and inspire a few to cross themselves in reverence.

Outside the Global Union headquarters, I saw many signs of religious devotion. Inside the headquarters, I looked for signs of fervent belief and found none. The lack of religious affiliation didn't bother me; it just struck me as odd. How could you live next to the head of the largest church in the world and not be affected by it?

I broached the topic with Maura Casale one day at lunch. We were eating outside in the courtyard, and the whirling white helicopter passed over our heads in a slow loop, then disappeared behind a stand of trees. I pointed in the direction of the Vatican and made a casual

—

remark about how much she must enjoy being near the heart of the world's church.

A blasé expression crossed Maura's face. "The pope is valued for economic reasons only," she said. "Many people yearn for the coveted prize of a Vatican job. The pay is low, but the perks are very good—if you are willing to sacrifice."

"Sacrifice went out a long time ago, signora."

The older woman rolled her eyes. "Not here. To work for the Vatican, you have to adhere to an antiquated moral code and list of prohibitions. No cohabitation or pregnancy without marriage. No abortion. No skirts above the knee. No bare arms in the basilica. Vatican employment is slavery disguised as religious honor."

I stared at the gleaming dome of St. Peter's. "I thought all Romans loved the pope. I used to watch him on television, waving to huge crowds in the square—"

"Tourists," Signora Casale spit out the word, then opened her mouth and shoveled in a generous forkful of gnocchi.

I fell silent and quietly adjusted my preconceptions. I had imagined Italy a devout and religious country, but I was beginning to understand that many Romans did not even pretend to practice their religion. I later learned that the United States actually has a higher percentage of professing believers within its population than Italy.

Italians were not as simple or as obvious as I had first imagined they were. Yet, after three weeks among them, I had to admit that I enjoyed them.

I've always enjoyed a challenge.

Six weeks after my arrival in Rome, I met with Reverend Synn for an evaluation of the concorso process. It was October 31, the day before the national holiday of *Tutti i Santi,* or All Saints' Day. Synn had requested the meeting before the holiday to "review our employment records and see where we stand." I interpreted that as "if we should be rid of you or keep you around for a while."

We sat at a concrete table in the piazza outside the Global Union building. The sky was a faultless wide curve of blue over our heads, and the sun felt good on my face. It was eleven o'clock, the hour of the espresso break, and several Global Union employees milled around us at a respectful distance.

"I must compliment you, signorina; you have done a marvelous job," Synn said, sniffing with satisfaction as he crossed his thick arms on the table. "All departments report complete satisfaction with their employees. We can truly change the world with such people."

The breeze freshened, and I wrapped my jacket closer around me. "How is Asher Genzano working out?"

"Ah, Signor Genzano is hard at work translating several of Il Presidente's speeches. I tried to get him to use our computer translation program, but he insists upon doing them manually. He has a quick mind, though, and I must admit his work is far superior to the computer's."

"I knew he would be a hard worker, but . . ." Weary of supposings about the inexplicable Asher Genzano, I let my voice trail off.

A gleam of interest flickered in Synn's eyes. "You have doubts about his character?"

"Not really. He is an honorable man, certainly, and definitely capable of being deeply committed to a cause. But there was something about his eyes . . ."

Blinded by the bright morning sun, I shaded my eyes with my hand and studied the memory of that night in the coffee shop. He had been considerate of me, helpful to the Somali woman, kind to the woman from the Philippines—who, I now realized, had recognized him as her employer. And yet there had been no haughtiness in his expression, no rebuke for the harried mother, and no judgment of me, the American who would not hire him. In his eyes I had seen infinite patience, remarkable for a man in any culture, but especially unusual in Italy . . .

The silence lengthened, then Il Direttore prodded me back to attention. "What about his eyes?"

"I don't know." I lowered my hand. "His eyes don't seem to match his face, I suppose. He is a young man, but his eyes seem old, as if he has seen all the world's sufferings. But he did say he has traveled in many foreign countries."

Synn nodded slowly. "Perhaps his travels led him to understand the heartbreak of war . . . and ultimately brought him to us." He gentled his voice. "There are many things, signorina, that have the power to age a man—sorrow, loss, and fear. And poverty, of course."

I bit my tongue, silencing a tart comment about Asher Genzano's noteworthy lack of poverty, while Synn's eyes went soft and gray. His mouth softened, and I knew he was on the verge of making one of his improve-the-world speeches. Glancing at my pocket watch, I mumbled something about needing to meet with Signora Casale to see if any new applications had been entered into the system.

"There are no new applicants," Synn said, his eyes still focused on some thought I couldn't discern. "We have filled all our present positions."

I digested this piece of information in silence. If there were no other positions to be filled, why was I still in Rome? Why had they asked me to set aside six months if they only needed me six weeks?

I opened my mouth to speak, but before I could utter a sound, Synn's age-spotted hand fell over mine. "Il Presidente has asked me to

—

invite you to dine with him today. We will eat lunch in his office, if that suits your schedule."

Too surprised to do anything else, I nodded in agreement.

As the hour approached noon, I peered into the tiny mirror of my compact to be sure I didn't have lipstick or coffee stains on my teeth. My mind had been roiling with questions ever since Synn's invitation, and I had come to the conclusion that this luncheon meeting was probably a token gesture of appreciation. Justus would thank me for my hard work and send me on my way with a considerably smaller fee than we had originally negotiated. I couldn't ask for more, however, if they no longer needed me.

At five minutes until twelve I stood, smoothed my skirt, and raked my fingers through the short layers of my hair, hoping I could evoke some semblance of the fashionably tousled look I saw on so many women in Rome. I paused at the doorway as another possibility reared its head. What if Justus *didn't* want to send me home? The quick question needed a thoughtful answer. What if he wanted to keep me on staff permanently? He had once mentioned the possibility of my working with him in Brussels, but since he never mentioned it again, I had dismissed the idea.

I rehearsed a dozen polite replies to that question as I rode the elevator up to the seventh floor. *Thank you for the honor, Il Presidente, but I have a business at home.* Or, *I have tremendously enjoyed my time with your organization, Signor Justus, but I have too many ties in the United States*—no, that reply broke one of the Global Union commandments: Don't mention a country. Better to claim family ties. Though I had never heard anyone mention Justus's family, the man had to have one.

As the elevator opened on the seventh floor, I stepped out into a space so bright it literally hurt my eyes. The floor here was white marble, the wall ahead of me clear glass, and the two walls at my sides were covered in full-length mirrors. The bright sunlight from the full-length window poured into the space with dazzling intensity, and for a moment I was too overcome to speak.

The sound of polite laughter cut through my bewilderment. I turned in time to see Reverend Synn coming through a glass door to the right of the elevator. Beyond the door I could see a secretary's desk.

"It is a bit bright when one first arrives," he said, extending his hand. "Come, the dining room is this way."

I followed him into a chamber unlike any corporate dining room I had ever seen. The walls were painted with a detailed garden scene; the cloth-covered ceiling elaborately gathered like a sultan's tent. A waiter in a white jacket and black bow tie stood to one side and bowed respectfully as Reverend Synn pulled out my chair.

A sense of unease crept into my mood like a wisp of smoke. "Signor Justus is joining us, right?"

"Of course." Synn took the chair next to me and gestured toward the only other remaining seat. "He will be with us shortly." We sat there for a long moment, pretending to listen to the odd chant playing on the sound system, then Il Presidente came through another door, this one disguised by the multicolored mural.

"A thousand apologies for my tardiness," he said, the warmth of his smile echoing in his voice. Synn stood when Justus entered the room, and the two embraced and exchanged kisses on the cheek. Justus took my hand when I stood too, then carelessly pressed a kiss into my palm. "Ah, Signorina Fischer. You have made the past few weeks so pleasurable. I have not heard one complaint from any of the department heads. The new personnel are all we could have asked, and more."

I thanked him, we sat, and the waiter began to serve the first course, a pasta-laden bean soup that smelled wonderful.

Shaking out his napkin, Justus looked at me and smiled like a child with a secret. "You're probably wondering why I asked to see you today."

I nodded and placed my napkin in my lap, a little surprised that Il Presidente would break the Italian prohibition of discussing business at mealtime. But if he wanted to live dangerously . . .

"I am curious." I kept my tone light and casual, in case he decided to steer the conversation away from our work. "It is not every day I am invited to dine with Il Presidente."

The sound of his laughter warmed the room. "Indeed, sometimes I wish I could duplicate myself many times over and spend time with each employee, but"—he shrugged—"such things are not possible, at least not yet. Perhaps when technology has improved a bit, my image can appear in many places at once. Until then, however, I shall simply have to work with my excellent deputies."

He lifted his wine glass and extended it toward Synn. "To you, dear Darien, for all you have meant to me. The future looks brighter than ever. With you at my side, the world cannot help but be a better place."

I lifted my glass as well but couldn't quite agree with the exuberant toast. Such a toast at home, coupled with the enthusiastic and physical greeting I'd witnessed, would have caused me to wonder about the kind of relationship existing between these two. But in Italy, men routinely greeted each other with loud exclamations, embraces, and kisses.

I shrugged away my concern and sipped from my glass. Justus picked up his spoon and began to eat from the bowl of aromatic *pasta e fagioli,* so the director and I followed suit.

"Signorina," Justus said, a thin smile on his lips, "Signor Synn informs me that all our current positions are filled, in part due to your hard work and earnest effort. We are grateful for your assistance."

I swallowed and smiled my thanks, bracing for the dismissal to come.

Justus scooped up a spoonful of soup and held it, regarding me for a moment. "We would now like to ask you, signorina, to move into another area."

I reached for my glass and struggled to overcome my surprise. "What did you have in mind?"

"Actually"—a dark flush mantled Justus's cheeks as he lowered his gaze to his soup bowl—"we had you in mind for this project from the beginning but wanted to be certain of your motivation. We can only trust those who are loyal, signorina. But in the last six weeks you have proved your dedication."

A chorus of *I told you sos* began to chant in my brain. I had wondered why Santos Justus would bring me in for something so basic as personnel management. He had wanted me for something else from the first, so he must be in legal trouble or facing some sort of lawsuit.

I sipped from my glass, then smoothed my features and lowered my glass to the table. "Why don't you tell me what the problem is?" I caught Synn's eye and smiled. "I must admit, gentlemen, that I thought our arrangement a bit odd. Why don't you tell me what you really want from me."

"It is a most delicate situation," Justus began.

"Most legal cases are."

Justus gave me an upper smile, polite and reserved. "It is not a legal case. The situation revolves around my work in the international arena."

—

I caught my breath as a thrill shot through me. The Roman connection had been exciting enough, but to work on a *truly* international level . . . I had only dared to dream of such possibilities.

Justus lowered his spoon to the table, then tented his fingers and looked directly at me. "As you have probably heard, signorina, I represent *Italia* in the Western European Union. Within the WEU there now exists an underground effort to demilitarize our organization, but those who would have us ground our planes and retire our armed forces have not considered the assets of a strong defense."

"History has shown that strong nations do not have to be *aggressive* nations," Synn interjected. "We do not want the WEU to lay down its arms. We are not warmongers; we are committed to peace. But total disarmament would be foolish."

"Three of the ten nations allied with us," Justus continued, "have elected new leadership to the WEU, and these three have formed an ad hoc committee whose purpose is to initiate wholesale and complete disarmament. Officially they deny this, of course, for a formal partnership with such a purpose would violate the bylaws of the WEU."

"But we have our suspicions," Synn said, his blue eyes sinking into nets of wrinkles as he smiled.

"We have our informers," Justus added. His eyes were flat and unreadable in the dim light. "We know they are making plans to influence the other nations to vote against us. Even as president, I could do nothing to overcome a majority vote. I am hoping they will not wield enough influence to do any real harm, but I do not know these newcomers well. Thus far they have refused all my invitations to meet and talk through our differences."

Both men had stopped eating. An unnatural silence prevailed as they stared at me, waiting for—what?

"I'm not sure I understand how I can help you." I spoke calmly, but with that eerie sense of detachment that comes with an awareness of impending risk. "I know very little about international politics and would not feel comfortable—"

"You know people," Justus interrupted. "And in the last few weeks you have learned a great deal about Europeans in particular. You would be able, wouldn't you, to watch the interaction of these men from a distance and read their body language? Would you, for instance, be able to tell if they are speaking truthfully or purposefully being secretive?"

I faltered in the silence engulfing me. "Perhaps. But it would be very difficult, and impossible if I could not understand their language. An individual reveals a great deal in his choice of words. Body language alone, no matter how expressive, cannot paint an entire picture. I would not want to make a mistake in something as important as this."

"We would, of course, send Signor Genzano with you as interpreter." A glint of wonder filled Justus's eyes. "I must compliment you, signorina, on your approval of that gentleman. He is a wonder! Last week I spoke to a tourist contingent from Zimbabwe, and he translated every word. I have yet to discover a language he cannot speak."

I smiled, anxious to abandon the subject of Asher Genzano. "May I ask how, where, and when I am to read these men from the WEU? I must warn you: They are likely to avoid sensitive topics if they are speaking in a public arena."

"You are not to worry, signorina." Synn showed his teeth in an expression that was not a smile. "Everything will be taken care of, and you will not be noticed in the gathering. But say nothing of this to anyone. This is—how would you say it?—*top-secret* work. No one will think your presence remarkable, nor will they know Global Union is involved."

Justus touched Synn's arm, effectively taking control of the conversation. "The next public meeting is in two days, in Brussels. These men are not only members of the WEU, but also of the European Union, and they will be present for a public councilors' meeting on Thursday. That is where you will observe them."

The thought of a clandestine operation brought a frisson of excitement. I had worked trials for clients suspected of industrial spying, but never had anything seemed as stimulating as what Justus and Synn were now proposing. And it would be safe, for Synn had said I would be watching in a public gathering.

"This isn't"—I hesitated, anxious to select the right word—"*illegal,* is it?"

My question seemed to amuse both men. "Of course not," Justus assured me. "You will be attending an assembly where every word is intended for the record. And you may consider your work an effort to reach our goal of international security and peace. If we are to live in safety, we must know what our opposition is thinking. I assure you, signorina, you will not find yourself in a compromising situation."

I blinked at that comment, not certain how reading people would help bring about world peace, but Justus picked up a little silver bell on the table and shook it. Within a moment, the waiter appeared to remove our largely untouched bowls of soup.

Justus leaned forward and pressed his palms together, smiling at me over his fingertips. "You will love the next course—*baccalà.* I believe the English word is *codfish.*"

I dipped my head and gave him what I hoped was an appreciative smile, though my thoughts had nothing whatsoever to do with food.

I woke with the sun on Wednesday morning, then remembered that it was November 1 and a legal holiday. All Saints' Day, Signora Casale had told me, had been observed since the seventh century, when the

—

Pantheon was consecrated as the Church of the Blessed Virgin and All Martyrs.

I cared nothing for churches or saints, but I was grateful for the day off. I pulled myself out from under the covers and fumbled for the phone on the bedstand. I couldn't wait to tell Kurt about Justus's latest proposition, and my excitement seemed to justify the exorbitant cost of an overseas call.

I glanced at the clock as the phone clicked in my ear. Seven in the morning in Rome was one in the morning in New York—late, but not so late that Kurt would be dead to the world. I knew he kept late hours on the weekends, so if he had already gone to bed, odds were good that he hadn't been asleep long.

I shivered in anticipation when the phone finally began to ring. He'd be so surprised to hear from me! Though I had e-mailed him nearly every day, filling my messages with details of life in Rome and describing my colorful coworkers, I had not yet managed to telephone him at home. The time difference made it difficult to catch him, and the expense was another consideration. Though Kurt could easily afford to call me, I wanted to be financially responsible until Rory and I safely pulled Fischer Consulting out of the red.

On the third ring, I heard the muffled sounds of someone fumbling with the receiver, then a husky hello.

A woman's voice.

I felt my breath being suddenly whipped away. Had I misdialed?

Obeying an instinct born of perverse pride, I resorted to subterfuge: "May I speak to Dr. Welton, please? This is his service calling."

I held my breath, hoping the woman would complain or curse at my mistake, but then I heard more fumbling sounds and a woman saying, "Kurt, it's for you."

I nearly dropped the phone as something inside me deflated and

—

153

began to drain away. Even the soft, reassuring sound of Kurt's greeting could not stop the nauseating sinking of despair that flowed from my heart.

I probably should have hung up. I should have replaced the phone and gone back to bed, letting my subconscious wrestle with the problem in my dreams. My clients would have expected that reaction; they always said I was unflappable in a crisis. But hurt and pride took the reins of my tongue and whipped it into an abrupt fury.

"Kurt!" Steely anger edged my voice. "Who is with you?"

"Claudia?" I heard surprise, alarm, and a note of panic in his reply. I closed my eyes, wishing I could see him, wanting to read the evidence of guilt and betrayal on his face. Then again, if he was leaning over this woman in an effort to reach the bedside phone, perhaps I was better off not seeing him. I'd never be able to shake that image out of my memory.

I shivered in the coolness of my bedroom. "Kurt, the engagement is off."

"Hold on a minute, Claude. Surely we can talk this out when you come back to New York."

"Is she a patient, Kurt? Is this some sort of new therapy—for you?" Seething with anger and humiliation, I threw the words at him like stones, not really caring if they made sense or not.

"Claudia, be reasonable. You were planning to be away for a *very* long time."

"No." A tremor filled my voice, and I closed my eyes, hating the weak sound of it. "I was planning to be *married* for a very long time. But if you can't be faithful for six weeks, I can't give you a lifetime."

"Aw, Claude—"

"Good-bye, Kurt." I slammed the phone down, then wrapped my arms around my knees and rested my head against them, realizing that for the first time in the length of our relationship, Kurt's blue eyes hadn't been able to dazzle me into overlooking his blunder.

Those eyes—would they ever look at me again?

"Buck up," I told myself. "This is a good thing. You learned the truth before it was too late."

Apparently, my charming Kurt was about as steadfast as a wall of mud—and I ought to be thanking my lucky stars. A man like that, Kirsten would say, wasn't worth the time and trouble it would take to train him as a husband. Good riddance to bad trouble. I would be better off without him.

I fell over onto the bed, burying my face in the feather pillow. With one phone call, my plans for the future had evaporated. I no longer had a fiancé in New York, a date for Lincoln Center, or someone to share Chinese with on long, leisurely weekends.

I rolled over and looked at the diamond winking on my left hand. With a shuddering sigh, I pulled it from my finger and dropped it on the nightstand by the bed.

Never had I felt so alone.

SEVENTEEN

MY LITTLE RESIDENZA SEEMED DARK AND GLOOMY WHEN I FINALLY dragged myself out of bed, and a quick glance out the window revealed a sun as weak as yesterday's dreams. I dressed in black slacks and a sweater (even on weekends and holidays, in Rome only teenagers seemed to wear jeans), then stepped out into the hallway. Mario and Marco sat at the end of the hall, the contents of their mother's mailbag spread all over the carpeted floor.

I slipped my hands into my pockets and morosely reflected that my love life was about as dependable as my landlady's mail route. Since my arrival at the residenza, I had learned that the twins' mother was a mail carrier for the city of Rome. Though the city promised two mail deliveries on weekdays and one on Sundays, Benedetta Donatelli's patrons were lucky if they got mail four times a week. They were luckier still if their cards, letters, and magazines survived the sticky hands of two inquisitive six-year-old boys.

I thought about asking the boys if they'd seen any mail for me, then thought the better of it. No telling what they'd hand me. After giving the twins a weakly tolerant smile, I stepped over the scattered mail, left the house, and walked down to my favorite espresso shop. After eating a tasteless croissant and downing a cup of the strongest concoction they offered, some of the feeling seemed to return to my body. Instead of returning to the scene of my humiliation, however, I turned and walked up the Via di Ripetta.

—

The prevailing sidewalk traffic seemed to be moving in the opposite direction, and I knew most people in this neighborhood would attend church, then spend their holiday in the Piazza del Popolo. The tourists would gawk at the three-thousand-year-old obelisk that Augustus had brought to Rome after the conquest of Egypt, while the locals gathered around the marble lions and fountains to exchange gossip with their neighbors.

Strange, that I now counted myself among the latter group. Immediately after arriving in Rome I'd spent my weekends visiting all the tourist sites, and I no longer wanted to fight crowds and look at ancient architecture. I wanted the comfort of the familiar—so maybe that's why I was walking toward Global Union headquarters, the red palace.

How pitiful! I stopped abruptly in the wide space of the Piazza della Rotonda, startling the man walking a scant two steps behind me. He muttered something about Americans as he changed his pace and passed on my right side, but I didn't care. I stood in the center of the sidewalk, floundering in an agonizing maelstrom of emotion, searching for something solid to cling to . . .

And then I saw Asher Genzano seated at a table outside the Café Giolitti with the morning newspaper in his hands. A cup of coffee sat on the table near his elbow, and a black-and-white tuxedo cat crouched at his feet, playfully swatting the laces of Genzano's shoes.

I may never understand why I sank into the empty chair facing him. I didn't particularly want to talk to him; perhaps the sight of a familiar face drew me to his table. Genzano looked up immediately, of course, and greeted me with a quiet, *"Buon giorno."* I answered him with the same phrase, then defensively crossed my arms and my legs and stared at the milling crowds in the piazza. I could feel the pressure of Genzano's eyes upon me, but after a moment he looked away and continued reading his paper. While I sat in lonely silence and mentally replayed my conversation with Kurt at least another dozen times, Genzano said nothing but flipped the pages of his paper until he reached the last page. When he had finished reading, he folded the paper, lowered it to the table, and picked up his coffee cup.

Watching from the corner of my eye, I felt a pain squeeze my heart as he leaned toward me. "Are you well, signorina?"

I wanted to lift my arms and scream no! at the top of my lungs— an action that probably wouldn't draw much attention in Manhattan *or* Rome. But an air of old-world gentility clung to Genzano, and I didn't think he'd want a bloodcurdling scream to shatter the serenity of his morning.

I swallowed the despair in my throat and tried to maintain an even, professional tone. "I'm fine—had a bit of bad news this morning, though."

"I'm sorry to hear that." Genzano spoke in a tone of surprised respect. "Family trouble?"

I nearly choked on the word. "Family? Not quite. My fiancé." I bent toward the ground and pretended to brush dirt from my shoe. "My engagement is off."

Genzano crossed his arms and pasted on a thoughtful expression. "I'm sorry to hear that. But I know you would not make a rash decision."

He was so calm, so matter-of-fact, that I wondered how many other women had wandered up to him and sat in pouting silence while he tried to enjoy his paper and espresso. His behavior was properly compassionate and supportive, but he was probably counting the minutes until I decided to leave . . .

He'd have to wait a few minutes more.

"Breaking up with Kurt was the rashest decision I've ever made,"

I told him, turning to look directly at him. "But I think it was also the rightest, if there is such a word. Trouble is, now I don't know what to do with myself. I had so many plans—things Kurt and I were going to do together. Now I feel a little lost."

His mouth quirked with wry humor. "Many are the plans in a man's heart, but it is the LORD's purpose that prevails."

I cut him a quick glance. "What's that supposed to mean?"

Genzano shrugged and shifted in the chair. "Only that we are often part of a bigger picture without knowing it."

I sighed, weary of Asher Genzano and his riddles. I hadn't seen much of him since he came to work at Global Union. Signora Casale had assigned him to work with the Publications Department on the fourth floor, so our paths rarely crossed during the day. I hadn't forgotten about him, though. Some back room of my brain not occupied with whatever task lay at hand speculated that perhaps I'd been right about Asher Genzano all along. Though everyone praised his work, his humble attitude, and his unflagging commitment to The Cause, I had a niggling feeling that some off-kilter aspect of his personality would pop that illusionary bubble one day . . .

Until then, I could do nothing but watch for signs of impending implosion.

I looked up at him, grateful that he provided a meaningful distraction from my pity party. During our interviews, Genzano had not displayed any signs of religious devotion—at least, no more than other Romans, most of whom merely paid lip service to the religious trappings surrounding them. This reference to "the Lord" offered a clue to a side of Genzano I hadn't seen.

I smiled. "Were you quoting the Bible?"

"It's a wonderful book. You ought to read it." He leaned forward and rested his elbows on his knees, his face dangerously close to

—

mine. "One of the men who penned the Bible wrote, 'My days have passed, my plans are shattered, and so are the desires of my heart.'" He hesitated a moment as if weighing my reaction. "Sound familiar?"

"I suppose that's how I feel." I scanned my memory, reluctantly trying to recall a Bible character with major problems in his love life, but my childhood Sunday school teacher must have skipped all the really juicy stories. "Who wrote that?"

"Job."

I nodded, not wanting to reveal my ignorance, then pulled back so a much more comfortable—and American—distance lay between us.

"What happened to Job?"

Genzano turned and propped his elbow on the back of the chair— a relaxed posture, so he obviously felt comfortable discussing religious figures. "Job was a righteous man who thought he had lived an honest and honorable life. God had blessed him and protected him. But Satan decided to test Job, and God permitted the testing, allowing Satan to take everything but Job's life."

I made a face. "Sounds like a pretty brutal test."

"It was. Satan left Job with only one thing, a nagging wife, while he took Job's children, his riches, and his health. Everyone in the city came around to commiserate with poor Job, but most of his friends spent more time criticizing than they did helping. They all figured Job must have committed the worst kind of sin to earn that kind of punishment."

"Did he?"

"Not outwardly; he had lived a blameless life before his fellow men. But Job battled the sin of pride, and it was only after he humbled himself before God that his health, wealth, and family were restored."

"Sounds like a tough way to learn a lesson."

—

"It is."

I found myself suddenly stunned by the weary, wounded look that appeared in his eyes. My disappointment and hurt faded to triviality in the light of that look. *What happened to this man?* The question snapped into my thoughts like a whip, making me flinch, but I had no time to consider it.

"Ask yourself," Genzano went on, looking away, "whether you are upset because you loved this man greatly or because he has wounded your pride. Are you hurt because you are angry or because he has broken your heart?"

I took a deep breath, feeling a dozen different emotions collide. I was angry and hurt and disappointed, and I had liked Kurt tremendously. We were great friends and perhaps, if I could work through my feelings, we could be friends again. But now I felt the sting of humiliation most. Was he taking this other woman to the diners and restaurants we had visited together? Were our friends whispering about me, even *pitying* me? If they knew about Kurt's lady friend, they probably thought me the worst kind of fool—

My mind came to an abrupt halt, like hitting a wall. "You're right. My heart isn't broken. I'm just . . . embarrassed. My pride is hurt more than anything, and I can fix that. I can call my secretary, and he'll be sure to spread the word around. I want everyone to know the engagement is off, and I'm the one who ended it."

Genzano gave me a look that said his brain was working hard at an entirely new set of problems. "That's your answer? If you save your pride, you'll feel better?"

To my annoyance, I felt a blush burn my cheeks. "Works for me."

He looked away and shook his head slightly. "I knew you did not love this man. So perhaps you are right, a little anger, a little pride, and you will feel better."

"You knew—" I closed my mouth, clamping off the words that threatened to rise from a geyser of indignation. I wanted to know why he thought I didn't love Kurt and by what right he had presumed to read *me*, when *I* was the professional people reader and jury consultant extraordinaire. But people read each other every day, reason assured me, and Asher Genzano seemed more observant and thoughtful than the average man . . .

He seemed to realize he had offended me, for he gave me an apologetic smile and gestured toward the piazza. "Would you like me to show you the city?" His smile crinkled the corners of his fascinating eyes. "I can guarantee no one will give you a better tour of Rome."

Suddenly uncomfortable, I slid toward the edge of my chair. "I've seen most of the sights."

"You've seen the tourist spots. Let me show you the real city."

I looked up. The morning sun had driven the clouds away and now bathed the piazza with dazzling light. "I don't want to spoil your holiday. You probably have other plans."

"Signorina Fischer," he said, examining my face with considerable absorption, "trust me. I have all the time in the world."

Before I could think of another excuse, Genzano had taken my hand and was leading me toward the Pantheon. His touch surprised me, though I should have expected that he would hold my hand; Italians held hands all the time. Yet there was something strangely intimate in the warm gesture that placed us palm to palm, and not even Kurt held my hand routinely. I was trying to remember the last time Kurt had impulsively caught my hand when Asher stopped abruptly and pointed toward the behemoth that, he assured me, had originally been built by Marcus Agrippa, the stuttering son-in-law of Caesar Augustus. Credit for the awe-inspiring dome belonged to the emperor Hadrian, but Agrippa got the project off the ground.

—

"How do they know Agrippa stuttered?" I asked, looking up at the immense portico, enclosed by stately granite columns. On the pediment overhead I could read the letters M A G R I P P A.

"*I* know he stuttered," Genzano answered, gently pulling me around a pastry vendor's cart. "He was an insecure fellow, even after he gained the throne. I think he believed history would be merciful to his memory if he created buildings like this. No one would care that he stuttered like a boy caught with his hand in the cookie jar."

"Signor Genzano—"

"Please. Call me Asher."

"All right. Asher." I glanced up at him, warmed by his effort to lighten my spirits and annoyed by his outright fibbing. "You don't have to embroider the history to make it interesting. The notion that Agrippa was a nervous kid is funny, but we probably shouldn't mock his memory."

His faint smile held a touch of sadness. "I'm not mocking anything. I knew the lad, and I heard him stutter myself." He lifted his free hand in the Italian gesture that seemed to mean, *I can't help it,* then gestured toward the steps of the Pantheon.

My mind whirled at his response, but perhaps I had misunderstood. Shaking my head, I sighed and followed him.

November 2, All Souls' Day, followed the feasting of All Saints' Day, but the latter day was not a holiday. On *Tutti i Santi,* people went to church and prayed to the saints with the government's blessing; on *Tutti i Morti,* they went to cemeteries and prayed for the dead on their own time. As I left my *residenza* for work, I saw that Benedetta had sacrificed her mail route for the sake of the dearly departed. Her boys wore matching dark suits and petulant expressions. Each carried a small bouquet of flowers destined, I knew, for the graves of ancestors.

Leaving the boys and their flowers, I went out the door in a flood of relief, grateful to go to work instead of the graveyard. I wore a black wool skirt, a gray sweater, and a black jacket—dull colors to fit into a soberly dressed European crowd. Today I was to fly to Brussels for the European Union conference.

My stomach did a little flip-flop when I saw Asher at the airport. With wit, charm, and an incomparable knowledge of Rome, yesterday he had succeeded in doing the impossible—he scattered my melancholy thoughts of Kurt to the four winds. And he was right—he did give me a better tour of the city than any of the regular tourist guides. He showed me the Ara Pacis, a detailed monument erected after Augustus Caesar secured peace in A.D. 13; he even pointed out the boundaries of Rome when the city burned during Nero's rule. We saw the Colosseum together; I touched the mosaics from the Baths of Caracalla; I marveled at a standing section of the Aurelian Wall. Asher opened my eyes to the Rome of the common people, and I inhaled its scents—of diesel fuel, cooking foods, ancient sewers, and ancient stones.

During my tour, Asher Genzano revealed himself as a man of culture. Without any help whatsoever he could detail the history of Rome, list the papal progression, and recite the epic poetry of Virgil. Yet this learned man of letters was sensitive enough to stand in wistful silence before Michelangelo's *Pietà*.

According to a brochure I picked up about St. Peter's, the sculptor finished the statue in 1499, when he was only twenty-five years old. "Hard to believe he was so young when he did this," I said as we stood before the *Pietà*.

"Yes," Asher answered, not taking his gaze from the statue of Mary with the body of Christ draped across her lap. I watched as water rose in his eyes, like a slow fountain filling up. "He was very young . . . to suffer so much. But God showed him mercy."

His comment made no sense, but I shrugged to hide my confusion and moved away. Asher Genzano was often mysterious. Out of gratitude for his time and concern, I had decided to leave it at that.

Now we sat aboard Justus's private jet with Reverend Synn. Asher sat in a seat by the far window, but Synn sat next to me, his elbow nudging my shoulder as he explained our assignment for the day. "The task is very simple," he said, his yeasty breath blowing over me as he leaned in my direction. "You will be home tonight with the job well done."

I leaned on the opposite armrest and tried to avoid crinkling my nose as he continued. Asher and I were to sit in the observer's gallery of the EU's Council of Ministers' building and make notes on the demeanor of three particular men: Vail Billaud, the ambassador from Luxembourg; Marlon Dutetre, the ambassador from Belgium; and Jan Dekker, the representative from the Netherlands. The EU provided an interpreter and headsets for those who needed them, but I was not to rely upon the official translators. Instead, I would have Asher Genzano seated next to me. He would speak into a tiny microphone fastened to his cuff, and the sound would instantly be transmitted to an earpiece in my ear.

Synn placed the dime-sized receiver in my palm. "It has been thoroughly tested," he said, transferring his gaze to Asher as he handed over the inch-long microphone. "You, Signor Genzano, will speak in a casual whisper. No one will suspect anything."

I shook my head. "Won't he attract attention if he's talking to himself?"

Synn laughed softly. "Not in the visitors' gallery, signorina. Trust me. Signor Genzano will be practically invisible."

—

166

After arriving at the airport, Synn left in a long, dark limo. Asher and I waited until a handful of officials and reporters wandered away, then we crept off the plane and walked into the airport terminal. With the ease of a veteran traveler, Asher hailed a cab and in fluent French gave directions to the EU Council of Ministers' building.

The European Union headquarters was located in an area of the city known as Euro-Brussels. We alighted from the cab in front of a gleaming building that rose from a colorful, cacophonous city like a modern-day Tower of Babel. People of every race and tongue milled in the crowds around us.

Asher paid the taxi driver as I drank in the scenery, then together we climbed the steps, entered the building, and crossed a polished foyer. I was about to ask a security guard for help when Asher gestured toward a sign that pointed the way to the visitors' gallery. He pulled two passes from his pocket, and I realized that while the gallery was open to anyone, seating was limited. Justus must have reserved these seats before he even approached me with the idea.

The upstairs visitors' area featured curving rows in a balcony overlooking the cavernous councilors' meeting room. Though the polished circular desk below was brilliantly lighted, with each seat well identified by a nameplate, there were no lights in the gallery, making us all but invisible to the council participants. For security reasons, a wall of glass panels, probably bulletproof, stood between us and the ambassadors. The sound poured in through a series of audio speakers, one mounted in each corner of the gallery.

I discovered the reason for Synn's confident assertion that no one would notice us soon after we had taken our seats. Without warning, the double doors blew open and a series of children—probably a class of ten-year-olds, judging by the giggly look of the boys and the superior look of the girls—pushed and shoved and stomped their way into the rows behind us. A trio of exhausted-looking adults filed in with them, then the chaperones split up—two kept an eye on the unruly young ones from opposite corners, while another stood guard at the door. There were about half a dozen other adults in the gallery—journalists, I supposed, because, like me, they carried steno pads and briefcases.

The subdued lighting in the gallery dimmed like the lights in a movie theater, and the children stilled. As the hush settled over the gathering, the councilors filed in and took their seats below us, then the president of the European Union stood before the lectern. He spoke in English, which made things easier for Asher and allowed me to direct my attention to the three men whose motives concerned Santos Justus. I knew these first few unguarded moments could tell me volumes.

Scanning the nameplates on each desk, I located the three men Justus had instructed me to watch. They sat just to the right of the lectern and next to each other—an interesting fact, considering that the names were not arranged in any sort of alphabetical order. Close seating therefore implied friendship, or at least cooperation.

While the president droned on in formal welcome, two of the men—Dutetre and Billaud—looked at each other and exchanged an eyebrow flash. Within sixty seconds, they each looked at the third man, Dekker, and received a brow flash and a simple smile in return.

I noted the fact in my notebook. An eyebrow flash, as any student of body language will tell you, is an international greeting, an action most people take completely for granted. If you are talking to a friend on the street and you see another friend pass by, even if you can't speak, you will certainly flash your brows at the approaching friend when your eyes meet. To refuse the flash is an outward sign of avoidance or hostility, often intended to provoke a response. The simple fact that these three had greeted each other with silent eyebrow flashes bore strong testimony to their acquaintance and implied a viable friendship.

As the president continued, I sketched a diagram of the furniture arrangement. The circular table featured a lectern at each end, and it was entirely possible the three men who sat practically in the first lectern's shadow were fairly concealed from the dozen or so ambassadors to the president's left. This concealment might lead to a sense of security, even persuade them that they could exchange comments without being spotted.

I leaned forward when the center man, Dutetre, leaned sideways to whisper something to Billaud. Billaud smiled and nodded slightly, then looked at the papers on the desk and shuffled a few pages without appearing to focus on them.

Distracted? I wrote.

The meeting went from boring to soporific, and before the president's speech ended I had to elbow Asher and wake him from a sound sleep. But by the time we left the building, I had gathered a host of impressions, all of which convinced me Justus was right. The three representatives in question were friendly, cooperative, and very likely in league with one another.

I presented my report to Reverend Synn on the jet. He listened to my observations, smiled at a couple of the finer points, then nodded in satisfaction. "We will proceed with our plans at once. You have done an excellent job, and I know you will be even more useful in the next phase."

"The next phase?" I stared at him in confusion. "Surely you won't need me—"

"We need you more than ever." Synn brought his hand down upon his knee, startling me with the sharp sound of the blow. "You said it yourself, signorina—these men would never completely reveal themselves in a public arena. Now that our fears have been confirmed, we must find out *exactly* what they are up to."

I glanced across the cabin at Asher. He had settled back in his seat and closed his eyes after boarding the plane, but he was wide awake now, his eyes wide and dark with alarm.

"You have nothing to fear." Synn took my hand and held it firmly. "Our men will set up a command post in another building; you will never even be near the targets. We will bring you in, you will watch and listen, Signor Genzano will interpret, and we will learn what we need to know. You will be out of the city within a few hours, and no one will ever know you were involved."

My adrenaline level had begun to rise when he used the word *target,* and the purposeful, intent look on his face did nothing to lower my blood pressure.

I looked away and blinked in stunned silence. Last week I had been a little thrilled by the thought of a mild cloak-and-dagger operation, but today's little day trip was nothing compared to what Synn was suggesting now. If he was telling the truth, we would probably be perfectly safe, but what he had described was nothing less than a covert operation. What was I thinking? I was a jury consultant, not an international spy! I didn't even like James Bond movies.

"Reverend Synn." With an effort, I pulled my hand from his grasp. "I'm not sure I'm entirely comfortable with this." I glanced up at Asher and saw that his pupils had dilated, his eyes filling with some stark, troubling emotion. What was it, fear? Uncertainty? Why had I never been able to read him?

"If you are uncomfortable, we will *make* you comfortable." The minister of whatever church claimed him leaned closer, vigorously invading my space and forcing me to tilt my head back at an awkward angle. "We will do everything in our power to be sure you are safe and content. You will be well rewarded."

"Money is not the issue."

His strong jaw wobbled, and I knew I had committed a faux pas. Italians did not like to bargain or talk about money in blunt terms. Negotiation was a dance, I'd learned, and I'd just stepped on his toes.

I drew a deep breath and tried to begin again. "Signor Synn, I'm not sure I can do what you are asking me to do. Observe people in another building? It would be difficult. Even with three or four cameras in the room I could not see everything—"

"We will make sure you have the best picture possible. You did so well today; we know you can do as well in this other situation."

"Well, I didn't want to mention this, but there is a personal matter I need to consider." I caught Asher's eye for a moment, smiled weakly, then turned my attention back to Il Direttore. "My fiancé and I are having problems. I must be getting back to New York to settle things between us. We have a wedding planned for May 13, and whether or not it goes off there are things I must attend to—"

"You cannot leave us." The soft note of entreaty had vanished from Synn's voice. "You signed an agreement to work with Unione Globale for six months. If you leave any sooner without our permission, you will be in breach of that contract."

I looked at him, surprised by the flat tone of his voice and the hostile gleam in his eye. In all my hours at Global Union headquarters I had never heard him utter a harsh word, not even when a nervous young Japanese student spilled espresso all over Synn's gray suit. But this—the narrow eyes, the furrowed brow, the flattened lips—these were unmistakable signs of anger. He would not let me go without a fight.

—

Too stunned to reply, I nodded slowly. Synn searched my face for a moment as if judging my sincerity, then smiled, his good humor restored. Wiping his hands on his trousers, he murmured something about being hungry, then made his way toward the galley at the back of the jet.

Totally bewildered, I looked across the aisle at Asher and read a new emotion in his face, as well—determination, marked by the strong stamp of fear.

Back in my two-room residenza, I sipped a lukewarm diet soda and paced before the brick fireplace in my sitting room, trying to think of some way I could walk away from Global Union. Reading people at the EU Council of Ministers' building had provided an interesting challenge, but reading people through an eavesdropping network would provide a challenge I didn't want. I knew the real world of espionage was nothing like a Hollywood movie—it was dangerous (no one ever thinks the movie star spy is *really* going to get hurt) and undoubtedly illegal. Furthermore, Fischer Consulting's lifeblood depended upon politicians and lawyers and judges in the States, so I couldn't afford to have my reputation smeared. Using hidden cameras and microphones to spy on three European ambassadors felt more than a little disreputable.

Tired of pacing, I sat on the edge of the small sofa and stared at the telephone. Every particle of my being wanted to call a friend. I could call Kirsten, but she wouldn't understand what I was feeling. Her world revolved around her family and life in the Hamptons, and I doubted if she knew what the WEU was or why it mattered. Political organizations didn't touch her world, and neither would my problems. She'd just tell me to pack my bags and come home.

I could call Rory . . . but long ago I'd decided it would be unprofessional to bring my personal problems into the office. Rory and I were great friends, and I ate dinner with him and his wife a couple of times a month, but I wouldn't let myself cry on his shoulder just because I'd run out of friends.

No, I couldn't call Rory . . . I wanted to call Kurt.

Maybe Asher was right and I never had really loved Kurt. But I had *liked* him tremendously, and I respected his opinion. Kurt had a marvelously clear way of looking through the emotions that clouded troublesome situations. But I couldn't call him, not after the scene I'd made the last time we spoke. If I called, I'd have to hear a list of excuses for his horrible behavior, and then I'd have to decide whether or not to forgive him when I really didn't care about the marriage anymore. Breaking off the engagement was the right thing to do. Breaking off our friendship would be foolish.

The thought of breaking away from Global Union appealed to me, though. Why couldn't I just pack my bags and take a cab to the airport? I could be back in New York by tomorrow morning, and Darien could sue me for breach of contract if he wanted to. The case would probably be thrown out of court.

I stood, about to bolt for the bedroom, then cold, clear reality swept over me in a terrible wave. I couldn't pack my bags if I wanted to. My passport was locked in a safe at Global Union headquarters and had been since my arrival in Rome. Because hoteliers were legally required to register all foreigners with the police, all guests of Global Union surrendered their passports upon arrival and received a Global Union identity card in exchange. "It is the best thing, especially with the purse snatchers and pickpockets," Maura Casale had explained as she took my passport. "Do not worry. We will keep it safe for you." Given Synn's mood the last time we talked, I didn't think he'd allow security to hand my passport over without comment.

—

Frustrated by my lack of options, I slammed the nearly empty soda can down on the little table that stood in my kitchenette, then slipped on my jacket. Maybe a walk would help clear my brain.

Darkness already shadowed the eastern sky, while deep orange and purple light streaked the western horizon. Shadows pooled and thickened around the bases of the monuments I passed, and the crisp wind bit at the exposed areas of my skin. Somewhere in the distance an ambulance wailed in the eerie *weee-oh, weee-oh* cadence of European emergency vehicles, while from a balcony overlooking the street a group of men engaged in catcalls as I passed beneath them.

Hunched into my heavy jacket, I thrust my hands deep into my pockets, ignoring the calls and barely acknowledging the friendly smiles of people I'd come to think of as my neighbors. I lengthened my stride, marching past the tiny shops on the Via Ara Pacis, then stopped at the end of the street and stared at the silver-spangled river.

I had only one friend in Rome—only one person knew what I had been asked to do. He knew because he had been asked to do the same thing.

The sluggish river slapped rhythmically against the concrete walls that restrained it. Could I go to Asher and vent my feelings? Would he even understand my reservations?

As I turned, my eyes fell upon the Ara Pacis, the "Altar of Peace" that had been erected by the Roman Senate in A.D. 13. The monument now stood beneath a large glass hangar, shining like a jewel in a pool of electric light. As tears of frustration filled my eyes, the highly detailed faces sculpted into the marble frieze seemed to shimmer with life.

Curling my frozen fingers into fists, I crossed my arms and moved toward the monument, studying the faces as I walked. I had visited the Ara Pacis in daylight, marveling over the incredible craftsmanship, but the figures had not seemed as animated as they did now. The brass plaque outside the entrance told me that the people depicted in the procession were the Roman royal family, ranked by position in the succession. In the royal lineup, Marcus Agrippa, builder of the Pantheon, stood next to the emperor Augustus, and Augustus's toddling grandson, Lucius, clung to the folds of his mother's gown.

The thought of Marcus Agrippa as a stuttering youth brought a twisted smile to my face. Asher's insane assertion must have been some kind of joke, but apparently I hadn't picked up all the nuances of Italian humor.

Leaving the monument, I turned onto the Via di Ripetta, accidentally stepping into the path of a moped on the sidewalk. As the rider swerved and filled the air with a stream of enthusiastic curses, I ignored him and hurried southward toward the Pantheon. I didn't know that Asher would even be home, but perhaps someone at the hotel might know where I could find him.

Half an hour later, the brisk walk had warmed me considerably. I cautiously crossed the large Piazza della Rotonda, then stood outside the Sole al Pantheon, not certain how to ask for Asher Genzano. Would the owner live in a detached building? In a penthouse?

The stately four-story building looked as though it had been painted with a thin wash of moonlight. Three rows of arched windows looked down upon the street, parallel slits of light marking their closed shutters. No sidewalk separated the building and the piazza, but a maroon awning jutted out protectively to shelter those who would find rest within the dignified walls. As I passed beneath its shadow, I noticed a brass plaque near the well-lit entrance. Though my Italian was still not all it should have been, I recognized the names of writers Jean-Paul Sartre and Simone de Beauvoir. Rome, too, offered versions of "George Washington slept here."

I walked through the long, narrow lobby and drank in the scents of live flowers, then approached the marble desk. I stood silently for a moment until the female clerk looked up and gave me a bland smile.

"*Vorrei vedere,*" I began, mentally searching for the correct Italian phrases, "Signor Genzano."

The woman lifted a brow. "Signor *Asher* Genzano?"

"Si." Was there more than one Genzano in the house?

The woman leaned forward and pointed toward the end of the desk, then began to rattle off directions so fluently I didn't stand a chance.

"In English, per favore?" I asked, hoping for the best. "I am a friend of Signor Genzano's."

I saw the tightening cheek muscles that turned her upper smile from a mechanical civility to a rictus of necessity. "To the end of the desk," she said, "into the hall. Walk until you cannot walk further. There is a door. That is the entrance to Signor Genzano's apartment."

"Grazie." Feeling suddenly chilly again, I put my hands back into my pockets and walked in the direction she had pointed.

A hallway opened up at the end of the desk, and I followed it, grateful for the dim glow of the brass wall sconces that provided narrow cones of light about every ten yards. Several doors opened off this hallway, but I passed them, recognizing from their nameplates that they led to offices of the hotel staff. The hallway was papered in russet and gold—a gaudy design from an earlier age, but I doubted that hotel patrons often walked through this corridor.

Finally the passageway ended at a single door, unmarked and unadorned. I stood in the silent hallway for a moment, wondering if Asher would think I had completely lost my mind, then I tapped on the door.

I locked my hands behind my back, glancing around as I waited for a response. Had I misunderstood the receptionist's directions? A patch of peeling plaster loomed above my head; the carpet beneath my feet was faded and worn. The elegant lobby had sparkled with grandeur, but I couldn't imagine a hotel owner choosing to live in this obscure corner . . .

I straightened at the sound of approaching footsteps, then tried on a smile as the door swung open. Asher's eyes widened when he saw me standing there.

"Per favore"—I tilted my head in the universal body language of winsome pleading—"may I speak with you, Signor Genzano?"

He gaped at me like a man faced with a hard sum in arithmetic, then he swung the door wider and gestured toward the tiny foyer beyond. "Come in, signorina."

I don't know what I expected of Asher Genzano's apartment, but I had never imagined the man might live in a library. For that was what I found in his foyer and sitting room—a veritable fortress of books. Heavily laden bookshelves lined every wall. Leather volumes filled the window sill and stood at attention upon the counters of his small kitchen. The scents of dust and age and paper permeated the room, underlined by the faint odor of dried leather.

I turned in speechless silence.

"I know." Asher lifted both shoulders in a shrug. "I have too many books in too small a space. The—what would you call him?—the *fire marshal* would not approve."

I smiled in bewilderment. "Have you read all these?"

"Once." He looked at me, his eyes shimmering in the light from a small lamp on a writing desk. "But you did not come here to talk about books."

"No. I came to talk about Global Union." I looked for a place to sit, and Asher hurried to remove a stack of newspapers from a velvet-covered settee with ornate carved feet.

"Excuse the mess; I do not often entertain visitors. Please, sit down."

"Thanks." I sat, smoothing the velvet fabric as I did so. I don't know much about antiques, but this piece looked positively priceless.

I waited until Asher seated himself in a chair next to the desk. "I am concerned about this latest job Justus has asked us to do. I don't feel comfortable with spying. When I took this job, I never intended to break *any* laws—international or moral. I'm worried about what might happen if we are caught."

Asher smiled, but with a distracted, inward look, as though he were thinking about something else altogether. After a moment, he crossed his arms and met my gaze. "I am afraid we cannot escape the nature of evil. It slowly creeps upon us until we are stained with sin. And then, when we are tainted, we can do nothing but try to scrub the stain out. That effort can take a lifetime, or even longer." The timbre of his voice changed, and I heard bitterness spill into his words. "Sometimes I think it is impossible to escape the consequences of sin."

"Asher." My tone was sharper than I had intended it to be. "I didn't come here for philosophical arguments. I came because I need to know if you are as worried as I am. Is there some way we can get out of this?"

Lines of concentration deepened along his brows and under his eyes as he looked at me. "It all depends."

"On what?"

He turned, resting one arm on the back of the chair and propping his head against his hand. "What is your ultimate purpose, Claudia Fischer? If doing what Justus demands will help you reach your goal, go ahead and be done with it. But if it is contrary to your purpose, walk away."

—

Annoyed, I glared at him. "I can't walk away! And I don't see what purposes and goals have to do with anything. Furthermore, I can't understand why *you* haven't objected. Don't you think what Synn's asking us to do is wrong?"

Asher studied me for a moment, then looked at the ceiling as if appealing to a higher authority. "I will do what Justus asks," he said finally, closing his eyes, "because it is what I must do. I must fulfill my purpose, and he must fulfill his."

I swallowed the scream of frustration that rose at the back of my throat. What was it with Italian men? Why couldn't any of them give me a straight answer?

"Would you please explain yourself?" I couldn't disguise the air of irritation in my voice. "I don't have the patience for riddles or religious dogma right now. I'm very serious about finding a way out of Global Union—"

"There is no way out of God's will." His face suddenly rippled with anguish. "Through all the years of my life I have sought a way of escape, and I can assure you there is none. We must follow our destiny, just as Santos Justus follows his. We have only one hope, and that is the blessed blood of Jesus Christ. If Santos accepts the Savior, then and only then can he be turned from the road laid out before him."

"Stop!" I put my hands over my ears, not willing to hear any more. Fear and anger knotted inside me as I looked up and saw the ferocity of passion glittering in Asher's dark eyes.

What had happened to the calm, reliable, good-natured man I hired? I would never have guessed that a religious zealot lived inside Asher Genzano; there had been nothing in his demeanor to suggest this streak of fanaticism.

He said nothing but leaned back in his chair, his gaze moving

—

toward the floor. Reassured by his demeanor, I lowered my hands and leaned forward. "Asher," I said, trying to reason with the gentle man I knew, "I respect religious conviction, really I do. But there is no place for it in the office or in Global Union. Even Reverend Synn makes a point of leaving his religious beliefs outside the organization."

Asher kept his gaze on the floor, but his mouth twisted in bitter amusement. "You really believe that?"

"I've seen no reason to think otherwise."

He looked at me then, his eyes damp with pain. "Claudia," he said, his voice calm and soothing, "do you believe in God?"

I nodded, grateful that I could at least placate him with a partially affirmative answer. "I went to Sunday school as a kid and got a pretty thorough indoctrination."

"Do you believe the Bible is the inspired Word of God?"

I bit my lip, realizing that I couldn't even hedge my way out of this one. "I believe the Bible is a great book." I glanced down at my hands. "It contains some of the world's finest literature. But I can't say I believe it is literally *inspired.*"

"Do you believe it is prophetic?"

"I'm not sure what that means."

His voice, so calm an instant before, filled with sudden vibrancy. "Do you believe it contains the future as well as the past? That events described in the books of Daniel and Ezekiel and Matthew and Revelation will come to pass in the near future?"

The thread of fervor in his voice was enough to make me shake my head. "No, I don't."

"Suppose I toldl you"—Asher leaned forward to pull a leather volume from a desk drawer—"that Santos D. Justus is described, in detail, in Holy Scripture."

As he flipped the thin pages of the book—a Bible—I pressed my lips together, not certain whether to laugh or cry. Had I allowed a lunatic into Global Union? Apparently something had triggered this change in Asher; some recent situation or someone's remark had caused a repressed religious fanaticism to surface. But, thank God, at least I had discovered his derangement away from Global Union headquarters. Tomorrow I could quietly tell Reverend Synn that Asher Genzano would no longer be available to serve as interpreter. I'd ask Signora Casale to find us another interpreter/translator—

"Here." Asher tapped a passage in the open Bible. "Revelation 13:1—John says, 'And now in my vision I saw a beast rising up out of the sea. It had seven heads and ten horns, with ten crowns on its horns. And written on each head were names that blasphemed God.'"

I hesitated, blinking with bafflement. Much of the Bible had never made sense to me, and this reading made even less sense than the *verilys* and *withersoevers* that confused me as a child.

"I don't understand," I finally said, giving Asher a small smile. "And I don't think most people do. I've heard that Revelation is allegorical; it was never meant to be understood."

"Why would God give it to us if he did not want us to understand it?" Something that looked like righteous indignation flared in Asher's eyes, then cooled. "It's very simple, Claudia, but it *is* symbolic. In prophetic symbolism, the sea always represents the Gentile world. The beast therefore comes from a Gentile nation, from a country or confederation that was once part of the ancient Roman Empire." He flipped the pages of the Bible. "Daniel 8:25 tells us that the beast will destroy many through peace—and Santos Justus has just organized an international peace organization headquartered in Rome."

"I'm sorry, but that's completely illogical. Peace can't destroy anything. Peace is the opposite of war."

—

181

"Peace made through concession can destroy a great deal." Asher flipped another page. "Daniel 11:16 tells us that his federation will be ruled by absolute authority. The Antichrist will do as he pleases, and no one will stop him. Haven't you noticed that no one within Unione Globale dares to question Justus?"

I gaped at him. My stomach had dropped at the word *Antichrist,* and now my mind reeled with confusion. Asher's paranoia was worse than I feared. In the space of five minutes, he'd gone from being a religious zealot to a conspiracy nut. What would Synn say if he learned that Asher Genzano, who moved through Global Union headquarters with a top-level security pass, believed our international peacemaker to be the Antichrist?

I closed my eyes, envisioning Justus asleep on the jet while Asher tiptoed up behind him with a wooden stake in his hand—but no, a wooden stake was the remedy for vampires, and a silver bullet dispatched werewolves. How, exactly, did one deal with an antichrist?

I had to stay calm. I would make a graceful exit, then go back to my residenza and call Kurt. He'd know what to do.

I propped my elbow on my crossed knee, then rested my chin in my hand, trying to assume a thoughtful, yet relaxed posture. "If Justus is the Antichrist," I said, choosing my words carefully, "what should we do about it?"

I felt his eyes grazing my face, reading me as thoroughly as I've ever read anybody. "You don't believe me," he finally said, his voice flat. "You don't believe any of this."

"My mind is open." I lifted my chin. "You just haven't convinced me. And I'll have to be convinced before I'd—well, before I could act on this supposition."

Before I could even allow you through the door of Global Union headquarters again.

—

A tide of hurt washed through his eyes, and I felt a sharp stab of guilt. I didn't want to injure our friendship. I had come to respect Asher, and I still did, for many reasons . . . but I couldn't allow him to jeopardize my client with this kind of religious insanity.

He closed the Bible. After a long, exhausted sigh, he began to recite what I assumed was another verse: "'Dear children, the last hour is here. You have heard that the Antichrist is coming, and already many such antichrists have appeared. From this we know that the end of the world has come.'" Asher's eyes sparkled with weariness when he looked at me again. "First John 2:18."

The wings of shadowy foreboding brushed my spirit. This was not good. The *something* that had bothered me about Asher Genzano had just revealed itself, and this character flaw could spell disaster for me if he spread these tales throughout Global Union . . .

"I need to go now," I said, trying to keep my voice nonchalant. "But before I go, I wanted to let you know that Il Direttore wants you to take tomorrow off. We both get the day off—a reward, I guess, for a job well done in Brussels."

Asher shook his head, causing me to wonder if he knew I was lying, then he gave me a strained smile and walked me to the door.

Eighteen

A THOUSAND REGRETS ROSE IN ASHER'S THOUGHTS AS HE WATCHED Claudia walk away. He shouldn't have told her so much—but she had been trying to draw him away from the coming confrontation, and he could not allow anyone to weaken his resolve. And he had not lied to her, not once. He certainly wasn't about to lie about something as important as the world's destiny. He would not have lied about his own destiny, either . . . had she asked.

He moved into his sitting room, walking on legs that felt as heavy as stone. He thought of opening a window to let some fresh air into the dusty space, but a trace of Claudia's perfume lingered in the atmosphere and the night breeze might have driven it away.

He breathed deeply of the floral scent and sat down at his desk, lost for a moment in memories. She had looked at him with fear in her eyes, and she had lied to him just before leaving. He hadn't earned a day off—but he might have lost his job. He would have to report to work in the morning as usual and carry on as if nothing was amiss. Claudia would be embarrassed to be caught in a lie, but he couldn't risk losing his position now.

Sighing, he pulled his journal to him and began to write:

Today I spoke with Claudia Fischer about the Antichrist. Her unbelief is as deeply rooted as that of the ancient Greeks, and, like them, she finds the concept laughable. But she did not laugh in my

face like the others. Our friendship—as tenuous and new as it is—
would not allow her to do so.

Despite her unbelief, I am even more convinced that Santos D.
Justus is the one spoken of by the prophets. Today we learned that
we are to spy upon three heads of government who might be resisting him. Is this not a clear reference to the three heads the
Antichrist will overcome in his rise to power? It is yet early and not
all the prophecies have been fulfilled, but I must confront him
before his heart is so hardened he cannot change.

There are so many signs that point to Justus and the end. The
Scriptures foretell that the evil one will worship the god of forces,
of military might, and Justus heads a military organization even
while he speaks of peace. Nations are listening to him; men are
coming to heap praises upon his head.

I waited too long with the others, but God has been merciful. In
this age of international communication and information, I have
been able to see the signs as they unfolded, before the root of corruption could flower into fullness.

May God give me the strength to do what I must. And may he
help me to know if and when I should be more honest with Claudia
Fischer.

Nineteen

In light of the very real possibility that I had installed a loose cannon near the top level of Global Union administration, all my qualms about calling Kurt vanished. It was twenty-two o'clock when I returned to my room, four in the afternoon New York time, but I dialed his office number without hesitation. I didn't care if I interrupted him, and if I caused him to miss a date . . . well, he deserved it.

His receptionist put me straight through when I told her the call was urgent. "Kurt, I need your help," I said, spacing my words evenly. "I know we're sort of not speaking, but this is really important."

"Claudia? Good grief, what's happened?"

"Nothing, I'm fine. But I need an expert psychological opinion, and I need it now. I think I have to fire an employee in the morning."

"So you've forgiven me?" he asked, his voice slow with contentment.

"Not really. But I think we can still be friends. I think that's all we were all along."

"You may be right." He spoke in an odd, yet gentle tone, and I knew he would give me the help I needed. We might not have made a great husband-and-wife team, but we had shared too much to abandon each other.

I sat on the edge of the bed and raked my hand through my hair. "I think I made a huge mistake. There was a man—Asher Genzano—and when I interviewed him, I sensed there was something . . . not quite right. I called him back for another interview and still couldn't put my finger on it, but his test scores were great, his talent remarkable, and he happens to be rich and some kind of local bigwig. Anyway, he won over the personnel director, so I approved him. I chalked up my uneasiness to my unfamiliarity with the Italian male."

Kurt chuckled easily. "And now?"

"Now I think he's a raving lunatic."

I heard shifting sounds and could almost see Kurt sitting up in his chair, pulling out a notebook for this unofficial therapy session. "*Lunatic* is a strong word, Claude. Maybe he's just neurotic. If you fire him without just cause, you'll be opening yourself up for trouble. Why do you think he's unbalanced?"

I lifted my hand and began counting on my fingers. "First, he seems to be overly religious. I've only seen one other sign of it, but that was away from the office. He doesn't pray in public, he doesn't wear a cross or a crucifix or anything like that, but tonight he started rambling about his destiny and God's will. Then he pulled out a Bible and started quoting verses about beasts and Gentile nations."

"Lots of people are religious, Claude, but that doesn't mean they need psychiatric help. If every street-corner preacher in Manhattan needed a shrink, I'd be working twenty-four hours a day." Kurt hesitated, and when he spoke again his voice was more intense. "You said you saw him tonight? Did you meet him away from the office?"

The question caught me off guard. "I, uh, needed to talk to him about this job we were asked to do together. Justus has asked me to read some people without their knowledge, and I'm a little nervous about it. Asher is the interpreter, so he's involved too." Though Kurt couldn't see me, I shrugged. "It's just professional. But this guy has a top security clearance and access to Justus, so I can't have him go loopy on me at the office."

—

"Do you think he might?"

I considered the question, remembering the passionate look in Asher's eyes. "I don't know. He looked pretty intense tonight, but at the office he keeps to himself and seems very laid back. Plus, he doesn't really have access to the executives unless we're traveling, and then there are always other people around."

"OK, Claude." I smiled at the degree of concern I heard in his voice. "I think I can assure you this guy is fine. He probably brought up his religion because you were away from the office; therefore he felt safe. As long as he keeps quiet in the workplace, write it off as harmless eccentricity."

"Kurt, it didn't feel harmless. He called Santos Justus the *Antichrist*."

He chuckled with a dry and cynical sound. "Some of my patients call their employers much worse. Don't sweat it, Claude, unless he brings his delusions into the office. That's when you really ought to worry."

"So—I shouldn't have him dismissed?"

"The guy was probably trying to impress you. Let it go, and you probably won't hear another peep out of him."

"OK." I wrapped the telephone cord around my wrist. "Thanks, Kurt. I appreciate it. Sorry for bothering you at the office."

"Forget it. I owe you one."

We said good-bye, and I disconnected the call, then sat with the heavy telephone in my lap. Kurt was probably right. I had spent enough time with Asher to trust him, and didn't everyone have at least one quirk? Besides, the idea of Asher threatening Justus seemed illogical. He was a wealthy man, despite his rather odd living conditions, which meant he had to be working at Global Union because he *believed* in Justus and world peace. Maybe he had mentioned the Bible

—

to me because he was troubled by the apparent contradiction between his beliefs and the good he saw Global Union accomplishing . . .

And what had he said to me? *If doing what Justus demands will help you reach your goal, go ahead and be done with it. But if it is contrary to your purpose, walk away.*

Asher clearly wanted to stay with Justus, so he must believe in the cause, but he didn't seem to care if I wanted to walk away.

Could I? I had taken this job because I thought it might boost my reputation to an international level. But if I was arrested for spying on political officials, the international stink might bury my career forever. Even the *hint* of a scandal would sink Fischer Consulting beyond any salvageable depth, and if I participated in what Justus suggested, quite a few people in powerful positions would know what I had done.

I would walk away. Let Synn accuse me of breaking my contract. I would ask Rory to find a new client—it wouldn't have to be anyone powerful or famous, just someone in legitimate need—and I'd tell Synn and Justus that I had to go home. Fischer Consulting needed me. And, after all, I had fulfilled the basic terms of my contract with Global Union. Though I hadn't served the full six months, I had remained long enough to completely staff their Rome headquarters.

I had left my laptop at the office, so I picked up the telephone and dialed the number for my Manhattan office. After three rings the answering machine clicked on: *Hello, you've reached Fischer Consulting. We apologize for being unable to take your call, but if you'll leave your name and number . . ."*

As I feared, Rory had already gone for the day. I waited for the beep, then launched into my spiel. "Rory, I hate to bother you with a message, but I didn't want to wait until our daylight hours converge again. Listen, I know we're in a holding pattern until I return from

Rome, but if you have any interesting cases in your pending file, check them out, will you? I'd settle for defending a New York City councilman. I think I might need an excuse to exit Rome, and a trial might be my ticket out. Let me know what you come up with, OK? Thanks."

I hung up the phone, feeling strangely comforted. My ex-fiancé was still speaking to me, my secretary would find me a new job, and it didn't matter that my closest Roman friend had just developed a case of bats in the belfry.

I was going home.

You could have knocked me over with a raw linguine noodle the next morning when I stepped into the crowded elevator at Global Union headquarters and saw Asher standing against the back wall. I flushed miserably, almost certain he knew I had lied about his day off, but if he did see through me, he gave no sign of it. "I was in the middle of a big translation project," he said, lifting a manila folder. "I decided to come in today and finish it up."

I nodded in numb silence, then turned and stared at the polished doors until we reached the fourth floor.

"Permesso." Asher shouldered his way through the crowd, tossed a pleasant smile over his shoulder, and walked calmly toward the Publications Department.

I sighed in relief as the elevator doors closed. For a couple of hours last night I had planned to go straight to Signora Casale and explain that we had to fire her favorite translator, but Kurt had put my fears to rest. Now I wanted to go, but getting myself dismissed would not be so simple. Rory would have to come up with a case so convincing that Synn and Justus would understand that my presence was absolutely required in New York. Even if they complained and threatened, which they might, as long as I had a compelling case waiting in Manhattan, they would surely sympathize with my situation and allow me to escape with my reputation untarnished.

I went to my office and followed up my telephone message with an e-mail, reminding Rory to check on the flurry of inquiries that had arrived right after the Mitchell verdict. Less than two months had passed, so it was entirely possible that some of those lawyers were still looking for a jury consultant. And there was always the Boston mayor and his indictment for racketeering . . .

I sighed as I clicked the send button. I had dreamed of international prospects when I first came to Rome, but right now the Manhattan Courthouse seemed imposing enough for me. Kirsten would say I had bitten off more than I could chew, and, for once, I was willing to admit she'd be right.

Rory responded to my e-mail midafternoon, assuring me he'd received my telephone message and had begun to make calls. He was planning to work over the weekend and hoped to have a couple of good leads by Monday morning. The mayor of Boston had already hired Elaine Dawson.

I drew a long, quivering breath, mastering the shock that shook me. Why was Elaine working the East Coast? Had she warned me away from Global Union in hopes that I'd take the job out of sheer stubbornness? It'd be just like her to do something so underhanded and conniving . . .

But it didn't matter. Racketeering meant extortion, loansharking, bribery, and obstruction of justice, and I knew the mayor of Boston wouldn't have been indicted unless the prosecution had piled up a mountain of evidence against him. I didn't have to read the mayor to be 98 percent sure he was guilty. When I got home, I'd find a *noble* cause to champion—maybe I could find a group of orphans fighting eviction or a breast cancer patient suing her tight-fisted HMO. With the sweet scent of world peace about me, I'd turn my case into a cause célèbre. Elaine could have the dirt bags; from this day forward I was only going to work for noble causes and innocent parties.

I typed Rory a quick thank-you note, then turned and began to rummage through my desk drawers, searching for personal items I didn't want to leave behind. If all went well, by this time next week I'd be sitting at my desk in Manhattan, maybe planning a trip to Kirsten's for the weekend. My sister was entering her eighth month now and was bound to be grumpy . . .

I smiled, relishing the thought.

I spent the weekend in a kind of contented fog. I sent my clothes out to be laundered, polished my leather shoes, and spent all Sunday afternoon trying to determine the best way to arrange things in my suitcases. I used my laptop to check for e-mail every hour, hoping Rory would send a message. Being a devoted churchgoer, he didn't. By Sunday midnight, six in the evening in Manhattan, I felt like a volcano on the verge of erupting.

On Monday morning, I caught a cab to work and greeted the receptionist as I always did, hoping she wouldn't notice the frayed edges of my smile. I slipped into my office without exchanging the usual morning pleasantries with the fifth-floor staff hovering around the coffee maker, then pressed the power button on my computer monitor. These computers remained connected to the Internet at all times, so if Rory had sent a message, it should be in my mailbox . . .

Bingo, I had mail. I clicked on the mailbox icon and saw three interdepartmental memos from Global Union, a note from Kirsten, and two pieces of spam, each offering me the chance to become a millionaire through Internet stocks. These I deleted without a second glance, then I took a moment to read Kirsten's note. She and family were fine, and the babe-to-be was giving her fits at night.

"But I can't help being in love with the little guy," she wrote. "I could sit for hours and play the pushing game. When I know he's awake, I'll push on my belly and he'll kick back. I can almost see him swimming in his little sac, pumping those little legs to let me know he's doing well."

While I was reading Kirsten's note, another letter appeared in my mailbox. I smiled with relief when I recognized Rory's address, but I wondered at the timing. Either the message had been hung up for a while in cyberspace, or Rory was awake and on the computer at four in the morning.

Typing a quick reply to Kirsten, I wished her well and promised to write more later. Then, hoping for good news, I clicked on Rory's note:

Claudia—
   Rory was murdered last night.

The computer screen wavered before my eyes. A tide of goose flesh rippled up each arm and raced across my shoulders. I closed my eyes and took a deep breath, then slowly exhaled it.

Somehow I'd misunderstood, misread the message. It couldn't say what I thought it said.

As fear blew down the back of my neck, I opened my eyes and continued reading:

Rory went to the office Saturday afternoon to go through some
   files—he said something about drumming up some work for you.

—
194

I've always told him to take a cab if he's coming home after midnight, but he took the subway . . . and someone stabbed him near the Hoyt Street station. That's where they found him and where he died.

I know you will want to come home, but don't make the journey just for me. I'm going to have him cremated after the autopsy, and we're going to have a small memorial service at the church. I don't want the kids to remember the violence of his death—I want them to celebrate his life and his journey to heaven. Thankfully, he spent a wonderful morning with us that day, and the kids and I will always have those memories. No one—not even the monster who took his life—can rob us of those.

Rory always said you weren't a religious person, so I don't know if you can understand how we feel, but I mean it when I say you don't have to rush back on our account. We are grieving our loss, but we believe Rory is waiting for us in heaven. His hope was secure in Christ, and to die, for him, was to gain far more than this world could offer. Jesus will be our comfort until we see Rory again.

Rory thought a great deal of you. I know he would tell you not to mourn, but to rejoice at his promotion.

Alice Metcalf

I stared at the computer terminal for a moment woven of eternity, then began to tremble as fearful images materialized in my mind: Rory with his family on Saturday morning, taking out the trash for Alice, playing with his two sons, maybe taking the family to the zoo . . . and then, once Jared and Jason were busy with the Nintendo, he had gone to the office. For me. To search the files for some quick job I could use as an excuse to come home. And though every New Yorker knew the subways weren't safe after midnight, he had decided to save the cab

—

fare and spring for the buck-fifty subway ride to Brooklyn . . . and that bargain had cost him his life.

I gripped the edge of the desk as ice began to spread through my stomach. Now I needed to go home more than ever. Despite Alice's reassurances, I wanted to see her, to throw my arms around her neck and apologize for sending Rory to the office on a Saturday. Though she would say it wasn't my fault, I knew it was. Rory was ultra-responsible; he always went the extra mile. So when I called and asked him to find a compelling reason for me to come home, he had done just that.

I shuddered at the irony.

When I had managed to rein in my emotions so that I could talk without my chin wobbling, I took the elevator to the executive offices on the sixth floor. I knocked on Reverend Synn's door, and his secretary ushered me in to see him at once. I was glad to find Il Direttore at his desk.

Without taking a chair, I came directly to the point. "Signor, I must go home. My business associate has been murdered."

"*E orribile!*" The thin line of Synn's mouth clamped tight for a moment, and his thick throat bobbed once as he swallowed. "When did this happen?"

"Yesterday—that is, early Sunday morning in New York. He was attacked on a subway. Robbed, I suppose." My voice quavered, so I looked down and clenched my fists in an effort to get a grip on my emotions. I did not want to cry before any of these people.

Synn made quiet clucking sounds of sympathy. "We will send a tribute to his family, of course. Would they appreciate a spray of flowers?"

"You don't have to do that." I lifted my gaze and saw him staring at me with a curious expression on his face. "I'll take care of all those details when I arrive in New York."

—

Slowly, Synn shook his head. "I am sorry, signorina, but you cannot leave. The arrangements have all been made—you are to depart for Brussels tomorrow morning."

I stared at him across a sudden ringing silence. "But—I can't. The family will expect me to come."

"We will take care of everything. I'll personally call the New York office of Unione Globale and see that a representative attends the memorial service."

His hand fell upon the telephone, and as I stared at it something clicked in my brain. Memorial service? How did he know there would be a memorial service instead of a funeral? I certainly hadn't mentioned it, and there'd been no word from New York except the message from Alice this morning.

Rory's voice rose from the fog of memory: *Whatever you do, don't send personal information through an intranet. Anyone with a master password to the server will be able to read your mail.*

With pulse-pounding certainty I knew Synn had read my e-mail. Why? Did he routinely read my correspondence? I grasped the back of his guest chair and held it tightly. I'd never worried about anyone reading my mail because I had no secrets worth hiding from do-gooders concerned about nothing but global peace . . .

I shook my head and forced a smile. Asher Genzano's paranoia was rubbing off on me. I was probably imagining everything. Maybe Synn mentioned a memorial service because that's what Italians called such things. I didn't know enough to feel sure of anything, but I knew I didn't like feeling ignorant and insecure and paranoid.

"I'm sorry, but the trip to Brussels cannot be postponed or rearranged," Synn was saying, his eyes narrowing as he stared at me. "You and Signor Genzano will leave tomorrow morning. You should carry a small suitcase, just for appearances. Our representatives will

—

meet you at the train station and walk you through the entire opera-tion." One corner of his mouth pulled into a slight smile. "I am sorry about your associate, signorina. But you should take comfort in knowing what you will do tomorrow will help the entire world. Surely your friend would have approved."

"When I come back from this trip"—my voice sounded flat in my own ears—"will we be able to negotiate an end to my contract? I would like to return to New York as soon as possible. There are things I must handle personally."

His brows shot up. "But of course, signorina! As long as Il Presidente agrees. I can do nothing, however, without his approval."

Keenly aware of his scrutiny, I took a step toward the door. "I don't suppose," I said, glancing at him over my shoulder, "that you could return my passport . . . just in case an emergency arises."

His face twisted in a phony wince of remorse. "I am sorry, signo-rina, but I cannot release your travel documents until you are cleared for departure."

I stared at him, stung by the undeniable and dreadful fact. I was a prisoner until Santos Justus decided to release me.

"For global peace, then." I pressed my lips together, then nodded farewell and turned on my heel, leaving him alone.

I spent the day reviewing a stack of personnel files Maura Casale had brought up to my office. She said it was most important that I write a summary of my interview with each employee, but I suspected the files were nothing but busywork Synn had suggested to keep me occupied. I went through the files as quickly as I could and made per-functory notes on each.

At seventeen o'clock, just as I was preparing to leave, I heard a knock on my office door. Before I could respond, the door opened and Asher thrust his head through the opening. "Signorina," he gave me a tentative smile, "I wondered if I might invite you to dinner. I feel I should . . . I feel I owe you a fuller explanation of my opinions. You left rather abruptly the other night."

I glanced quickly up and down, reading his body language. He seemed calm, confident, and entirely sane, even apologetic. His eyes were sincere, his smile genuine, his posture relaxed.

I offered him a forgiving smile. "That's very kind, Asher, but I'm afraid I won't be very good company tonight. We have the Brussels trip tomorrow, and this morning I received some very sad news. A friend of mine has died."

An odd expression settled over him—if it hadn't been completely illogical, I would have said a quiver of *jealousy* flickered across his face. He quickly lowered his gaze, though, and kicked at the carpet with the toe of his shoe. "Do they not say misery loves company? I would hate for you to be alone if you need to talk."

I pressed my fingertips to my lips, a little overcome by his offer. This morning I had shared the terrible news about Rory's death with Maura Casale, virtually guaranteeing that the entire Global Union organization would know about the tragedy by lunchtime, but Asher was the first to offer sincere condolences.

And, when he wasn't ranting about the end of the world, he could be pleasant company.

I looked up at him. "That's very kind of you, Asher. When would you like to go?"

"As soon as you are available. I will wait downstairs near the reception area."

"I'll be down soon."

He left, and I turned my chair toward the window, considering his

—

request. Perhaps Kurt was right, and Asher was a harmless eccentric. I had encountered him on his own turf last Thursday night, and *any* conversation might have seemed a little odd in his library of a living room. Besides, compared to dealing with the horror of Rory's death and my indentured servitude to Santos Justus, Asher's bizarre beliefs seemed almost insignificant.

Outside my window, the light was fading fast, color bleeding out of the air. By the time the sun rose again, Asher and I would be on our way to Brussels for a covert mission that Synn and Justus considered important. I would feel tense enough without worrying about Asher's mental competence, so dinner with him tonight might set my mind at rest.

I placed the last personnel file in my out basket, then touched the power button on my computer monitor. I stared at the screen for a moment after it had gone dark. Knowing Synn's penchant for security, I didn't doubt that he or one of his minions regularly screened incoming e-mails. And, since the computers and the network belonged to Global Union, he was perfectly within his rights to do so.

I'd just have to make sure that any other personal correspondence came through my laptop at my old address, Pplreader@worldnet.com. The Global Union mailbox would only be for interoffice memos.

I was in a strangely mellow mood as Asher and I left the Global Union building. The last few hours had drained me, and I was sure it showed in the drooping slope of my shoulders and the pockets under my eyes. I dragged along at Asher's side, content to let him take the lead, and in my apathetic state I noticed that more than one woman turned her head to look at us—or rather, to look at Asher. One particularly lovely girl stood in the doorway of her shop, offering him a slanted brow and a pouting smile that he seemed not to notice.

—

He was, I decided as I stared at him with newly distracted eyes, handsome in an Antonio Banderas fashion. Though he was not as careful about his appearance as Santos Justus, I thought him even more attractive than Il Presidente. Kirsten certainly would have thought so.

Another charming signorina coming toward us smiled at Asher, then gave me the ears-back look two female dogs give each other before deciding to fight. I smiled smoothly, betraying nothing of my annoyance, then slipped my hand through the crook of Asher's arm, well aware of the proprietary message I was sending. Let the woman think he was off-limits. I was in no mood for a challenge.

After nearly two months in Rome, I was becoming used to the rather bold manner of Italian men—they are not at all shy about telling a beautiful woman they appreciate her. I don't consider myself especially beautiful, but during my first few days in Rome the constant awareness of dark, smoldering eyes raking my form made me a little uncomfortable. With one glance, some Italian men seemed able to take in every detail of a woman's appearance, process it, and then, with a provocative tilt of a brow, flash forth an invitation. I had met flirtatious men before, but few men in America are that bold . . . or that confident. Italian men didn't seem to know the meaning of *inhibited*.

Apparently, some Italian women were equally as brazen. On the other occasions I had walked with Asher, we had been deep in conversation and I had paid little attention to passersby. Now, however, we walked like two old friends who were comfortable with each other, and I couldn't help noticing that other women found my companion worth a second glance.

Ignoring the more expensive *ristorantes* catering to tourists, I pointed toward a trattoria, knowing it would offer good food at reasonable prices. Asher shook his head and placed his hand in the small of my back, steering me to a small doorway from which wafted a symphony of wonderful scents—garlic, meat fat, and the faint tang of a wood fire.

"This place is better," he said, smiling at a bald man who appeared a moment after we entered. After greeting Asher like a long-lost cousin, he gestured to an empty table, and Asher thanked him. A moment later we were seated with huge napkins in our laps.

"How did you know about this place?" I asked, glancing around. "There was no sign outside."

"You live in Rome long enough," he answered, his face smooth with secrets, "and you will learn where all the best cooks live."

"I don't intend to live in Rome much longer." I took pains to keep my voice light. "I am planning to go home soon. I'll do what Justus wants us to do tomorrow—but then I think my work here will be finished."

"I know you're thinking about your friend." Asher's eyes were gentle and contemplative. "I am very sorry for your grief . . . but I must admit, I am almost envious."

His admission shocked me. "Why would you say that?"

The arrival of our dinner put a halt to the conversation. The man who had welcomed us stepped out of the kitchen with two steaming plates in his hands. True to Italian form, Asher waved away the topic under discussion in anticipation of the meal. "I'll explain later. After we eat."

I would have pressed him, but the heaping plate before me assaulted my senses and set my stomach to rumbling. Sick with the news of Rory's death, I had skipped lunch. The plump sausage before me looked utterly delicious.

"*Zampone*," Asher said, picking up his knife and fork. He nodded toward the meat. "It is a specialty of the house. We will also have fresh vegetables and mozzarella cheese made just last night. If you like, Georgio will make you a pizza."

I smiled at the cook, who hovered nearby as if waiting for my critique. "This looks wonderful."

Georgio clapped his hands and turned toward the kitchen. *"Buon appetito!"*

Asher cut a slice of sausage. "After dinner, we will have *fritelle* for dessert—perhaps we will take it with us and eat while we walk. I have something important to tell you."

For no reason I could name, his words raised the hairs on the back of my neck.

After dinner, the cook brought each of us a waxed paper bag of *fritelle,* which turned out to be chunks of sweet dough deep-fried in olive oil, then coated with powdered sugar. The sweet concoction reminded me of the funnel cakes my sister and I used to buy at the county fair when we were kids, and I said as much to Asher as we began the walk home.

"When were you born?" he asked.

I laughed at the unexpected question. "I'm twenty-eight, if that's what you really want to know. I'm one of those women who doesn't mind telling her age."

He nodded as a thoughtful expression filled his eyes.

"You wanted to tell me something after dinner," I reminded him. "Well—the time is right, and I'm curious."

"Let us sit." He motioned toward a stone bench at the edge of the Piazza della Rotonda, and I sat down, feeling strangely at home when he sat next to me. The atmosphere around us was nearly carnival, for the night was clear and cool, and crowds had come out to celebrate the end of a workday. A bevy of fat, placid pigeons waddled over the stone piazza, hoping for a handout, and from the next block I heard the frustrated wailing of an automobile, probably trapped behind a row of double-parked cars. A horde of high-school students in jeans, leather jackets, and sneakers clustered around the steps leading to the Pantheon, the herd mentality as evident in Rome as it was in New York. Above the dome of the ancient temple, an attenuated moon hung amid a jumble of stars, and the ristorantes and clubs in the streets beyond offered a mix of the ancient, the contemporary, and the tacky. I gratefully drank in the atmosphere, hoping that the prevailing mood of gaiety would prevent Asher from bringing up Justus and antichrists and primeval prophecies . . .

Asher's dark eyes flitted over the milling crowd. "I am older than you."

"I know that. You're what—thirty-three? Thirty-four?"

"No. I am *much* older."

"That doesn't really matter, does it?" I looked away and pretended indifference, though my mind bulged with a heavy unasked question. Did his comment about our age difference mean he was entertaining some sort of romantic feeling for me? I liked him a lot, I considered him a friend, albeit a slightly odd one, but the thought of a more personal relationship had not even crossed my mind. My thoughts jetted back to an hour ago when I took his arm on the sidewalk. Surely he was not so unsophisticated that he interpreted my gesture as anything significant. An affectionate touch meant virtually nothing, especially in Italy.

"I was born in Rome," his gaze moved over the crowd, "in the year of our Lord."

I lifted a brow, waiting. A boy rode by on a bicycle, his radio humming with the relentlessly cheerful cadences of Europop, but Asher didn't finish his sentence.

I leaned closer, urging him on. "In the year of our Lord . . . what?"

Lifting his gaze to the star-spangled sky, Asher pulled back his shoulders and raised his jaw. "In the year of our Lord," he repeated. "In the same year as Jesus the Christ. He was born in Bethlehem; I was born in a village just outside Rome. He grew up in Nazareth; after being orphaned, I grew up in a house on Patrician Street, a major road leading southwest from the *Castra Praetoria* toward the heart of the Eternal City. My adoptive father was not a great man as the Romans counted greatness, but he had connections in high places. In A.D. 26, I left my father's house and journeyed to Palestine in the service of one called Pontius Pilate, the man Caesar appointed as *prafectus Iudaeae*—governor of Judea."

I listened with a vague sense of disbelief. For an instant I thought he wanted me to take him seriously, but the words rolled off his tongue like a well-rehearsed poem, and I realized I was listening to an oft-repeated story. This, then, was not a conversation, but a performance.

He glanced briefly over his shoulder, probably checking my reaction. Though I had no idea what he was reciting or why he felt impressed to recite it, Asher had never been predictable. "Go on," I urged him, reserving my judgment for the end of this recital. "I want to hear all of it."

For a moment his face seemed to open, and I saw surprise and relief in his eyes. "Have you heard, Claudia, of the Legend of the Wandering Jew?"

I crossed my arms. "I know a plant by that name. My mother used to have a big pot of it hanging on our front porch."

He sighed, rubbing the back of his neck with his hand. "Not the plant—the man. The one who is doomed to wander the earth until Christ comes again."

I looked away, regretting my decision to encourage him. "I was never big on fairy tales or legends."

"You should learn about this one. According to the legend, after Pontius Pilate sentenced Christ to death by crucifixion, soldiers led the Savior out through the city of Jerusalem. When he came to the house of a cobbler named Ahasuerus, Christ put out his hand to rest upon the wall of the house. But the cobbler came out and urged Christ to hurry, saying, 'Get on there! Get moving!' But Christ, bearing the weight of the world upon his shoulders, looked at the man and replied, 'I will go, and I will rest. But you will walk until you see me come again.'"

Asher fell silent for a moment, then took a deep breath. "The details are incorrect, of course. First of all, the man was neither a Jew nor a cobbler. He was a Roman called Cartaphilus, a porter in the service of Pontius Pilate. And this Cartaphilus, in an effort to show off for the soldiers who were escorting the prisoner, did not only speak harshly to Christ, but actually *struck* him. Finally, Christ did not say what is commonly reported. After feeling the sting of Cartaphilus's blow upon his cheek, he looked at the offending servant and said, "You see me now, but you will live until the day you see me clearly."

Asher pushed his hair back, his gaze focused on some distant image. I waited a moment to be sure he had come to the end of his recitation, then I shifted on the bench. That story wasn't so bad. I definitely preferred it to the Antichrist saga. "That's an interesting story, Asher. How did you learn so much about it?"

"I didn't learn it; I lived it. I am *Errante L'Ebreo*."

I swallowed to bring my heart down from my throat, then crossed my arms. "You're going to have to translate that one." I forced a laugh. "It almost sounds like you're asking me to believe you are two thousand years old."

He looked at me then, and in the dim glow of the streetlights an aura of melancholy radiated from his striking features. "I would not lie to you, signorina. I am the one they call the Wandering Jew. I am Cartaphilus, the one who struck the Savior, and I have been journeying through the earth since the year of his death. I cannot age, I cannot die, and I must beg you to believe I would not lie."

—

Somewhere nearby a woman laughed shrilly and a trumpet blared, but I could not turn toward the sound. Transfixed, I sat in a paralysis of astonishment and stared at a man whose direct eyes, erect posture, relaxed mouth, and motionless hands told me he spoke the truth.

But professional liars are extremely difficult to detect. And psychotics cannot distinguish reality from fantasy.

Who was this man?

"Asher," I spoke slowly, not wanting to provoke him, "it's getting late. If you don't mind, I think I'll walk home now."

His face filled with distress. "I've upset you."

I lifted a hand in denial, then looked down and shook my head. "You have given me a lot to think about. And tomorrow is an important day for us—we have to go to Brussels and do this job for Justus. What I need to know is—can you do it?"

His eyes went thin as he looked at me. "You mean, do I feel capable of keeping my thoughts to myself?"

Afraid to speak, I nodded.

He looked away, his eyes as flat and unreadable as stone. "I will not disappoint you."

He did not protest as I slowly stood. I pulled my purse strap over my head, the way one should always carry a purse in crowds, the only way to be sure a purse-snatcher will not yank it from your shoulder—

Heaven help me, is he truly mad?

A muscle clenched along his jaw as he watched me take a tentative step, and at the sight of that involuntary reaction, I took another half step back. "I'll see you in the morning," I called, not wanting to upset him. "Buona notte, Asher."

Then, before he could object or call me back, I turned and hurried through the crowd.

TWENTY

I FRETTED ABOUT ASHER ALL NIGHT, TOSSING AND TURNING UNTIL I wore myself out with worry. Finally, at six, I picked up the phone and dialed New York. I wasn't about to go to Brussels with Asher until I had talked to Kurt.

"Kurt," I switched the phone from one hand to the other, as if trying a new approach would help him understand that this wasn't a prank call, "you've got to help me. I'm sorry for the late hour, but I need your advice. I think I might be in serious trouble with the employee I told you about."

Kurt yawned noisily. I closed my eyes, wishing he could see how desperate I was. I held my breath and tried to be patient—after all, it was midnight in New York and I had awakened Kurt from a sound sleep.

"I don't need this," I whispered, dismayed to hear the sound of tears in my voice. "Not coming so soon after Rory's death. In a few hours we're supposed to go to Brussels and read some people for Justus. I'm nervous enough about that; I don't want to worry about traveling with a psychotic."

"Is this the guy who thinks he's the Antichrist?"

"He doesn't think *he's* the Antichrist. He thinks our boss is. Come on, Kurt, wake up. I need help here."

"I'm awake." Kurt cleared his throat. "And I was sorry to hear about Rory. Terrible break."

209

I swallowed hard. "I know. But I can't talk about him right now. I'm trying to focus on one disaster at a time."

"OK, tell me about this employee." Kurt's voice was even now, and deepening into his professional tone. "Does he function well within his work environment? What's his official role?"

I closed my eyes in relief. "He's an interpreter/translator, and yes, he's fine in the office, though I've had reservations about him from the beginning. But he never spins these bizarre stories unless we're alone."

Kurt fell silent for a moment, and I thought I could hear the sound of drumming fingernails on a bedstand. "Have you considered the possibility that this man might be infatuated with you? Perhaps these incredible tales are nothing but a ploy to get your attention."

I thought a moment. "I've wondered about that, but I don't get any sense of infatuation from him. I know all the courtship signals, Kurt, even the Italian versions, and this guy uses none of them." I felt a wry smile cross my face. "He's probably the only man in Rome who *doesn't* flirt with every woman under fifty."

Kurt made a grunting noise, then I heard the sound of rustling paper, as if he were searching for something. "You're gonna owe me for this, Claude. Like dinner at Chanterelle when you get back."

"I'll pay. Just help me out on this."

"Do you think he sincerely believes these bizarre stories?"

"I don't see any of the usual signs of deception. He could always be a chronic liar, but I think someone in Publications would have noticed before this." Sitting on the bed, I bent my knees, then propped my forehead on my hand. "From his body language and manner, I'd say he believes he's telling the truth. That's why he's got to be psychotic. He has to be out of touch with reality, but unless I can prove it—"

"Here it is," Kurt interrupted. "I knew I had recently read something. This is a case summary from a medical journal." The sounds over the phone grew muffled for a moment, then Kurt spoke in the even, slightly stuffy tone he used for reading aloud: "'Once Mr. Jones came to my office and identified himself to the receptionist as the honorable Frederick Jones—but he worked as a plumber. He sat in the waiting room and told my receptionist one incredible tale after another, amazing my staff with his detailed stories. He seemed to have been everywhere, done everything, and met everyone of consequence. My nurse remarked that he seemed to have squeezed ten lifetimes into one.'"

"That's him!" I could barely contain my excitement. "That sounds just like Asher. He is always talking about the places he's been and the people he's seen."

"I was reading a description of a man with Korsakov's Syndrome. When a patient has entered a state of permanent lostness, he must call forth powers of invention and fancy. He must literally re-create himself and his world in every moment. Of course he sees nothing wrong with himself. He will remember nothing for more than a few seconds—"

"That's *not* him." Disappointment hit me like a blow in the stomach. "Asher remembers everything."

"No defects in memory at all?"

"Not that I can tell."

"Could he be an alcoholic?"

I considered the possibility, recalling that nearly everyone in Rome enjoyed a glass of wine with lunch and dinner. But Asher seemed to drink more coffee than wine, and I had never detected the scent of alcohol on his breath.

"Highly unlikely."

"Any severe emotional changes or mood swings? Any pronounced lack of initiative in recent days or weeks?"

"Nothing. He is a very conscientious employee. Everyone is pleased with his work."

"Then I wouldn't lean toward a diagnosis of Korsakov's. His condition could result from any number of things—incontinent nostalgia, reminiscence, a delusional disorder, or retrograde amnesia."

"It's not amnesia, Kurt. He remembers things, but they're *impossible* things."

"That's the point. He invents memories because he can't recall his own memories. Each of us, you see, owns a particular past, our own individual lifetime. These memories shape us, color our thoughts, and make us who we are. If a man forgets his past, he has no sense of himself. So, as a means of self-preservation, the amnesiac or Korsakov's patient is forced to continually *invent* a past. He will ramble on, sometimes divulging fascinating stories, all in an effort to place himself inside the world."

"So,—" I said, struggling with the concept, "if Asher tells me the same story tomorrow—"

"If he's a Korsakov's patient, he won't tell you the same story. Since your man has a taste for religious personalities, he'll say he was Noah on the ark, or even the pope himself. But he won't remember what he told you today. That's the trademark of a Korsakov's sufferer—no long-term memory. That's the driving force behind the bizarre stories."

"But someone like that wouldn't be able to function in an office. They wouldn't know who they were from day to day."

Kurt grunted his agreement.

"So that doesn't fit Asher Genzano. He knows who he is."

Kurt sighed wearily. "Listen, Claude, it's really impossible to make a diagnosis on the phone and in the middle of the night. I'm just guessing. But from what you've told me, I'd say you're looking at one of three situations: the guy is either spinning a story just to impress you, he's mildly neurotic with a flair for the dramatic, or he suffers from a delusional disorder."

I sprang for the latter possibility. "Tell me about delusions. That sounds like it might fit."

I heard the rumble of the telephone as he adjusted it. "A delusion is a false belief strongly held despite evidence to the contrary. Patients who suffer from paranoia, for instance, often experience delusions of persecution or grandeur."

"He's not paranoid—I don't think. He's got some wild ideas, but I don't think he fantasizes about people out to get him."

"Perhaps his case is not severe. A simple delusional disorder, on the other hand, is characterized by the presence of nonbizarre delusions that have persisted for at least one month."

A cockroach began crawling up the wall in my room. I stared at it, too engrossed in the conversation to care about bugs. "What's a nonbizarre delusion?"

"Something not outside the realm of possibility. A woman may think her child is about to die, or a husband may be convinced his wife is being unfaithful." He chuckled. "One of my patients was convinced his wife was a government agent. Any nonbizarre delusion could be true, of course, but they are highly unlikely. And the patient persists in believing them even when presented with evidence to the contrary. Delusionals can be cured, Claude, but you've got to make them face reality one step at a time."

I tapped my nails on my kneecap, staring at the roach. Asher's belief certainly seemed bizarre, but perhaps *bizarre* was relative. I mean, if a man *could* live two thousand years, I supposed his stories about meeting Agrippa and Jesus could be true.

"Would a person with a delusional disorder be able to work in an office?"

—

213

"Definitely. People who suffer from a delusional disorder would not experience a marked impairment in their daily lives. Their outward behavior is not noticeably out of the ordinary."

"That sounds like Asher . . . but his delusion seems out of the ordinary."

"What is it?"

I hesitated. "He thinks he's been alive for two thousand years."

Kurt couldn't keep the laughter from his voice. "That's a new one, at least. Very creative."

"But how can I *prove* he's suffering from a delusion?

"Doesn't Rome have government offices? Ask for the man's birth certificate. Set the paper chasers to work on his case and assemble a case file. And get on it quickly, before he embarrasses you in front of your boss."

I felt a curious, tingling shock. "You mean he might—"

"Delusionals are capable, but they're not always discreet. If you value your reputation, Claudia, you'd better get this guy cured or replaced. I don't think Santos Justus would be pleased if his interpreter casually mentioned that he'd just celebrated his two-thousandth birthday."

I had to agree Kurt was right. If I wanted to leave Global Union with my reputation intact, I'd have to do something about Asher Genzano.

Asher and I could not take the jet to Brussels, Synn explained, because the appearance of Justus's jet would excite media attention. We could travel by train, however, and no one would notice our arrival or departure.

I stared wordlessly as he placed false national identification cards into our hands, gave us our train tickets, and told us to take a cab to

—

the station. "There must be no records of any Unione Globale employee present in Brussels," he explained, folding his arms on his desk as he looked at us. "You will go to the Eurovillage Brussels Hotel and take a room under the name of Signor and Signora Pax. You will wait there for further instructions." He glanced at the suitcase by my feet. "Thank you, signorina, for remembering to play the part. You must be careful not to speak to anyone to whom you must show the ID card."

I ignored the insult to my Italian language skills and studied the identification card. The picture was a copy of my own passport photo, but the name printed underneath was *Maria Pax.* I noted without amusement that *pax* was Latin for *peace.*

"Why husband and wife?" I asked.

Synn smiled, a roguish twinkle in his blue eyes. "What better cover for a couple traveling together?" He stood and gestured toward the door. "You'd better leave now. The train departs in less than an hour."

I glanced at Asher, half-afraid to meet his eye after our talk last night, but he smiled at me with calm confidence and politely opened the door.

"So tell me more about your life." I transferred my gaze from the wide train window to Asher, who sat silently across from me in the private compartment. We had not spoken much more than polite "excuse me's" and "after you's" since boarding the train, but ten minutes of strained silence were all my tattered nerves could handle. If I was traveling with a man who couldn't discern fantasy from reality, I wanted to know the depth of his delusion before we got into real trouble.

"I'd like to hear more of your stories," I said. I leaned my elbow on the armrest, then parked my chin in my hand, affecting the posture of casual interest. "If you have lived as long as you say, you must have some interesting tales to share."

Asher hauled his gaze from the sky beyond the window and looked at me. I don't know what I expected to read in his eyes—craziness, maybe, or confusion—but when he smiled I saw nothing but weariness tinged with patient amusement.

"People of the twentieth century are not quick to believe." He lowered his thick black lashes, momentarily hiding his eyes from me. "They see fantastic things in film and on the television, so they tend to believe miracles happen only in the imagination. But they are wrong, Claudia. Miracles happen every day to those who have eyes to see."

Riddles again. Was this a sign of Korsakov's? Kurt had said Asher wouldn't be able to remember his stories of the previous night, and he certainly seemed to be heading off on another tangent . . .

I lifted a brow and smiled, silently urging him to continue. I would not give him any clues about what he told me last night; I could not allow myself to feed any particular fancy.

"I was once married." He gave me a brief, distracted glance and tried to smile. "Her name was Claudia too—in fact, in many ways you remind me of her. She worked in the governor's palace, as a handmaid for the Lady Procula, Pilate's wife. We considered ourselves fortunate to have such good positions with an important family. We might have had a very pleasant life, if not for the Nazarene."

So he did remember. I froze, my mouth going dry as he shifted his gaze to the window.

"The afternoon of the trial, Jesus the Nazarene stood before Pilate, condemned of treason. The leaders of the Sanhedrin wanted him dead, of course, but Pilate could not find any evidence to prove the man had violated Roman law. The chief priest screamed that Jesus had broken their Jewish laws, but Pilate cared nothing for any religion but Rome's. And then, almost as an afterthought, Caiaphas reminded Pilate that the Nazarene had claimed to be a king. And that was enough to prevent Pilate from releasing the man outright. Judea was not an easy place to govern, you see, and Tiberius Caesar Augustus not an easy man to please."

I lowered my eyelids, slowly submerging myself into the memory of stories learned in my childhood Sunday school classes. The rhythmic sound and sway of the train provided a soothing background to Asher's voice, blocking out everything but the picture he painted with words.

"My master Pilate faced the most difficult confrontation of his career. Rome had recently chastised him for upsetting the Jewish religious leaders, so he could not summarily dismiss their complaints. And yet his honor forbade him to send an innocent man to death. Finally, in a brilliant attempt to sway public opinion, Pilate ordered that the prisoner be flogged in the outer court. He was certain the flogging would break Jesus' stubborn spirit and move the strident crowd to pity—or at least satisfy their blood lust."

Asher's eyes sought mine. "A Roman flogging, as you must know, was no routine matter. This Jesus, who remained silent throughout the ordeal, was stripped of his robes and forced to stand beneath a boiling sun in front of a hostile crowd. The captain of the Roman guard beat him with the *fustigatio*. From an alcove, I watched as the skin of his back bruised and ripped beneath the blows. When the beating was done, someone found a purple mantle and draped it over his bleeding shoulders. The captain fashioned a crown from a thorny vine growing near the stables, then made great sport of pretending to crown the prisoner like a king. Someone else thrust a reed into his

—

hand, a sorry substitute for a scepter, and one by one the company of guards fell on their knees and saluted him, the king who was no king, the rabbi rejected by his own people. Finally, in a single line, the guards filed by him. Some spat in his face, others slapped his cheek and jaw. But the worst—at least for me—was yet to come."

I watched Asher in silence, knowing he believed every word he spoke. His strong face and darkly powerful eyes, which could intimidate most people even from across a room, filled with a beaten sadness while his voice grew rough. Though I had heard the story of Jesus' crucifixion many times, I did not believe Asher told it often. From the look in his eyes and the tension in his clenched fists, I received the distinct impression his soul couldn't bear the black memories—whether real or imagined—that had scorched it once.

"You must understand," he said, looking at me as if he believed I actually could, "I was a mere servant, and I looked up to the Roman soldiers. Pilate's Praetorian Guard was renown for its bravery; every merchant in Jerusalem offered the men in his command free food and drinks. These men were superhuman, blessed by the gods and honored by Rome. I wanted nothing more than to earn their respect . . . and so, as the spectacle with the Nazarene continued, I lingered in the shadows, watching and applauding their efforts.

"When the prisoner looked as though he could no longer stand, the soldiers tied him to a post. One man blindfolded the Nazarene while a small group of men moved around the post, still calling out jests and insults. As they passed before the prisoner, one would hit him with all his might, then the circle would move and another would call out, 'Who hit you? Tell us, if you can!' I watched for several minutes, laughing and jesting, until I was called away to a duty in the house."

Asher lowered his gaze to the floor as fresh misery darkened his face. "I did not see the man again until much later. By then Pilate had washed his hands of the judgment, the people had chosen to release Barabbas in honor of the Passover festival, and the Sanhedrin had demanded crucifixion for the Nazarene.

"I saw Jesus again in the courtyard of Pilate's palace. He had been stripped of the purple robe, but still he wore the crown of thorns. He carried the *patibulum,* the wooden beam that would later be fastened to one of the stakes already mounted at the place of the skull. A contingent of Pilate's guards walked before, beside, and behind him, leading him to the place of execution outside the city. My heart thrilled when I realized they would walk right by the place where I stood.

"I don't know if you can understand how I felt in that moment. My heart brimmed with pride—the pride of Rome, of leadership, of position. I also coveted the admiration of the soldiers with whom I worked. And so, full of pride, covetousness, and bravado, I curled my hand into a fist and waited for the Nazarene to approach.

"I wanted to throw one blow that might knock him off his feet and set the soldiers to cheering. With one punch I could earn myself a round of drinks in the garrison, and my name would be on every soldier's lips. Even Pilate, who usually did not condone violence, might see a brash aspect of my personality that duty forced me to repress.

"A thrill of fear shot through me at the thought of my own audacity, but I waited, my hand and my will forged to one purpose. And when the Nazarene was as close to me as I am to you, I stepped forward, cursed his name, and swung with all my might. My hand hit his jaw and moved forward over his damp flesh, slamming against his temple and knocking the crown of thorns to the ground. My ring scraped his skin—sometimes I can close my eyes and still see the red welt it raised from his cheek to his hairline. He staggered beneath the blow, but he did not fall."

—

Out in the hallway, a gaggle of giggling girls passed our compartment. Asher waited for silence to fall before speaking again.

"I expected to hear cheering, shouts of approval, applause, and congratulations. But the guards around me seemed stupefied—as if they couldn't believe a mere servant had acted so impetuously. As I rubbed my injured hand—a thorn had torn a long scratch upon my knuckle—Jesus the Nazarene looked directly into my eyes and said, 'You see me now, but you will live until the day you see me clearly.'

"For a moment I thought time had stopped. The Nazarene and I stood frozen in place, like statues, while he looked at me with an expression in his eyes that brought the blood rushing to my face and made me feel as though the world whirled madly around us. A thick silence settled upon the courtyard, a choking absence of sound, yet all the while his words echoed in the stillness—*you will live until the day you see me clearly.*

"The pain in my hand disappeared. The bleeding stopped. And then, through the dark arch made by his sweat-soaked hair I saw a tear run upon that bruised cheek. He was weeping, yet there was no self-pity in his expression. He wept . . . for me."

The conductor of the rushing train blew the whistle, a blunt, blaring sound, but I scarcely heard it, so intent was I upon Asher. He seemed to huddle in his seat and stared out the window with somber eyes, a mournful face, and sagging shoulders—the body language of sorrow.

Finally, he drew a deep breath and continued. "I was confused, and pride concealed my inner turmoil. Why would he weep for me? I was Pilate's personal servant, and he nothing but a condemned and conquered Jew. I lifted my hand, wondering if I should strike him again for his impertinence, and the silence broke. The soldiers jeered and pushed him forward, and one of them clapped me on the shoulder. But I scarcely felt it, for the condemned man's puzzling words remained uppermost in my mind. He had made strange statements before Pilate too, neither confirming nor denying his accusers, and claiming to have a kingship 'not of this world.'

"They led him away, and I returned to my duties, still thinking about the Nazarene. The weather did little to lift my pensive mood. The sky grew dark and the birds fell silent, and at one point the earth itself trembled until the stones of Pilate's palace shuddered and broke the bonds of mortar that held them together. Claudia came running to find me, and I held her in my arms as she whimpered.

"Both of us breathed a sigh of relief when the trembling earth finally stood still. My wife was convinced the strange portents had something to do with the Nazarene, for her mistress, the Lady Procula, had suffered greatly in a dream about the man, going so far as to warn her husband not to have anything to do with judging him.

"But by the time the execution detail completed their work, I had convinced myself that the Nazarene was more philosopher than prophet. Rome was filled with wits who loved to turn a phrase and confound the casual listener. I decided that this Jesus was like them, neither more nor less.

"By sunset, the Jews had cleared the streets to observe their Sabbath and Passover feast. No one in Pilate's palace dared to speak of the Nazarene. The master himself seemed relieved that he had narrowly avoided a riot, but a shadow lay behind his smile, and I knew Jesus' death troubled him. Lady Procula made no attempt to hide her distress. She took to her bed with a headache and would not come to dinner.

"When all the servants had gone to bed, Claudia and I lay in each other's arms and whispered about the day's events. I told her what Jesus said to me. The meaning of his riddle disturbed her so much she

—

221

climbed out of bed and insisted upon making an offering to the household gods whose altar stood in a niche inside the wall. While I lay on my back and tried to erase the afternoon from my memory, Claudia scattered grain and salt upon the altar of our little chamber, then murmured prayers for our continued well-being.

"I think Claudia expected me to be struck dead by the Jew's God, but nothing out of the ordinary happened. The next day passed in subdued silence, as if the city were holding its breath. We went about our duties as usual. The Jews continued with their festival; the Romans thanked their gods for the lull. A bit of trouble reared its head the third day when the Jewish leaders appeared at Pilate's door and complained that the Nazarene's body had been stolen in the night.

"Pilate only chastised them for their own incompetence. Rome had no interest in safeguarding a criminal's corpse, and the leaders of the Sanhedrin had insisted upon using temple guards to seal the tomb. Another earthquake had scattered the frightened guards and apparently broken the tomb's seal. Any fool could see, Pilate said, that the Nazarene's disciples had crept in and stolen their teacher's body.

"The rumors flew through Jerusalem. Some repeated the story about the stolen body; others said the rabbi had risen from the dead as he prophesied. His followers proclaimed the resurrection tale with great zeal, though many still clung to shadows for fear of the Romans. But Pilate cared nothing about dead Jews. He and Procula had grown weary of Jerusalem and wanted more than anything to earn permission to return home.

"Three years later Pilate was recalled to Rome. Claudia and I went with him, of course, as did several of the household staff. After ten years in the dusty, dry lands of Judea, the cool winds of Rome felt like heaven. We encountered a substantial tumult as we arrived, for Tiberius had just died and Caligula was named emperor. My master

—

Pilate wanted nothing more than to retreat into anonymity, and Claudia and I wished to retreat with him.

"I was thirty-six years old, a mature man in those days. Silver strands had already begun to color my lovely wife's hair, and her step was not as quick as it once was. As we went about the business of day-to-day life, I began to notice that my wife was growing older."

Asher's hand lifted and traced the air between us, outlining a woman's cheek, neck, and shoulder. When he spoke again, his low and passionate voice commanded the compartment. "I loved my wife as man loves only one woman in a lifetime. I gave her my heart, emptying all my adoration and devotion and worship at her feet, wanting nothing more than to live at her side and die in her arms." His mouth spread into a thin-lipped smile. "As years passed, however, I began to understand part of the meaning behind the Nazarene's riddle. Time was passing for my beloved Claudia, but for me, it stood still."

His gaze shifted and he stared out the window, his expression darkening with unreadable emotions. "Ten years passed, then twenty. Claudia grew stooped and tired more easily. Pilate died, followed by Lady Procula. My wife, the love of my life who used to tease me about my youthful appearance, stopped joking. Her laughter evolved into bitter cries, her songs into storms of weeping. In an effort to escape the people who knew us, we moved to Antioch. The citizens of that city thought we were mother and son, not husband and wife."

His voice faded to a hushed stillness. "One day in summer, my beloved Claudia died in my arms. Her lovely face was lined with hate, her hands curled into knots that for years had resisted my touch. She could not believe that I did not see decay and ugliness when I looked at her, and her disbelief destroyed our happiness in the remaining years of her lifetime."

Asher turned and gave me a wintry smile. "I buried her in Antioch."

He fell silent. I said nothing but reflected on his story even as I watched him for signs of deception. He had created this thoughtful and detailed story some time ago, I was certain, and had probably recited it before. The telling included details any mediocre history student would recognize—the crucifixion of Christ in A.D. 33, the names of Pilate and his wife—yet the emotion behind the story seemed genuine.

Could a man—even one as ostensibly brilliant as Asher Genzano—manufacture such a tale?

I sat for a moment, listening to the gentle rhythm of the rails, then lowered my head to intercept his gaze. "What did you do then—after Antioch?"

He blinked, staring at me as if I had brought him back from some faraway place. "I returned to Rome, of course. It was the only home I knew. Nero was emperor, however, and his cruelty inspired revolts in Rome and the outlying dominions. He began to persecute those who called themselves Christians, and I heard rumors that he actually started the great fire that devoured Rome in A.D. 64. Life in Rome was barely tolerable, but I had no roots elsewhere. Though my old friends were dead and gone, I did meet a few people I had known in years past; they immediately assumed I was the son of their old friend. Not wanting to explain my curse—for that's how I saw it, nothing less than a malediction—I allowed them to believe whatever they wished.

"I continued to live in Rome, working in the employ of old family friends, for another twenty years. When it became apparent that my unchanging appearance might arouse suspicion, I left, this time for Galatia."

He bent his head and studied his hands. "That is where I learned the entire truth. I had heard, you see, that the Nazarene claimed to be the son of a god, and by the time Claudia died I realized he must have spoken the truth—no one else could inflict the curse of immortality upon another living soul. But in Galatia I heard the entire story—how Jesus was born of a virgin, lived a simple life, preached repentance and good works, and died to pay the penalty for mankind's sin. The Christians in Galatia had given themselves over to good works, and I labored among them for many years, hoping that God would see my labor and my earnest heart. But after thirty years, as my companions grew gray and bent, I remained strong and upright. And so I left Galatia too, before anyone could discover my shameful secret.

"Not long afterward I realized something else—my curse was particular and meaningful. Every man is born under the curse of sin, and every man can find release through Christ. But not every man has struck the face of God in such pride as mine, and Jesus never told any other man what he told me. I had been singled out to remain on earth until I saw him again. The Christians who understood his teachings explained that he would come again at the end of days. So it was in Galatia that I realized I would wander the earth until Christ comes again . . . until the evil one is revealed."

I stared at him in dazed exasperation. "You've lost me, Asher. What evil one?"

He gave me the smile one gives a dull-witted child. "The Antichrist. I have spoken of him to you before."

From far away the train whistle stretched across the concentrated silence in our compartment. He *had* mentioned the Antichrist before and had apparently retained a perfectly good memory of the occasion—so he did not fit Kurt's profile of an amnesiac.

I'd been trying to force Asher into a psychological box all morning, but I could no longer deny the truth: Asher Genzano was not psychotic. Neurotic, perhaps, or an accomplished liar. But he appeared to be in complete possession of his memory and mental faculties.

—

"So," I began, deliberately changing the subject, "what did you do after you left Galatia?"

His tight expression relaxed into a simple smile. "I wandered from place to place, working at various jobs, learning as much as I could about the people who called themselves Christians. Nero had begun to pursue them, and the apostle Peter was executed in A.D. 67, in Rome, of course. The persecution of Christians continued for 250 years. Not until the emperor Constantine granted Christians freedom of worship were those who followed the Nazarene able to feel safe in the city that had crucified Peter."

He lowered his head into his hands and kneaded his forehead as though his head ached with memories. "I saw it all, Claudia. The great plague that swept through Rome in the second century, the division of the Roman Empire, the fall of Western Rome and the rise of Byzantium. I have lived throughout the lifetime of every pope. I witnessed Charlemagne's crowning in St. Peter's, the Normans' attack upon Rome, and thousands of Roman citizens gasping for their last breath in the plague called Black Death. I met Michelangelo; I once spent an entire morning watching him paint in the Sistine Chapel. I saw the Spanish troops of Charles V pillage the city and destroy countless works of art. I stood in the crowd as Galileo was condemned to death for heresy; I heard the shouts of acclamation when England's Bonnie Prince Charlie was born in my native city. I fought for Rome when Napoleon captured it, I worried when Italy entered the First World War, and I wept when the *Fascisti* marched on the city and Mussolini became prime minister. I cheered with thousands when Rome hosted the Olympic games; I was standing in St. Peter's Square the day a wild-eyed fanatic tried to assassinate Pope John Paul II. Though I have traveled the world over, I have never stayed away from Rome for long, for in Rome beats the heart of the world. I can take her pulse through the city's streets; I can read her future in the newspaper headlines. And what I see today, Claudia, troubles me more than anything has ever troubled me in the past."

His face betrayed a certain tension, a secret passion held rigidly under control, and I felt a tiny tremor of fear when he met my gaze. I swallowed against an unfamiliar constriction in my throat. "What do you see?"

He smiled, but it was the kind of stiff grimace an undertaker would fix on the face of a corpse. "I see the fulfillment of the vision spoken of by Daniel the prophet: 'Its ten horns are ten kings that will rule that empire. Then another king will arise, different from the other ten, who will subdue three of them.'"

I felt my own smile stiffening. "Asher, I don't know what you're talking about."

"A confederation of ten nations—another king will rise and subdue three of the nations. He will destroy their leaders and set himself in their place."

"*Who* will?"

"The Antichrist."

I snapped my mouth shut and leaned back in my seat, amazed that he had managed to bring the conversation back around to this particular obsession. What fed his fascination with the Antichrist?

Something in me wanted to crack him open like a Russian nesting doll, opening shell after shell, searching for the man inside the mystery. Had he once been a guide in one of Rome's historic buildings? Perhaps he was the son of literature professors, or he had majored in history in his college years. Perhaps one of his professors had cheated him, or jilted him, or hurt him and left a deep psychological scar . . .

I tucked the thought away as the train whistle blew and the rhythmic clacking of the rails began to slow. We were nearing Brussels, and we had risky work to do. I didn't dare upset Asher until we were safely rid of our obligation to Santos Justus.

"I'd like to hear more on the way back." I gripped the edge of my briefcase and gave Asher a careful smile. "But for now, let's concentrate on the job we're here to do, OK?"

He smiled, ruefully accepting my decision to set the subject aside. "Whatever you say, signorina."

Twenty-one

WE DID AS SYNN HAD INSTRUCTED, TAKING A CAB FROM THE TRAIN station to the Eurovillage Brussels Hotel. I was not entirely comfortable being alone with Asher in the hotel room, but he seemed to sense my unease and took pains to respect my desire for physical space. While I sat at the desk and riffled through the drawers, trying to find a suitable piece of stationery, he sat in a wing chair and turned on the television, thoughtfully lowering the volume. While he watched a local news station, I stared at a blank sheet of beige cotton bond and tried to write a sympathy note to Rory's wife. No matter how hard I tried to summon the words, my thoughts kept returning to an imagined scene in which Asher and I were detained by angry Belgian nationals who had discovered that our national identification cards were false.

Scarcely ten minutes after our arrival, the telephone rang. Asher picked up the phone, murmured "Oui" in a restrained voice, listened for a moment, then hung up. "They will pick us up outside in a black sedan," he said, a faint glint of humor in his eyes. "The driver will"— he tugged on the lapel of his jacket—"wear a red flower on his coat."

I brought my hand to my mouth, smothering an incredulous smile. There was something strangely ludicrous about this entire situation, and I felt a wave of gratitude toward Asher for helping me see it.

"I'll be just a moment," I said, moving toward the bathroom. "I just want to freshen up before we go."

—

229

He nodded, and I stepped into the bathroom and closed the door, pausing a moment to stare at my reflection in the smoky mirror. My eyes looked like black holes in my face; no condemned criminal could have looked guiltier.

"Shape up, Fischer," I told my ghostly reflection. "Just do this and get out. Nothing's going to happen, and no one's going to care."

Five minutes later, Asher and I were walking through the hotel lobby, where a man in a dark coat lounged against a marble pillar. After spotting the clichéd red flower, Asher walked over to the man, murmured something in French, and the two shook hands. Asher beckoned to me, so I followed them through the lobby and into the bitterly cold wind. After seating us in the backseat of a sedan, the driver whisked us through the streets of Belgium.

Asher and I didn't speak until we stopped outside a concrete and glass building. I barely had time to ask, "Are we here?" when another man opened my door and practically pulled me onto the sidewalk.

This man, a tall, thin fellow with long brown hair and a long face to match, gestured toward the building entrance. "This way, mademoiselle." I glanced back for Asher, saw that he stood right behind me, and together we followed the man into the building and through a maze of hallways.

Finally he led us into a small, windowless room with bare walls. The air smelled of sweat and pulsed faintly with fluorescent light. A fax machine rasped on a stand against the wall, spitting curled paper into the room. Above a utilitarian table, a column of dust rose toward the ceiling in a column of greenish light. A computer monitor sat on the table; a still image filled the screen. A heavy bald man with a pair of headphones on his ears sat at the end of the table and fretted with some sort of electrical control panel. His neck was so thick that his head appeared to rest directly on his substantial shoulders.

—

Our escort pointed toward two steel folding chairs, then moved toward the fax machine. "The meeting is to begin in ten minutes," he said, gesturing that we should be seated. "We wanted you here early so you can understand how to direct our cameras. We have six cameras in the room. If you tell us what you want to see, you shall see it."

I looked up at our guide and decided his mustache was more intention than fact. "What about the sound?" I asked.

Mr. Thin Face nodded. "We have excellent audio reception."

He scanned the fax for a moment, then folded it and tucked it into his pocket. Without another word, he leaned back and flipped a switch, plunging the stuffy room into a silent darkness lit only by the soft gray light from the computer monitor. The technician's hands floated over his controls, magically changing the picture on the screen so I could see the room from several different vantage points. The room under observation seemed to be a parlor in a deluxe hotel suite, or perhaps a drawing room in a private home. The curtains were heavy and of luxurious fabric, probably velvet; the sofa and chairs were likewise of fine quality. Several lovely paintings hung on the walls, and an ornate carved door appeared to be the main entrance.

"Where are the cameras hidden?" I asked, a little amazed by the technical setup.

"Inside the impressionistic paintings." A smile ruffled our host's shadow of a mustache. "The camera itself is nothing but a tiny dot. In such a painting it is practically invisible."

"And where is the meeting taking place? A hotel?"

The smile disappeared. "That, mademoiselle, you do not need to know."

I sat back, feeling abruptly rebuffed. Asher filled the awkward silence. "The microphones—are they hidden with the cameras?"

"No. The listening devices are tucked behind the electrical switch plates. The fools did not think to have the room swept before arranging this meeting."

We sat in silence for at least another five minutes, watching the monitor like terriers at a rat's hole. Then we saw the door open. The technician's hands stilled, and three men entered. One had his hand clasped upon another's shoulder, and all three displayed a generous amount of teeth in casual, relaxed smiles. Right away I realized these were the same three ambassadors I had read at the EU Council of Ministers' meeting five days before.

"They are friends; they are comfortable; they are sincere," I murmured, tilting my head as one of the men moved to a cabinet to pour drinks for the other two. "And this one considers himself a host."

The thin man peered at the screen over my shoulder. "That is Dutetre."

"Well," I drawled, "at least I know they're meeting in Belgium. It is only natural that Dutetre would feel obliged to serve his guests in his home country."

The thin man said nothing but crossed his arms and stared at the monitor. I returned my gaze to the screen as the camera zoomed in for a closer view.

After serving his guests, Dutetre sat in a wing chair facing the others, who had seated themselves on the sofa—another signal that he had arranged this meeting. Leaders usually situated themselves at the end of a table or in the center. In the absence of a table, the wing chair served as a substitute.

Dutetre crossed his legs, a sign of confidence, and said something to the others in French. Immediately, the smiles disappeared.

"How do you feel things are going?" Asher said, translating Dutetre's comment.

He paused as Dekker, the ambassador from the Netherlands,

answered, then translated his comments as well. "Not well. Justus is meddling in our affairs. He has already proposed that a WEU peace-keeping force be installed in Amsterdam to quell the recent student uprisings."

"Have you investigated the cause of the riots?"

"Of course. All the rioting students are either affiliated with Unione Globale or have been influenced by the organization's literature."

Asher pointed to Vail Billaud as the representative from Luxembourg spoke. "Are any other countries having trouble with students from Unione Globale? I've heard the organization now has branch offices in every country, even the United States."

"They only cause trouble when Justus gives the word," Dekker said. Anyone could have read the bitterness in his face. "Justus is applying pressure to us alone, my friends, and I do not know how we can stop him. If we resist his ideas, we will be reprimanded by the other nations of the WEU. And how can we justify resisting *peace?*"

"Justus defines peace as power." Billaud's eyes narrowed with fury. "And I do not want him to have power. It is already difficult to resist him."

On and on they talked, with Asher translating in a rough whisper. The atmosphere in our little spy post grew tenser with each passing moment. I pulled out my notebook and made notes on body language when appropriate, but once I had ascertained that these men trusted each other and were speaking truthfully, anyone could see they were worried. Their conversation left no doubt that the force worrying them most was Santos Justus.

The conversation lasted for half an hour, then Dekker glanced at his watch and stood, announcing that he was late for another appointment. All three men embraced in farewell, and when the camera zoomed in upon Vail Billaud's face, I thought I saw the glint of tears in his eyes. These men were not only worried . . . they were terrified. For themselves, and for their countries.

One sudden, lucid memory broke into my thoughts: *A confederation of ten nations—another king will rise and subdue three of the nations. He will destroy their leaders, and set himself in their place.*

Asher's words washed through me, shivering my skin like the touch of a ghost. The WEU was comprised of ten nations. Was Santos Justus planning to overthrow the leadership of these three countries? I had seen nothing in Justus's personality to indicate he was capable of such ruthlessness, but I had spent little personal time with the man. Yet here I was, locked in a secret room, spying upon three unwary diplomats for him.

As a bead of perspiration traced a cold path down my spine, I pushed away from the table. "If you have no further need of me, monsieur, I am not feeling well." I must have sounded as weak as I felt, for Asher's arm went around my shoulder, supporting me as I stood. The lights came back on in the room, and I saw that the thin man had filled a page of notes too. "Wait, mademoiselle," he said, looking at his notebook. "You must explain to me everything you saw and what it means."

"I can't." I was breathing in shallow gasps, trying not to inhale the sickly sweet stench of body odor. I had the feeling Monsieur No-Neck had not bathed in a week.

"You must stay." The thin man looked up at me, his brows arching. "You will tell me all I need to know, and I will report it to my superior—"

Asher fairly growled at the man. "Mademoiselle Fischer will make her report to Justus alone. Can't you see she is not well? Take us out of this place at once, or Il Presidente will hear that his representative was mistreated."

The thin man measured Asher with a cool, appraising look for a

—

long moment, then abruptly closed his notebook. "One moment, mademoiselle, I'll have to take you out."

Swallowing against the nausea threatening my throat, I picked up my notebook and slipped it in my purse, then moved toward the doorway.

Lengthening his stride, the thin man led us out of the building and to the car. Safe in the backseat, I closed my eyes and leaned against Asher's solid shoulder as the engine roared to life.

Like tourists returning from sightseeing, Asher and I went back to the hotel, picked up my suitcase, and took a cab back to the train station. I didn't know what the hotel would think of our abrupt departure, and I didn't care. Mr. Thin Man and his cronies could handle the dirty details.

Asher sank into his seat across from me. "Are you all right?" he asked, a note of uneasiness in his voice.

"It's just a nervous stomach." I pressed my hand to my middle. "I'll be fine in a few minutes—I just wanted out of there." I gave him a look of gratitude, which he acknowledged with just the smallest softening of his eyes.

As the train pulled out of the station, Asher settled back in his seat and opened the Belgian magazine he'd picked up as we boarded. I sat across from him with a pillow over my eyes and a hand pressed to my still-queasy belly. One moment slid seamlessly into the next, and though the train roared through the darkness and only a soft over-head light burned in our compartment, sleep would not come to a brain as bothered as mine.

Until this afternoon, I had been certain—convinced—that his were the ravings of a conspiracy nut, or at least a paranoid neurotic. And though I found the idea of spying for Justus unwise and unethical,

I had managed to rationalize my actions by thinking of my work as an effort to further world peace.

But what I heard in that darkened listening post shattered my illusions. Those three men—speaking truthfully and with complete candor—had testified of Santos Justus's manipulation and treachery. From Rico Triccoli's weekly convocation reports I knew Justus had planted Global Union chapters in every nation and now they were working to have a Global Union office in every major city. Justus appealed to idealists, he spoke of freedom and an end to war, and droves of young people signed on to aid his cause.

I hadn't picked up an English newspaper since arriving in Rome, so I hadn't heard anything about student riots in the Netherlands, Belgium, or Luxembourg. But I knew riots in the name of peace would be hard to put down—my own country could not forget what happened at Kent State in 1970. National Guardsmen, called in to put down a student protest against the Vietnam War, shot into a crowd of students, killing four and injuring nine. Kent State happened two years before I was born, but years later I studied the black-and-white photograph of a girl screaming at her fallen friend's side . . . and you didn't have to be a people reader to see the heart rending horror in the tragedy.

Surely Dekker, Dutetre, and Billaud had heard of Kent State . . . and now they faced the same situation. It was a challenging conundrum—what could they do to resist *peace?*

I heard the sound of Asher shifting in his seat, and when I opened my eyes I saw that he had put the magazine aside. He was staring out the window, his arms folded across his chest, his thoughts apparently a million miles away. Perhaps, like me, he was thinking about Justus's army of idealistic students.

"Tell me more," I whispered, reluctant to break the silence. "About why you think Santos Justus is the Antichrist."

—

Without looking at me, Asher lifted one shoulder in a shrug. "I don't know that he is. I only know that he could be. No one can be certain of the evil one's identity until after the day of the Lord."

I sighed, knowing that I'd signed on for a long conversation. "Maybe you'd better start with the basics. What's the day of the Lord?"

He looked at me then, a thoughtful smile curving his mouth. "Are you ready to believe?"

I felt a blush stain my cheeks. Had he known all along that I thought he was crazy?

"I don't know what I think, Asher. I just want to understand your reasons. I know you're intelligent and well educated. So I want to know why you believe the things you do about Justus—and about yourself."

My doubts didn't seem to upset him; he merely smiled and looked back at his reflection in the black window. "After I became a follower of Christ," he said, his voice velvet-edged and strong, "I joined a monastery and spent several years studying the Holy Scriptures under Ephraem the Syrian, an important theologian of the early Byzantine Eastern Church. It was Ephraem who told me about the end of the world and the evil one who will appear. The Lord will gather his elect from the earth in order to deliver them from the tribulation to come. After that, the Antichrist will arise. He will seduce the world through intelligence and persuasiveness, subtlety and craft. For seven years he will attempt to rule the earth, and during that time the earth will know great tribulation unlike any that has ever scourged the planet. At the end of the seven years, the Lord will appear with great power and majesty and glory. Then he, Jesus the Christ, will vanquish the Antichrist forever."

I propped the small pillow behind my head and thoughtfully considered Asher's words. My childhood Sunday school teacher never taught about tribulation and antichrists, and the sermons I heard in church—those I could remember, anyway—seemed to revolve around having faith in God and the goodness of man. I knew some ministers preached all sorts of prophecy; at the turn of the millennium the tabloids had been filled with stories of doomsday cults and photos from people who snapped Jesus peeping out through the clouds. The *New York Times* had reported that at least a dozen respected ministers believed that Jesus might return to earth in the year 2000, but that year had come and gone without any sign of Christ's appearing.

Was Asher just another prophecy nut? A leftover zany from the millennium craze?

"So," I said, speaking slowly, feeling my way, "you think the Antichrist is here, so Jesus is coming back soon—"

Asher shot me a warning glance. "The Antichrist won't be revealed until *after* all believers are taken to heaven. Some people call that event the Rapture. Others call it the Ingathering. Whatever you call it, it's going to happen."

I waved a hand in confusion. "OK. But it hasn't happened yet—right?"

"You'll know when it happens. The world won't be able to ignore the day millions of people vanish."

I nodded quickly, hurrying him past that particular prediction. "If it hasn't happened, why do you think Justus is the Antichrist?" Another more troubling question suddenly popped into my brain. "And if you think he's such an evil person, why are you *working* for him?"

"I didn't say he was the Antichrist, and I'm not sure he's evil. But I know he is ambitious. And I think he might become the Antichrist one day if—well, if I do not succeed."

My internal warning systems went on full alert. "Succeed at *what*, Asher?"

"In leading him to the Lord."

I pinched the bridge of my nose and groaned as a sudden tide of weariness engulfed me.

Asher leaned forward, eagerness shining from his eyes. "Claudia, you must understand. The apostle John told us that the Antichrist is coming in the future. But he also wrote that *many* antichrists have already come. In the first century he told his readers that the *spirit* of the Antichrist was already in the world."

Totally disoriented, I looked up at him.

"Claudia." He slid to the edge of his seat, then reached out and clasped my hand. "Satan is not like God. He is powerful; he is clever; he is the most proud and ambitious being ever created. But he is not omniscient. He does not know when the Rapture will occur. Jesus said no man knows the day or the hour; only God the Father knows. And God, in his mercy, is waiting for more souls to repent. He is long-suffering and ever-patient, and with every day he waits, more people have an opportunity to accept the truth of who the Nazarene was and what he came to do."

I sat very still. "So—you are telling me . . . what?"

Asher didn't miss a beat. "I believe that in every generation Satan prepares a man who will rise to world power if the Rapture occurs. Once the believers are delivered, Satan will not want to waste a moment. He will have his man ready, and that man, *the Antichrist,* will step onto the world's stage and begin to implement Satan's agenda. By that time, his heart will be hardened, his mind resolute, and his spirit owned by *il diavolo.*"

I didn't need my Italian-English dictionary to know he was talking about the devil. There was a blank moment when my head swarmed with words, and then my uppermost thought slipped out: "Why did I ever hire you?"

—

Asher smiled and squeezed my hand. "Because God knew you would become my ally. Because I will need help to confront Santos Justus. Because, you see, I need time alone with him to share the good news of Jesus Christ. If I do not, his path could be set. Reverend Synn will never tell him, for he does not understand the gospel himself. Signora Casale will never tell him, nor will Rico Triccoli. They are too busy working to further Justus's power, and they tell him only what he wants to hear."

"Asher"— I firmly pulled my hand free of his—"I can't let you harass Justus. First of all, he's not going to believe your story—I don't believe it myself. Second, I'm sure he's quite happy in his religion, whatever it is. And third, politics and religion don't mix. Why do you think the Holy See is a separate country?"

Asher leaned back and gave an irritable tug at his sleeve. "What I plan to do is not *harassment*. It is an act of mercy, for the world and for Justus himself."

"I just don't see how—"

"What would have happened," Asher interrupted, visibly trembling with intensity, "if someone had confronted Adolf Hitler when he was a young and impressionable child? What if someone had convinced him that the Jewish nation is beloved of God and that Christianity means love in action, not genocide?"

"I suppose—" My voice faltered before his steady gaze. "I suppose history would be changed."

Asher nodded. "Of course it would. And the lives of more than six million innocent people would have continued, populating today's world with their children and grandchildren and great-grandchildren." He leaned forward again as a glazed look of despair spread over his face. "I tried to reach *der Führer.* By the time I recognized him as the candidate for that generation, the security around him was tight. I had to join the SS in an attempt to reach him. In '34, by the time Hitler was ruling as absolute dictator, I got close enough to speak with him, but he laughed in my face when I mentioned Christ's love."

I absorbed this unbelievable news in silence, then drew a deep breath: "You worked for Hitler."

He answered with an impersonal nod. "In the press office, but only for a short time. Over my lifetimes I have borne witness of the gospel to scores of would-be antichrists. With the Holy Scriptures as my guide, I have testified of Christ before Richard II in England, Cosmo Medici of Florence, and Henry VIII. For a while I believed Philip II of Spain would certainly be the one to do Satan's bidding after the departure of the believers, for he and the bloody Inquisition he inherited strove to mold Spain into a society marked by religious unity and social conformity—a one-world system beginning in Spain."

He spread his hands, palms upward, a sure sign of sincerity.

"In the seventeenth century, I journeyed back to England to bear witness to Oliver Cromwell, who killed a king, ended the monarchy, and created a dictatorship more absolute than any kingdom. I was nearly convinced he would be the Antichrist when in 1653 he met with Rabbi Menassah Ben-Israel to discuss the readmission of Jews to Britain—they had been expelled in 1290. Cromwell met many of the criteria—he was a soldier, he had divided the British Isles into six military commands, and he seemed determined to crush his people, going so far as to outlaw dramatic performances, horse races, and even stained-glass windows. He was nothing short of a tyrant, but he, too, met his end before the end of time.

"Napoleon rose as the next obvious candidate. Though he was a French subject, he was born of an Italian family in Corsica, thus springing from the people of ancient Rome. He, too, was a military man and a most ambitious soldier. He used the advances gained during the

—

French Revolution to promote himself, then systematically limited the freedoms the French people had gained, violating the liberty of speech and the press. After he came to power, the number of newspapers in France fell from seventy-three to four. His laws denied equality to women and reinstituted slavery, which had been abolished during the Revolution. In the name of freedom he set out to conquer Europe, but he desired to increase his power above all else. Like most men of authority, he played at religion, courting church leaders in public and living for pleasure in private. I did not think I would ever be allowed to see him, but finally I found a way . . . and Napoleon joined the ranks of those who would not listen.

"When Napoleon died, I returned to Italy and discovered Count Camillo Benso di Cavour, prime minister of Sardinia-Piedmont and Italy. During his first tenure in the Piedmontese cabinet in 1851, he secured the portfolios of Agriculture, Navy, and Finance." Asher shifted his position and lifted a brow. "Can you see why that was significant?"

I nodded slowly, a little amazed that I could follow his thoughts. "Three divisions of government . . . three heads. He took over three heads."

Asher's face lit with a sudden smile. "Exactly. I was certain Cavour would be the one. He, too, hungered for authority, and he grasped the reins of power tightly. He believed the main occupation of a ruler should be the art of war, and he accomplished the near impossible—the unification of Italy—through force. Like the Scripture foretells, Cavour was a man of cunning and persuasion, orchestrating 'spontaneous' riots in the Italian duchies. He achieved power through deceit, conquest, and broken promises, but I was never able to penetrate his inner circle. He died in 1861, at the relatively young age of fifty-one."

Asher rubbed a hand over his face, then sighed heavily. "With every decade of the nineteenth century, a new candidate for antichrist seemed to arise. Lenin ruled in Russia, Leopold II in Belgium, and Napoleon III in France. Wilhelm II, who believed he ruled by the grace of God, came to power in Germany. He was also enamored of the military, loving uniforms so much that he changed his own several times a day. Looking far beyond the boundaries of Germany, he established a 'world policy,' creating a framework of defensive alliances and promising to come to the aid of his allied countries. He was partly responsible for the beginning of World War I and stepped down only when it became clear Germany and her allies could not win. Shortly after his abdication, the Social Democrats proclaimed the existence of the German Republic.

"In the twentieth century, I watched Khrushchev, Gorbachev, and Pierre Laval in France. *Time* magazine proclaimed Laval 'Man of the Year' in 1931, but he worked hand in hand with Hitler during the Nazi occupation of France, exporting thousands of Jews to German extermination camps. That was significant, for anti-Semitism will be another characteristic of the Antichrist."

A smile tugged at Asher's lips. "For a long time I studied Ronald Reagan. I was about to take a trip to America but changed my mind when I learned more about him. He was neither ambitious nor military."

I couldn't stop a burst of laughter. "Why in the world would you suspect Reagan of being the Antichrist?"

A faintly mischievous look entered Asher's eyes. "His name—Ronald Wilson Reagan. There are six letters in each name—six-six-six. The Bible says the number of the beast is the number of a man, and that number is six-six-six."

A shiver of panic ran through me as I mentally counted the letters in Santos Justus's name. Six letters in the first name and the last, but the middle—

I leaned back and grinned in a surge of confidence. "If that's true, you're wrong about Justus. I've heard that his middle name is David, and that's only five letters."

"His middle name," Asher responded, his voice dissolving into a thready whisper, "is spelled the Italian way—with an *e* on the end. So that's six letters—Santos Davide Justus."

The train rolled through a tunnel, blanketing our compartment with a roaring wall of sound. I took advantage of the noise to try corral my thoughts, but nothing in Asher's story made logical sense. *Actually, it makes perfect sense,* some other part of my brain argued, *but none of it is possible.* Even if everything he told me was true, none of it could have happened. People didn't live for two thousand years without aging. End of discussion.

We shot out of the tunnel and settled back into the gentle rhythm of the rails. The dense darkness outside the train made me feel as though we were moving through a sea of India ink. Like characters in a science-fiction novel, complete with the arch-villain of fantasy, we shot toward our destination and our destiny . . .

"We'll be arriving at the station soon." Asher straightened in his seat and leaned toward me, his deep-set eyes gleaming. "Tomorrow you'll be expected to give a full report to Justus. Let me come with you, Claudia. Let tomorrow be the day when I tell him it's not too late. This man I found early; there is still time to turn his heart toward the Savior."

I crossed my arms over my chest. "Asher, I can't do that."

He bit his lip, signaling that his mood was shifting toward irritation, but I pushed on. "Even if I did get you in to see him, what do you think he will do? Do you think he'll just drop to his knees and repent? I don't think Il Presidente sees himself as a bad man, Asher. You're asking him to turn from a horrible future he doesn't believe in toward a God he sees as responsible for much of the world's struggle and strife. And think of the risks! You could lose your job. You *would* lose your job.

—

And then he'd turn on me. Justus has the power to harm my reputation on an international level, don't you understand that?"

Unspoken pain glowed in his eyes when he looked at me. "Then I'll wait," he said, leaning back in his seat. He crossed his arms and turned to look out the window again. The marks of grief were clear, etched in the lines beside his mouth and eyes, thrown into shadow by the overhead lamp. "I'll wait until you believe . . . or I will find another way to reach him. Because it is important, Claudia. It is what I must do. It's my task."

"I'm tired, Asher. I think I'll try to get some sleep." I reached up and turned off the dim lamp, then turned away from the distressing sight of him at the window.

Where was Kurt when I needed him? I felt reasonably sure he had never encountered anything like this in his practice. As far as I could tell, Asher suffered from only one delusion, but he believed it with utter resoluteness.

What should I do? I didn't think I could talk Asher out of his fascination with Justus—his argument was so persuasive he had nearly convinced *me* that Justus could be the Antichrist. Perhaps I could distract him. If I could convince him that the American president presented an equally valid prospect for a future puppet of Satan, perhaps I could persuade him to join me when I went back to New York. Once there, Asher could get professional psychological help. He was far too charming and intelligent a man to be allowed to waste his gifts in delusion . . .

I turned slightly and opened one eye, peeking at him. He had curled his tall frame in the chair, but his eyes were open and fixed on the black horizon beyond the window.

What a novelist he would make! Each historical name he had so casually rattled off would make a book in itself. In his delusion he had

—

cast himself as a modern Indiana Jones who always managed to survive despite overwhelming odds.

"By the way," I whispered through the semi darkness, "how did you escape from all those encounters with dictators? I can't imagine any of them hearing your story and then just letting you go."

"I didn't always escape." A small grimace of pain rippled across his face. "A few times I was imprisoned and beaten, once I was exiled. Most often, however, I was executed."

I opened my mouth, then quietly closed it again. For a few moments his delusion had almost seemed minor.

"Of course you were," I murmured, then turned to snuggle into the cushions and sleep.

Twenty-two

Asher was right. I was summoned to Justus's office the next morning, where I gave him my report. I needn't have bothered. From the calm, knowing look in his eyes I gathered he had already heard from his operatives in Brussels. He listened to me merely out of politeness, or perhaps he wanted to test the truthfulness of the thin man and his cohorts.

When I had finished, Justus thanked me, then stood and came around from behind his desk. "I am told you are anxious to get back to New York," he said, his dark eyes creasing in an expression of admiration. "I understand, of course, but we would like you to remain with us for at least another two or three months. In the very near future we plan to establish an office in Brussels, and we will need to hire more staff. I'm sure I don't have to tell you that they must be the sharpest, most excellent people available."

"My office in New York," I began, but Justus cut me off with an uplifted hand. He sank onto the edge of his desk, then crossed his arms and gave me a sympathetic upper smile. "I was sorry to hear about your associate, and I know it won't be easy to go home and pick up the pieces. That's why I think you should remain in Rome for a while. My people are fond of you, and your work is respected. If you remain, signorina, I could help you find enough work in the international arena that you may never have to go back to New York." He arched a brow. "Would work of an international scope suit you? I should think that working for peace would be far more appealing than jury consulting for murderous senators who want to escape justice."

For an instant I wondered if he had been reading my thoughts and knew about my vow to work for more noble causes. But had I been hard of hearing, I could not have missed the note of sarcasm in his voice, and his cynicism brought up my defenses. "My work in the States has merit, Il Presidente. Every citizen is entitled to a fair defense."

"But is every citizen entitled to buy his way out of the system? I am well acquainted with the details of your last case. Senator Mitchell hired the best defense lawyer he could find, and that lawyer hired you, the best jury consultant in the business. You practically read the jurors' minds during voir dire. You knew the verdict weeks before the jury did. Is that not unfair? Can you honestly tell me Senator Mitchell did not buy himself an acquittal?"

His voice was dusty and nearly as deep as the tide of guilt that threatened to pull me under. I sat in silence under his penetrating gaze, recognizing the truth in his words. We had perfected the art of jury selection, and people of wealth could buy better lawyers than the average man on the street. The poor fared worst of all. All too often, court-appointed public defenders were recent law school graduates, young men and women who didn't have the connections or where-withal to land a spot in a choice firm . . .

"We'd make it worth your while to remain in Rome," Justus said, his voice low and seductive. "What are we paying you now—$5,000 per week? We could double that if you'll agree to remain until the Belgium office is fully staffed."

"Would I have to work in Brussels?"

"No. All prospective staff will go through the concorso here. We just want you to continue doing what you do so well."

—

I drew a deep breath and lowered my gaze, taking advantage of the quiet to wrestle with my reservations. Now that I stood on the brink of a decision, I had to admit that among my swirling emotions was a sense of reluctance to return to New York. Without Rory, I'd be lost in a sea of scribbled telephone messages and unpaid bills. I'd already been away seven weeks, and I had absolutely no idea what currents were running through the Manhattan legal system. I did know Elaine Dawson had moved in during my absence, and if I went back now, at the start of her new trial, I'd be fighting a turf war without an assistant and without clients.

Why not remain in Rome for a few more months? I had been nervous about the clandestine trip to Brussels, but Justus had been right—we hadn't encountered even a hint of danger. Last night I had been quite willing to believe that Justus's ambition was rooted in evil, but that belief had been fueled by the darkness and Asher's mystical stories of world tyrants. Asher's proclamation that he suffered through numerous executions broke the spell that nearly captivated me.

Looking up at my employer, I saw a remarkable man sitting on the edge of his desk, a charming, optimistic politician who wanted peace for the world. Nothing more. Nothing less.

My reservations could not prevail against double pay and two additional months of job security. "I wouldn't want to do anything else like the job in Belgium." I met Justus's gaze without flinching. "I was nervous the entire time. It felt . . . not right somehow."

"You will not have to do anything that causes you distress." Justus laced his hands together. "We want you to be happy."

"Then . . . I will stay." I smiled and gave him a nod. "I'll stay through January, but then I really must get home. My sister is expecting a baby at the end of December, and I've promised to get home as soon as I can."

—

Laugh lines radiated from the corners of Justus's eyes as he chuckled. "I have a sister myself. And though I've never been a parent, she has ten children who keep me on my toes. I cannot visit on a Saturday night without the little ones hanging from my neck and demanding to know what sort of presents I have brought them."

Something in my heart lifted as I stood to leave. Justus had never mentioned his family, and for the first time I felt I had been allowed to glimpse the man behind the polished mask he wore almost constantly. Perhaps I had finally won his trust.

He walked me to the door, and just before leaving I turned to face him. "I want you to know, sir, that I have really enjoyed my time here. You have attracted the most wonderful people to Global Union." I paused, wondering if I should tell him about Asher Genzano. If the world ever learned that one of the Global Union employees suffered from a rather creative delusion, at least Justus could say I had warned him.

I took a breath, ready to speak, but Justus had opened the door and was beckoning to Reverend Synn, who stood outside in the foyer. He was no longer looking at or listening to me; the moment of camaraderie had passed.

"Buon giorno, signor," I murmured politely, then moved out of the way.

Alone in my office, I bounced the rubber tip of my pencil against the desk while staring at the telephone. Should I call Kurt? A cynical voice in my brain kept telling me I should call an Italian psychologist, and fast, because Asher's delusion was more than slightly abnormal. But I knew enough about people, and about Asher, to feel reasonably sure he wasn't dangerous. I had also grown fond of him and couldn't bear the thought of hurting or embarrassing him.

I pressed my lips together and shifted my gaze to the window, recalling the many sorts of people I had seen on the streets of Rome—ragged beggars and Gypsies and religious pilgrims traversing St. Peter's Square on their knees. In the past few weeks I had encountered homeless men who talked to themselves and religious penitents who flogged themselves in the shadows, of the Vatican walls. Who could say Asher was more disturbed than any of them? He had a home, he held a job, and he knew more about everything than I knew about anything.

My hand moved toward the phone, curled around the receiver, and stopped. Kurt would be alarmed if I shared Asher's entire story. He'd say I owed it to Global Union to have a potentially dangerous employee committed. I could almost hear him: *A man who says he's been executed by world tyrants? Good grief, Claudia, you sat there and encouraged that nonsense? You're not a psychologist. Get the man to a doctor.*

But the story didn't seem like nonsense when Asher told it. I haven't had much experience with the mentally ill, but I saw nothing in his demeanor to indicate that he was telling me anything but the truth—no revealing tics, no touching his nose or ears or other disguising gestures. He spoke honestly and openly, with a clear voice and direct eye contact. I doubted whether even a habitual liar could have maintained as perfect an illusion of honesty.

Well. I lifted my hand from the phone and picked up my notebook. There was more than one way to prove the truth, and I believed in Asher's innate sense of reason. Last night he had rattled off a long list of names and dates and places, and after arriving home I had jotted down as many of them as I could remember. If I could confront him with proof that just one of his supposed "recollections" was false, perhaps I could place a solid dent in his delusion. After all, Kurt had urged me to present Asher with facts.

With a sense of purpose I hadn't felt in days, I scooped my notebook off the desk and walked to the elevator, then pushed the button for the second floor. Monsieur and Madame Curvier had made good progress organizing the library's archived files, I'd heard, and I thought they might be able to give me some information. After all, they were French, as were several of Asher's suspected antichrists . . .

The elevator dinged softly, and I stepped onto the second floor, then pushed my way through the double glass door that led to the archives. Dr. Millard Curvier sat on a stool facing the door, a folder in his hand. He lifted his head when I came in. Not knowing any sign language, I smiled and wriggled my fingers in a wave, then pointed toward the door that led to the doctors' private offices. "Your wife?" I said, feeling slightly silly as I exaggerated the movement of my lips. I didn't speak sign language, but he most certainly didn't lipread English, so my attempt to communicate was laughable, at best.

He pointed to the door, either intuiting what I meant or resorting to a habitual gesture for guests. I hurried forward and called out, "Dr. Curvier?"

I found Patrice seated at her desk. She looked up from a stack of typed pages when I came in, then pulled her glasses down her nose. "Oui? Can I help you?"

"I hope so." I glanced at my notebook, not certain where to start. "I'm searching for some information on dictators . . . particularly European dictators. I thought there might be something in the files about Hitler, Wilhelm II of Germany, or even Napoleon."

"Oui, the Communists kept files on everybody, living and dead." She pushed her glasses back as she stood and moved past me. "We have lists; we have biographical files; we have photographs. We have a file on Tito of Yugoslavia thirty centimeters thick."

"Really?" I mentally cross-checked the name against my list and didn't find a match.

I followed her to a long bank of filing cabinets that traversed the room. Fortunately, each cabinet was only four feet high, which made for a convenient reading height when files were spread over the solid surface. Mounds of paper lay scattered across the top of the cabinets, some pages wrapped in folders, others spread out like a crazy quilt, punctuated here and there with grainy black-and-white photographs.

"Hitler is there, file fifteen, third drawer," she said, pointing to a cabinet near the center of the room. "But we have scarcely begun to archive all the information about him. His troops occupied Rome, you know, after Mussolini's fall. They were hated. In 1944, someone set off a bomb near a marching column of SS police in the center of Rome and 31 Germans died. In retaliation, Hitler ordered 335 Italian hostages shot by the Gestapo on the old Ardeatine Road. His pride demanded vengeance." She paused. "In whom else were you interested?"

I glanced at my list, searching for one of the more obscure names. "Laval, from France?"

"*Vous plaisantez!* I remember hearing about him. He was a devil." She walked away, muttering about the man who had controlled France for Hitler, and I stopped in front of file cabinet number fifteen. A pile of black-and-white photographs covered the cabinet, and I found myself studying the first one, a shot of Hitler sitting in an open car, his eyes fixed upon the road before him, a bevy of SS men clustered around the vehicle like obedient priests around a stern-faced demigod.

I picked up the photograph and ran my finger over the face of the man who sent millions of people to their death. Somehow, in the light of Hitler's unspeakable deeds, Asher's story about a man doing the work of the devil did not seem so ludicrous. A man would almost have to be possessed by the spirit of pure evil to send babies and their mothers into the ovens . . .

—

I set the photograph aside and stared at another. The camera placed Hitler front and center, as always, but in this photo he posed at the bottom of what looked like an outdoor staircase. His men, three solid rows of somber-looking soldiers in dark uniforms, stood around and behind him, each wearing an expression of resolute determination.

I brought the photograph closer to my face and searched each man's face for some sign of conscience. People tended to reveal a lot about themselves even in photographs, but I could not detect a single derivation from the stiff, focused status quo. Not a man's arm hung bent; not a single chin was lifted in a disobedient wayward glance. Every eye was focused upon the camera, every profile turned at the proper angle to favor the Führer who had become the center of their universe . . .

I was about to set the photograph aside when a memorable pair of dark eyes caught my attention. I knew the man standing in the second row, scarcely six feet from Adolf Hitler.

My heart began to pound like a kettledrum as my fingertip traced the image of Asher Genzano.

Twenty-three

Tired and irritable after a nearly sleepless night, I stood outside the American Academy Library and wondered if Kurt would approve of my plan. After finding Asher's face in the Nazi photo, I had silently carried my questions and bewilderment back to my apartment, where I tossed and turned throughout the hours of darkness. By the time daylight at last fringed the blinds, I had formulated a two-pronged plan—first, I would go to the library and look up references to this Wandering Jew character, the better to prove to Asher that he couldn't possibly be a living legend, then I would return to Global Union headquarters and search for information that might explain how a man who looked exactly like the current Asher Genzano came to be employed in Hitler's army. *Perhaps*, my tired brain told me, *the man in the photograph is one of Asher's relatives.* Even if that was the case, I doubted that Santos Justus would welcome the news that one of his employees was related to a Nazi war criminal.

I crossed the Via Angelo Masina in a flood of pedestrians, then entered the library, one of the few in Rome that catered to English-speaking residents. Accustomed to the large, expansive stacks of the New York Public Library, this building seemed small and crowded. A gate prevented entrance to the large hall where the books were shelved. A small woman sat behind a dark wooden desk next to the gate, her pink scalp glowing through a tight white perm like a warning.

"Buon giorno," I said, giving her the brightest smile I could muster after a sleepless night. "*Parla inglese?*"

She made a faint moue of distaste, then switched to English. "How may I help you?"

I placed my hands on the railing and cast a covetous glance toward the books on the shelves behind her. "I'm searching for information about the man called the Wandering Jew. I don't have a library card, but perhaps I could just look at a few materials here in the library."

Her mouth took on an unpleasant twist. "Signorina, we do things differently here. In Italy, you do not *join* a library, you *gain access* to it. And the extent of your access depends upon whether or not you have a sponsor to support your work."

Momentarily speechless with surprise, I gaped at the woman.

"You must go to the *Ufficio Orientamento* and present your passport or other official identification, then you'll be given a *permesso di entrata* for however long we estimate your work will require. If you want access to rare books or *manoscritti*—"

I flagged her to a halt, afraid she had somehow moved on to the discussion of pasta without answering my question. "Wait, please. I must go where to get what? And what are *manoscritti?*"

"Manuscripts." Her brows drew downward in a frown. "You must go to the admissions office and get an entrance pass before you will be allowed access to the library. And once you have gained access, you will need help from one of the *bibliotecari*. We do not have computerized card catalogs, and only our *bibliotecari* understand the filing system."

She had lost me again, but by the second mention of the b-word I deduced her meaning: *Bibliotecari* were librarians, and apparently I wouldn't get anywhere without one. I wouldn't even get through the gate without some sort of entrance pass.

—

I smiled and struggled to maintain control of my temper. Most Italians I met were polite, if a little relaxed and phlegmatic, but this woman had definitely risen on the wrong side of the bed. "Thank you for your help." I returned her icy smile in full measure. "I'll be back."

Two hours later, armed with my Global Union identity card and a letter from Reverend Synn—I had vaguely explained that I was working on a research project—I approached the library's admissions office. It took twenty minutes for them to examine my ID and fill out a form that gave me permission to pass the guarded wooden gate, but by noon I found myself standing before the library's white-haired watch poodle again.

"Here is my permesso di entrata," I said, handing her the library form, "and I also have a letter from Darien Synn of Global Union. He asks that you allow me to search through the library this week."

She took both documents, scanned them, then gave me a frosty, tight-lipped smile. After handing the documents back to me, she picked up the receiver of the heavy black telephone on her desk and murmured something in Italian. A moment later a younger woman, this one soft and smiling, came up to the gate and invited me in. Upon her fuzzy sweater she wore a nameplate that told me her name was Carmela. "How may we help you?" she asked, speaking perfect English as she opened the swinging gate.

"I'm researching the legend of the Wandering Jew," I answered, happily moving into the forbidden territory. "I'd be interested in anything you have on the subject, no matter how old."

Carmela and I spent the rest of the afternoon playing find the needle in the haystack. The watch poodle wasn't kidding when she told me only librarians could understand the cataloging system, and Carmela often seemed as baffled as I by the sprawling cursive script on the file cards. In one section of the library, bound volumes of

—

257

handwritten pages functioned as a catalog. On its pages the books were organized *per autore* (author), *per soggetto* (subject), and *per titolo* (title).

I've always loved libraries, and I can find practically anything in the New York Public Library within minutes. But in Rome, for some mysterious reason only librarians are allowed to access the stacks. When in the handwritten catalog I found a book I wanted to examine, I had to fill out a *modulo* on which I wrote the call number, title, publication place, and date. I then had to give the modulo to Carmela, who gave me a receipt and went to search for the book. More than once she returned after a lengthy search, only to tell me the book was out on loan or *irreperibile*—impossible to find.

By the end of the first day, I wondered why the Romans, who profess admiration of many American institutions, had not thought to visit an American library.

By the end of the second day, I was convinced the Romans had instituted their library system solely to encourage the ownership of *household* libraries.

As I neared the end of the third day, I was ready to commit arson upon the American Academy Library so that Carmela and the watch poodle could have a new and efficient one.

I was nearly ready to give up for another day when Carmela approached and placed a heavy, leather-bound volume on the catalog desk. "I found this," she said, a blush of pleasure tinting her cheeks. "It seems quite complete. Such a pity the book has been damaged."

The book was titled *The Legend of the Wandering Jew,* and the author's name was all but obscured by a water stain on the front cover. I thanked Carmela, then carried the book to the reading room where I could devour whatever information it held.

The scents of mold and earth and leather rose from the pages as I

—

cracked open the book and scanned the copyright page. The publication date was 1942. In the eternal scheme of things, this work was fairly recent.

I smoothed the yellowed first page and began to read:

The Legend of the Wandering Jew is an amalgamation of the traditions of Malchus and St. John. Malchus is identified in John 18:4–10 as the servant of the high priest—the unfortunate soul who lost his ear in the face of Peter's eagerness to defend the Savior in the Garden of Gethsemane. Later the apostle John tells us that a servant of the high priest struck Jesus with the palm of his hand (18:20–22). Though we cannot be certain of the abuser's identity, he has traditionally been identified as Malchus. One fact is certain: a man struck Jesus at his trial, and in the following years those who repeated the story felt such a blasphemous act deserved a suitably horrible punishment—the curse of immortality.

Consider now the Legend of St. John, which has its roots in Matthew 16:28 and John 21:20–22. In the Matthew passage, Christ said, "Verily I say unto you, There be some standing here, which shall not taste of death, till they see the Son of man coming in his kingdom." Theologians have long debated what Jesus meant, but many people of Jesus' day thought the Savior meant to honor John with the *gift* of immortality.

According to tradition, John the dearly beloved disciple did not die either in Ephesus, where he worked after Christ's ascension, or on Patmos, where he spent time in exile. According to the Legend of St. John, the disciple's grave was opened after his supposed death, but his body had mysteriously disappeared. Proponents of the legend say John is a wanderer and a prophet, still waiting for the day of Christ's second coming.

These two ideas—the story of John and the tale of Malchus—

—

met and married, bringing forth the Legend of the Wandering Jew. Throughout history, the legend has served as a vehicle for anti-Semitism, though some early versions maintain that the Wanderer was not Jewish, but Roman.

The legend first appeared shortly after A.D. 1200, when a Latin chronicle recorded the Wanderer's appearance in Armenia. The old man, who called himself Joseph, told the people of that city that he had been a Roman porter in the house of Pilate. There he witnessed the "passion of the Lord" and drove the Savior away with a blow and wicked words. The Lord reportedly answered him, "I go, and you will await me till I come again."

The Wanderer is said to wear sandals with seven holes in the bottom of each shoe. The holes form two lines, horizontal and vertical, so that the Wanderer leaves the imprint of the cross with every footstep. Several versions of the legend recount his trek across blazing desert sands, imprinting the cross upon the dunes. In some versions he is called Joseph, in others Cartaphilus or Ahasuerus. In a German legend, he is called John Buttadaeus, whose appearance is recorded in the thirteenth, fifteenth, and sixteenth centuries. John Buttadaeus's last recorded appearance was in Brussels in 1774.

Paul von Eitzen, Bishop of Schleswig, was said to have encountered the Wandering Jew in Hamburg in 1542. During his interview with the Wanderer he learned the man's name was Ahasuerus. A shoemaker in Jerusalem, Ahasuerus had cried out in anger when Jesus, carrying his cross, stopped to rest against the wall of Ahasuerus's house. Jesus replied, "I will stand and rest, but you must walk." Ahasuerus reportedly felt compelled to follow Jesus and witness his execution, then he left Jerusalem to wander about the world, miserably but reverently providing a witness to Christ's power and teaching.

Throughout countless generations, the Legend of the Wandering Jew has been retold and embellished. The Wanderer has, on occasion, represented the futility of questing for the fountain of youth and personified the wandering nation of Israel. He has embodied world-weariness and nostalgia and served as a symbol of the entire human race. His tale has been set in ancient times and contemporary; a 1940 novel by Nelson Bond even launched him into outer space.

Though within the following pages I will attempt to give as complete a rendering of the legend as possible, space will not permit me to describe all the different versions of the legend. In some stories he ages until he reaches one hundred years, then he falls asleep and awakens as a thirty-year-old. In nearly all stories he refuses gifts and speaks of the coming of the Lord, telling his tale with great sorrow and repentance. In some stories he is a shoemaker, in others a servant. He is supposed to have visited several of the crowned heads of Europe, impressing them all with his knowledge of the events surrounding Christ's crucifixion. In 1604 he was reportedly seen in France; he visited Saxony in 1603–4 and spoke with several noblemen there. His story has blossomed in poetry and song; his fame has spread throughout Europe and the Western world.

He is as much a man for our time as he is a man for the ages.

Looking up from the book, I found that my brain had become a lightning rod for ideas. Was it possible that Asher had read this book, or one like it, and adopted the role of the Wandering Jew for himself? He certainly knew the story of Ahasuerus; he had recited it for me.

And he said he was an orphan. In seeking his identity, why couldn't he have latched onto this persona of the Wanderer? Without parents to give him the foundation of a family, he could easily have looked elsewhere for emotional and psychological support. And in a city like Rome, where the stones of the streets themselves attest to the elegance of generations past, who wouldn't want to be known as "a man for the ages"?

I flipped through the following pages, skimming stories and poetry and supposed eyewitness accounts of encounters with the man called "the eternal wanderer" or the Wandering Jew. One stanza of a seventeenth-century poem caught my eye:

Desiring still to be dissolv'd, and yield his mortal breath;
But as the Lord had thus decreed, he shall not yet see death.
For neither looks he Old or Young, but as he did those times
When Christ did suffer on the Cross, for mortal sinners' crimes . . .
"If thou had'st seen grim Death," said he, "as these mine eyes have done,
Ten thousand thousand times, would ye his Torments think upon;
And suffer for His sake all pains, all torments, and all woes."
These are his words, and this his Life, where'er he comes and goes.

Something in my heart constricted as I read the words *for neither looks he Old or Young*. Asher looked exactly the same today as he did in the photograph taken with Adolf Hitler . . . if that was Asher in the photograph.

Shaking my head, I dismissed the possibility, then turned the page and found myself staring at a photograph of a man with swarthy features, narrow eyes, and a dark goatee. The caption told me the black-and-white photo was from a 1933 film about the Wandering Jew, but the fierce-looking man in the picture bore little resemblance to Asher Genzano.

Smiling at the moviemaker's caricature of the villainous wanderer, I turned the page, then froze, my heart beating hard enough to be heard a yard away. Two photos faced me, one on each page, and each portrayed an ancient image. The first featured a woodcutting titled "The Wanderer on the Road," and though the man in the primitive cutting could have been anyone, there was something in the Wanderer's posture that reminded me of my delusional friend. The slim body and long hands were Asher's, as were the broad shoulders and the unique way his hair curled over his forehead . . .

The second photo slammed into my consciousness with all the delicacy of a charging bull. I stared at a marble statue sculpted in the tradition of Michelangelo. The stunning bust revealed a man with broad shoulders, a cleft chin, and wide white eyes that seemed to gaze upon a world filled with tragedy and sorrow. The chin was Asher's, as was the jaw; the nose could have belonged to no one else. The sculptor had caught every detail of the face I had studied for hours, even the cowlick that forced the curl over his left brow to stand slightly apart from the others.

Feeling as though I moved in slow motion, I lowered my hands to my lap, wiped my damp palms on my skirt, and sent my thoughts scrambling for a reasonable explanation. Could this image be the result of some sort of genetic fluke that resulted in identical men born hundreds of years apart? Why not? After all, how many combinations of eyes and nose and mouth and forehead could the human body fashion? Sooner or later, nature was bound to duplicate a creation. This statue looked like Asher, but it was an eerie coincidence, period. Perhaps Asher Genzano had passed a lazy summer afternoon looking at this book and he noticed the resemblance himself. Perhaps he had been an impressionable youth at the time. His fantasies and an unstable family situation rendered him susceptible to suggestion, leading him over the years to believe he was this eternal wanderer . . .

Grasping for an answer, I read the caption beneath the photograph.

—

According to the author, the bust had been sculpted between 1501 and 1505. Some art experts claimed Michelangelo himself had carved the sculpture, but others doubted it, since his marble *David* was created at the same time. One odd peculiarity, the caption noted, was a small initial chiseled into the base of the bust, a tiny letter A.

I felt a cold hand pass down my spine. A—for Asher. Or Ahasuerus.

I shivered and drew the edges of my sweater together as a horrifying realization washed over me. My suppositions and wild conjectures were more far-fetched than the story Asher had related. Why was I more willing to give credence to random genetic coincidence than to the man who asked nothing of me but belief? Believing that the man who posed for this marble bust was Asher's genetic duplicate required far more faith than accepting the obvious—I was staring at a bust of Asher himself.

I dredged that admission from a place far beyond logic and reason, and the resulting flood of relief surprised me. With sudden clarity I understood that I *wanted* to believe Asher. Despite my fears and misgivings, he had done nothing to hurt my standing at Global Union, and he had proved himself capable, honorable, trustworthy . . . and a good friend. I liked him. Why, then, couldn't I accept his story?

"Because men don't live forever." I whispered the words, rubbing my cold hands together as I stared at the photo of the marble bust. "Because to believe Asher, I would have to believe in God and curses and eternal punishment. And I don't believe in any of those things."

Sighing heavily, I closed the book, then stood and took it back to the librarians' desk. I had spent three days searching for the truth, and my head now bulged with more questions than when I started. But at least I knew where to go next—I needed to speak to a minister, and I knew right where to find one.

TWENTY-FOUR

I PAUSED OUTSIDE REVEREND SYNN'S DOOR, THEN QUIETLY KNOCKED. When I heard him call, I turned the knob and stepped inside. "Il Direttore, I hate to bother you—"

"Nonsense, signorina, come in, please." Synn had been leaning back in his chair with a book on his lap, but at my approach he closed the book and leaned forward, a welcoming smile on his face. "I have been wondering about your research project. I have scarcely seen you these last few days."

"I've been very busy." I sank into the padded guest chair in front of his desk, then gave him an uncertain smile. "I've been a little concerned about one of our employees and had to do some background research before I approached anyone. And now, if you have the time to spare, I have a few questions to ask you."

"I shall always have time for a lovely signorina." A relaxed smile played at the corners of his mouth, and I felt some of my uneasiness begin to melt away.

"If I may speak of a confidential matter," I lowered my voice, "I'd rather this not go any further, if you don't mind. The employee in question has never done anything to jeopardize his work, and thus far he has been valuable to Global Union. But his beliefs are a bit unsettling, and I thought I'd ask you about them."

Synn's smile vanished as he raised his eyes to my face in an oddly keen, swift look. "But of course, I will keep your concerns to myself . . . unless you convince me there is cause for alarm."

"There is no cause—at present. I just want to make certain there is no reason for alarm in the future."

Synn nodded, his gaze never leaving my face.

"One of our employees," I began, averting my eyes lest he read Asher's name there, "is very religious. He believes, I think, every word written in the Bible and clings to it as if it were as fresh as the morning newspaper. He has interpreted certain portions of the Bible as predictions, and he believes a terrifically evil person will rise in the last days."

Synn drew his lips into a tight smile. "You are speaking of the Antichrist. It is an old prophecy and common in many cultures."

I smiled in relief, grateful that I had not been the first to say the word. "Yes—that's what he called it, the Antichrist. In any case, he is quite serious in his belief that this antichrist will rise soon . . . and possibly from our own organization."

Synn's brow wrinkled and something moved in his eyes. I felt an instant's panic, then he smiled, his blue eyes glowing with humor. "*The* Antichrist—coming from among us? How delightful! I shall have to tell Santos. He'll be amazed anyone could think such a thing."

I felt an unwelcome blush creep onto my cheeks. "Please, no. This is quite confidential."

Synn's smile deepened into genuine laughter, and no amount of protest from me could stem his hilarity. He giggled, his bulk shaking his chair, until tears ran down his round cheeks. I watched, perplexed and helpless, until he palmed the wetness from his face and looked at me with streaming eyes. "All right." His voice wavered. "I'll keep the story to myself . . . at least until Santos and I need a good laugh."

I raked my hand through my hair, torn between being relieved that he'd found the idea hilarious and concerned that Asher was right. Synn's response was overblown, and his exaggerated reaction might have been intended to cover embarrassment or discomfort.

"Reverend Synn"—I shifted in my chair to try a new tack—"do you believe the Bible contains prophecies that will come true in the future?"

"Ah, signorina." He wiped more water from his eyes, then took a deep breath. "Of course the Bible is a holy book, and holy books are always relevant. It contains truth, certainly. It speaks wisdom and comfort to millions of people who have nothing else to guide them. But is it a crystal ball with which we can foretell the future? Definitely not. We are to live by faith, and faith does not rely upon fortune-telling and superstition."

Listening intently, I nodded.

"You see, signorina, enlightenment must come from within a man or woman. When we look for God and giftedness in ourselves, we invariably find it. Jesus himself said, 'Seek, and you shall find. Knock, and it shall be opened to you. You have not because you ask not, because you seek not.'"

The words sounded familiar, so I nodded again. "I'm sure you're right," I murmured, looking at my hands as a wave of guilt flooded my cheeks. "I ought to know more about these things, but I stopped going to church when I was eleven or twelve. I remember so little of what I learned as a child."

"That's the beauty of Holy Scripture—it remains with us, like a treasure in our hearts. And if you will look within, Claudia, you will find the beauty, the strength, and the peace you will need to survive in this hectic world. You will find God if you take the time to meditate on his love and unity. Think about him. Think about men like Santos Justus, who are leading mankind to a new world of harmony

—

and peace. Think about the day when not even a child will be afraid to walk down the street at midnight because all will know the power of peace and goodness."

He tilted his head in an expression of pleading, and I was surprised to see a trace of unguarded tenderness in his eyes. He had never spoken to me with such affection. His words warmed my heart and gave me the courage to ask a more pointed question.

"Do you believe in miracles?" I asked, thinking of Asher's resemblance to the marble bust.

"I see miracles every day." Synn leaned back in his chair, his eyes misty and wistful. "When I go down to the cafeteria and see Englishmen and Italians and Danes eating together, that's a miracle. When I hear Rico announce the birth of so many new international chapters of Unione Globale, I know I am witnessing a miracle. And when I see the growth of love between a man and a woman . . . that is perhaps the greatest miracle of all."

My fingers tensed in my lap. Was he referring to something specific?

Synn noted my expression and laughed. "Don't look so frightened, signorina. Love is not shameful. But we have all noticed how you seek out Signor Genzano's company. Signora Casale told me just the other day that you and your fiancé have called off the wedding, and now I understand why."

My brittle laugh sounded more like a yelp. "Oh no, Il Direttore, Asher had nothing to do with my engagement. We are only friends."

"Of course, I could be wrong," Synn said, but with a significant lifting of his brows. "So it's *ti voglio bene* and not *ti amo?*"

"Um . . . I think so."

My confusion must have shown on my face, for Synn laughed. "*Ti voglio bene* means *I care about you,* and the expression is used for friends and family. *Ti amo,* of course, is reserved for romance."

—

268

"Well, then, it's *ti voglio bene.*" I grinned in relief. "And don't worry—I would not allow my personal feelings to interfere with my work."

"We never thought you would. You have done a fine job, and I'm delighted you'll be remaining with us a few more weeks."

His last statement felt like a dismissal, so I slid to the end of my chair. "Thank you for your time, Reverend. I will try to explain these things to the employee in question. I'm sure he's just confused."

"Do you really understand, signorina? Happiness is not to be found in following a creed or clinging to an outdated book of rules. Peace and contentment are found through the simplicity of truth—in living authentically, simply, peacefully. Seek the peaceful life, and you will find it."

I smiled as an inexplicable feeling of contentment rose inside me. "I think I understand, Il Direttore. Thank you for explaining."

He stood and came from behind the desk, taking my hand as he helped me to my feet. "If you seek, you will find," he repeated, his dark eyes jumping in their quick, electric way. "I promise you this and more, if you will follow my guidance."

After leaving Synn's office, I decided my task was clear—I would find Asher, present him with what I'd learned at the library, and explain how he had probably latched onto the legend as a child. With patience and compassion, I would tell him he didn't need to be ashamed of his insignificant background. Lots of people invented personal histories; Hollywood starlets and politicians embellished their biographies all the time. Faced with facts presented with love and concern, perhaps I could weaken his delusion.

Feeling more resolute than I had in weeks, I visited the small cubicle

Asher used for an office but saw that he had already left for the day. Brimming with determination, I left the building and hailed a cab, directing the driver to the Sole al Pantheon. If Asher had decided to walk home, I would certainly arrive first, but I didn't care. I could use the time alone to gather my thoughts.

After paying the taxi driver, I walked through the lobby of the ornate hotel, uncomfortably aware of my wooden heels clacking on the marble floor. The desk clerk, a full-figured woman with piercing eyes, lifted her brows as I walked past, but I lifted my chin and obeyed one of the most basic laws of body language—walk confidently and act like you know what you're doing, and most people will leave you alone.

I turned the corner into the darkened hallway, then made my way over the worn carpet to Asher's door. On the off chance that he had arrived first, I knocked, then stared in surprise when a uniformed maid opened the door.

"*S-scusi,*" I stuttered, wondering if I had inadvertently interrupted something I'd rather not know about. "I am looking for Signor Genzano."

The maid gave me a knowing smile, then pulled a vacuum cleaner through the doorway, babbling in Italian so fluent I couldn't catch a word. She conveyed her meaning, though, in a sly wink, then she practically pushed me through the doorway and into the foyer. When she closed the door behind me, I pressed my hands to my sides and looked around, amused by the hotel gossips' assumptions. I had obviously been noticed in the building before, and apparently some people were eager for me to spend some time with the bachelor hotel owner.

I shouldn't have been surprised. After all, several people at Global Union had painted us as a pair.

—

I checked my necklace watch, then sighed and moved into the front room. A cool breeze came through the half-opened window and fluttered the linen curtain, casting shadows around the book-lined space. With nothing else to do, I scanned the shelves of leather volumes, expecting to see titles printed in gold leaf like the aged books I'd explored in the library. Cracked spines and faded leather I saw, in various sizes and colors, but not a single book was marked on the outside. Curious, I drew a volume from the shelf and opened to the flyleaf.

Journal 1155, Asher's bold hand had written, *in the year of our Lord 1203. My journeys in England.* I riffled through the book and saw that every page had been filled in.

Amazed, I lowered that book to the writing desk and tugged on the one next to it. The second book was journal 1154, dated 1202. *My journeys in Normandy.* The pages that followed were written in French.

Ripples of shock were spreading from an epicenter in my stomach, making the tips of my fingers tingle. I reached for another book on a high shelf and saw that the inscription on the flyleaf was written in Latin and Roman numerals.

"No."

I shoved all three books back to the shelves and hastily stepped away. Asher's delusion could not have progressed this far. Why, there were *hundreds* of books on these shelves, and through the doorway I could see more in the bedroom beyond.

Two thousand years . . . two thousand books?

Impossible. I ran my hand through my hair and drew a deep breath, then moved to the window and lifted the curtain, hoping for a glimpse of Asher on the street. He would explain this when he came home. I couldn't wait to hear how he had written stories in all these journals, and how he managed to make some of them look positively ancient . . .

I sank onto the settee and clasped my hands together, then found myself at eye level with another row of books lined up like planks in a solid fence. What if he *hadn't* written in all the journals? Or what if they all contained the same story?

A scene from an American horror movie flashed across my brain—Jack the would-be author typing "All work and no play makes Jack a dull boy" over and over and over again as he slowly sank into madness.

I reached out and pulled another volume from the shelf, a single black binding among so many in red and blue and brown leather, then lifted the cover and smoothed the first page. The binding cracked as I read *Journal 1615, in the year of our Lord 1690. My Journeys in Madrid.*

I quickly scanned through the pages and saw that they were written in English. Well—Asher had once told me he liked the language.

I shifted my position until the gray window light fell across the faded pages, then began to read.

TWENTY-FIVE

I HAD NEVER IMAGINED I WOULD OPPOSE THE HOLY INQUISITION in Spain, nor dared to think I might run afoul of it. But I am writing this in chains. The book itself was furnished by a faithful servant from my house in Madrid. I am writing in the language of the English so my fellow prisoners cannot read this book—though I doubt many of the poor fellows can read at all.

I do not understand all the reasons for my presence in this prison, but despite the official papers served upon my arrest, I know the matter stems from a speech I gave in an inn not far from here. For years now the Holy Church has sought to settle the problem of Jewish converts to Christianity—to test their souls, as it were. The matter seemed fair to me when I first considered it. At the time Columbus sailed for the New World, Their Majesties Ferdinand and Isabella gave the Jewish population of Spain four months to leave the country. Many of Abraham's children departed during that time of grace, leaving their homes and belongings and paying dearly for safe passage away from Spain. The Jews who remained professed to convert. They married into all classes and races, and many of them eventually obtained considerable wealth, status, and power—power that Spanish officials now seem determined to test.

The Council of the Inquisition—known here as the Supreme— has sworn to stamp out heresy in all its forms. I applauded their efforts at first—what Christian could not stand against heresy?—

but soon the Supreme was denouncing people for such innocent offenses as smiling at the mention of the Virgin Mary, eating meat on Friday, and urinating against the walls of a church. One man privately confided to his wife that he did not believe fornication was a sin; she denounced him, and now he sits beside me in this cell. If you will recall, in 1622 the entire Enrique family was tossed into prison and chained for two years because secret witnesses claimed their father, the Duke of Alva, had been buried according to Jewish rites. No one could prove he had been buried in such a manner, but neither could anyone prove he had not.

If you will recall—I frowned, uncertain whom the *you* referred to. Had Asher written this journal for himself? Or had he intended to give it to a friend? I rechecked the date on the front page, then did the math. Sixty-eight years had passed since the supposed writing of this journal and the imprisonment of the Enrique family, so Asher was either writing to a *very* old friend or he persisted in his delusion even here . . .

I glanced at the doorway as voices sounded outside in the hallway, then relaxed as they faded. Interested in spite of my fears for Asher's mental health, I kept reading.

I am here because I defended my neighbor, Señora Melendez. She was arrested after someone accused her of not eating pork and not changing her linens on Saturdays; these innocent activities resulted in a charge of Jewishness. I went to the trial to protest that Señora Melendez had not changed her linens or eaten pork since I have known her; she is too poor to buy a pig and too lazy for cleanliness. But before I could speak, I learned that Señora Melendez had already signed a confession. Placed upon the rack, she confessed to her alleged crimes, confessed to being a Jew, confessed to anything they repeated to her. The Supreme sentenced her to a hundred lashes, to be bestowed while she made her way through the streets on foot.

The sight of tears in that helpless woman's eyes roused my passion. Her eyes were not like those of Christ, who bore my blow without self-pity, but I knew she was innocent of any crime. Like the Nazarene, she did not deserve to suffer. Filled with the wrath of holy indignation, I stood and proclaimed that the inquisitor, the local bishop, and the attending doctor were false and evil fellows.

Had I been a mortal man, I would have turned and hurried from the place, for in the first shock of my words the authorities did not move. Had I been a wiser man, I would have held my peace and kept my thoughts to myself. But being neither mortal nor wise, I spoke out, and within a moment I was surrounded by a number of the king's men. Grinning like the thoughtless fools they are, they grasped my arms and led me to stand before the offended bishop.

He asked my name; I gave it truthfully.

He asked my occupation; I told him I was a wanderer.

He declared me a heathen and infidel; I told him I loved God and followed the faith, but nonetheless I was taken to the dungeon, where I waited in darkness for many days and nights. Listening to the soughing of the wind through the prison casements, I considered that confinement might be the only sentence my immortal body could not bear. Others had tried to kill me, and always, within hours after death, my heart resumed its rhythm and my chest rose and fell with breath. Threats hold no fear for me, for I have been drowned, speared, and starved. But never has my spirit been allowed to take its place in the silent halls of Death. Always I am returned to my weary body, which heals in time and resumes its course over the earth.

—

Yesterday they came for me. In the presence of a public executioner, a representative of the local bishop, a doctor, and an official notary, I was told that I would be examined in the light of God's laws. Oh, if they only knew how I had already been judged and found wanting!

After being roughly thrust into the room, I was stripped to the skin and brought to the rack, as cruel an instrument as mankind ever invented. The executioner bade me mount it—using his sword to encourage me onward—and there I was hung by the bare shoulders with two small cords, which went under both my arms and ran on two iron rings fixed in the wall above my head. After being hoisted to the appointed height, the executioner moved to my legs. Tying a cord about each of my ankles, he placed one of the rack's planks over my knees, then stood upon the plank and pulled upon the cords, drawing my ankles upward at an unnatural angle. The sinews of my hams burst asunder, the lids of my knees shattered, and the cords remained taut. There I hung in agony for more than an hour.

Then the executioner, laying my right arm above my left, did wind a cord over both arms seven times. Then lying down upon his back, he set both his feet on my stretched belly. He charged and drew violently with his hands, making my womb suffer the force of his feet, until the seven cords combined in one place of my arm, cutting the crown, sinews, and flesh to the bare bones. He did pull my fingers in close to the palm of my hands, leaving the left hand limp and numb so that I felt nothing for hours.

Then, by command of the Justice, my trembling body was laid upon the face of the rack, with my head downward and enclosed within a circled hole; my belly upmost, and my heels upward toward the top of the rack. My legs and arms, being drawn apart, were fastened with pins and cords to both sides of the outward planks, for now I was to receive my main torments.

What good does it to do to record these horrors? You shall not want to relive them when you awaken next in the dawn of a new day, and every man forgets what he has lived. Yet herein is a lesson you must not forget: Do not forget the water device through which water was poured in your belly until you strangled on the taste of it. Do not forget the injustice of being declared guilty at the moment of your arrest and being tortured only to gain a confession. Do not forget that you were held without precise charge and no possible defense. Do not forget that many were required to confess to crimes they struggled desperately to imagine, though you knew full well how you erred. You spoke the truth, and for that they will decree that you must die.

Go then to the stake as steadily and with as great a determination as the Nazarene whom you injured. If by dying you command the time and attention of the Inquisitors, you may prevent them from harassing one of the others whom Jesus loved. If so, you have not borne the agony in vain.

A wide blank space followed the last paragraph, and when the story resumed on the next page, the handwriting seemed to waver with weakness. Caught up in the story, I pressed on.

The execution took place within the auto-de-fé, a spectacular occasion held in the elegant Plaza Mayor, a square in the center of Madrid. The king and his court assembled for the spectacle, each man and lady dressed in full regalia. How well I remember it! While I knelt upon the slave-wagon, my skin grimed in filth and crusty with vermin, a gentle breeze blew over the gathering, fluttering the ribbons on the ladies' headdresses and ruffling the men's wigs. I remember one lovely girl—she leaned over the railing that sheltered her from the place of execution and waved at me in a small token of pity. I can still see the white lace at her wrist fluttering in the breeze . . .

But to continue my recital of events—before us marched the officers of the Inquisition, preceded by trumpets, kettledrums, and the royal banner. In the center of the square a high scaffold loomed, and thither, from seven in the morning until sunset, were brought criminals of both sexes; all the Inquisitions in the kingdom sending their prisoners to Madrid. Twenty men and women out of these prisoners were ordered to be burned, myself among them. Fifty Jews and Jewesses, having never been imprisoned, were sentenced to long confinement and to wear always a yellow cap. Ten others, indicted for bigamy, witchcraft, and other crimes, were sentenced to be whipped, then to serve in the king's galleys. These last wore large pasteboard caps and halters around their necks as befitted those who would serve in the yoke of bondage.

On this solemn occasion the entire court of Spain had gathered. The grand inquisitor's chair rose above that of the king, resting in a sort of tribunal to which we were led like sheep to the slaughter. A thick cord was bound about my neck, by this I was yanked off the wagon and led to stand before the king, the inquisitor, and the curious host.

At the place of execution there were many stakes set about— one for each prisoner to be burned. A large quantity of dry furze had been piled about the stakes. The stakes of the Protestants, or, as the inquisitors call us, the professed, rise about four yards into the air, and each has a small board where the prisoner is seated within half a yard of the top. Each of us was prodded up a ladder between two priests, and when we came to the board, we were commanded to turn and face the people. The priests then spent nearly a quarter of an hour exhorting us to be reconciled to the Holy See of Rome, but though I knew of Peter and respected him, I had decided I could not ever again be a party to the death and destruction of innocents. The observers nearby mimicked our stalwart courage, and upon our refusal to submit, the priests came down and the executioner ascended, one by one turning us off the ladder and chaining our bodies close to the stakes. The priests then came up the ladder a second time, renewing their obnoxious exhortations. The man three stakes down from my position did yield to this last entreaty, and for his piety and devotion the executioner granted mercy. In the sight of God and the assembled company, the executioner climbed the ladder with a noose of thin cord, looped it around the penitent's neck, and strangled him.

Is that mercy?

Finding their last exhortations ineffectual, the priests proclaimed that they would leave us to the devil, who was standing at our elbows, ready to receive our souls and carry us to flames of hell fire. A general shout arose as they descended the ladders, and the universal cry echoed from the observation stands: "Let the dogs' beards be made!"

My intentions were resolute, but I did not relish the thought of what came next. If Jesus could pray "Let this cup pass from me," could I not cringe from the torture of the fire? While the crowds jeered, the executioners lit torches upon poles, then pressed them in to touch the beards that grew upon every man's face. The barbarity was repeated for each prisoner in the line, and my flesh recoiled at the knowledge of what I would soon endure.

But even as I saw the torch approaching, I wondered at the sight that met my eyes. In the flames blossoming to my right, I saw dauntless men and women thrusting their hands and feet into the flames with courageous fortitude, yielding to their fate with such resolution that many of the spectators lamented that such heroic souls had not been more enlightened. Just before the flames licked at my own beard, I saw the face of the Spanish king, who sat with dull eyes and doubtless a heavy heart. I did not doubt that he yearned to be elsewhere, but his presence was required to sanction that mockery of a tribunal.

On June 30, 1690, my body was burnt to bone and ashes. I do not know—or do not remember, I know not which—what they did with the charred remains, but I awoke three days later on the banks of the Tajo River. My skin felt tender and fragile; the gentle rays of the sun seemed to blister and scorch my very soul. I found solace and comfort by coating my flesh with mud from the riverbank, then remained hidden under a bridge for nearly a week, eating small insects and drinking from the flowing river.

Today I shall hail a passing boat and beg assistance. And tomorrow night I shall return to my house, gather whatever remains of my belongings, and begin the journey back to Rome. I am tired and sick in body and soul.

Would that God had collected my soul while my body fell into ashes and embers! I would not have gone willingly to the devil no matter how earnestly the inquisitor wished me to do so, but I would have given ten lifetimes to remain in the oblivion of peace.

I am jealous of my fellows at the stake. They resisted to the end, they stood for truth, and today they are with God. Jealousy is an ugly sin, yet I am often consumed with it. I am jealous of the hundreds who died in the Naples earthquake nearly sixty years ago. In prison I heard that plague, war, and famine stalk the land of Germany; more than eight million souls have died there in this generation alone.

—

Perhaps I should save Rome for another journey—indeed, I think I shall. Tomorrow, I will set my feet upon the road westward and not stop until I reach the land where death dwells.

Another wide blank space followed this entry. I pressed my hand over the page as the wind blew in from the window and whipped the curtains toward me. Asher's story—real or fiction—had shattered my soul. As I read, I could almost smell the scent of burning wood and hear the agonized screams as the flames devoured the condemned prisoners' faces. Delusional or not, the man was a talented storyteller.

I supposed any good writer could create that story if he had researched the Spanish Inquisition. I did not want to believe a man could survive burning at the stake and numerous other executions, but wouldn't that kind of trial account for the resignation I sometimes heard in Asher's voice and the world-weariness in his eyes?

I shivered as a shadow fell across the room. I lifted my face toward the window, seeking the light, and saw Asher standing outside, his gaze mystified and somber—

My breath caught in my lungs. He had seen me with the book.

Before I could speak, Asher turned and walked away. Mortified, I closed the journal and with trembling fingers set it back in its place. I stood and paced before the bookshelf, wondering whether I should leave or remain here to face him—

The sound of a key in the lock settled the question. As I stood there, as embarrassed as a judge caught in a lie, Asher came through the door, his eyes downcast, his shoulders hunched. Not looking at me, he shrugged out of his coat and hung it on a hook, then slipped his hands into his pockets and looked up, his gentle brown eyes sparking with some emotion I couldn't read.

"Asher, I'm sorry—"

—

"Did you find what you were looking for?" He spoke softly, and I could read no trace of condemnation or anger in his eyes.

I pressed my fingertips to my lips, not certain how to respond. I had come here to make Asher face the truth, yet what I had just read convinced me he was either telling the truth or far more involved in his delusion than I had supposed. If it was the latter, he needed serious professional help.

"Asher"—my smile wavered—"I don't know what you want me to do. You tell me things, and everything you say sounds accurate, but your stories cannot be true. It's impossible. Nobody lives two thousand years, and nobody dies and wakes up again a few days later."

He walked past me toward the kitchen, then opened a small refrigerator tucked under the counter. "Would you like a soft drink?"

I shook my head in exasperation. "No. What I want is answers, Asher. You've convinced me you're either telling the truth or you're"— I gulped—"in need of psychological help. So unless you want me to call a shrink, you'd better explain some things."

The corner of his mouth lifted in a wry smile as he popped the ring on a can of soda. "You think I'm crazy?" He leaned back against the counter, then lifted the soda can in an informal toast. "You wouldn't be the first to think so, signorina."

"Asher, please." I walked to him and caught his free hand, cradling it between my palms. "I want to understand. I want to help you, but you've got to see that these things just can't happen. Even God is logical, and Reverend Synn says—"

His brows rose, graceful wings of scorn. "Reverend Synn knows nothing about faith. But I will tell you everything, and you can make your own decision about my sanity. But whether you believe or not, nothing will change."

His hand caught mine then, and with surprising tenderness he led me to the antique settee. We sat together like two nervous teenagers on a first date, then he turned slightly and looked at me, his eyes filled with a curious deep longing. "What do you want to know?"

I took a deep breath, grateful that we were finally being honest with one another. If I could fully understand the foundation of his fantasy, perhaps I could gently chip away at that delusional underpinning, leading him step by step toward reality . . .

I smiled in the calm strength of compassion. "All right. You've told me what happened in the beginning. But tell me why God would want to punish you."

"Why shouldn't he punish me? I struck God's only Son in his hour of weakness."

"Others struck him too. And the Romans crucified him. So why aren't they wandering the earth like you?"

His gaze dropped like a stone. "I asked myself the same question many times, and then I found the answer in Scripture. As the Roman guards injured him, Jesus said, 'Father, forgive them; for they know not what they do.'"

"So—he forgave the Roman soldiers, but not you?"

"I was not at the cross. He was not speaking of me."

I bit my lip, wishing I'd paid more attention to my Sunday school teacher. "So you think," I began, "that the man who taught his followers to forgive and love and turn the other cheek has borne a grudge against you for two thousand years."

An inexplicable smile swept over Asher's face. "You're looking at things from the wrong perspective, Claudia. I used to think God was angry with me. For two or three hundred years I railed against his injustice, then I began to realize that what I saw as a curse could be a blessing. In the tradition of Jesus, who died so that others may live, I was cursed so others could be blessed."

—

I narrowed my eyes at him, trying to find the meaning in his riddle. "I can't see God cursing anybody. After all, don't they say God is love?"

"God is also a judge. Jesus cursed a fig tree for not bearing fruit. God cursed creation after man's disobedience. He is a righteous judge, and he cannot tolerate sin." Sensing my confusion, Asher spread his hands in a gesture of openness. "You must understand God's eternal plan, Claudia. The Scriptures plainly say that God allows the world to continue because every new day brings another opportunity for men to come to Christ. The Lord isn't being slow about his promise to return, but he is being patient with mankind. He does not want anyone to perish, so he is allowing more time for people to repent. But soon his patience will end, Jesus will call the church to heaven, and those who remain will endure severe tribulation. The evil one, the Antichrist, will step to the center of the world's stage, and all who remain on earth will be forced to submit to him or pay the consequences."

I pressed my hand to my forehead and struggled to still my spinning thoughts. It was hard to remain coherent when seated so close to Asher's persuasive eyes.

"So," I said, speaking slowly, measuring each word, "you think God has left you here . . . to preach?" I forced a smile. "I hate to be the one to tell you this, Asher, but you're not exactly what I think of when I think *preacher.*"

"I'm not a preacher." His eyes brimmed with tenderness and regret. "Not in the usual sense, at least. The gospel of Jesus Christ is preached in every nation today; God doesn't need me to evangelize the world. My purpose, as I have come to understand it, is to bear witness to one individual in each generation."

"Just one person?"

"One *particular* person. The one who would be Antichrist. The one who would rise to world dominion if Jesus were to call the church away."

—

With a shiver of vivid recollection, I remembered the passion in Asher's eyes when he told me he wanted to lead Santos Justus to the Lord—and he wanted me to help him.

"Oh, no." I threw up my hands in a defensive posture. "We're not going back to that topic. I'm not going to let you share all this with Justus. He—well, he won't be as understanding as I've been. In fact, if I hadn't been engaged to a psychologist who thinks you can be cured, I don't think I'd have listened to this much of your story."

His chin lifted. "You think I need to be *cured?*"

"Yes—and no." I was babbling to cover my confusion, and I didn't like feeling out of control. I stopped, gripped the edge of the settee, and looked him directly in the eye. "I think you will do yourself real harm if you persist in this idea of confronting Justus."

"Will you have me dismissed if I persist?"

"Probably." I nodded with a taut jerk of my head. "Definitely, yes. I don't know why you're working, anyway. You obviously don't need the extra income."

"No, I don't." He squinted in embarrassment. "You know about the money?"

"I know you own this hotel. Signora Casale told me."

He looked away, a betraying blush brightening his face. "I bought it shortly after it was built, mainly because I wanted a place to call home. A place to store my life's work." He gestured to the books surrounding us. "A man needs roots, no matter how often he wanders." He shrugged. "A little money, invested over several lifetimes, can easily grow into a fortune. I have never lacked for worldly wealth."

I crossed my arms, a little stunned at how easily he could cross the boundary between reality and fantasy. "And I suppose the employees think you are the great-great-great-grandson of the original owner."

Featherlike laugh lines crinkled around his eyes. "Something like that."

Silence overtook us. A light rain had begun to fall, and tires hissed on the wet asphalt outside the window. Some women walked by in the hotel hallway, leaving a trail of laughter that seeped in under the door. In the kitchen, a faucet dripped in a slow, rhythmic patter.

Asher must have been gathering his thoughts because he shifted on the settee and suddenly filled the silence with a stream of words. "I began this work in the medieval age, you see. Churchmen of that time divided the world into two realms, the kingdom of God and the kingdom of Satan. For every light there was a corresponding darkness. There were two sides to every issue: good and evil. And I began to consider a theory: Since Satan would prepare a man to do his bidding in each generation, why shouldn't God prepare a man as well?"

Feeling unqualified to theorize about spiritual matters, I said nothing. Asher must have interpreted my silence as understanding or agreement, for he continued. "Thomas Aquinas and Albertus Magnus, two of the greatest medieval theologians, declared that the Antichrist would be born in Babylon, he would proceed to Jerusalem, and there persuade the people that he was a Messiah. This son of Satan would rule the earth, then Enoch and Elijah would be sent to confront him. This belief dominated the medieval age, continuing into the Protestant Reformation in the sixteenth century. The theology changed somewhat with the tenor of the times—the Protestants called the pope Antichrist; the pope returned the favor and identified the Antichrist as Martin Luther. But then something remarkable happened—a German tract, printed after 1550, announced that the Antichrist had been born in Babylon. According to this tract, the newborn child was abnormally large, had cat's teeth, spoke after eight days, and possessed the power to make manna fall from heaven."

—

I winced. "Surely you didn't—you don't—believe that."

Asher lifted one shoulder in a shrug. "Men believed strange things in those days. By the time the story reached me it had been embroidered, so I did not know what was true and what was not. But I became convinced of one thing: The Antichrist was neither a figment of men's imagination nor a spiritual symbol. The Scriptures speak of him as a living man, so as a living man he will come. Since the devil cannot know when the Father will remove the believers, he must have a candidate waiting in each generation."

My mind vibrated with a million thoughts. "And so you set out to confront these men?"

"I tried. In the beginning it was difficult. The world was a bigger place, and communication slow and unreliable. I had no way of knowing what forces were stirring in the kingdoms beyond my own, so I traveled a great deal, listened to people, and visited the courts of learned men. I entertained kings with my tales of travel and history. I shared the true story of my past with anyone who would listen."

From out of nowhere, like a careening vehicle, came a name. "Paul von Eitzen, Bishop of Schleswig," I whispered, recalling the words I had read only a few days earlier. "You visited him in . . . Hapsburg."

"Hamburg," Asher corrected, glancing at me with a glimmer of hope in his eyes. "I believe it was around . . . the mid–sixteenth century. My memory is as faulty as any man's; that's why I began keeping my journals."

I waved a hand at the shelves lining the walls. "You wrote all these."

"Yes."

"Every word is true?"

He nodded thoughtfully. "Every word is a true testimony of how I remembered the events. There were periods of dark days . . . when my memory clouded."

"After your executions."

His pupils dilated, his eyes going dark with hope and wonder. "You read quite a bit."

"I read enough."

"Then you understand."

"Not much, I'm afraid." I rubbed my hand hard through my hair, half hoping a scalp massage might stimulate my sluggish brain. "Asher, I'm confused. What are you hoping to accomplish by confronting these men?"

He rubbed a hand over his face, and I heard the faint rasp of his evening stubble. "Two things—first, I hope to save their immortal souls. If they turn from evil to Christ, I have helped keep them from hell. And if they choose God"—two deep lines appeared between his brows—"I hope I will have gained time for all mankind. If there is no Antichrist to rise after the departure of the church, the timing will not be right, so—"

"The Scriptures cannot be fulfilled." I finished the sentence for him, understanding his logic but not his rationale. "Let me see if I understand—you want to turn the Antichrist from his appointed path—"

"I'm not sure it is appointed," he interrupted. "All men have free will, so until he submits his soul to Satan, he will be free to choose God and reject evil."

I sat back, momentarily confused by the mismatch between what I had read of the Wandering Jew and what Asher was saying. "If you really believe this, why don't you just sit back and let the prophecies unfold? After all, won't your curse be broken when Christ returns?"

The corners of Asher's mouth went tight with distress as he looked away. "Only a truly selfish man would seek to end his suffering when he could bring God's mercy to others." A tremor passed over his face. "This is the price I must pay for my sin it is my penance. I will wander the earth, and I will seek the one who will be Satan's pawn. And if I can turn him toward the Savior, my suffering will extend God's patient mercy to another generation."

The room swelled with silence as I tried to make sense of what he was saying. "Do you have any proof that your theory is true?" I finally asked, reaching out to touch his shoulder. "You're so fond of quoting Scripture—is there a verse that mentions your role? Your purpose?"

He shook his head. "But I know the man who walks by faith is blessed. So I try to live a righteous life, and I keep my eyes and ears tuned to world events, always looking for the one man who best fits the description found in Scripture." He turned to look at me again. "The man for this generation is Santos Justus, and that's why I need you to get me an appointment. I must share the gospel with him before it is too late, but I am only a translator. He would never see me without your recommendation."

I leaned back and propped my arm on the settee, confused and more worried than ever. None of this made any practical sense, but I was no theology expert. One thing, though, was clear: Asher was prepared to give his life for others, and he would do almost anything, including humiliating me, to meet with Justus. My career and reputation probably counted for very little in Asher's view of past, present, and future.

If Asher was suffering from a delusional disorder, perhaps a few practical questions would point out the incongruities in his story.

"Asher," I began, my voice calm, my gaze steady. "I want to help you, but I'm not sure I can believe your story yet—there are too many unanswered questions. For instance, how could you live in a town and have no one notice that you never aged?"

"I traveled a great deal." He leaned forward and rested his elbows on his knees, and for a fleeting moment I caught the impression that he intended to walk out the door and start yet another journey. "And people did not live so long in generations past. A man who lived fifty years was counted as an elder. I kept moving, I used different names in different places, and no one was the wiser."

"What about your family?" Several times I had wanted to ask this question but had never felt comfortable enough to approach the topic from within his fantasy. "Did you never remarry?"

His face twisted into an expression of utter wretchedness. "I could not. I learned my lesson with Claudia. We should have grown old together, but when she aged and I did not—" He clasped his hands together and stared at them. "I am willing to do penance for my sin. I am not willing to put a woman through that kind of exquisite torture."

"It just doesn't seem fair," I insisted. "And if God is anything, he should be fair."

"God is not *fair.*" His voice took on a bitter edge. "He is *just.* There is a difference."

"I don't see a difference."

"You won't . . . as long as you look with earthly eyes."

I bit down hard on my lower lip, resisting the urge to smack his shoulder. Why did he always have to speak in riddles? "Tell me," I said, leaning forward to look into his eyes, "did you say you met Michelangelo?"

His gaze shifted and thawed slightly. I followed his eyes and saw that he looked at a lower shelf laden with dusty journals. "Twice. I met him in Rome and watched him paint the Sistine Chapel. And in Florence, while he was sculpting his *David.*"

"Did he—" The words caught in my throat, but I pushed them out. "Did he ever sculpt a bust of you?"

The heavy lashes that shadowed his cheeks flew up. "Not that I know of. Why would he?"

Was it possible he didn't know? Could Michelangelo have sculpted a bust of Asher at the same time he worked on *David*? I closed my eyes, visualizing two young men enjoying dinner in a piazza, then the artist going off to sculpt a bust of his fascinating friend, while the scholar returned to his books and journals. Clearly, Asher had no idea how deep an impression he made upon the people he met . . . including me.

I leaned back, blinking hard to stop the sudden rush of tears that flooded my eyes.

"You believe me." He smiled, and I knew his comment was not a question.

"I'm not sure."

"You do. Something has convinced you my story is true." He waved his hand and lifted his gaze to the ceiling. "Whatever it was, I thank God for it."

I sighed, resigned to the fact that my research only reinforced Asher's story. "Asher, you said it yourself. My belief doesn't change anything. But as things stand, I either have to believe you or have you committed."

Surprise siphoned the blood from his face. "You would never do that . . . would you?"

I laughed. "Believe me, I've thought about it. You're just crazy enough to get me into real trouble."

His dark brown eyes softened, then he reached out to push a stray strand of hair away from my forehead. His warm palm cupped my cheek for a moment as something that looked like affection glowed strong in his eyes, then his hand fell to my elbow and urged me upward. "Come," he said, leading me toward his bedroom. "I have something to show you."

Something—modesty or fear or simple nervousness—caused me to hang back, but Asher caught my hand and pulled me along. My apprehensions faded when he stopped before a wooden chest by the side of his bed. The dark wooden box gleamed in the light, as if a loving hand polished it every day.

Almost reverently, Asher knelt before the chest, pulling me down with him. He released my hand after I sank to the tiled floor, then he leaned forward and lifted the lid. As I breathed in the scents of age and dust and wood, Asher lowered his arms into the depths of the box and pulled out an object I had never imagined I would see.

A crown of thorns.

I held my breath as Asher gingerly lifted it between his fingertips, then turned and lowered it to the quilt covering his bed. When it rested there, he leaned back and dropped his hands to his knees, his gaze intent upon the relic.

"I have never shown it to anyone else," he said, his voice a low rumble at once powerful and gentle. "No one else seemed to require visual proof. But you . . . look at it, Claudia, and tell me what you see."

What did I see? I saw a vine, covered in spiky thorns and the white dust of age, curled into a circular shape the size of a man's head. Several of the thorns were dark, and parts of the thin vine seemed hollow, as though decay and corruption had begun to destroy the woody stem from within.

"I have kept it safe," Asher said. "Shielded it from light and humidity and prying eyes. If I had surrendered it to the church, it would have been venerated as a holy relic or destroyed by those who would tear it apart in a quest for authenticity."

"If it hasn't been examined or dated," I said, my mind congesting with doubts, "how do I know it is genuine?"

"You don't know." Asher looked at me with an invitation in the smoldering depths of his eyes. "I can tell you that this is the crown Jesus was wearing when I struck him in Pilate's hall. My blow knocked the thing from his head, and when the guards pushed him forward, the crown was left behind. I picked it up, and I have kept it all these years." His words came out hoarse, as if forced through a tight throat. "Believe me or not, the choice is yours."

He rose to his feet then and walked away, leaving me alone with the fragile crown of thorns and a decision I could not make. I sat silently on the floor, weighing what I had heard in the last hour with what I had believed my entire adult life, comparing faith in Asher with faith in the man who had supposedly worn this wicked circlet of pain.

Never had my senses and abilities seemed so inadequate to the task. Everything I knew of Asher and every physical sign I read in his tone and posture and expression assured me he spoke the truth, so why couldn't I believe? Why was it easier to believe in a two-thousand-year-old Roman than to believe Jesus Christ truly lived and died for all mankind . . . and for me?

I bowed my head. Tears ran down my cheeks, as warm and soothing as summer rain, but I was not really crying, they sprang from a simple overflow of feeling. Asher had shown me this treasure because he wanted me to believe . . . not in him, but in Christ. How long had it been since someone cared so much for me? None of my close friends gave a flying fig about where I stood with God, probably because they didn't think about spiritual things at all. Kurt had proved unfaithful. Elaine Dawson plotted against me. Even Kirsten was distracted by her family and the coming baby. Rory had occasionally talked about God, but the boundaries between employer and employee restrained any really personal questions.

Asher, my only true friend in Italy, was probably as nutty as a peanut bar, but he cared enough to want me to believe in his Jesus. I read his concern in his eyes and in his actions. He had supported me when I learned of Kurt's defection; he had been my steady right hand when we traveled to Brussels. And during all the weeks I had known him, he had

—

293

asked only one thing of me—trust. He had shared his incredible story, trusting me to believe and help him accomplish his goal.

Well. I swallowed hard and thumbed the wetness from my face. I would help him, if I could. But first I wanted to be sure I was doing the right thing.

I rose and walked slowly into the front room. Asher sat at his desk, an open journal spread before him, an ink pen in his hand. He looked up as I came in, a question in his eyes.

"I'm going now, Asher," I said, reaching for my purse on the settee. "I want to make a couple of inquiries. And then, perhaps tomorrow, I'll let you know what I think about your meeting with Justus."

"Thank you." He eased into a slow smile. "I will pray that God will guide your footsteps."

"You do that." I tried to smile in return, but the corners of my mouth only wobbled precariously. Averting my eyes, I hurried to the door and left him alone.

TWENTY-SIX

As I passed under the hotel awning, a few lingering raindrops fell in soft spatters that dampened my hair and caught in my lashes, blurring my vision like tears. The clear sky beyond the Vatican was awash with crimson and gold, but I thrust my hands into the pockets of my jacket and walked with my gaze lowered to the wet stone pavement. I had become inured to the dangers of Roman pedestrian traffic, so when several bicycles and a motor scooter whizzed by, missing me by inches, my heart didn't skip a beat.

As much as I hated to admit it, Asher's tale made a rudimentary sort of sense. A man strikes God and is doomed to walk the earth until God pulls the plug on the planet. As penance for his impudent deed, the thoroughly contrite fellow decides to spend his time seeking the one man necessary for the final battle between good and evil—the devil's pawn, the Antichrist. The heroic wanderer studies and works and travels, gleaning all the information he can, so he will be prepared to persuade evil's representative to switch sides before the battle can begin, thus leaving the devil without an agent. He figures that God, in his sense of fair play, will stall the game until the opposing team can bring in another player.

I stopped on a street corner, rubbing my temple as I watched three cars ignore the red light and press forward in the traffic. If I kept thinking about this, in an hour I'd have a migraine. Even now a fuzzy glow surrounded the streetlights in my field of vision, and the wet stones beneath my feet had gone indistinct and blurry.

The pedestrian *walk* light blinked at me from across the street. I left the curb and had taken four steps, maybe five, when from out of nowhere a Vespa buzzed up from my right and passed directly in front of me. Some part of man or motor scooter hit my shoulder, spinning me with such force that I fell and tumbled over the asphalt, finally coming to rest beside a heap of garbage bags near the curb. Sprawled with my legs spread and my arms akimbo, I felt more irritable than hurt. I was about to open my mouth and loose a stream of invectives when a small man stepped out of the pedestrian crowd and hurried toward me.

"Togliti dai piedi!" he yelled, his face lit by the beams of an approaching car. *"Muoviti!"*

Brushing grit from my wet palms, I tried to follow his words. He was telling me to get out of the way and to hurry . . .

I felt a sudden chill as realization struck. I was sprawled in the right lane of a busy street, at dusk, with nothing but this little old man between me and the oncoming traffic.

I struggled to stand, but for some reason my arms and legs wouldn't respond to my panicked commands. Then the little man's arms slid under mine, and he lifted upward, dragging me out of the path of an oncoming BMW sedan.

A moment later, I was seated on a bench, wet, embarrassed, and angry. I leaned forward, taking inventory of my scraped knees and torn hose, while my elderly savior removed his hat, then pulled a handkerchief from his pocket and sopped beads of perspiration from his forehead. When he had finished these ministrations, he replaced his hat and pinned me in a long, admonishing scrutiny. I opened my mouth, but he lifted a silencing finger and proceeded to chastise me in firm and expressive Italian.

I pressed my palm to my forehead, certain that I had somehow wandered into the second act of a bizarre nightmare. I must have fallen asleep in Asher's apartment. Tomorrow I would awaken on his settee and realize that my fertile subconscious had conjured up this scolding man, the car, and the blasted motor scooter.

The old man ended his tirade with a grand flourish of his arms, but in the ensuing silence I could still feel the burning pressure of his eyes. *"Mi dispiace,* signor," I mumbled, hoping that I had remembered the correct phrase for *I'm sorry. "Non parlo italiano."*

"Ah." He sank onto the bench next to me, and his brows lifted. "Americana?"

"Si." I rubbed my aching wrist; I must have fallen on it. "I'm sorry for causing you trouble, but I didn't see the motor scooter."

"It's a miracle you were not killed." The English words surprised me, as did the strong suggestion of reproach still in his voice. "One must be careful at night, signorina. The streets are dangerous to the unwary."

"I know. I'm usually careful . . . but I was preoccupied."

My bantamweight rescuer rose and planted himself on the sidewalk before me like a guardian grandfather. "Stand, then, and let me see if you are all right."

"I'm fine," I protested, but I stood anyway. Apart from torn nylons, a tender wrist, a wet skirt, and a black smudge upon my left palm, I seemed none the worse for wear. My elderly hero must have thought so too, for after scanning me from head to toe, he nodded abruptly, then pointed toward the building behind our bench.

"You will come in for a cup of espresso." His tone left no room for argument. "After you have refreshed yourself, we will see how you feel. And then I will call a cab to take you to your hotel."

I opened my mouth, about to correct his impression that I was a mere tourist, then clamped it shut again. Let him think what he wanted. I was too tired for explanations.

—

Nodding in mute agreement, I stood and followed the man. As we entered the building he had indicated, I glanced at a sign on the wall. My white-haired knight in sensible wool armor had not come from a castle, but from the Rome Baptist Church.

I did feel better after a cup of espresso. My champion, who introduced himself as Vittorio Pace, was a silver-haired man of about sixty. He must have been about five feet two, for he came up to my shoulder, and though his frame was slender, he carried a round little tummy above his belt. When he removed his hat, thinning silver hair spilled onto his forehead above wide eyes that watched me from beneath tufts of graying eyebrows.

The interior of the church was plain by Italian standards. There were no paintings, no shrines, statues, or relics. Four wooden pews sat on each side of the rectangular building, and a carpeted platform stood before the pews, occupied by a single wooden lectern. A piano sat off to the side of the platform, and beside the piano a lonely looking microphone perched upon a silver stand. I couldn't imagine why anyone would need a microphone in a room this small.

Signor Pace had seated me in a chair beside a table near the doorway, and it seemed to me that I recalled a similar table in the small church I attended as a child. The church of my childhood had offered free leaflets and small Bibles on their table; the Italian Baptists offered espresso. Which, I thought, lifting the fragrant cup to my lips, could not have been more welcome on a night like this.

Like a guardian angel, Pace watched me drink and smiled in satisfaction only when I could lower my cup back to the table without trembling. He asked if I wanted more, and I nodded. I didn't really need the drink—I certainly didn't need the caffeine—but I wasn't ready to go back into the night. This little church, as sparse as it was, seemed warm and comforting.

"So," he said, handing me the second cup, "you are an American."

I accepted the cup and took a perfunctory sip. "I'm in Rome on business. I've been here nearly two months."

He lifted a brow but said nothing.

I glanced pointedly around the room. "Is this your church?"

He grimaced in good humor. "Mine? I am only the—how do you say it?—the caretaker. I tend the church and feed the cats."

"The church has cats?"

He leaned upon the back of the last pew and crossed his legs at the ankle. "Surely you have noticed the cats of Rome?"

I tilted my head and considered the question. "Now that you mention it, I have seen quite a few cats around the city. I always assumed Romans were fond of them."

"Romans hate rats far more than they like cats. That's why there are so many cats lounging on cars in the sun—they help keep the rat population from going *kaboom.*"

Exploding. I smiled and resisted the urge to shudder at the thought of rats. "So who owns all these cats?"

His thin shoulders rose in a faint shrug. "I suppose the city does, though it will not protect or feed them. That is the job of the *gattara.*" He bowed his head in an imitation of an almost courtly bow, and something in the gesture touched me.

"Gattara?" I tried the word out on my tongue and stumbled at the last syllable. Most Italian words that refer to men end in the masculine *o*, so if Signor Pace took care of the cats, he should have been a *gattaro.*

"Most of our volunteer cat people are elderly women," he said, the hint of a smile acknowledging his success in reading my thoughts. "So the language recognizes this truth. More espresso?"

"No, grazie." I held up my still-brimming cup, then took another sip, inwardly smiling at the thought that a man who apparently spent his life looking after strays had rescued me.

"God is good." Signor Pace crossed his arms as he watched me drink. "The night is a very dangerous time to cross the street, very dangerous indeed—"

"Signor," I interrupted, not wanting to hear another lecture on the dangers of nighttime street crossing. "Why do you believe in God?"

A glow rose in his face, as though my question had lit a candle within him. "Why believe in God?" he whispered, his voice fainter than air. "Signorina, he is my life and breath."

I tilted my head. He spoke so fervently, he could be a pastor. I gestured at the building around us. "So this is your church."

"It is Christ's church," he said, verbally underlining the word *Christ*. "I care for the building and the sheep of the Master's flock."

I lifted a brow, now reading a far deeper meaning into his previous answer. He was referring to the people of this church . . . who, judging by the plain and simple surroundings, were neither very numerous nor very wealthy.

"How many members have you?" I asked, wondering how a Baptist church could prosper in the shadow of the Vatican.

Signor Pace gave me an easy, relaxed smile with a good deal of confidence behind it. "All of them." His eyes radiated joy and peace. "I am happy to say we have not lost a soul. God has called a few home, but for that we are always grateful."

I crossed one arm across my middle and smiled at my new friend. He was an odd little man, but he certainly seemed confident of his role in the church . . . and he was sure to know more than I about spiritual matters.

"Signor Pace," I said, placing my cup on the table, "do you mind if I ask a question? I need to know if God would ever curse a person."

His abrupt intake of breath told me the question caught him by surprise. He leaned back for a moment, turned his head and looked away as if to consider another voice, then returned his gaze to me. "That is an odd question for a pretty signorina to ask," he said, looking at me with a smile hidden deep in his eyes. "Was it this question that blinded you to the oncoming traffic?"

My mouth curved in a faint smile. "Probably."

"Then we must find an answer so you will not be struck and killed tomorrow." Lifting himself from his perch, he turned and walked into the pew, then sat down and turned halfway to face me, making himself comfortable. "You do not ask easy questions, signorina."

A blush burned my cheeks. "I'm sorry."

"Do not apologize. Questions that require digging for deep answers may reveal an unexpected treasure or two for the effort." He paused a moment and shifted his gaze to the side window, a golden panel of textured glass. "Do you think God has cursed you?"

"No—not really." I bit my lip, wondering how much of the truth I should tell. "A friend of mine believes God has cursed him. He once committed a great sin, and he thinks he must do something—make an exceptional sacrifice, I suppose—in order to make things right."

"I see." Signor Pace kept his gaze upon the window, and in his profile I could see the long, silken fringes that framed his eyes. "Your answer, signorina, is that God does not curse people—not as you and I would think of cursing. We are born under the curse of sin, and those who die without God are never released from that condition. But Christ, in his great mercy and love, died to free us from the bondage of sin. His love is not enslaving—it is liberating. His grace sets men free."

He turned, his gray eyes blazing into mine with the most extraordinary expression of compassion. "Do you understand? Words are such crude tools when we attempt to explain the great gift of God . . ."

—

His voice drifted away, and in the ensuing silence I groped for understanding. And then, like unwelcome guests, Asher's words came crowding back into my thoughts. "What about the fig tree?" I asked. "And the curse of creation? Didn't God curse those things?"

Signor Pace lifted his hand and absently fluttered his fingers at me. "You must understand, signorina, God's 'curses' are not the consequence of passion or spoken out of a desire for revenge. They are predictions. When God cursed creation and Jesus spoke to the barren fruit tree, they were predicting the negative consequences that would result from sin. Because man sinned, paradise was lost. Because the fig tree had no fruit buds, it could not live and produce. Both God and Christ recognized negative conditions; they did not impose them."

"Still," I whispered, recalling the story from some place in my childhood memory, "the fig tree withered."

"Si. It did. But that was a miracle, a demonstration of Christ's power to those who followed him." Signor Pace tapped his fingers on the back of the pew in a meditative rhythm. "My daughter, why must you worry about such things? You are like a child, fretting about the color of the ribbon on a gift while not caring about the precious item beneath the bright wrapping. God's grace is the gift, signorina. We can do nothing to earn or deserve it, but still God gives it to us." He turned and leaned over the back of the pew, his outstretched hands outlining the shape of a box in the air. "The gift comes wrapped in forgiveness. If you accept the gift, you are forgiven, and God's grace is yours. When you possess grace, you become like a beautiful lamp through whom God's holiness and truth can shine out upon the world."

I felt the corner of my mouth droop at the mention of the word *holiness*. I used to consider myself a moral person—as close to holiness as a human can come, I suppose—but then I walked into a career where I mingled with murderers and drug dealers and lawyers who redefined morality to suit their purposes. Things weren't any better in Rome, even working for a humanitarian organization like Global Union. In my two months here I had spied on foreign ambassadors and relayed confidential information to men whose motives were definitely suspect. The lampshade of my life was clouded with soot, so the light of God's holiness wouldn't shine very brightly through me.

"I'm afraid"—I managed a choking laugh—"that I'm not very holy. I'm not sure God would want to give me any of his gifts."

"And there you are wrong, my young friend. None of us are holy in ourselves. And if God would be gracious to me, he will be gracious to anyone." For an instant the pastor's gray eyes darkened and shone with an unpleasant light. "I do not share my story with many people, but I believe God would have me tell you the truth."

His pupils dilated with intensity, and I forced a laugh, not certain I wanted to hear what would come next. I glanced over my shoulder; the door was only a few feet away. If I could come up with a good reason to exit, I might not have to hear this wizened old man's confession. What great sin had he committed—jaywalking?

Pace's voice cut through my thoughts. "Have you heard, signorina, of the Magliana gang?"

Awkwardly, I cleared my throat. "No, signor."

He shrugged. "It is just as well. I am not proud of the things we used to do. The Magliana gang is the largest criminal organization in Rome. I believe they still control many of the city's fences, moneylenders, drug pushers, and pimps. In '77, I was one of several family members—"

"Mafia?" The word burst from me in a gasp.

One corner of the reverend's mouth drooped in a wry grimace. "As I was saying, in '77, we kidnapped a Roman nobleman, Duke Massimiliano

—

303

Grazioli, and held him captive for over a month, eventually extorting $2.5 million American from his family. Then, instead of returning the duke to his wife and children, we sold him to a Naples gang who tried to squeeze even more money from the man's family. The family could not pay, and the Duke was murdered. We broke the code of honor. The family had paid—they deserved to have the Duke back, but someone in our family decided that honor meant nothing."

I looked down at the floor, growing more uncomfortable by the minute. Why was he telling me these things? I wrapped my palm around my foam coffee cup, wondering how effective a weapon hot espresso might be if a pack of Italian Mafioso came through the doors.

"For the first time in my life," Signor Pace continued, his voice drifting into a hushed whisper, "I felt guilty about an act I had committed. Despite warnings from my family, I went to the authorities and confessed to my part in the abduction scheme. My brother, my wife, and my children had to leave Rome. I served twenty years in prison and was released. Because I maintained my silence about my co-conspirators, the Magliana gang leaves me alone. And I am grateful to serve my Lord as caretaker of this church and the *gatti*—the cats."

"So—your work is your penance?" At least this concept was familiar; I'd heard Asher voice the same sentiment at least a half-dozen times.

He gave me an indulgent smile, like a parent amused by the thoughts of a child. "This work is my *offering*. It cannot save me, but it might lead to the salvation of others. While I was in prison, you see, a minister shared the gospel of Jesus Christ, and I accepted the gift of grace. My salvation rests upon what Christ did two thousand years ago at Calvary."

Two thousand years ago . . . I closed my eyes as my mind traveled back to the day Asher rose up in pride and struck the face of God. He had been doing penance ever since that dark day, and yet he had never found the peace I saw in the lined face of this elderly ex-convict.

Vittorio Pace. A man of peace.

"Thank you, Reverend Pace. I shall never forget your story." I stood and brushed the wrinkles from my damp skirt, then gave him a formal smile. "You are a most remarkable man."

"Call me Vittorio, please. Everyone else does." For an instant, a measure of wistfulness stole into his expression. "I did not tell you the truth to earn your praise, signorina. Will you think about what I have said?"

I nodded, trying to maintain a measure of dignity as I reached for my purse. "I owe you my thanks, Vittorio. Can I make a contribution to your church?"

He rose from the pew, shaking his head. "You are still confused, signorina. God does not want an offering from you . . . until you have accepted the gift he offers. He longs to give you freedom. He longs to tell you there is no condemnation and no curse for those who belong to Christ Jesus."

Something in his gentle smile cut me, spreading an infection of doubt. Hesitating, I nearly sat down again, but I was so tired my nerves throbbed. Besides, if I wanted a theological discussion, I could always provoke Asher into another argument.

Smiling my thanks to my diminutive hero, I pushed the door open and walked out to the busy street.

A note from Signora Donatelli hung on my door when I returned. "Please find me," it said, and as I pulled the sticky note from the door, I wondered what sort of emergency could require my presence. Had Global Union failed to make one of the weekly payments for my

—

residenza? Or had one of her twins broken something in my room?

I crossed the tiled hallway and knocked at the heavy wooden door that led to the Donatelli family's private corners. I heard the protest of a chair as it scraped across the floor, then a little round face with a pair of too-big teeth peered up at me through a crack in the doorway. "Mama! La signorina!"

He—either Mario or Marco, I couldn't tell which—left the door open, and the warm scents of tomato sauce and herbs wafted out to greet me. I crossed one arm across my belt and silently hoped my landlady's note had resulted from an overabundance of pasta. Maybe she'd offer me a bowl, then send me up to bed. The experiences of the day had drained me, and I wanted nothing more than to fill my rumbling stomach and then crawl between her stiff sheets. I was ready to close my eyes to thoughts of Rome and Asher and events of the past two thousand years . . .

I think my countenance fell when Benedetta appeared in the doorway with only a yellow envelope in her hand. She pinched her lower lip with her teeth in a worried expression, then handed me the letter with all the gravity of a military general exchanging his command.

Not a letter—a telegram. From New York.

I thanked Benedetta, then took a step back to the wall as I ripped the envelope open. The message inside was brief:

Kirsten in accident; lost the baby. Thoughts and prayers appreciated.

Sean

Like a slippery snake, grief rippled through my churning stomach, swimming up my throat and almost surging into my mouth. I choked it down, crumpling the featherweight yellow page as my hand contracted into a fist.

—

Through my peripheral vision I saw Benedetta and her son staring at me even as my eyes clouded with tears. Benedetta said something in Italian, but my benumbed brain refused to decipher the words.

I nodded, not having the faintest idea why, and moved toward my room on legs that suddenly felt as though they belonged to someone else. After unlocking my door, I dropped my purse and the wadded page onto the table, then moved to the bed.

I should have been with my sister. Though some feeble voice in my brain kept repeating that I couldn't have prevented the accident, a stronger voice insisted that everything would have been different if I had been home. If you drop a pebble into a pond, every part of the pond experiences the ripple, and things would definitely have been different if I had been in New York. She might not have been driving; she might have even been with me. A woman eight months pregnant had no business behind the wheel of a car, anyway. Why wasn't Sean driving?

I moved toward my laptop and pressed the power button, then plugged the modem into the telephone switch and waited for it to complete the Internet connection. E-mail was faster than a telegram, but I had been away from the computer all day. Sean must have tried to contact me and then called Western Union only when I didn't respond via computer . . .

I winced at the sight of a message in my mailbox, then clicked on it. Sean had signed on using Kirsten's screen name, but here, at least, were the details I sought:

Claudia—

I'm so sorry to tell you that Kirsten was injured in a car accident last night. She was on her way to pick me up at the train station when some idiot ran a red light and hit her. Travis is fine, thank God, but Kirsten was pretty banged up. She's fine, except for some bruises, but the trauma sent her into labor. The baby would have been fine, if a bit small, but he wasn't in the correct position for birth, and the umbilical cord somehow wrapped around his neck.

He was beautiful . . . and I'm pretty sure we'll bury him next to your parents.

Kirsten is upset, of course, and she wanted me to contact you. She's at Southampton Hospital and will be there for at least a few more days. Call if you can—I know she'd appreciate hearing from you.

Sean

I turned to the telephone and mentally clicked the time difference off on my fingers. It was two in the afternoon in New York, so the hospital should be accepting telephone calls. Sure enough, when I finally got through I was transferred to Kirsten's room immediately. Sean answered. We spoke for a moment, I thanked him for the telegram and the message, then he handed the phone to Kirsten.

I didn't know what to say to her, but right after I said hello, she burst into tears. I made soothing sounds and quiet clucking noises, and she finally calmed down. I told her I was sorry, I said I wished I'd been there, and she said I shouldn't blame myself, it was a freak accident. We wept together, and then Kirsten mumbled something about not coming home on her account.

"But I want to."

"No. There's nothing you can do, and I don't want to get in the way of your work. Stay where you are, Claude. When you've made your mark on the world, then you can come home. Until then, at least—"

She fell silent, and I knew she had choked on her emotion. "At least what, K?"

The answer came in a hoarse whisper: "Sean's here."

Fresh tears stung my eyes as I grasped her meaning. *Sean was with her*. It had taken a tragedy to pull him away from his practice, but if he was with her in the middle of a weekday, he had canceled appointments and reordered his universe to be there.

Good.

I told her I loved her, she said the same, then we hung up.

I don't know how long I sat there staring at the phone and drowning in a sea of conflicting emotions. Part of me wanted to be away on the next flight, but the pragmatic voice that ruled my days said, *Stay, there's nothing you can do*. I couldn't ease Kirsten's pain, nor could I bring that beautiful baby back.

I hunched forward, feeling myself compressed into an ever-shrinking space between the weight of my sister's grief and my own ambition. What should I do? Emotion-driven Asher would probably tell me to go; practical Maura Casale would advise me to stay. And Kurt, though he'd be quick to acknowledge the emotions involved, would say Kirsten would grieve until she healed and nothing I could say or do would speed that process.

Slowly, I stretched out on the bed, burrowing into the heavy feather pillow. Asher would undoubtedly pray about the decision. And then, no matter what happened, he'd say it was God's will.

Maybe I should do the same.

My heart was squeezed so tight I could barely draw breath to speak, but I hugged the pillow to me and forced the words out: "God, if you're there, show me what to do. Make the way clear for me, please."

My mind drifted into a fuzzy haze and then into sleep. If God answered, he didn't speak loud enough to wake me.

Twenty-seven

THE NEXT MORNING DAWNED BRIGHT AND CLEAR, THE KISS OF SUNRISE painting a rosy blush on the stately structures of the city. For a change, it didn't rain, though gray skies would have been more in keeping with my mood. I had awakened in a fog of regret and sadness, and only by focusing on the task ahead could I keep my thoughts from centering on Kirsten and home.

I took a cab to Global Union headquarters, rode the elevator to my office, and dropped my purse and briefcase into my desk drawer. After quickly checking my e-mail to be certain there was no urgent news from Kirsten or Sean, I placed a call to Santos Justus's office, spoke to his secretary, and made a note in my desk calendar.

Ready or not, Asher, here I come.

I tugged down the hem of my jacket—*a nervous gesture*, my brain noted—and walked to the elevator. As the doors slid closed and I found myself staring at my reflection in the brass surface, I pressed the button for the fourth floor and met my own determined gaze straight on.

Last night, I'd dreamed of lamps and lights and Inquisition fires. I found myself in a long line of condemned heretics before a cheering crowd in the Global Union cafeteria. Though I protested that I had done nothing to promote heresy, when Reverend Synn lifted the torch and asked if I would confess Christ and receive his grace, my mouth went dry and I could not speak.

—

311

The flame came toward me, dancing upon the end of a long wooden pole while Signora Casale sang the Global Union anthem: *Peace, Peace, follow me to peace!* But death had never brought peace to Asher, just as it did not now bring peace to Kirsten and Sean and Travis . . .

As the ends of my hair sizzled and blackened in the crackling flames, I awakened.

I still didn't understand what Signor Pace meant about receiving God's grace, but I was ready to stop doubting Asher Genzano. I have always trusted the evidence gathered by my eyes and ears, and everything I saw in Asher attested to the truth of his testimony and his journals. For eight weeks I had been poking and prodding at his story, and not once had I discovered a weak spot or rattled his composure. And I had discovered other proofs as well—the statue by Michelangelo, the eyewitness accounts of others who met Asher in centuries past, the photograph with Hitler.

As impossible as it seemed, Asher Genzano had told me the truth . . . and right now I needed truth more than I had ever needed anything.

I had no answers for Kirsten; I couldn't explain why God, if he truly existed, would allow a loving mother to lose her innocent child. But Asher claimed to know God, and if he believed God wanted him to speak privately with Santos Justus, he would speak with Il Presidente today.

I would wait and see what God would do . . . or if he could do anything at all.

The elevator chimed softly as the doors opened again, then I stepped off and went in search of my friend.

Twenty-eight

"Is Asher Genzano in yet?"

Asher's pulse quickened as Claudia's soft voice floated over the wall of his cubicle. The receptionist must have nodded, for Asher heard nothing else until Claudia stood in the doorway, gazing at him with a chilling intensity.

"I've made an appointment for you," she said, her blue eyes focused and direct. "Will you be ready to speak to Il Presidente at fourteen o'clock?"

Asher swallowed his surprise and pushed back from his desk. "I will be ready."

She looked at him a moment, her mouth tipping in a mirthless smile. "I thought you'd be more excited. Isn't this what you've wanted all along?"

"Yes. But it is never easy." With an effort, he tore his gaze from her face and stared at the pages he had been translating. He would put this work aside until later; everything else could wait. An eel of apprehension wriggled in his bowels, reminding him that he needed time to prepare.

"I'll go with you."

Asher jerked his head around. "That's not necessary."

"I think it is. Justus only agreed to see you because I told him you have discovered some interesting information about a possible role for Global Union in the future. So he'll see both of us after lunch."

The apprehension stirred again, twisting in his guts. "Claudia, I've done this many times, and it doesn't always go well. You may not like the result."

"It doesn't matter." She leaned her shoulder against the wall of the cubicle and lowered her voice. "I've decided to think of this as a little experiment. If God is in control, things will work out as they should, right?"

"What about your contract?"

She shrugged slightly and made a face. "Perhaps Rome has influenced me, Asher. Don't you have a saying, *Que sera, sera?*"

Before he could object again, she turned lightly on her heel and moved away.

Asher spent the next three hours planning his strategy, scribbling notes on slips of paper, then tossing them into the waste bin. What sort of approach would work best with Santos Justus? After noticing Hitler's care for his niece, Asher had appealed to Hitler's mercy, only to discover the man had none. With Napoleon he attempted an intellectual approach, only to find that the little man's great mind remained closed to the truth of God. He had tried to argue the Scriptures with the inquisitors; he had wept before the emotional Wilhelm II to no avail.

How should he approach Santos Justus?

Through the grace of God and the miracle of technology, he had caught this man at an early stage of his career. Asher could not shame him; the man's public record was nearly spotless and his private encounters no worse than any other politician's. He could not speak of the organized church, for Justus was irreligious. He could always point out the similarities between Justus and the Antichrist as portrayed in Scripture, but Justus would undoubtedly take offense at being likened to one called "the son of perdition."

Perhaps he should not rely on a specialized approach. Perhaps he should just speak the truth, simply and honestly. That's how Claudia dealt with people.

At lunchtime he did not go out to eat in the piazza with the others but remained at his desk, jotting notes on a card. Claudia would probably be alarmed at these signs of his nervousness, but at least she had arranged the interview. He had been prepared to wait months, if necessary, until a door of opportunity opened. But waiting carried the risk of speaking up too late.

A shadow fell across his desk at 13:55. Asher looked up to see Claudia standing behind him. She did not speak but lifted a questioning brow.

He slipped the scribbled note cards into his coat pocket. He probably wouldn't use them, but he liked knowing they were within reach. "I'm ready."

How odd, he thought as he followed her to the elevator, that he should be nervous while Claudia remained calm. Something had happened since he last saw her, for as recently as yesterday she had believed Justus would view this meeting as nothing less than harassment. Either something had convinced her otherwise, or she no longer cared what Justus thought.

They rode the elevator to the seventh floor. "Are you really ready?" Claudia whispered, turning to face him. She reached out and plucked a piece of lint from his shoulder.

Despite his apprehension, Asher felt a hot and awful joy at her touch. *She cared.* The depth of her concern echoed in her voice as she whispered, "I'll be right beside you."

Clinging to his purpose, Asher prayed he would not betray his

—

315

agitation. The elevator doors opened, then he strode forward and opened the door that led into Justus's private office. A blonde secretary seated at the reception desk flashed a brief smile at him, then nodded to Claudia. "Grazie, you are right on time. If you will wait but one moment . . ." She rose and stepped into the inner office, then returned a moment later, holding the door open for them to enter.

Asher drew a deep breath as a tremor of mingled fear and anticipation shot through him, then closed his eyes to focus his thoughts. *Holy God, for this I have waited and worked. Send your Spirit to convict Justus's heart. And speak through me, I beg you.*

He lifted his head, saw Claudia looking at him with a question in her eyes, then gave her a confident nod and led the way into the inner office.

Justus was seated at his desk, a telephone pressed to his ear, his chair turned toward the window. Asher stood before the desk and clasped his hands at his waist, waiting. Somehow it didn't seem polite to stand here listening to the man's telephone conversation, but the secretary *had* ushered them in.

Behind him, Claudia cleared her throat. He glanced back long enough to give her a smile, then looked up as the chair squealed and Justus turned.

"See to it, then," Justus said, then replaced the telephone in the receiver. He looked first at Claudia, then focused the full intensity of his gaze upon Asher. "Welcome, both of you. Please, Signor Genzano, sit and tell me all that is on your mind. Signorina Fischer tells me you have a unique idea about Unione Globale's role in future world affairs."

Asher glanced at Claudia as they sank into the guest chairs, then his gaze moved into Justus's, seeing nothing else. "Thank you for seeing me, sir. I believe I have news that will interest you."

—

"If I wasn't interested," Justus said, his voice as cool as the smoke off dry ice, "you wouldn't be here."

Claudia laughed softly, and Asher allowed himself to smile. Like a swimmer about to plunge into icy water, he took a deep breath. "You may not know, Il Presidente, that I am a student of history. I have studied many ancient works, among them the Greek and Hebrew texts of the Bible."

The smile remained on Justus's face, but Asher saw a flash of cold enter the man's eyes.

"You may not know, Il Presidente, that the ancient prophets spoke often of a great leader who will come to power in the latter days of the planet. A charismatic and intelligent man will rise from the ancient Roman Empire to become the head of the last form of Gentile world government."

Justus lifted his hand, his eyes as black and polished as obsidian beads. "Excuse me, signor, but are you going somewhere with this? All this talk about ancient Romans and Gentiles seems a little irrelevant to our work."

"I was speaking of the ruler to come. For a few months the world will believe him to be a great leader, but in truth, he will be the pawn of Satan himself . . . and I believe *you* may be that man." The words seemed to flow out of him, and Asher paused as they filled the silent room. For an instant, Justus did not respond, then shock flickered over his face like summer lightning.

He leaned forward across his desk. *"Sei pazzo?"*

Asher slowly shook his head. "No, I'm not crazy. Signorina Fischer used to think so, but she knows I am speaking the truth."

Justus glared at Claudia with burning, reproachful eyes, then crossed his arms and turned his gaze back to Asher.

"I am the greatest of sinners," Asher continued quickly, "so it is in

---

total humility that I come before you today. I have come to Unione Globale for one reason only—to tell you that God demands repentance from every man who would accept salvation. Jesus Christ offers eternal life, but first you must renounce your sinful ways. Jesus Christ came into the world and was executed at Calvary to atone for the sins of mankind. His salvation is available to any who will accept it, and today he is ready and willing to accept you."

Justus said nothing but sat motionless, radiating disapproval. Asher felt it like a chilly breeze on the back of his neck.

"Grazie, Signor Genzano," Justus said, bridled anger in his voice. "You are dismissed."

Asher stood and turned to go, with Claudia following, but Justus stopped her with a command: "Signorina—you will remain."

Asher moved through the doorway, then turned in the reception area in time to steal a glance at Claudia's face. She looked at him with an almost imperceptible note of pleading in her face, like a hunted animal peering out from the brush.

Twenty-nine

"WHY HAVE YOU HUMILIATED ME IN THIS WAY?"

I resisted the urge to cringe as Justus's voice rolled over me with all the thunder and fury of an old-time preacher.

"Signor Genzano did not intend to embarrass you, Il Presidente." I spoke quickly, the words running together as I pulled them out of thin air. "He is concerned for Global Union. He is concerned for your soul." I heard Justus take a deep, angry, and insulted breath, but he didn't speak, so I continued. "Asher is a man of deep religious conviction. He has spoken to me of many things over the past few days, and I honestly believe he only wants what is best for you and Global Union."

Justus's face went quite pale, with a deep red patch over his cheekbones, as though someone had slapped him hard on both cheeks. "The man is a lunatic! And you—whatever possessed you to bring him up here?"

"I—" For the first time in years, words failed me. I had been depending on Asher's ability to make Justus see the truth. It should have been simple, but it took time for Asher to convince me, and it might take time for Justus to come around.

But time was something Justus did not seem inclined to give either of us. Neither did God seem inclined to grant a miracle.

A thunderous scowl darkened his brow as his gaze fell upon me. "You are finished here. Your employment shall terminate in one hour, and I expect you to have your office cleared of all personal belongings. Leave your badge with the security officer in the reception area."

My stomach dropped like a hanged man. I had never been fired from a job, nor had I ever had a client look at me the way Santos Justus did. He eyed me as if I were a bad smell.

I lifted my chin and met his gaze. "Anything else?"

"If you think the matter ends here, you're sadly mistaken. You will never work again in Europe. The hot breath of religion is the last thing we need in the sensitive atmosphere of global politics. For two thousand years we have been striving to rid ourselves of religion's poisonous stench, and yet you have the audacity to hire a zealous bigot and drag his nonsense even into my office!"

From some reserve of strength I didn't know I possessed, I summoned the courage to answer him. "Asher Genzano is neither a bigot nor a lunatic. He is only a Christian."

Justus's gaze locked on mine, focusing on me with predatory intensity. "I suppose you are one of those fanatics too."

I swallowed hard. "I want very much to be."

"Then *va al diavolo* to you both!" He flung out his hand, literally sending me away. I turned and left the room, giving the unnaturally blonde secretary a stiff nod as I passed from the outer office into the lobby. And as I pressed the elevator button and tried to stop my knees from trembling, I wondered how I had managed to travel from the peaks of confidence to the pits of despair in less than a week. The man who would have paved my road to fame and fortune had just told me to go to the devil.

After stopping in a ladies' washroom to splash my hands and face with water, I went to my office and emptied my desk drawers of all personal items. I piled my pocket tape recorder, a half-dozen books, and my favorite Waterman pen into my leather briefcase, then pulled my laptop's plug from the electrical outlet with one smooth jerk. Into the briefcase it went as well, with a handful of personal files from the credenza. I picked up a framed photo of Kirsten and Travis and dropped it into the case, then settled the leather strap onto my shoulder and turned for a last look around.

"Signorina Fischer?" Maura Casale's husky voice caught me by surprise. "Is something wrong?"

"I'm leaving, signora." I gave her an abrupt nod, then gestured toward my desk. "If I have left anything of personal value, will you send it to me? I expect I'll be leaving Rome soon." I slipped a business card from my wallet. "Here's my New York address."

The personnel director merely stared, apparently tongue-tied, as I pressed my card against her palm and moved through the doorway. "By the way, signora"—I turned in the hall—"have you seen Signor Genzano in the last five minutes? I'd like to speak to him before I go."

Wordlessly, she pointed toward the elevator.

I stopped on the fourth floor and looked for Asher, but the Publications secretary said he had already left for the day. I thanked her and strode away, determined to leave the building before my fragile facade cracked and shattered into a million tears.

The rush of adrenaline supported me through my exit interview at the security station where I handed in my ID badge and requested my passport. The guard stepped back to his desk to place a telephone call, watching me through half-closed lids as he confirmed my story, then he returned my passport without ceremony. I took it, flipped through the pages to be sure it hadn't been altered, then slipped it into my bulging briefcase.

A surge of indignation carried me out of the building and northward for two blocks, then swirled away like water from an unclogged kitchen

—

sink. As the wind fingered my hair, I plodded forward with a couple of waddling pigeons for company. I felt empty without the rush of adrenaline, so I took a seat in a neighborhood trattoria and ordered a sandwich and a diet soda. I wasn't hungry but forced myself to eat. As I chewed the unusually tasteless meal, my eyes carelessly scanned the crowds moving on the sidewalk.

I should have been flooded with relief. I was free from my contract, so in a matter of days I could return to the life I had left behind. I could be with Kirsten and help her through her grief. I could go back to Manhattan and pick up the pieces of my practice, hire a new secretary, and prepare to defend my territory against Elaine Dawson's invasion. I could visit Rory's wife and offer my long-overdue condolences. Justus might very well prevent me from working in Europe again, but I had responsibilities aplenty in New York.

But my mind still burned from the encounter I'd witnessed in Justus's office. How surreal the situation now seemed! From reading Asher's journal, I knew he possessed great courage under pressure, but I read unmistakable signs of nervousness in his body when he confronted Justus. Did his anxiety stem from his conviction that he was speaking to the future Antichrist, or was it the simple tension anyone would experience when faced with a long-sought goal?

And why had Justus reacted so strongly? Why couldn't he accept Asher's concern at face value and, if he wasn't interested in religion, politely dismiss him? Asher's fears were not unfounded. Though Justus was not a particularly evil man, the potential for corruption and power undoubtedly yawned before him. How many other men had stood on the brink of world conquest? Hundreds. And how many kings and dictators and emperors had been corrupted by the power they wielded? Most, if not all. The few men who chose to govern with love and gentleness were no match for evil and ambition.

—

While I searched for references to the Wandering Jew in Germany, I found a quote where Hitler spoke for most would-be world rulers when he proclaimed that Jesus Christ was "a self-appointed rabbi whose teachings of meekness and love ended in the surrender of the will to survive." Hitler saw the Christian virtues of forgiveness, self-abnegation, weakness, and humility as "the seeds of decadence" and "the very denial of the evolutionary laws of survival of the fittest, the most courageous and talented."

I stirred the straw in my soft drink. Hitler spoke as one who believed nothing existed outside of life, but Asher certainly didn't feel that way. He yearned for death, evidenced real jealousy toward those who found it, and seemed convinced that the hereafter was infinitely more beautiful than the here and now.

Where had he gone? For some inexplicable reason, I worried about him. He was a grown man and quite capable of caring for himself, but in the last hour he had finally come face to face with his target . . . and failed to hit the mark.

What would he do now? Would he continue his pursuit of Justus or search for another man who might fit the role of Antichrist? I considered the latter option for a moment, then dismissed it. Asher had been convinced that Santos Davide Justus was the man who would be king, and I didn't think he'd give up as long as Justus lived.

He wouldn't be able to work through Global Union, though. If Justus had been furious enough to fire me, he certainly wouldn't allow Asher to remain at Union headquarters. A memo had probably already appeared on Signora Casale's computer: *Dismiss the translator and hire another. Alert security; Asher Genzano is not to enter the building . . .*

I crumpled the paper wrapping from my sandwich, then stood and tossed it into a waste bin. Keeping my soft drink cup, I slipped my briefcase strap back onto my shoulder and stepped into the parade of passing pedestrians, walking northward toward the Piazza della Rotonda and the Pantheon. With any luck, I'd find Asher sitting in an espresso shop or a trattoria along the way.

An unexpected weed of jealousy sprang up in my heart as I walked. Asher might have been doomed to a life he did not want, but at least he had managed to find a purpose. What purpose did I have? None—at least none that mattered. I had come to Rome with the goal of proving myself to be the world's leading people reader, but what did my personal ambition matter in the face of the world's needs? Asher had steered his life on a course to serve mankind; daily he poured himself out in an effort to buy a few more years for people he had never even met. For the sake of others he had endured pain, loneliness, sorrow, and suffering, while I had done nothing but attempt to polish my own rising star.

Santos Justus's goal of world peace was more noble than my ambition.

I abruptly changed directions, accidentally bumping another woman's shoulder. "Scusi!" I tossed the apology over my shoulder, then glanced up at the street sign. Asher once mentioned that he liked to visit the Pincio Gardens when he needed to think, and those gardens were just off this bus route and not far from my residenza.

I caught the bus, stared mindlessly through the windows until we reached the Piazza del Popolo, then exited. The hillside above Il Pincio was green with life even in November and the zigzagging path that climbed to the gardens all but invisible through the evergreens. Lengthening my stride, I cut across the piazza and entered the garden path, watching for Asher as I climbed. Beneath a canopy of umbrella pines, palm trees, and gnarled oaks, the garden's broad avenues seemed a quiet oasis in the midst of the city's bustle.

When I finally reached the Pincio's main square, I stood on the crest of a hill and stared in wonder at the panoramic view stretching before me. A signpost beside the path told me I could see from the

Monte Mario to the Janiculum. I didn't recognize either of those names; I only knew the view was extraordinary. Like a living organism, the city lay before me in all its glory, as alive with the throbbing sights and sounds of life as it had been when Asher first walked these streets two thousand years ago . . .

I will be your God throughout your lifetime—until your hair is white with age. I made you, and I will care for you. I will carry you along and save you.

The words crept into my mind, softly, like the poet says, on little cat feet. I don't know where they originated or why they crept into my consciousness, but they brought comfort in their wake.

It would be wonderful to believe as Asher did. To know that life had purpose, no matter how short or long, and that no matter what happened, God remained in control.

Signor Pace believed like that. That wise man had found happiness in something as simple as caring for a tiny church and the neighborhood's feline population . . . and I envied him.

If I could believe like that, I might be able to accept Rory's death and the loss of Kirsten's baby. I might never cease to mourn what might have been, but I'd know that evil couldn't separate us forever and that I'd see them again.

My childhood Sunday school teacher had been fond of teaching about heaven. She'd taught us prayers like "Now I lay me down to sleep, I pray the Lord my soul to keep . . ." I smiled as I flipped through my memory file for the rest of the prayer. Of course—"And if I die before I wake, I pray the Lord my soul to take."

God had taken Kirsten's baby to heaven. He hadn't caused the accident, but he was sheltering that child, and the accident had drawn Sean and Kirsten closer together. God had also taken Rory, and now Jesus was comforting Alice. I didn't understand how, but she did.

Yet for some reason God had steadfastly refused to take Asher's soul . . . why? So he would be here when Justus rose to power? Or so he would be here when I needed him?

A stone bench stood at the edge of the avenue, and I sat down, keeping my gaze fixed to the horizon. As a child, I had marveled at views like this. Every sunset filled my heart with ecstasy, and sunrise was a time of magic and unexpected delight. Kirsten always told me that every morning God opened his paint box and painted the colors of a new day. I believed her, just like I believed her story about thunder coming from God's bowling alley. I also believed everything the Sunday school teacher said, often taking her literally. When she explained that we put money in the offering plate in order to give it to God, I assumed the dark-suited men who took the overflowing plates down to the Communion table were like the priests in the Old Testament stories. Since I knew they couldn't very well take the money outside and toss it up to heaven, I figured they burned it, like the animal sacrifices, so God would smell the smoke and declare the offering a sweet scent . . .

But then I grew up and learned the difference between imagination and reality. I gave up sunrises in order to sleep late; schoolwork and studies filled my sunset hours. I learned that rapidly expanding air along the path of an electrical discharge of lightning created thunder, and I realized that no one in his or her right mind would burn money to please God. No, the money went to very practical, realistic needs: electricity, flowers for the altar table, and the pastor's salary.

My world shifted on its axis; my daydreams vanished, replaced by five-year goals and to-do lists. A pocket organizer replaced my girlish diary; meetings replaced my hours of contemplation. I didn't mind, for the person I became earned praises and awards and the admiration of her peers. I began to consider myself the ultimate pragmatist. Independent, self-contained, cool under pressure, and very private, I didn't need anyone and I certainly didn't need God. I wasn't interested in changing other people, and I didn't want anyone to change me.

Until now.

A faint wind sighed through the trees, and in its breath I felt my spirit stretch and soar. If nothing else, Asher had taught me to look beyond myself and my physical boundaries, to broaden my thinking. Through his eyes I had glimpsed a world that stretched like this panorama, from ancient history to a foreseeable future. Through his conviction I had begun to accept that it was all part of God's plan. In the beginning he created man, in the center of time he sent the One who would atone for all, and in the end he would set things right. And throughout the marvelous and varied tapestry of time, the simple scarlet cord of love ran like the foundation thread on a weaver's loom.

A wry smile tugged at the corners of my lips. God must have known I'd be a tough nut to crack. Into my world he first sent Rory, who lived a quiet and steady life of faith. When that didn't impress me, God sent the one person on earth who would pit my abilities against my reason. My eyes and ears told me Asher spoke the truth; my mind had never been able to believe it. With such a contest raging in my brain, it's a wonder *I* didn't need psychological help!

Behind me, the sun was coming down the sky but hadn't yet reached the row of pines that topped the hill. Watching the lengthening shadows, I exhaled a long sigh of contentment.

"God so loved the world that he gave his only begotten Son . . ."

My mind ran backward, picking up the strings of time. I think I learned that snippet of Scripture in the little wooden church where Kirsten and I were baptized as babies. I thought I was a Christian back then—after all, weren't all Americans? But later, when I thought I had grown too old for Bible stories and Sunday school songs, I put my spiritual training away, like a box of outgrown garments.

—

"Show me the way back, God."

In the distance, far beyond the gleaming man-made monuments, the wind herded dull-gray clouds over the mountains like a shepherd gathering in his wayward sheep. I lifted my chin and closed my eyes. "God—Signor Pace said you would give me salvation if I ask for it. So I'm asking. I don't know what else I'm supposed to do or say, but I chose to believe in Asher, and now I'd like to believe in you."

When I opened my eyes again, a little boy, probably three or four, stood at the end of my bench with a finger in his mouth. He looked at me with wide, curious eyes.

One corner of my mouth lifted in a smile. "I believe," I told the toddler, not caring whether or not he understood. It just felt good to say it.

The child looked away, then turned and ran off, calling for his mama.

I hunched into my jacket and scanned the wide horizon, not wanting to alarm the boy's parents. I wasn't a crazy American. For the first time in years, I felt I had found a way home.

—

Thirty

Alone in his sitting room, Asher slipped out of his coat and tossed it onto the settee, wishing he could cast aside his defeat as easily. Sighing in frustration, he slouched into his desk chair and pulled his journal toward him. As the wind hooted through the half-opened window, he uncapped his fountain pen and confessed his failure in the only way he knew how.

Today I spoke to Santos D. Justus, and he would not hear me. May God forgive me if the fault was mine, but I fear his heart was set against the truth before I even began to speak. He sees nothing but his own ambitions; he cares for nothing but his own schemes. And now I am at a loss—what should I do? I was certain I had caught this one sooner than the others.

Oh, God, have I failed you yet again? My hand still bears the scars from your crown of thorns. Must I bear the scar of your displeasure forever as well? I know I am cursed before you. My anger and pride were an abomination to you, an affront to the humble Lamb of God who was preparing to give his life.

Can Justus not see the truth? He lives in the most holy city in the world; he walks upon the streets where saints have trod, yet his eyes are blind to the truth of the gospel. He is Antichrist, if not in fact, then certainly in deed and attitude.

I pray he is not the one, yet I am almost certain he is. Never

—

have the times been more ripe for the Lord's coming. You spoke, blessed Lord, of wars and rumors of wars; I see them on every hand. You spoke of famines in various places, of earthquakes and death and destruction. These, too, I see behind and before me.

You said the sons of Abraham would return to the Promised Land, and they have. I know now why Adolf Hitler could never have been the Antichrist—the time was not right; your people did not safely dwell in the land promised to Abraham's seed. But now they are there, with more arriving every day, and they have signed peace accords that allow them to dwell in relative safety. They are even preparing to rebuild the holy temple that will be the scene of abomination and desolation in the time of tribulation.

I understand, heavenly God, that man's time of groaning and travail is nearing an end. I myself am weary and weak in spirit. My tongue is not as eloquent as it once was, and the men and women of this day and age are not easily impressed by knowledge. Their minds are too full of useless things; their minds are cluttered with images and sound bites from around the globe. They hurry and scurry and chat by telephone and e-mail. They communicate more information in a minute than an ancient scribe could in a year . . . yet they accomplish nothing of eternal value or consequence.

I cannot help feeling that I failed today. Santos Davide Justus must be the man who will lead the world once your church has departed, yet I could not persuade him to hear the truth.

Have I presumed upon your eternal plan? Will you come so quickly, Lord Jesus? Your children would rejoice to see you burst through the clouds to call them to their heavenly reward, but the rest of the earth would mourn. They are still lost, holy God; they are still groping in spiritual darkness. For their sakes, have mercy

and postpone your coming. For them, withhold your righteous
anger for another generation. For them—

Let me stop Santos Justus.

Asher dropped his pen to the desk, pinched the bridge of his nose, and closed his eyes. A thought occurred to him—a thought he dared not write in his journals or even confess aloud. The idea might have arisen from the pit of hell itself, but in the light of the day's defeat, it seemed the only logical alternative to surrender.

He had a choice—God always provided a choice—but Asher could not step back and let Santos Justus continue to lead Unione Globale. Already the organization had spread its tentacles throughout the world, and by sending Asher and Claudia to Brussels, Justus had demonstrated that he was not an honorable man. Just like Napoleon, Wilhelm II, and Hitler, Santos Justus craved power. And he would increase his power, through fair means and foul, until he controlled the mightiest empire the world had ever known. Like a great, dark spider sitting atop a web, he would manipulate the media, the economy, the government, and the church. It was only a matter of time . . . and time was running out.

Asher opened his eyes, blinked, and raked his hand through his hair. In Old Testament times, God allowed his people to kill their enemies; at times he demanded it in order to purge the land of idolatry. Wasn't this the same situation? Santos Justus would lead the world to idolatry when he set himself up as god, for the Scripture plainly prophesied that the Antichrist would erect a statue of himself within Jerusalem's holy temple. Anyone who did not worship the beast would be martyred, and thousands of people would die, just as they had in the Inquisition . . .

Asher could not wait. Even if God did not protect him, still he would act. Not for his own sake, but for the ones who still wandered in darkness.

Pressing his lips together, Asher picked up his pen.

Give me strength, holy God, and guide my hand. Even if you will not, then clear the way so my aim is true. Let me rid the world of this one who would lead it to death and destruction and desolation.

Thank you, Father, for your mercy. I pray you will heap it upon the dark soul of Santos Justus tomorrow.

Asher lowered his pen, waited a moment for the ink to dry, then closed his journal. Moving slowly in the dim lamplight, he moved to the bureau in his bedroom, then knelt and opened the bottom drawer. From beneath a stack of sweaters that smelled of wool and mothballs, he pulled a bundle of gray felt, secured with strips of leather.

Carrying the bundle to his bed, he carefully unknotted the leather strings, then wound the felt away from the object it protected. The gray material fell away, leaving a seven-inch metal tube in his hand.

Asher stared at the olive green weapon, reacquainting himself with its features and purpose. He had not unwrapped it since 1959, when it fell into his possession shortly after the assassination of Ukrainian dissident Stefan Bandera. Asher had not known Bandera or the assassin, a KGB officer called Stashinsky, but he had been standing in the shadows on a snowy night in Munich when a Russian officer crept out of an underground tunnel and dropped the felt package into a waste bin. As the officer crept away, Asher retrieved the bundle.

—

A week later he read in the German papers that Stefan Bandera had been murdered with a Soviet gas gun, a short tube containing an ampule of acid. When the firing lever activated a firing pin, the percussion cap detonated, vaporizing the acid into a poisonous gas that would be propelled out of a small hole in the tube. According to eyewitnesses, the papers added, Bandera fell dead just after KGB officer Stashinsky approached and pointed a rolled-up newspaper toward his face.

Now, as the thick black sky pressed against his window, Asher studied the assassination gun. The felt had kept the mechanism clean and dry; he found no evidence of rust. The cocking rod lay at one end, the muzzle at the other. The designer had placed a rubber ring between the cocking rod and the bend of the firing lever. The rubber had deteriorated somewhat, so the shooter might feel the recoil.

Carefully, Asher twisted the muzzle end, then pulled out the firing chamber. A single cartridge lay within, its end still sealed with a gas ampule that would spell certain death for whomever the shooter selected as a target.

In the rush of a busy Roman street, it was unlikely anyone would notice the encounter, much less hear the short bark of the shot. And Asher doubted that an assassination gun had been used in more than forty years—the authorities might even conclude that Santos Justus had suffered a heart attack.

The thought of murder was like a rock dropped into the quiet pool of his heart, sending ripples of anguish in all directions. But what else was he to do? God had allowed him access to Santos Justus, and Justus had spurned the gospel. If Asher did nothing, Justus would rise to power and begin a bloody inquisition unlike anything the world had ever seen. The barbarity of Hitler's ovens would pale in comparison to the guillotines of the Antichrist, and no one would be able to buy or sell or work without swearing allegiance to him and accepting his mark on the hand or forehead.

And all who did so would be consigned to eternal torment.

Though his hands were slick with sweat, Asher's mind had sharpened to an ice pick's point. He alone could stop Justus and secure a reprieve for the earth.

He wiped his right hand on the leg of his trousers, then carefully screwed the firing chamber back into the hollow tube.

THIRTY-ONE

CLAUDIA.

Darkness pressed against my open eyes, as if I were swimming underwater. An instant of sheer black fright swept through me—had someone come in through the window? Had I remembered to lock the door? But as I lay in bed with my head off the pillow, my body tense and rigid, I heard only the dull rumble of traffic outside my closed window.

I let my head fall back to the pillow and sighed in relief. The day had been stressful, the walk home long and thoughtful. I had not seen any sign of Asher at Pincio Gardens, and since the gardens were well north of his apartment and only a few blocks from mine, I had walked home, taken a hot bath, and eaten a pizza strewn with arugula.

I closed my eyes and patted my stomach. The arugula must not have agreed with me.

I turned onto my side and stretched out, willing myself back to sleep. I had just withdrawn into that vague grayness between wakefulness and sleep when I heard the voice again, as insistent and unfamiliar as before: *Claudia.*

I sat up, clutching the sheets to my chest. "Who's there?" I whispered, peering into the darkness. I could see nothing but the neon glow of the electric numbers on the alarm clock: 12:15. My glands dumped such a dose of adrenaline into my bloodstream that my heart contracted like a fist, but still I saw nothing in the blackness. I heard a dull thump overhead and looked up, then someone upstairs flushed a toilet and the pipes in the wall began to sing.

The twins. They were romping around, bedeviling their mother, and refusing to go to sleep. Nothing unusual; nothing to worry about.

I closed my eyes and felt my shoulders relax. I must have been more stressed than I realized if every little sound had the power to spook me.

I lay down again, but this time I pulled the spare pillow to my chest and hugged it, then pulled the blanket up to my earlobes with my free hand. On the off chance I was wrong and an intruder *had* entered my room, maybe he'd just take my laptop and wallet and leave. As long as I played possum, he wouldn't bother me.

If there was someone.

But there wasn't.

After lying awake for what felt like an eternity, I drifted into a shallow doze in which memories of the day mingled with inchoate fragments of dreams. I saw Asher standing before Justus, Justus's angry face and blazing eyes, the gardens upon the hillside, the vast panorama of the city lit by the orange rays of the setting sun. A little boy stood beside me, and I heard his mother call, "Samuel!" and then suddenly it seemed to me that the city itself was aflame, the ancient walls burning in an orange and scarlet conflagration, and Justus was there, thirty feet tall, standing with one foot on the rooftop of the Global Union headquarters and another on the non-descript office building next door. "I am not a lunatic," he bellowed, his uplifted fist piercing the swirling gray clouds overhead. "I am the Antichrist!"

Hatred radiated from him like a halo around the moon while ambition, stark and vivid, glittered in his eyes. Watching him from my bench in the garden, all I could feel was fear, growing and swelling like a balloon in my chest. A scream rose in my throat, but I clapped my hand across my mouth, choking it off—

Claudia.

Drowning in my nightmare, I swam upward toward the soft and insistent voice, finally crossing the void between sleeping and waking. When I opened my eyes this time, nothing in the room had changed. I felt so grateful to be in a safe and secure place that tears of relief flooded my eyes.

Then I remembered. *Samuel.*

The name stirred the nearly forgotten memories of a shadowy night in my childhood. I was spending the night at my grandmother's house, sleeping in the room where the big brass bed reminded me of a jail, and something flew past the window and sent shadows racing across the wall. I screamed, and Grandmother came running, then held me close to her heart while she soothed my fears and combed her fingers through my hair. And then, while I breathed in the whisper of rose sachet and felt her cool hand upon my brow, she told me the story of a little boy who heard noises in the night and decided God was calling him. The boy's name was Samuel, and the third time he heard the voice of God, he said, "Speak, Lord; for thy servant heareth."

And God spoke to him.

A cold shiver spread over me. I sat in the stillness for a moment, then cautiously brought up one hand and peeled the covers from my chin. The room was silent, the numbers 1:16 were glowing in the dark, and nothing had changed . . . except my willingness to face the unknown and unlikely.

"Speak, Lord." My voice emerged as a hoarse croak, crusty with swallowed apprehension. "For thy servant heareth."

I can't really describe what happened in the next moment. The voice wasn't audible, and nothing changed in my physical surroundings, but suddenly I knew God was speaking to my heart in a way he never had before. The air beside my bed stirred with the inaudible vibration of angel wings, and my heart thrilled to know I was a beloved child, entrusted with a command. I had been given a simple task, and when I lay back down to sleep a moment later, I knew I would obey.

Once the sun rose, I had to find Asher as soon as possible. He would need me.

THIRTY-TWO

A DELIVERY TRUCK GRUMBLED BY ON THE ROAD OUTSIDE ASHER'S window and he sat bolt upright, as wide-awake as if he'd just been given an intravenous dose of pure caffeine. For an instant he felt as though the events of the previous day had been nothing but a dream, then he lowered his feet and the cool kiss of the tile floor established reality. He glanced across the room. The assassination gun rested on the bureau, visible even in the gray shadows of dawn.

Asher slid his feet into slippers and pulled his robe from the foot of the bed, shivering as he belted it around his waist. Raking his hands through his hair, he walked through the front room and foyer, then opened the door and saw his newspaper on the carpeted floor.

He lifted a brow. If God had not wanted him to proceed, it would have been a simple thing to prevent the delivery of the newspaper he planned to use as a prop.

Asher stooped, picked up the paper, and closed the door, then made his way to the kitchen. He tossed the paper onto the counter and switched on the coffee maker, then leaned against the counter and crossed his arms, staring at the floor.

It all might end today. This cozy little existence, this link in a chain of lifetimes, might be shattered by sunset. His plan would end in one of several possible results: He would either succeed and be caught, fail and be caught, or succeed and escape to be captured later. In this modern world, technology virtually guaranteed punishment, and if by some miracle Santos Justus lived, he would know that Asher had approached and pointed a weapon at his face. So this would almost certainly be Asher's last morning in this quiet kitchen.

A niggling fear wormed its way through the crowded thoughts in his mind. Was it even *possible* for Justus to be killed? A careful study of Scripture seemed to indicate that the Antichrist would be a mortal man, and all of the other possible antichrists had died easily enough after falling from leadership to corruption. But perhaps the power of evil guarded Justus's life even as the power of God guarded Asher's.

The muscles of his forearm hardened beneath the sleeve of his robe. Guarded or not, he had to make this attempt. In all the years since his repentance, he had never knowingly lied or stolen or committed harm to anyone, but this situation demanded action. Always before there had been room for doubt, but yesterday Asher had seen honest fear in Justus's eyes when he spoke the name of Jesus. Why would a man fear the Savior unless he had already sold his soul to il diavolo?

Asher took a deep breath in an effort to steady his erratic pulse. He would take action, but this time he had more to fear than an execution squad. After his first death experience, he had learned to endure pain, knowing it would soon pass into the oblivion of time and forgetfulness, but Italy had not executed a prisoner since 1947. The government had abolished the death penalty in 1994, so if Asher was captured and sentenced for attempted murder, he would remain in prison for life. And if the Lord should delay his coming . . .

"Half of forever," he whispered, the room swimming before his eyes, "is still forever."

He reached out and braced himself against the edge of the kitchen counter, his anguish almost overcoming his resolve. His life had been endurable only because he always managed to find his way back to freedom. How could he endure an immortal lifetime behind bars? And what could he do in prison when evil assumed authority and God sent tribulation and judgment upon the earth? Asher earnestly hoped to join the other believers in the Rapture, but he had no guarantee that he would be included in the ingathering. Somehow, in the deepest part of his soul, he had always felt unworthy of inclusion. He was a sinner, the lowest of the low, and though he had spent nearly thirty mortal lifetimes trying to do penance for his crime against Deity, could *anything* atone for his sin?

Asher pressed his hand over his face in a convulsive gesture of resignation, then slowly sank to his knees on the tile floor. For a long moment he knelt there, his forehead pressed to the sharp edge of the countertop, his fingertips clinging to the rim of a drawer.

He swallowed, his throat raw with unuttered shouts and protests, then beat his fist against his chest, resigned to the irony of his situation. If he was successful today, he might buy time, perhaps another entire generation, for a world lost in spiritual darkness.

If he had to spend the remainder of his forever in prison, he would. He would pay the full price for his sin and bear whatever he had to bear.

He could do no less.

THIRTY-THREE

I SLEPT SOUNDLY, THEN WOKE AT SIX. FOR A MOMENT I LAY IN A QUIET cocoon of anguish for Kirsten, then a more recent memory hit me like a punch in the stomach. Asher, wherever he was, would need me today.

I slipped out of bed, staggered to the shower, yanked the hot water on, and grabbed one of the towels from the rack. As the hot water pipes groaned, I dashed back into the bedroom to pull a pair of black slacks and a matching turtleneck from a bureau drawer, then locked myself in the bathroom.

Twenty minutes later, I stood before the mirror, dressed and with a towel on my head. I finished applying my makeup in a couple of deft strokes, then unwrapped my hair, tousled it with my fingertips, and blew it dry.

Asher needed me.

The thought kept running through my brain like some sort of commercial jingle. I didn't know why he needed me, or where I was supposed to find him, but the urge to locate him grew more intense with each passing moment. I don't know how to explain it—if you've ever felt the same thing, you'll know what I'm talking about, but I'd never felt anything like it before.

As I grabbed my red cardigan from the back of a chair and ran for the door, I knew Kurt would say I had joined my Italian friend in his delusion. "When in Rome, do as the Romans do," I muttered, closing the door behind me.

It was a cold day, but a bright one, with the sun pouring buckets of yellow light onto the Roman streets. Obeying a sudden impulse, I hailed a cab and told him to drive me to the Piazza della Rotonda, which meant I'd exit right across the street from Asher's hotel. I glanced at my watch. It was now 7:30, and the sidewalks were already clogged with pedestrians. Cars and motorcycles jammed the streets, and the silence I had enjoyed only an hour earlier had vanished.

I leaned back against the cab's vinyl upholstery and tried to force my confused thoughts into order. What might Asher do now that Justus had turned him away? I knew he was upset—his abrupt disappearance yesterday had proved that. I had tried to call him last night, but he never answered his cell phone. Which meant he had either left it someplace or he was steadfastly refusing to answer its continual chirping . . .

We had reached the piazza. "Please stop here." I leaned forward and tapped the driver on the shoulder, then tried my request in Italian. "Ah—*si fermi qui, per favore.*"

The driver flashed me an obliging grin, then thrust out his hand for the fare. Too anxious even to count out the right change, I pressed a handful of lire into his palm and slid out the door, joining the pedestrians in the piazza. I stood for a long moment, slowly turning to examine the tables and benches where dozens of men and women were enjoying their morning espresso. I didn't see Asher.

Obeying that insistent inner urging, I sprinted across the piazza and entered the lobby of the Sole al Pantheon. A trim young woman in a navy blazer looked up as I approached the reservations desk. "Is Signor Genzano in?" I asked, panting to catch my breath. "Could you ring his room, please?"

She lifted a brow, probably wondering why Signor Genzano would want to entertain a breathless American at this early hour, then moved to the telephone. After a moment, she came back to me. "Signor Genzano does not answer. Would you like to leave a message?"

"No, grazie."

I turned from the desk and pressed my hand to my brow, thinking. Asher left abruptly yesterday, so he might not even know he had been officially dismissed. In any case, he hadn't had a chance to clean out his desk, so he might be walking to Global Union headquarters even now. The offices did not officially open until nine, but perhaps he had gone to work early, hoping to catch Signora Casale and plead for his job . . .

I knew the personnel director often arrived before the office officially opened. Justus and Reverend Synn did too, in order to avoid the mass of adoring employees. A security guard would let them in, but for a moment or two they would have to wait outside on the piazza . . .

Perhaps Asher hoped to confront Justus again.

The five-block walk to Global Union headquarters had never seemed so long. I set out at a quick pace, zigzagging through the crowd while I scanned the people in front of me, hoping for a glimpse of Asher's dark head. But nearly every man on the street had dark hair, and most wore navy trench coats just like Asher's . . .

I had just rounded the corner and stepped onto Via delle Botteghe Oscure when I saw him. He was sitting on a bench across the street from Global Union's glass entrance doors with a white foam cup in one hand and a rolled-up newspaper under his arm. He seemed relaxed and content to wait for nine o'clock.

Relief flooded my soul, and I slowed my steps to catch my breath. At least a hundred yards remained between us, but with the curve of the road I could keep my eye on him, and there was no sign of Signora Casale, Justus, or Synn. So if Asher had planned another confrontation,

I would have time to talk to him and make certain he planned to proceed in a reasonable manner.

I smiled at my fears. Asher was one of the gentlest people I knew, so why was I concerned? He would laugh when he saw me, and then I'd have to try to explain why I had rushed over here like a dog after a rabbit.

A long blue car with tinted windows swept around the corner and passed me, then slowed to a stop outside the building. The driver stepped out and took a moment to lift his arms in a sleepy stretch, and I recognized the lanky figure of Angelo Mazzone, Justus's driver.

My heart leaped uncomfortably into the back of my throat. Lengthening my stride, I lifted my hand, waving to catch Asher's attention. But Asher had lowered his cup to the bench, and now he was standing, the newspaper moving from under his arm into both hands, one hand supporting the far end, the other working at the edge near Asher's body.

Something was wrong. Asher never wore this determined look, and his hands were usually loose and limber, not taut and mechanical.

Panic rioted within me. By some miracle my feet kept moving even as my lips parted to call his name, but Asher didn't turn. Staring at the car, he moved toward the door Angelo had bent to open. In a moment he would be within inches of whomever rode in the backseat—

I let out a tiny whine of mounting dread as Angelo began to open Justus's door, then Il Presidente himself stepped out, looking to the left, and then Asher was upon him, the newspaper only inches away from Justus's face . . .

I experienced a moment of empty-bellied terror, then stopped in midstride and screamed. The sound rose and echoed down the street, overpowering the rush of the moving cars, the blare of horns, and the puttering noises of the motor scooters, and suddenly Justus, Angelo,

Asher, and about a thousand other Italians were staring at me. Justus wore a look of complete surprise, marked by the hint of fear, but Asher stared at me as if he'd never seen me before. Silence sifted down like a snowfall for a profound instant, then Angelo's gaze dropped to the newspaper in Asher's hand.

Before I could draw another breath, Asher lay facedown on the pavement, his arms twisted behind his back. The Global Union security guard flew from the building and picked up the fallen newspaper, revealing not the gun I had feared, but an odd green stick.

Justus retreated inside the car as the guard pulled a gun from his coat and used both hands to point it at Asher's head. Angelo sat on Asher's back, trembling with fear and adrenaline. Like a man stricken with Tourette's, he shouted the same Italian profanity over and over again.

I sank to the sidewalk and braced my back against a stone wall, gulping air to fill my starving lungs with oxygen. I deliberately averted my eyes from the scene to my right, not wanting to believe what I had just witnessed.

Asher had tried to kill Justus. I didn't know what sort of weapon that green stick was, but from the bodyguard's anxious expression, I knew it might be lethal. And, if not for my scream, Asher just might have accomplished what he set out to do today.

"Is this why you sent me here, God?" I covered my eyes with my hand, then peered through my fingers toward the blue sky. "Did you want me to stop Asher—or prevent him from trying? Was I too late?"

There was no answer, no quiet voice, but after a moment I heard the pulsing wail of sirens in the distance. The police would arrive at any moment, and though the scene was confused with screams and shouting, soon someone would remember what had happened . . . and they might want to talk to me.

—

What could I tell them? Nothing. They wouldn't understand—or believe—a single word of the true story.

With an effort, I roused myself from the numbness that weighed me down and stood. Turning away from the hubbub on the sidewalk, I retraced my steps and left Asher alone.

The natives say a man isn't a genuine Roman if he hasn't done time in the *Regina Coeli*. The institution with that stately name is a prison located on an embankment of the Tiber River. The ancient complex is situated between the silver river and the green slope of the Janiculum Hill—a beast between two beauties. Though the "Queen of Heaven" jail once served as a monastery, little has been done to preserve its original lofty intention. The street vendors who hawk souvenirs on the river embankment assure me that the prison cells lack heat, adequate ventilation, and modern conveniences. It is, they say, shrugging, a place of punishment after all.

For three days I stood outside the stone bastion, waiting to see the man I considered a friend. The first day I stood across the street on the Via della Lungara for more than an hour, just summoning the nerve to approach the forbidding fortress. When I finally did grasp my slippery courage and enter the main office, I was told I would have to wait until the staff psychologist had completed the prisoner's mental evaluation. I flinched at this, imagining the psychologist's horror if Asher volunteered his complete history, but I later learned it was Asher's choice of weapon, not his background, that signaled the need for a psych consult.

On Sunday, the third day of my vigil, I met Ricardo, the espresso vendor who operated a stand outside the prison. Ricardo had a cousin who worked in the system, and through the family grapevine I learned that the weapon used in the attempt to assassinate Santos Justus was a type of gas gun not seen in Italy since World War II. The alarmed authorities were keeping Asher Genzano under strict guard with a "no visitors" policy until they were certain the Italian Mafia had not decided to resurrect an old and sadistic weapon.

After recovering from the shock of this news, I was not surprised Asher had used a World War II–era relic. I wouldn't have been surprised if he had tried to wield a medieval sword or an ancient spear. I was astounded, however, that he had tried to commit murder.

After thanking Ricardo, I lowered my head and walked away from the depressing sight of the jail, wanting to put as much distance between it and me as possible. Sadness pooled in my heart, an acute despondency I'd never felt before. Until this point, everything in my life seemed to have a concrete reason and/or a rational cure—I was depressed because something bad had happened; I was elated because things were going well. Never before had my unease sprung from such unearthly causes. I wasn't even certain I ever would feel better— weren't Christians supposed to suffer?

Find Vittorio Pace.

There it was again, that insistent, inaudible voice. Suddenly Signor Pace's little stone church seemed the only solid reality in a nebulous world. I looked up, struggled to think where I was on a city map, then stepped to the curb and lifted my arm to hail a cab.

The cab driver wasn't familiar with the Rome Baptist Church, but eventually we found the place off the Piazza San Lorenzo. I paid the driver and stepped out of the car, noticing that the church looked smaller and a bit run down in the bright afternoon light. The wooden door was unlocked, so I lifted the iron handle and stepped inside.

—

I expected to see people—after all, it was Sunday—but it was nearly fourteen o'clock, so I assumed the worshipers had gone home. The interior was as plain and simple as I remembered, but I saw no sign of Vittorio Pace. I paced up and down the aisle and called his name a couple of times, then stood still and heard the rumble of a masculine voice from outside the building. Following the sound, I stepped through a side door that led to a small courtyard.

To my astonishment, the church courtyard seemed exclusively devoted to cats. Except for a winter-bare tree in one corner, any plant life that had existed in the walled space had long surrendered to the feline occupants. At least a half-dozen cats sat atop the stone wall, their front paws tucked neatly beneath their breasts, their tails swinging lazily into empty space. One of them, a yellow-eyed beast that must have weighed at least twenty pounds, turned to stare at me as I slipped through the doorway, but Signor Pace stood with his back to me. He was pulling pieces of white meat—chicken, I suppose—from a plastic bag and dropping them into ceramic bowls in the center of the courtyard. At least a dozen scrawny cats crouched around the bowls, sharing their feast in surprising harmony, and others were leaping from the wall to join their fellows.

"*Fate piano, lasciate un po per gli altri.*" I wasn't sure what he said, but Signor Pace spoke to the cats in soothing tones. "*Rufio, stai sempre a litigare?*"

I smiled at the scene and leaned against the doorframe, content to wait until Signor Pace had finished his work. He had told me he was one of the volunteers who fed the homeless cats of Rome, but I hadn't realized just how many cats depended upon him for their daily meals. I took a brief head count and came up with forty-two, but in the constantly shifting diorama I could have missed another dozen.

—

A black-and-white tuxedo cat brushed against Signor Pace's legs, then plopped down on the ground and exposed his belly. "*Ah, Stash, vuoi la pancia grattata?*" Signor Pace emptied the last of his bag, then stooped to rub the cat's stomach. "*E come sono oggi le pulci?*"

"He behaves just like a dog," I called, startling several of the animals.

Signor Pace turned, then a smile gathered up the wrinkles by his ancient mouth. "He may think he *is* a dog," he answered as the cat rolled back to his feet and slunk away. "He is certainly one of the leaders of this group. Look how he waits for the others to eat."

He wadded the plastic bag in his hand, then came toward me. "I was hoping to see you again, signorina. Are you well?"

"Very well, thank you." I transferred my gaze from the cats to the elderly minister. "I thought a lot about what you told me the other night. And I want you to know that I understand now. And I am happy to call myself a Christian."

"God be praised." His expressive eyes searched my face, reaching into my thoughts. "I am happy for you, my daughter. But something tells me you have come for a different reason today."

I cast my gaze downward, a little startled by his discernment. Reverend Pace was in the wrong line of work; he could make a fortune in jury consulting.

I told him the truth. "I have come on behalf of a friend in trouble. He has an unusual story, and I hope you can help me help him. I don't know anyone else who would understand, because his trouble is . . . well, it's spiritual."

Signor Pace gave me a look of faint amusement. "Shall we go inside? Your friend sounds interesting."

"He is more than interesting, Vittorio." I turned to follow as the minister opened the door. "He's downright unbelievable."

"My friend," I began after we had seated ourselves on the front pew, "has made a life's work out of watching for the Antichrist—you know, the evil leader who will rise in the last days."

"I know about the Antichrist," Signor Pace said smoothly, with no expression on his face. "But he will not be revealed until after the believers have been taken from the earth. It will be as it was in the days of Noah—the righteous preached repentance, the faithful were delivered, and judgment fell upon those who did not heed the warning." A twinkle of sunlight caught his eye as he glanced up at me. "If your friend has trusted Christ, his concerns about the Antichrist are pointless. All believers will be gone by the time the Antichrist rises to power."

"He thinks," I spread my hands, "that if the man who will be Antichrist is removed, God will postpone his decision to take the believers."

The minister's face contorted into a brief grimace of disbelief. "But how can anyone know who the Antichrist is? There are many who oppose the things of God, and they are all anti-Christ—"

"He believes the Antichrist will be Santos Justus."

Signor Pace recoiled from my steady gaze and tried on a smile that seemed a size too small. "I can understand his concern. There are many who worry about Justus. The man has gained considerable power in a short period of time, and his influence is spreading throughout the world."

"My friend tried to kill Justus three days ago. He is now awaiting trial in Regina Coeli prison."

The minister stared blandly at me. Only a tiny unconscious twitch of his eye revealed his surprise.

"The man I saw on the news—that is your friend?"

I nodded.

—

"And did you have anything to do with this, my daughter?"

I had expected the question—the police had asked me the same thing two days before. In the barest possible terms I told the investigating officer that I had been walking to Global Union, saw a man in a trench coat approach Justus with what looked like a weapon, and screamed. I volunteered nothing about my relationship with Asher, and the investigator didn't ask for further details. When the case went to trial, though, I knew he'd be back with more questions.

"No, Vittorio, I had nothing to do with it—in fact, I think I may have saved Signor Justus's life. Three times in the night before that morning I heard a voice calling me. When I finally listened, I knew I was supposed to find Asher as soon as possible." I looked down at my hands, which trembled despite my resolve to remain calm. "I couldn't stop Asher, but I screamed loud enough to distract Signor Justus. So Asher did not kill him."

Signor Pace leaned back against the wooden pew, a frown puckering the skin between his dark eyes into fine wrinkles. "Perhaps you should give me the entire story."

"The story is almost unexplainable, signore. I would not believe it myself, except—well, sometimes I can't believe I *do* believe."

The grim line of the minister's mouth relaxed as he folded his hands. "I deal with the unbelievable every day, signorina. Now—begin at the beginning and tell me everything. I will make no judgments until you have finished."

After a long pause, I drew a deep breath and forbade my voice to quiver. "It all began when I took a job for Global Union and met Asher Genzano . . ."

An hour later, thick shadows had begun to stretch across the church. I finished my tale, ending with a simple question: "Can you believe God would allow a man to live two thousand years?"

—

Signor Pace sat in silence. He had not interrupted once during the telling, nor did he seem inclined to react quickly. He simply sat there, his eyes unfocused, his mouth set in a straight line, his forehead wrinkled in thought. Finally he looked up with a burning, faraway look in his eyes. "Long ago I learned never to predict what God can or cannot do. He can do whatever he pleases. You, however, must go to your friend and give him the truth. He has been laboring under a lie."

I blinked in surprise. I had expected doubts and arguments, not an outright command.

"But I don't know what to tell him. I've only been a Christian for three days!"

"You are the one God has chosen to minister to him." Vittorio's pale gray eyes lifted to meet mine. "Would you refuse God?"

"But . . . I'm unworthy. Unqualified. Asher knows so much more about the Bible; he can quote it chapter and verse. So how am *I* supposed to give *him* truth?"

"I will teach you some things you need to know. And when you enter the prison, don't worry about what to say. Just say what God tells you to. Then it is not you who will be speaking, but the Holy Spirit." He uttered these words through a confident smile. And though I did not find much comfort in the words, his quiet, certain manner soothed my spirit like a balm. Without asking, I knew I was listening to a man who had staked his life upon the Word of God and found that it completely satisfied.

We spent another hour together, Vittorio teaching while I listened, and by the time I left the church I felt I could do the same.

On Monday, the fourth day following Asher's arrest, the prison officials allowed me to visit him. A uniformed guard led me into a large, windowless room filled with air that had been breathed far too many times. He gestured to a small, wooden table with a red line painted down the center, and I sat in the wooden chair on one side. A moment later another guard led Asher in, and something in my heart twisted when I heard the metallic chink of the fetters on his ankles.

He smiled as he shuffled toward me. "It was good of you to come," he said, lowering himself into the wooden chair. "I wasn't sure I would have any visitors."

"I've been trying to get in for four days. They said you had to talk to a psychologist first."

Asher shrugged. "I tried to tell him why I did it, but he wasn't really interested. He just wanted to know about the gas gun."

I nodded, wanting to say more, but not knowing quite how to begin. I knew why he was here, and I understood the desperation that drove him to attempt murder. In the past four days I had come to understand many things I suspected even Asher himself did not know.

Asher leaned forward, dropping his manacled wrists upon the table. "I have heard things in this prison." His eyes cut a glance from left to right, as though he expected someone to jump out at any moment and silence him. "Two days ago I shared a cell with a man from Florence who had just returned from New York. He was imprisoned here for drug smuggling, but as we talked he bragged that the authorities had no idea of his true crime."

I hadn't come to talk about criminals and drug smugglers, but something in Asher's furtive manner piqued my interest.

"He confessed something to you?"

Asher looked at me then, his smile strained, his eyes hard and wary. "This man—his name is Carlos—went to New York to commit a murder. He followed his victim from his workplace in Manhattan, then dragged him off the subway and killed him in a dark alley."

—

Hot as it was in the stuffy room, I felt a sliver of ice begin to slide down my spine. I stared at Asher as thoughts I dared not utter aloud began to assemble in my head.

Asher's burning eyes held me still throughout a long, brittle silence. "Can you guess who sent him?" he finally asked, the question underlined with a delicate ferocity that made it abundantly clear that he expected me to know the answer.

"N-not Santos Justus," I stammered.

"No. Darien Synn. Carlos did not know him by that name, of course, but he described the man, and the description fits Synn perfectly. And the timing was right. Carlos killed the man during the first weekend of November, which is when your friend died—"

"No." The word came from my mouth reflexively, in the same way I'd seen a hundred mothers insist that their sons couldn't possibly have committed the heinous crime for which they had been indicted . . . but I knew Asher was telling me the truth. The pieces fit. I had spoken to Synn about leaving Rome on November 2; I had even e-mailed Rory and asked him to find a case that would require my presence back in the States. Synn had read my e-mail, then sent someone to New York to remove my secretary. Synn had visited my Manhattan office, and he knew that without Rory, I had no other associates to look after my interests. Finally, by holding my passport and sending me to Brussels, he had guaranteed I wouldn't bolt for New York on the next available flight.

Asher opened his mouth to speak again, but I held up my hand, needing a moment more to organize my thoughts. "Have you said anything to anyone?" I asked, finally meeting his gaze. "I want justice for Rory. And I want Synn exposed."

Asher's dark brows slanted in a frown. "I have not spoken to anyone in authority. And I want to be careful—when they do send me in to face the magistrate, I do not want it to appear that I am offering the information in an attempt to lessen my own sentence." His face furrowed with contrition. "I am willing to pay the full price for my crime, even if I must spend the next thousand years in prison." A melancholy smile flitted across his features. "I will be the marvel of the prison community."

The sight of that sad smile gave me courage. "Asher," I began, glancing down at my hands, "I've something to tell you, and I don't know where to begin."

An expression of weary resignation settled upon his face. "You've come to say you're leaving Rome."

I shriveled a little at his expression. "No, Asher, I won't leave until your case is settled. Though I'm no longer employed by Global Union, I want to stay for your sake. I'll help your lawyer prepare your case, I'll stay through the trial . . . and then I'll go home." Like an old wound that ached on a rainy day, the mention of home reminded me of Kirsten. "I've had a bit of bad news since we last talked—my sister lost her baby, a little boy. She was eight months pregnant and in a car accident, and the trauma . . . well, it was an accident. So I'll go home and help her when I can."

Asher clamped his jaw tight and stared into the distance. "Fortunate baby," he murmured.

I couldn't believe I had heard him correctly. "Fortunate?" I whispered, my mood veering sharply to irritation. "How can you say such a thing?"

Asher returned his gaze to me. "He never had to endure the pain of life. He went from the womb to the arms of God."

"He never felt the joy of life, either," I snapped. "He never laughed; he never fell in love—"

"He never wept," Asher countered, his expression clouding. "He never held his dying wife in his arms and felt himself powerless to save her."

"So this is about you." I lifted a brow and crossed my arms. "You know what your problem is? You're angry with God. You think he's punishing you, so you're ticked off, but you won't admit it."

"I am not ticked off!" His brown eyes bored into mine, narrowed with fury. "I know I deserve my fate, and who am I to question God? But I cannot feel sorry for a child who will never have to endure what I have endured. I never weep at funerals, and I would *rejoice* to see death approaching in any form whatsoever. But I cannot. Because until I see Jesus, I have to remain here and suffer the lot of all mortals over and over again."

Our heated conversation had drawn the guard's attention. He peered in our direction, then pulled himself off the wall and took two steps toward our table. In a unanimous and silent conspiracy, Asher and I lowered our voices.

"I didn't come here to argue with you," I said, shaking my head. "I came because I think I've found an answer for your . . . situation."

Hoarse laughter rose from Asher's throat. "I've tried everything, Claudia. Unless you have Jesus waiting in the clerk's office, I don't think you can solve my problem."

"Just hear me out, OK?" I bit my lip, then took a deep breath and dived in. "I suppose I should start with the morning I saw you on the street with Justus. I was there, you see, because I knew you would need me that morning. It's hard to explain how I knew—I heard something that was almost, but not quite, a voice in the night. I tried to ignore it, but finally I realized the Spirit of God wanted to speak to my heart. And when I listened, Asher, I knew I had to find you as soon as I could. That's why I was running toward you that morning . . . and why I called out."

His face changed, the mask of resignation shattering in surprise. "You heard—"

I held up my hand, cutting him off. "God wanted me to stop you. And I'm very glad I did."

Asher stared, his lips parting slightly. "Why would God speak to you?"

"I don't know why he does what he does," I pressed on, "but I know I'm his child, and he's been leading me for the last few days. I paid a visit to a friend, a minister named Vittorio Pace. I asked him about many things, and I'd like to share some of his thoughts with you. The first and most important truth is this—you are not being punished, Asher. There is no condemnation for those who have trusted Christ Jesus."

His expression didn't change for a moment, then my words fell into place. He lifted a brow and looked at me as if I were a naive child. "Then tell me why I am alive. If God is not punishing me with immortality, who is?"

I slid my hands over the table until my fingertips kissed the edge of the red center line. "Perhaps God is not *punishing* you, Asher, but showing you mercy. Do you recall the story of the woman who covered Jesus' head with rare perfume and washed his feet with her tears?"

A flash of humor crossed his face. "Remember her? I met her when she traveled to Jerusalem and tried to speak with Lady Procula. She had been a village prostitute, but after the resurrection she became an ardent believer."

"Do you remember what Jesus said about her? Her sins—which were many—had been forgiven, so she showed the Lord much love. But a person who is forgiven little shows only a little love."

Asher tilted his brow and gave me an uncertain look.

—

"Think about it." I lowered my voice. "You feel you committed a severe sin and consequently earned a severe punishment. But God is rich in love, Asher, and to you he has extended a severe mercy. Don't you see how kind, tolerant, and patient God has been with you? Can't you see how merciful he has been in giving you time to turn from your sin?"

A cold, congested expression settled on his face. "My sin? I have turned from it. I turned from it scores of lifetimes ago, and since then I have done nothing but sacrifice myself in order to do God's work. I have studied, and worked, and allowed my body to be humiliated and tortured—"

"Stop." I shivered with a chill that had nothing to do with the weather outside. I knew very little about the Bible, but Vittorio had opened the Scriptures and explained several things in simple terms— enough that I now knew where Asher had erred in his thinking.

Ignoring the tight place of anxiety in my heart, I fixed Asher in my gaze. "Listen to yourself, Asher. *You* have worked; *you* have labored; *you* have sacrificed. Don't you see? You have tried to do everything yourself, and you have neglected the gift of God. It is by *grace* that we are saved through faith—and we do *nothing* to earn it. It is the gift of God. You turned from your sin, but you did not turn to Jesus."

He closed his eyes, literally blocking me out. "How could I go to him with empty hands? I struck the face of God, Claudia! In pride and audacity, the very sins of Satan, I cursed Christ!"

"Asher," my voice trembled, "suppose you do encounter *the* Antichrist and he rejects your testimony. Suppose the Lord then comes for the believers—what will happen to you?"

I strained to hear his soft answer. "I don't know."

"Everyone else who accepts Christ is assured a place in heaven." The words formed a traffic jam in my throat, battling each other to get out in the short time I would be allowed with Asher. "I look forward to his coming because I have no fear for the future. You, on the other hand, are working to *prevent* his coming. You say this is because you want to give others a chance to accept the gospel, but could it be that you're only fooling yourself? What will happen, Asher, when God moves and you realize *you* are not the referee and timekeeper? What will you do when you stand before God after pouring out the riches of your lifetime in an effort to avoid facing him again?"

Silence stretched between us, broken only by the hush of cars moving on the road outside. A change came over Asher's features, a sudden shock of sick realization.

"Do you realize what you are saying?" he whispered through stiff lips. "If you are right, for a lifetime of lifetimes I have worked and suffered and labored. Now you say I only have to *trust*? I can't. It would be easier for me to abandon my body than to abandon the purpose I have devoted years to following . . ."

As his words trailed away he pressed his hands to the tabletop, sliding them forward until our fingertips touched. "Claudia, this is the most grievous news you could have brought me."

"No, Asher." I gentled my voice. "It is the most wonderful news. Signor Pace showed me a verse that says God has every right to exercise his judgment and his power, but he also has the right to be patient with those who are the objects of his judgment and fit only for destruction. You recognized Jesus as the holy Son of God. You saw that his Word was true. But you never trusted him for your salvation, Asher. You strove to *earn* his forgiveness. And though you labor until the end of time, you can never earn salvation. It is a gift. It is free. It flows from mercy, not self-sacrifice."

He looked away, his chest heaving in a dry, choked way, but he did not weep.

Hoping I had struck some responsive chord, I continued: "You once shared with me a verse about the Lord waiting for people to repent before his return. Perhaps he has been patient for your sake all these years. He does not want you to perish, so he is giving you time to repent."

Tears gathered in the corners of his eyes and slowly spilled from the ends of his lashes. "Believing in grace is one thing," he whispered, a note halfway between disbelief and pleading in his voice, "living it is quite another."

"Exactly." Ignoring the guard's stern glance, I slid my hand forward until my fingertips overlapped his, covering him with my prayers as I did so. "God is waiting for you, Asher, with his arms outstretched. His mercy is rich and available . . . whenever you're ready to accept it."

A deep silence filled the room; even the sounds of traffic outside seemed to fade. "Can it be," he said finally, lifting his eyes to meet mine, "that I am the world's greatest fool? To have seen what I have seen, and yet not understand the meaning of it all—"

"Millions of people never see with spiritual eyes." I gave him an abashed smile. "I know I never would have, if not for you. You opened my eyes, Asher. You were stronger than I could ever be, and your labors were not in vain. You have to believe that."

He shot me a half-frightened look. "But what I did to Justus—or what I *almost* did. That was not a godly act, but I could see no other choice."

"You were operating under your own authority. You failed to trust God . . . and Signor Pace assures me that God has matters well in hand. He alone knows when the world will end; he alone knows who the Antichrist will be. We are not to run about searching for him. We are only to trust . . . and point others to grace. That's our calling, Asher. And that's what you did for me."

—

I would have said more, but the guard came to our table and rapped upon it with his knuckles. Reluctantly, I released Asher's hands and watched silently as he stood and turned to leave. His posture was bent, his shoulders hunched as though he carried the guilt of the world.

Tears came in a rush so strong my shoulders shook. *Dear God, show him the truth. Show him the riches of your miraculous grace.*

Thirty-four

WORKING OUT OF MY RESIDENZA, I SPENT THE NEXT TWO DAYS TRYING to find a lawyer who would represent Asher. Though he could well afford to hire any lawyer he chose, Asher seemed to have no interest in his defense. I had a terrible suspicion that he might plead guilty at his hearing. A guilty plea could only result in confinement, possibly for the rest of his life, and for Asher I could think of nothing worse.

Better to have him declared mentally incompetent than to have him locked up for life. I dialed Kurt's office, knowing that he already knew enough about the case to write a letter about Asher's mental state.

I had just hung up after leaving a message with the answering service when the phone jangled beneath my hand. Thinking it might be Kurt, I snatched it up before it had even finished ringing.

"Signorina Fischer?"

The Italian accent and female voice surprised me. "Yes?"

"Il Presidente would like to meet with you this afternoon, if possible."

I took a quick breath of utter astonishment. "Signor Justus wants to meet with me?"

"Can you come to his office? At fourteen o'clock?"

I glanced at my pocket watch. I would have less than an hour to make myself presentable—and for what? Did he intend to grill me on my association with Asher, or did he need me for another spy mission?

—

365

I cast about for a reason to refuse but remembered what Asher had said about Synn and Rory. Justus might know about his director's murderous methods, but perhaps he did not. In either case, I might be able to gather some useful information for the police. "I'll be there," I told the woman.

Thankfully, the hour of the appointment didn't leave much time for worrying. I took a quick shower, slipped into a wool skirt and sweater, then hurried out the door. I made it to Global Union headquarters with only five minutes to spare.

Maura Casale greeted me in the lobby. "I am so glad to see you," she said. After giving me a quick hug, she stepped back and gave me a swift appraisal. "And what is the meaning of those dark circles under your eyes?"

"I haven't been sleeping well," I answered, letting her escort me through the security checkpoint. "I've been trying to find a lawyer for Asher Genzano. No one seems to want his case."

"We've heard everything, of course." She led the way to the elevator, then pushed the button for the seventh floor. "Il Direttore keeps us informed. I was amazed when I heard the news. Signor Genzano seemed such a quiet, steady man—"

"He is." I met her gaze, determined that she understand the truth. "He wouldn't act without a reason."

She stared at me, uncertainty creeping into her expression. "You think he had a valid reason to kill Il Presidente?"

"I really can't say, signora." I glanced up at the flashing numbers above the elevator doors. "But I trust all will be made clear at his hearing."

I trust. If she only knew how desperately I was trusting God to set things right. Never had I felt less convinced about the outcome of a trial, and never had I cared more.

—

The doors opened. Signora Casale remained behind as I stepped onto the seventh floor. I flashed her a farewell smile, then moved through the marble lobby toward the secretary's desk. How long had it been since I stood here with Asher? Only a week, yet it felt like a lifetime ago.

"Signorina Fischer." The bottle-blonde behind the desk smiled, but her expression held only a trace of its former warmth. "Il Presidente is waiting for you. Please go in."

I felt my stomach sway as I approached the wide wooden door. I gave a tentative knock, then heard Justus's clipped reply: *"Entrano!"*

He was seated behind his desk, but he looked up when I came through the doorway. I saw his Adam's apple bob as he swallowed—a signal of nervousness—then he pasted on a smile and stood, extending his hand as if I were a long-lost friend. "Signorina Fischer! I am so pleased you could find time to come see me!"

Shock caused my greeting to wedge in my throat, but Justus didn't seem to care. "Come, have a seat," he said, guiding me to the leather sofa in the corner of the room instead of the guest chairs before his desk. The move spoke volumes. "Can I get you anything? White wine? Espresso?"

"No, thank you." I felt like a windup doll moving to a preset program, but I sank to the couch as gracefully as I could. "I don't need anything."

"Fine." Still smiling, he lowered his graceful frame into the chair next to the sofa, then draped one arm over the padded armrest. "I suppose you're wondering why I've asked to see you."

I lifted a brow, mutely acknowledging the truth.

"Actually"—He glanced away for an instant, and I marveled at the discreet sign of nervousness. I had never noticed any of the usual signals of unease in Santos Justus's body language, yet now he was displaying an entire gamut of the most obvious—crossed legs, aversion to direct eye contact, fidgety fingers . . .

"You are here, signorina," he said, looking back to me, "because I wanted to thank you. Your shout distracted my assailant the other morning, and I am convinced you saved my life. If not for you, well"—he made a vague dismissive gesture with his hands—"I would not be here. So I thank you from the bottom of my heart, and I apologize for my harsh words during our last meeting. Now I understand that you brought Asher Genzano into my office to demonstrate his instability. I did not give you an adequate chance to explain, nor did I fully consider the depth of his insanity."

He laughed, but I heard a note of hysteria in his voice.

"And so, signorina, I am offering you my deepest apologies and a new offer to work for Unione Globale. In order to make amends for my rush to judgment, I would like to hire you at double your most recent salary and extend your contract for another twelve months." His extraordinary eyes blazed and glowed as he smiled. "Please say you'll work with us, signorina. We need you. And we are prepared to make your name great."

His last words chafed across my soul. My name did not deserve to be great. Neither did Santos Justus's.

"I appreciate the confidence you have placed in me," I answered, taking charge of the conversation with quiet assurance. "But I will not work for you, Signor Justus. I have promised to see that Signor Genzano receives a fair trial. I am his friend, you see."

Justus blinked, his features hardening in a stare of disapproval. "You would defend that madman?"

"He is not what he appears to be." I looked away and smiled, thinking of my enigmatic friend. "Like you, he harbors a wealth of secrets."

"Secrets." Justus's voice grated in the silence. "Tell me, signorina—do you really believe what Genzano said? Surely you don't believe I am the pawn of the devil."

"I can't read your heart, Signor Justus, just as you can't read Asher Genzano's. But I do think you ought to take a closer look around your organization. After Asher's hearing, I intend to bring the murder of my associate in New York to the attention of the Italian police. I believe they will find a link between Global Union and Manhattan."

I stood, leaving him stunned and silent in his chair, then moved out of the office toward the lobby. The secretary snapped her gum in farewell as I stepped into the elevator and pressed the button.

I visited the jail after my appointment at Global Union, only to find that the visitors' entrance was locked. I stomped about in frustration for a moment, then caught the attention of Ricardo, the espresso vendor across the street. He waved me over.

"Can I help you, signorina?" he asked, a gleam in his eye. "Perhaps you want to get word to a prisoner inside the Regina Coeli?"

I raked my hand through my hair, amazed that I had forgotten that most Roman business takes place outside established operating procedures. In Rome, it doesn't always pay to follow the rules—it's usually more important to have friends in appropriate places.

I opened my purse and fumbled for the small notebook I always carried. "Could you get word to Signor Genzano? I am trying to find someone to help him."

"Genzano?" Ricardo's brows flickered. "I know the name. He is on the list for tomorrow."

My stomach went cold. "What list?"

"The transport list. They are taking him away tomorrow."

—

"To where?"

Ricardo lifted both hands up in the air. "City Hall, probably. The courthouse, for his hearing. They will take two vans, one for petty thieves and the like, the other for more serious criminals."

As my pulse began to beat erratically, I braced my notebook against my palm and scribbled a note, then ripped the page out and thrust it toward Ricardo. "Can your brother get this to Signor Genzano? It is very important."

Ricardo's eyes scanned the note, then met mine. "Maybe," he replied, his voice flat.

I'd been in Rome long enough to know his disinterest wasn't personal. I dug through my purse, found my wallet, and yanked out the largest bill I had, a hundred-thousand-lire note. According to the day's exchange rate, I figured I was offering Ricardo at least two days' espresso profits. "Can your brother get this to Signor Genzano?" I repeated, staring directly at Ricardo. "It is very important."

"Signorina," he said, accepting the money and the sheet of paper with a gracious little bow, "I will see to it. Do not fear."

I watched him fold the papers and tuck them into his pocket, then I turned to face the jail. "What time will they move him, do you think?"

Ricardo squinted toward the setting sun. "The vans usually leave the prison around nine o'clock." A smile nudged itself into a corner of his mouth. "If you want to speak to the prisoner, you might get here early. Sometimes these things can be arranged."

If you have the money and the connections. He didn't have to spell it out for me this time. I nodded and glared at the horrid prison one final time, then moved down the street where I'd be more likely to catch a cab.

THIRTY-FIVE

THE MAN IN THE CELL NEXT DOOR KEPT BABBLING AT THE MOON, BUT
Asher made no effort to block the sound. He clutched the unfolded
sheet of notebook paper and read the message again:

> *Tomorrow—I will do what I can. If I can't convince someone in*
> *Rome to help you, I will pray for a heavenly defender.*
> *Always, Claudia.*

Tears welled up in his eyes as he read the message a third time.
Dear Claudia. What a friend she had become! Faithful, loving, and
merciful. All the things Jesus was.

That thought brought another in its wake, with a chill that struck
deep in the pit of his stomach. *Claudia has become more like Jesus in*
the last week than I have in the last two thousand years.

He felt the bitter gall of envy burn the back of his throat. How
could one so young and inexperienced come to a fuller understanding
than he? He had been following the path of martyred saints for generations, subjugating his desires, denying his earthly impulses, avoiding
temptations of the flesh. He had shunned the spotlight, given himself
to study and research, and all for—what? To be rebuked by a young
American who could hardly quote Scripture without prompting?

Lifting his eyes to the cracked and stained ceiling, he whispered,
"My God, my God, why have you forsaken me?"

—

371

No answer came from heaven; he heard no sound at all but coarse laughter from the man in the next cell. Asher stretched out upon his bunk and folded his hands behind his head. Hearing wisdom from Claudia's lips and seeing the light of holiness in her eyes only amplified his feeling of estrangement. The chasm between himself and God yawned like an open wound.

Had he always been separated like this? Claudia said she felt the Spirit of God speak to her; he had actually awakened her in the night. Never in all the winding length of Asher's memory had the Spirit spoken to him. Never had he felt the confidence that lit Claudia's face as she spoke of grace and love and forgiveness.

But grace and love and forgiveness had to be earned! One had to labor to be worthy of the high calling of Christ Jesus. One had to live a holy and blameless life! Even Jesus said his followers would have to drink the cup of suffering . . .

He breathed deep and felt a stab of memory, a sharp shard of Scripture: *And if they are saved by God's kindness, then it is not by their good works. For in that case, God's wonderful kindness would not be what it really is—free and undeserved.*

The words made his throat ache with regret. Had he been so misled? Could the key to unlocking his life really lie in simple trust?

His mind filtered back to the afternoon. He and the other prisoners had filed into the dingy recreation room to watch an American movie, *The Wizard of Oz*. He had thought it a silly story until the end, when Dorothy discovered she didn't need the wizard, the witch, or the magic of Emerald City to return to her true home. She only had to close her eyes, tap her heels, and whisper, "There's no place like home . . ."

Dorothy had worked, risked death, and suffered for no reason . . . no, that wasn't true. In her journey, she had made friends and influenced people along the Yellow Brick Road. But it wasn't until she learned that the desires of her heart lay in her own backyard that she could find her way home.

Asher let his gaze rove over the stained ceiling, the crumbling walls, the filthy floor. He had been searching for a true home, a place of rest, all his life. Just as Dorothy had set out to disarm the Wicked Witch of the West; he had set out to disarm the Antichrist. Now Claudia wanted him to stop striving and rest.

The sound of crazed laughter filled the heavy air. Asher closed his eyes, bracing himself against the diabolical sound. Across the hall another man let a stream of curses fly, stunning the laughing simpleton into silence, at least for a moment. From another cellblock rose a shriek as thin as a paper cut, accompanied by pulsing sobs. Asher clapped his hands over his ears and rolled onto his side, trying desperately to block the vile sounds of human pain and madness. He'd grown soft in the last sixty years. After leaving Nazi Germany, he had wandered mostly in civilized countries, leaving behind the cries and whimpers of suffering men . . .

As unexpected as a ray of sunshine in the middle of a summer shower, another sound suddenly poured from a distant cell. A tenor voice, pure as mountain spring water, began to sing a hymn Asher had not heard in ages: *Grazia sorprendente, quanto dolce il sano che ha salvato un miserabile come me!* . . .

Asher rolled off his bunk and walked to the locked door, then folded his hands around the iron bars. He pressed his face into the narrow opening, trying to get as close as possible to the source of the sound. *Ero perso ma ora mi sono trovato . . . Ero cieco, ma ora vedo.*

The cursing stopped as the heavenly voice floated over the complex. *Attraverso molti pericoli, tormenti e difficolta gia sono passato . . .*

Asher could feel each separate thump of his heart against the wall of his chest. *Questa grazia é stata la mia salvezza e la mia guida.*

Would grace lead him home? Unable to control the spasmodic trembling within him, Asher clung to the bars and took a deep breath. "Father," he whispered, his mind curling lovingly around the thought of release. "Father, will you hear me?"

Asher waited, oblivious to everything but the certainty that he had found what he had been seeking for years. "Father, can it be so simple? Jesus said I would live until I saw him clearly—Father, I would see Jesus!"

And then, like a warm wind that stirred his soul, came a voice he had never heard or felt or sensed: *There is a path before each person that seems right, but it ends in death. Fear not, beloved. My grace is sufficient for you; my strength is made perfect in weakness.*

A hot tear rolled down Asher's face as his heart sang with delight. The truth was so simple even a child could grasp it. A blush of pleasure rose to his cheeks as he lifted his hands in praise and thanksgiving, then joined in the song.

> *Amazing grace, how sweet the sound that saved a wretch like me.*
> *I once was lost, but now am found, 'twas blind, but now I see.*
> *Through many dangers, toils, and snares, I have already come,*
> *'Tis grace hath brought me safe thus far, and grace will lead me home.*

THIRTY-SIX

CROSS AND FRUSTRATED BECAUSE IT TOOK FIFTEEN MINUTES TO FIND
a cab, I arrived at the prison at eight-thirty the next morning.
Clutching my purse, which I had stuffed with persuasive hundred-
thousand-lire notes, I approached the main entrance, then nearly
shrieked in disappointment when the officer at the desk told me guests
were not allowed to visit prisoners awaiting transport.

I told myself to calm down; I had prepared for this contingency.
Giving the officer my most beguiling smile, I pulled one of the colorful
currency notes from my purse and slid it over the desk. "Can't we make
one exception?" I asked, wishing I had looked up a few pertinent jail-
house expressions in my Italian phrase book. I could use all the sympathetic feelings I could arouse today.

I could tell from the guard's posture, however, that he was in no
mood to bargain. He gave the money a cold glance, then glared at me.
"No exceptions," he barked, rising from his chair like a jack-in-the-box.
"Now, if you will excuse me, signorina, I must attend to other work."

I picked up the money and crumpled it in my palm, struggling to
hold back tears of frustration. I had planned to ask Asher to name
Kurt Welton as his psychologist of record, so the court could at least
call Kurt and get an appropriate referral. But unless I had a chance to
speak to him—

A tall man with a mustache stepped out of a hall and stared
straight at me, his eyes narrowing. "Signorina Fischer?"

—

375

A cry of relief broke from my lips. "Si! Have you news for me?"

He came toward me with long strides, glancing over his shoulder as he approached. His furtive attitude immediately put a damper on my rising spirits. "I am Ricardo's brother." He whispered out of one side of his mouth, like a gangster in an old-fashioned movie. "I have a letter for you."

The hesitation in his hawk like eyes disturbed me. "A letter?"

"From Signor Genzano."

I put out my hand in silent expectation, then realized the man was waiting for money. Silently grumbling against the greasy-palm system of government, I pressed the crumpled hundred-thousand-lire note into the man's palm.

The money disappeared, then the tall officer reached into his coat and pulled out a long, white envelope. "I myself delivered the envelope, paper, and pen to Signor Genzano," he said, as if I should reward him further for his generosity. "He was most anxious to write you."

The noise level outside the prison suddenly increased, and Ricardo's brother politely steered me toward the door. "They are bringing out the prisoners now," he said, pushing the door open. "If you want to speak to your friend, you may be able to call to him."

I found myself caught up in a crowd of relatives and reporters moving toward an eight-foot chain-link fence. Within the fenced perimeter, a pair of dark blue police vans waited beside one of the prison blocks. Scanning the doorway of the prison, I saw a row of handcuffed and shackled prisoners. After being counted off, the prisoners were led to the first blue van.

After all these prisoners—the petty criminals, I assumed—were secure, the guards closed the doors and the van sped through the gate. The crowd surged forward as mothers and fathers and wives shouted and waved to loved ones within the vehicle, then the cries faded. Many people drifted away, some sobbing in heartbreak. Those of us who remained turned our attention back to the prison, where another van was revving its engine.

That's when I saw Asher. He came through a doorway and shuffled forward, a guard at each side. Though the restraints made his movements seem awkward and halting, he carried his head high. He turned as if to scan the crowd at the fence, but one of the guards shoved him toward the back of the open van. My heart pounded as I watched him sit on a bench, then a guard secured his manacles to an overhead bar that ran the length of the vehicle.

As the guards stepped away, I called out Asher's name, but at that exact moment every reporter in the crowd yelled to him as well. "Signor Genzano! *Avete provato ad uccidere Santos Justus?* Why would you try to kill the world's peacemaker?"

I stood on tiptoe, trying to see above a half-dozen other heads, then realized the task was impossible. Breaking free of the media mob, I followed the fence to the gate, then positioned myself next to the opening. Asher would see me when he passed by, and I would *not* let myself be pushed aside.

As I suspected, the mob of reporters moved as the van pulled out, and within a moment I was clinging to the fence, my eyes following the van. There were no windows in the side except for those of the driver and the guard, but two back windows allowed us to see inside as the van passed. Calling Asher's name, I held up my arms against the chain link, then froze as Asher's gaze met mine. I saw the flicker of a smile cross his face, then he swiveled slightly and opened his hands, showing me—what? That his hands were empty? That he would hold my hands if he could?

A sense of anticlimax visibly descended upon our group as the van

—

turned onto the main road. The reporters lowered their microphones; the cameramen shut off their cameras. I lowered my arms and moved away from the fence, my misery so acute it felt like physical pain. I'd have to be more positive when I arrived at the courthouse. I couldn't let Asher see me like this.

Beside me, an Italian journalist stood in front of her cameraman, recording a lead-in to her story. I walked directly behind her, too weary to care if I ruined her perfect shot. Below the curve of the hill I could see Asher's blue van cruising the street, then slowing to turn onto the bridge. A group of tourists at the bridge railing were posing for a picture with the Tiber River as a backdrop. Some fool with a camera stood in the middle of the road, apparently oblivious to all traffic.

As the van driver honked his horn, the tourist snapped his picture, then saluted the guards with a jaunty wave. As the driver shook his head in exasperation, the tourist jogged across the street to join his friends at the railing.

I found myself muttering, "E un americanata!" So typically American, so arrogant and thoughtless.

At the sound of a shrill cry, I slowed my steps. The newswoman who had been recording her sound bite was pointing toward the bridge, her face contorted in horror. As my eyes followed her trembling fingers, I saw that a small child—a toddler, probably not more than two or three years old—had wandered away from the distracted tourists. The van driver saw the child at the last moment and abruptly jerked the wheel. The sickening sound of a metal-to-metal impact slammed against my ears, and in astounded horror I watched the van teeter on the bent railing, then fall, end over end, into the silver waters of the swollen river.

I lurched toward the bridge with the pack of reporters and photographers. More screams chilled the air now, but I barely heard them, so loud was the roaring of blood in my ears.

I was one of the last to arrive at the wounded railing. The water beneath did not seem deep, for we could see the dark shadow of the overturned van in the waters below. The two guards had managed to release their seat belts by the time I arrived, and both bobbed in the water.

But I couldn't see Asher.

A wave of grayness passed over me, sapping my strength. I sank to a stone curb and stared mindlessly at the water, counting the minutes it had taken for me to run from the road to the bridge. Had it been three minutes? Four? How long could a person hold his breath underwater?

Tension descended upon the area like toxic gas, driving the crowd to panicked action. The tourists huddled together, some snapping pictures while others pressed their hands to their chests and gaped in horror. A handful of policemen ran from the prison and dived into the water to rescue their comrades, while the news cameras captured every moment.

I sat without moving as the moments passed one after the other, knowing I would never see Asher again. He had been handcuffed to a stationary railing, so he had drowned . . . or had he? I found myself hoping they would bring his body to the surface and take him to the morgue. I would speak for him, argue against an embalming, and wait until his heart began to beat again. Then someone would call a psychologist for *me*.

Surrounded by an ever-increasing crowd of reporters and curious onlookers, I sat numbly on the curb until the police divers surfaced for the last time, nearly three hours after the accident. One of the divers, his wet suit shining in the bright sun, climbed into a boat and spoke to a police captain; a few moments later the captain gave the news to the reporters. I stood and wandered through the crowd until I found a newscaster who spoke English.

"The police chief reports that the single casualty in today's accident was Asher Genzano, a lifetime resident of Rome," the newscaster said, offering his best look of concern to the camera. "Due to the currents in the river, the body has not been recovered."

Pressing my lips together, I backed away and left the reporters to their speculations. They might fool the public, but they couldn't fool me. I knew Asher's hands had been cuffed to the restraining pole; I saw that the van's door remained closed even after the vehicle submerged. Furthermore, I knew the currents of the Tiber were about as swift as molasses in winter.

The truth was unspeakable and unexplainable. Asher Genzano had vanished.

I had walked nearly a mile before I even remembered the letter. A moment of panic seized me as I felt for it in my pockets, then I discovered that I had stashed it in my purse at some point during the excitement.

I pulled it out, weighed its heft in my palm, then decided that Asher's letter would best be savored over a cup of espresso. I stepped into the nearest trattoria, ordered a sandwich and a cup of coffee, then took a quiet table in the corner of the building.

I broke the seal, unfolded the plain pages, and began to read:

My very dear friend Claudia:

I do not know what today will bring forth, but I know you are not meant to sorrow for me. I believe—indeed, I know—that God has restored me to my rightful place. Release will come for me in God's time, and I have never been more ready to face it. I find myself agreeing with Paul—I want to really live and yet I long to be with Christ. For the godly who die will rest in peace.

Tonight I thought about what you said and realized you were right. Tonight I have surrendered my work, my striving, and my goals to the One who has sought me relentlessly for over two thousand years. I thought I was doing the world a service by pursuing the Antichrist, and now I see that Christ has done me a greater service by pursuing me. I know others will find my story unbelievable, but I believe it is a testimony to the unfathomable riches of Christ's mercy. Tonight I saw the Savior even more clearly than I saw him in Pilate's palace. Then I saw a prisoner on his way to death. Tonight I saw the Lord of Grace, extending his love and forgiveness to one who could never deserve it. I saw him, Claudia, and in that moment I was freed.

A thought occurred to me last night—it may or may not be relevant, I do not know. Do you recall that Scripture tells us of other men who lived dozens of average lifetimes? Adam lived nine hundred thirty years; Methuselah lived to be nine hundred sixty-nine. Enoch and Elijah never died but were taken bodily to heaven. God used each man for his purposes. Every one of their earthly days was counted and appropriated by the Almighty.

Which brings me, dear one, to the real purpose of this letter. I am thick and slow, but God is gracious, and I am convinced he will soon welcome me home. This letter is to validate your claim to my journals. I will die without a will (how could I write one?), and I do not care how my property is disbursed. But my journals—I leave them to you. Whether I spend a week or a lifetime in prison, I leave my precious books in your hands. Take them

—

with you when you leave Rome. Use them as you will, dear friend.

Thank you, beloved sister, for having courage enough to speak truth to me. I leave you now with a quote from Job, who suffered many things, and yet did not turn his heart against God: "If mortals die, can they live again? This thought would give me hope, and through my struggle I would eagerly wait for release."

I await my release . . . and another encounter with my Savior. Even so, come, Lord Jesus!

Asher Genzano, signed this 23rd day of November, Regina Coeli Prison, Rome.

I stared at the signature, then ran my fingertip over the bold, sure strokes of the date. The fourth Thursday of November. Thanksgiving Day in America . . . and for at least one man in Rome.

So—Asher had found victory at last. What I had witnessed today was not an end, but a beginning.

The owner of the trattoria moved to a small black-and-white television above the counter and pressed the power button, providing the noon news for his patrons. The screen immediately filled with the face of an earnest reporter standing before the Tiber embankment. Behind her I could see the divers in their darkly gleaming wet suits and the somber-faced chief of police. A single phrase caught my ear: "*Temiamo che il prigioniero sia morto.*" We fear the prisoner is dead.

"No," I whispered, folding Asher's letter. "*Sappiamo che il prigioniero è libero.* We know the prisoner is free."

I was honestly happy for Asher, but my lower lip wobbled and my eyes filled in spite of myself.

I would miss him.

—

Epilogue

A week later, I stood inside the Fiumicino Airport with my luggage and forty-two cardboard boxes containing Asher's journals. The government had been delighted to get its hands on Asher's estate and agreed to give me what the court-appointed appraiser called "a heap of dusty diaries." After I found people to translate the foreign journals, I planned to study them carefully, beginning with the earliest entries.

I could already think of a hundred uses for Asher's writings. The journals were priceless for their historical value alone and would bring forgotten eras and peoples to life. Asher's testimony would also shine the bright light of truth upon certain dark episodes in the history of civilization—his experience in the Inquisition alone would make any churchman cringe. And what politician would not be interested in Asher's encounter with Hitler? In his misguided enthusiasm to find the Antichrist, Asher had encountered one of the most occult-driven personalities of the twentieth century.

Yes, his history would have much to teach anyone with a heart of faith. Most important, Asher's experiences could expose all the dead-end roads man has traveled in an effort to reach God. I planned to condense his story, close with his final letter to me, add a postscript about his release, and let the record speak for itself. After all, his journals had made a believer of me.

The airline attendant waved me forward to the desk. I checked my

—

383

luggage and the boxes, picked up my boarding pass, and made my way to the gate. As I settled down to wait with a book I had picked up in the airport bookshop, an image on the overhead television caught my eye. The screen featured a photograph of Santos Justus, with the words *Morti in scontro automobilistico* superimposed across the bottom of the screen.

"*Morti* . . ." My breath caught in my throat. *Morti* meant dead.

Trembling, I stared at the television screen in hypnotized horror. Santos Justus was dead?

Clutching the armrest of my seat, I strained to follow the news report. Footage of Justus and Synn rolled across the screen, then I saw a video clip of Angelo pulling the blue Alfa Romeo away from the curb. The next clip revealed an accident scene along a deserted country road. The Alfa Romeo was a mangled mess, a grisly metal sculpture wrapped around a tree. Two sheet-covered bodies lay on the ground. Darien Synn, however, was shown upon a stretcher being lifted into an ambulance.

I felt a sharp pang of sorrow for the people at Global Union. Some of them I had liked, others I had tolerated, but they had all been bound together by a shared wish for peace. Now Il Presidente was gone, and Il Direttore would have to carry on . . . if I couldn't have him arrested.

A thought suddenly froze in my brain. Asher had risked spending the rest of his immortal life behind bars because he was convinced that Santos Justus would become the Antichrist, but Asher was . . . wrong.

The thought was so absurd I couldn't stop a smile, though I felt a long way from genuine humor. "Ah, Signor Pace," I murmured, lowering my gaze from the carnage on the television screen. "You were right. It does us no good to look for evil when we ought to be looking for those who are lost."

—

As the flight attendant began to call for first-class passengers, I pulled out a photo of the brass plaque I had commissioned for the entry of the Sole al Pantheon, Asher's home. For as long as the hotel remained in the heart of Rome, all who entered would read my tribute to the man who had lived in the city longer than any other:

Grace comes into the soul, as the morning sun into the world: first a dawning, then a light; and at last the sun in his full and excellent brightness.

—Thomas Adams

I tucked the photo into my purse, dashed a tear from my eye, then stood to follow the line of passengers down the ramp to the plane. As I settled into my seat and fumbled for the safety belt, the woman next to me twiddled her fingers to get my attention.

"What a lovely necklace," she said, pointing to the watch dangling from the gold chain around my neck.

"Thank you." I snapped the seat buckle, then looked at my traveling companion. "It was my mother's. She always loved Rome."

"So do I," the woman answered, giving me a relaxed upper smile that indicated friendliness and honesty. "But I was only able to visit for the weekend. There was so much more I wanted to see."

I tilted my head, returning her smile in full measure. "I was in Rome ten weeks," I told her. "And I saw things you wouldn't believe."

"Will you tell me?" Her pupils dilated with interest. "It's a long flight, and I don't have anything to read."

I smoothed my skirt, then touched my watch, remembering the inscription, *Do not squander time, for that's the stuff life is made of . . .*

"I'd be happy to tell you all about my trip," I said, nodding. "I have a hunch you'll be a good listener."

RESOURCES

ASHER'S RECOLLECTIONS OF THE INQUISITION ARE ADAPTED FROM eyewitness accounts recorded in Edward Burman's *The Inquisition*. The two stanzas of poetry about the Wandering Jew are from John Ker Roxburghe's *Roxburghe Ballads* and quoted in *The Legend of the Wandering Jew* by George K. Anderson.

I owe a special thanks to novelists and friends Nancy Moser, Robert Elmer, Melody Carlson, and Molly Bull, who shared vivid memories of Rome. (Thanks, folks! I'll make it to Italy yet!) Also, special thanks to Grant Jeffrey, who shared many things about the Wandering Jew, and to Susan Richardson, who waded through a *very* rough draft and provided helpful feedback. *Grazie molto, amici!*

I am also indebted to the following authors and their informative books:

Anderson, George K. *The Legend of the Wandering Jew*. Hanover, N.H.: Brown University Press, 1991.

Blumberg, Arnold, ed. *Great Leaders, Great Tyrants*. Westport, Conn.: Greenwood Press, 1995.

Burman, Edward. *The Inquisition*. New York: Dorset Press, 1984.

Chirot, Daniel. *Modern Tyrants*. New York: The Free Press, 1994.

Dimitrius, Jo-Ellan and Mark Mazzarella. *Reading People*. New York: Random House, 1998.

Grun, Bernard. *The Timetables of History*. New York: Simon and Schuster, 1991.

Hindson, Ed. *Is the Antichrist Alive and Well?* Eugene, Ore.: Harvest House, 1998.

Hofmann, Paul. *The Seasons of Rome*. New York: Henry Holt and Company, 1997.

Jeffrey, Grant. *Final Warning*. Toronto: Frontier Research Publications, 1995.

Lewis, David. *The Secret Language of Success*. New York: Carroll & Graf Publishers, 1989.

Neighbor, Travis, and Monica Larner. *Living, Studying, and Working in Italy*. New York: Henry Holt and Company, 1998.

Pentecost, J. Dwight. *Things to Come*. Grand Rapids, Mich.: Zondervan, 1964.

Sacks, Oliver. *The Man Who Mistook His Wife for a Hat*. New York: Harper Perennial, 1985.

Stableford, Brian, ed. *Tales of the Wandering Jew*. Sawtry, U.K.: Daedalus Ltd., 1991.

Wild, Fiona, ed. *Rome*. New York: DK Publishing, 1997.

THE SPEAR OF TYRANNY

Grant Jeffrey & Angela Hunt

Will Isaac Ben-David learn the truth of
who Romulus is in time to stop the ultimate evil?

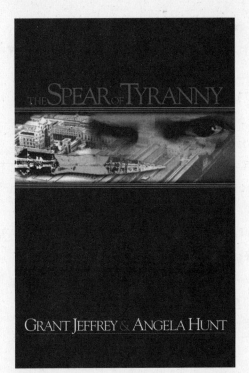

In the sequel to the popular fiction book *Against the Dawn*, evil ruler Adrian
Romulus has achieved what no other world leader could: the signing of a
peace treaty between Israel and her Arab neighbors and the rebuilding of the
Temple in Jerusalem. Romulus seems to have the world's political matters
firmly in control, but underneath his powerful facade is an evil madman bent
on destruction. When Isaac Ben-David (one of Romulus' inner circle and a
new believer in Christ) learns the truth, can he stop Romulus from destroying
the world?

 WORD PUBLISHING

AGAINST THE DAWN

Grant Jeffrey & Angela Hunt

Now retitled and repackaged in trade paper, part of
the popular millennium fiction series from prophecy expert Grant
Jeffrey and acclaimed fiction writer Angela Hunt.

Daniel Prentice's technological skill helped save the world from the deadly
impact of Y2K in the popular thriller *Flee the Darkness*. But that victory didn't
stop the evil or alter the ancient prophecies foretold in the book of Ezekiel.
Now Daniel must help as Israel faces the threat of nuclear war and invasion of
all four borders. The fates of nations and individuals hang in the balance.
Never have the forces of evil been stronger, the stakes higher, or the world's
possible destruction nearer.

 WORD PUBLISHING